THE MESSENGER

Leah Rose

Lands Atlantic
Publishing

The Messenger

Published through Lands Atlantic Publishing
www.landsatlantic.com

Copyright © 2012 by Leah Rose

ISBN: 978-0982500569

THE MESSENGER

Sierra,
I hope you enjoy
Jeilin's story. Best wishes
& happy reading.

Leah
Rose ♡

Prologue

J eilin was six years old the first time she saw a messenger.

It was a cold, grey, and early morning, but in Jeilin's eyes it was glorious. For the first time, she had been allowed to accompany her father to sell crops in the nearest town, seven miles away from the small cabin that was home to Jeilin, her two older brothers, and her parents.

A small grey gelding named Ash pulled their cart, which was overflowing with apples, pumpkins, and corn.

Jeilin reached behind herself and seized an apple. For a minute the only sounds were the steady beating of Ash's hooves on the dirt road, the squeaking of the cart's wheels, and Jeilin's crunching. "Can I give Ash an apple?" she asked, her breath hanging in the chilly air after she'd stopped speaking.

"When we get to Almrahn," her father replied.

In the next moment, a dark form appeared in the distance. Jeilin watched curiously as it drew closer, revealing itself to be a horse and rider.

The horse drew closer and closer, dust flying from beneath its hooves, the rider's cloak billowing in the wind.

Soon, it became clear that the horse was black and the rider was a man with a strong jaw and dark hair, also flying in the wind. Eventually they drew close enough for Jeilin to catch sight of a medal pinned to the mysterious rider's chest: a gold star. An identical decoration glimmered from the horse's bridle.

The pair sped past, and for a second, just a second, Jeilin caught the rider's eye. And then they were gone, reduced to the sound of hoof beats fading into the distance.

"Looks like we've seen a messenger!" Jeilin's father said. "He must be on an important run to be going that fast!"

"What's a messenger?" Jeilin asked.

"A messenger is someone the king, other royalty, and their military officers rely on to deliver important things," he said. "Messengers are the fastest of the fast, the best of the best! It's a great honor to be chosen as a messenger—did you see that gold star on his chest?"

Jeilin nodded.

"The king pinned that on there himself," he said. "He does it for every messenger."

Jeilin was spellbound. "Could I be a messenger?"

Her father chuckled. "Well, nothing's impossible, is it? But you have to be a great rider—you can never let the king down. You have to care more about your mission than you care about yourself, and you can't let anything stop you or stand in your way."

"I wouldn't!" Jeilin said, leaning forward at the edge of her seat.

"And you must have a horse," he added. "And not just any horse—one of the best."

"I could use Ash!" Jeilin declared.

Her father just looked down at her and smiled.

Chapter 1

A sh had pulled the family's plow and cart since Jeilin could remember and was still around by the time she was thirteen, though he had become more white than grey. "Here boy," Jeilin said, dumping half a pail of feed into his trough. Ash nickered appreciatively and began to eat. Jeilin left Ash standing at the end of his paddock, his nose buried in his oats, and turned to the hens. They were standing about in a group, cackling and beating their wings, waiting to be fed. She replaced the grain bucket in the small barn and grabbed a pail of chicken feed.

Glancing over to the orchard, she scattered the feed on the ground for the scrambling chickens. Her fifteen-year-old twin brothers, Ehryn and Emrys, were plucking fruit from the branches of an apple tree, filling large baskets that would be sold in the nearest town.

"Jeilin!" her father, Rab, called from behind her.

"What is it, father?"

He was carrying two buckets. "Could you run to the stream and fill these?" he asked.

Jeilin took the two pails, turned away from the barn and the little cabin, and walked across the field toward the small stream at the edge of the woods.

Ten minutes later she was there, kneeling on the stream's bank under the shade of pines and a few deciduous trees. The yellow plains stretched behind her, the house and barn hidden by a hill. Her reflection stared back at her from the water's surface. Her eyes were large and bright—maybe too large, she thought. Her shoulder-length sable hair had been pulled back and secured with a strip of leather. She wore an old cream-colored tunic and brown leggings. Her boots were smeared with mud.

She dipped the first bucket in the water and was just lifting it out when she heard an unexpected sound.

Startled, she jumped up and turned around, dropping the bucket. Everyone knew the woods were filled with dangerous animals, but the animal that had made the sound wasn't dangerous—if she'd heard what she thought she'd heard. She waited, her muscles tense, and then it came again. A horse's neigh. A young horse.

Jeilin knew there was a herd of wild horses that sometimes roamed through the area, but she hadn't seen any sign of them on her walk from the farm.

She stepped quietly out of the woods and scanned her surroundings.

She saw nothing.

And then—there it was—a golden flash of movement.

Jeilin's heart seemed to jump into her throat when she saw him: a lithe golden colt gleaming in the sun, nervously prancing back and forth and neighing shrilly. His tiny hooves—pink and topped by neat white socks—barely seemed to touch the ground.

Jeilin stepped carefully out of the trees, forgetting about the two pails, which fell onto the muddy bank with soft plunks.

The colt didn't see her. Unaware that she was holding her breath, Jeilin dared to take another couple of steps.

The colt froze, his muscles tense and his ears pricked forward. Jeilin stood as still as a statue, but the little colt turned on his heels and bolted anyway. He stopped several yards away and turned to peer over his hindquarters at Jeilin. He snorted and trotted away, out of sight over a small hill.

Jeilin dashed forward and scrambled to the top of the hill.

The colt stood a stone's throw away, eyeing Jeilin suspiciously.

For the first time since she'd seen the exciting flash of gold, something else caught Jeilin's eye: a dark lump some sixty feet away in the tall tan grass.

Jeilin started toward it curiously, keeping one eye on the strange, unidentified object and another on the colt, who was still eyeing her intently. When she was halfway there, Jeilin realized with a start what the black mound in the grass was—a still and bloated belly, belonging to some large animal, possibly...

A horse.

Jeilin stopped a few feet from the body. A black mare lay on her side in the grass, unmistakably dead, her belly bloated in the autumn sun and her sides motionless. What exactly had caused her death was a mystery to Jeilin, but she estimated that the mare had died a couple of days ago. Surely the colt was hers.

Jeilin cast a look over her shoulder at the colt. His gold coat and the mare's black one were polar opposites, but they shared nearly identical white stripes that ran from the center of their foreheads all the way to their lips.

They were wild horses from the local herd; Jeilin could tell. Several burrs were entwined in the mare's mane and tail, which showed no signs of ever having been brushed or trimmed. Likewise, her coat gave no sign of having ever been groomed. Her hooves were unshod, untrimmed, and chipped in places. Her udder was swollen, a tell-tale sign that she had been nursing a foal.

Jeilin turned to observe the golden colt. He was beautiful…the kind of horse that galloped through her dreams and raced through her mind whenever she could afford the small luxury of fantasizing. Ever since Jeilin had seen a messenger as a young girl, she had dreamed of one day becoming one, of having a golden star pinned to her chest by the king himself. Of living an adventure, her horse's flying hooves eating up the ground beneath them as they raced to deliver a royal letter or decree. If only she had a horse, she'd thought to herself so many times. If only…

Now the gorgeous colt stood before her, motherless and somehow separated from his herd. One of two things would most likely happen to him: he would become another animal's dinner or he would be snatched up by any person

6

with any amount of sense who discovered him. It occurred to Jeilin that she was probably the first to find him, but how long would that last? She looked to the right where a dirt road snaked through the fields; it was the only path from this rural area to the nearest village, Almrahn. It wasn't exactly bustling, but it saw a decent amount of traffic.

Jeilin couldn't remember ever having felt such an overwhelming sense of longing. A beautiful young horse of her very own! The thought was tantalizing to the point that it hurt. He could be kept in the paddock with Ash. Surely father would agree! She imagined what her family's faces would look like when she came home with such an outstanding find. Her father would stand with his arms crossed, bewildered and awaiting an explanation, her mother would come out of the house with her hands on her hips, still wearing her apron, and Ehryn and Emrys would probably fall right out of the apple tree! Jeilin nearly laughed at the thought, but another quickly stopped her. What if someone else were to discover him and take him first? A sense of urgency, of desperation, crowded her thoughts. How would she get the colt home?

There was no way he would allow her to approach and halter him, and simply trot by her side. If she was going to have a chance, she would need another horse.

She started abruptly back for the farm, startling the colt, who jumped and trotted several paces away, eyeing her reproachfully.

By the time the cabin loomed into view, Jeilin was clutching her side, which felt as if it had been pierced by a butcher's knife. However, she was in no position to succumb to pain. This was too important, much too important.

She dashed to Ash, who was standing lazily in his paddock, gazing curiously at her as if wondering why she was in such a hurry. Jeilin hopped over the fence in one fluid movement, simultaneously seizing a rope that had been draped over one of the posts.

"Hey!" her father called from the orchard, causing her to jump. "Where's the water?"

"I—I'm going back!" she shouted hastily.

Her father started toward her. "Oh no," Jeilin breathed, attaching the rope to Ash's halter. He would want an explanation, of course, which would waste valuable time. In her mind's eye, Jeilin could see a group of travelers coming down the road—all robust young men—and pointing out the little lost colt to one another.

Jeilin unlatched the gate hurriedly and led Ash toward the nearby barn.

Her father reached her just as she was heaving Ash's worn old saddle onto his back. "What's going on?" he asked, his brow furrowed.

"I found a colt!" Jeilin exclaimed as quickly as possible. "His dam's dead and he's been separated from the herd. I'm going to go get him before someone else does or before he's hunted down by a wild animal!" She drew the cinch tight, perhaps a little too tight, and Ash turned his head to give her a disapproving look. She ignored it and seized two spare lengths of rope that were hanging from pegs on a stall wall, looping them over the saddle horn.

"Wait just a minute," Rab said as Jeilin swung herself into the saddle. "You're sure he's wild?"

"Yes!" Jeilin declared. "Absolutely sure!"

"And how are you planning on getting him back here?" he asked.

"I—just—I just will!" Jeilin declared pleadingly. She placed her hands on her father's shoulders from her position in the saddle and leaned down to look into his face. "Father, *please*, let me go right now, just this once!" She stared into his eyes as hard as she could, hoping to somehow bore into his heart, into his sympathies.

He opened his mouth to object and Jeilin felt her stomach plummet horribly, but then he seemed to change his mind. His expression softened. "Don't do anything foolish. And don't be gone too long."

Jeilin grinned with relief and appreciation as she dug her heels into Ash's sides and started off at a bouncy trot.

Her mother, Almeda, watched from the doorway as she trotted past the cabin. "Where are you off to?" she called.

"Ask father!" Jeilin cried over her shoulder as she implored Ash to move faster.

The fields and tiny rolling hills seemed to stretch before Jeilin like an endless expanse, and Ash just couldn't move quickly enough. Every minute seemed to stretch itself into an eternity.

Finally, they slowed, and Jeilin could make out the mare's lifeless body a few hundred feet away. Her eyes

9

swept the fields in a surge of panic when she was unable to spot the colt. Then Ash suddenly became alert; his ears pricked forward as his head rose into the air. She followed his gaze straight toward the golden colt, who had stopped his nervous trotting by the edge of the woods to stare at Ash.

For a moment both horses stood stock-still, watching one another. Then the colt neighed shrilly, and Ash nickered back and started forward unbidden. Jeilin went to stop him, but then thought better of it. Maybe the colt would allow her to approach him on horseback.

The little horse neighed again as Ash and Jeilin continued their approach. It dared to take a step forward. Jeilin felt a pang of pity for the lonely colt, who seemed nervous, yet desperate to be in the company of another horse again.

Jeilin pulled Ash short a couple of yards away. The colt allowed her to come much closer than he would have let her if she'd been on foot. Even so, she didn't want to get too confident and send him bolting through the stream and into the forest. Curious, Ash tried to move forward, but Jeilin held him back. The colt stood with his tiny golden ears pricked forward in nervous interest.

After a moment of thought, Jeilin backed Ash several paces and turned him around, stopping several yards away. Both Jeilin and Ash turned to watch the little foal's reaction. He neighed, bobbed his small golden head, and took a couple of steps forward. Jeilin wondered if he might follow Ash back to the farm. She trotted a few yards farther to test him, but the foal watched them hesitantly.

Jeilin sighed. Perhaps wishing for the colt to follow Ash home was too much to hope for. She neared the foal again and prepared for a second try. The distinct sound of a twig snapping underfoot caught Jeilin's attention. She immediately followed the sound into the woods. The horses looked too.

Emerging from the thick shade cast by the forest canopy was a magnificently large, shaggy black bear. It lumbered nonchalantly toward the tiny stream, the only thing that stood between it, the two horses, and Jeilin.

Her heart pounded against her chest and she felt Ash tense beneath her. There was no need for her to give any direction; Ash had already turned and was sprinting for home. Gripping the saddle tightly between her knees, with her heart in her throat, Jeilin turned to look for the colt.

His tiny hooves pounded the earth, sending dirt and grass clods flying as he galloped full-speed behind Ash. Despite the panic, Jeilin felt a surge of hope. Maybe this was a stroke of luck—maybe the colt would follow Ash all the way home!

She dared another glance. The bear was nowhere to be seen, probably hunched over the stream for a drink. The horses, of course, did not turn to look, but continued to run as if their lives depended on it.

Soon the colt had caught up with Ash, and the farm, with its small barn and cabin, had come back into view. A grey ribbon of smoke snaked out of the stone chimney against the blue sky. Jeilin felt a rush of hope; they were almost there and the colt was still following!

It seemed that in no time at all they were rushing past the cabin in a blur, and Jeilin was pulling Ash to a stop behind it. She looked over her shoulder to see that the foal had stopped a hundred feet from the cabin, apparently unsure what to think of the strange structure.

Jeilin thought furiously—she would need a plan to get the colt inside the paddock.

Jeilin's father emerged from the barn with eyes wide. "I haven't seen old Ash move that fast in years!"

"We—the horses were spooked by a bear!" Jeilin declared.

Rab quickly peered around the corner of the cabin and spotted the colt. "So he followed you back?" he finished.

"Yes, and I need to think of a way to get him inside the paddock before he wanders off!" Jeilin panted.

Ehryn and Emrys came jogging over. "Where did that—" Emrys began.

"Shhh, you'll scare him away!" Jeilin snapped, desperate for her brothers to go back to their chores.

Emrys cast a sullen glance at his sister, but Rab spoke before he could say anything else.

"Why don't we throw some hay out for him?" he suggested. "I don't think he'll be quick to wander off then—not with food and Ash around."

Jeilin opened her mouth to object, but realized that she didn't have a better plan. She dismounted hastily and ran for the barn. A moment later, she emerged with her arms full of hay. She placed it carefully halfway between the cabin and

Ash's paddock. All the while, the colt watched from a distance.

Jeilin led Ash to the small pile and allowed him to take a mouthful. The colt continued to stare, so she let Ash have another before she led him into the paddock, where she removed his tack and tied him to a fencepost. By the time she had replaced the saddle, blanket, and bridle in the barn, it was time for her midday meal.

In the cabin, Jeilin positioned herself at the end of the table nearest the fireplace so that she would be able to see out the opposite window, where the small haystack was still visible. Her mother, a petite woman with light brown hair secured in a neat bun, busied herself around the table doling out biscuits, beans, and salted ham. Jeilin ate quickly, not because she was especially hungry but because she was anxious to be outside again.

"You'll choke if you don't slow down," Ehryn commented.

Jeilin ignored him.

"So," Almeda asked sharply as she took a seat at the table, "what's all this about a colt?"

Jeilin continued to chew ravenously and glanced hopefully up at her father.

He sighed and began to explain. "Jeilin found an abandoned colt this morning when she went to fetch water from the stream."

"An abandoned colt?" Almeda repeated.

"One from the feral herd," Rab replied. "Its dam was nearby, dead. The herd is nowhere to be seen. Right, Jeilin?"

Jeilin nodded.

"And somehow she got the colt to follow her and Ash back to the farm. She tells me that there was a bear involved."

Almeda's eyebrows shot up so high that Jeilin feared they might separate from her forehead. "A bear?"

Jeilin nodded again, still chewing ham. "Yes," she said with a gulp. "I think it was just coming to the stream for a drink, because it didn't chase us. But it really startled the horses, and the colt ran all the way back here behind Ash."

Suddenly, Jeilin jumped in her seat as a flash of gold outside the window caught her eye. The little colt was there, eating the hay.

3 Years Later

Chapter 2

The dawn was a vivid orange sliver rising over the yellowing autumn plains as Jeilin joined her family at the breakfast table. Over the past three years, Jeilin had grown, though not as much as she had hoped. She was scarcely her mother's size and was still completely dwarfed by her much larger father. Ehryn and Emrys towered over her as well, though they too ghter than their father.

"So, Jeilin," Al sat down to her own bowl of porri thought?"

"C asked between mouth

Alme posal."

Jeilin s at her porridge. Since she had turn .iother had taken to hinting frequently abo ge. Much to Jeilin's horror, a young man named Gadyn, who lived only a few miles from her own family's farm, had expressed his interest in Jeilin to her father. Gadyn was…all right in his own way, Jeilin supposed. Twenty-four, a hard-working farmer with enough gold saved to build a house and start a family. The problem was that the thought of marrying and bearing children made

17

Jeilin wonder whether or not she was going to be able to keep her porridge down.

"I'm only sixteen, mother," Jeilin replied.

"I was sixteen when I married your father," Almeda reminded her. "Most young women your age are thinking about marriage, although not all of them are lucky enough to have already had a proposal." She straightened in her seat and beamed smugly, as if proud that *her* daughter had been the one to catch Gadyn's eye.

"I don't even know why Gadyn would want to marry me," Jeilin mumbled.

Almeda's moment of happiness vanished like a drop of water thrown in a hot skillet as she cast a disapproving glance at her daughter's apparel. Jeilin wore a plain tunic over a pair of leggings, high boots, and the signature leather strap that kept her dark, shoulder-length hair out of her face. "Well, I think we can rule out feminine charm," Almeda answered.

Jeilin snorted, still hovering over her porridge. "Maybe I want to do more than just cook and have children," she said quietly.

"Like what?" Almeda asked.

Jeilin remained silent. If she were honest with her mother, she would tell her that what she truly desired more than anything else was to become a messenger. However, she wasn't about to admit it; she knew she would be scoffed at if she did. Even though, as far as she knew, there was no rule against them, Jeilin had never seen a female messenger. It was exceedingly difficult for anyone to become a messenger anyway; only the best made it and they had to prove themselves. Plus, tryouts to become a messenger were held randomly, whenever the king himself deemed them necessary.

"Are you coming to Almrahn with me today, Jeilin?" Rab asked, mercifully interrupting the awkward marriage debate.

"Of course!" Jeilin replied. She never missed a chance to go into town, where the hustle and bustle was an interesting change from the quiet life on the farm. Plus, it would be a good excuse to indulge in a nice long ride with Fringe.

"You'll wear a dress then?" Almeda asked in a would-be casual voice.

"A dress? What for?"

"A young lady should always look her best in public," her mother prodded.

"I can't wear a dress while riding."

Almeda sighed. "I guess you don't care that going into town would be a perfect opportunity to be seen by some eligible young men."

The family finished their breakfast a few silent minutes later.

"You know," Ehryn joked as they exited the cabin, "I have a friend who tells me he'd like to marry soon, but he just hasn't found the right woman yet..."

"Don't let mother hear you," Jeilin said. "Or he'll be sitting at the dinner table when we get back from Almrahn."

Jeilin and Ehryn went to the paddock together to retrieve Fringe and Ash. The little golden colt Jeilin had discovered along the fringe of the woods three years ago had grown into every bit of sixteen hands tall, and his cream-colored mane and tale glistened, as did his golden coat. He nuzzled Jeilin with his striped nose when she approached. "Ready for a day of riding?" she asked him. He nickered in response.

A couple yards away, Ehryn was leading Ash out of the paddock.

Jeilin groomed Fringe's shining coat, which was just beginning to grow longer as the air grew cooler. Afterward, she saddled him while Ehryn harnessed Ash to a cart loaded full of crops.

Emrys emerged from the cabin carrying two burlap sacks. "Lunch," he said, situating them in the back.

"Everyone ready then?" Rab asked, emerging from the barn as hungry chickens scratched and flapped around his feet.

Jeilin swung herself into the saddle. "Ready."

The journey from the farm to Almrahn was a somewhat lengthy one, spanning seven miles of a winding dirt road known as the Dusty Pass, which bordered the forest for the first half of the journey. Jeilin had to hold Fringe back to keep him from speeding down the road, leaving little Ash and his cart behind.

The cabin and small farm had barely faded from sight when it became apparent that a group of travelers was coming from the opposite direction. Within a few minutes, Jeilin could just make out the silhouette of a horse-drawn wagon much like their own, accompanied by two mounted riders.

It wasn't until the other travelers were within shouting distance that Jeilin recognized them. The rider on the left-hand side was none other than Gadyn, the one they had discussed at the breakfast table. The other rider was one of his brothers, whose name Jeilin couldn't recall. Their father drove the cart, which was being pulled by a fat brown cob.

Jeilin cast a quick sideways glance at her own cart. Both Ehryn and Emrys gave her teasing, knowing looks.

Jeilin scowled and sat up straighter in her saddle. She could count the number of times she'd actually conversed with Gadyn on one hand; surely he wouldn't say much to her...well, hopefully he wouldn't.

Gadyn, his brother, and father drew near with a jangling of bits and squeaking of wheels.

"Good morning!" Gadyn, of middling height and build, with a head of dark waves and deep brown eyes, called from atop his horse. The gelding was a handsome animal; a sleek sorrel with a wide band of white striping its face. Jeilin focused on the horse instead of its rider.

"Good morning," Rab replied as he slowed the cart to a halt.

Following suit, Jeilin stopped beside her father and brothers and wondered whether she could back Fringe up a few paces without anyone noticing. Gadyn and his sorrel were a bit too close for her comfort.

"Headed to sell your crops at Almrahn?" Gadyn asked.

Rab nodded.

"We sold ours yesterday, stayed the night, and now we're on our way back," Gadyn explained. "The harvest

21

was good to us," he added, seemingly speaking directly to Jeilin.

Jeilin's insides seemed to squirm. She didn't know what to say. She didn't *want* to say anything, but the silence was awkward.

"That's an excellent horse you've got," Gadyn said, eyeing Fringe from his pink hooves to the tips of his ears and nose. "He's the wild colt you tamed, right?"

Jeilin nodded.

"A true stroke of luck," Gadyn said with a grin that Jeilin couldn't bring herself to return.

"This is a new horse," Gadyn said, patting his mount's neck. "Bought him in Almrahn yesterday. Four years old. What do you think of him?"

Jeilin was taken aback by Gadyn's question; she hadn't expected him to ask her opinion.

"He's…really nice," Jeilin said. "Good conformation."

"I thought so too," Gadyn said with another of his unbearable grins.

"So the market's good in Almrahn, then?" Rab asked.

Jeilin mentally vowed to thank her father later for interrupting the awkward conversation.

"Very good," Gadyn's father piped up from his seat at the front of the cart. "We'll be heading back with another wagonload soon."

Fringe shifted anxiously under Jeilin, who knew that he was longing to stop all of the boring standing about and be on with the journey.

Gadyn, who had scarcely taken his eyes off of Jeilin, noticed. "We won't keep you then," he said. "Good luck selling your crops, though I don't think you'll need it."

Everyone muttered goodbyes, and then they were finally gone. Jeilin breathed a sigh of relief while Ehryn and Emrys laughed from their seats in the cart. "I don't think he paid enough attention to you," Emrys said. "You should have worn a dress!"

Jeilin scowled.

****

It was midmorning when they arrived at Almrahn, and the marketplace was bustling. Jeilin and Fringe moved slowly through the crowded streets into a square while Ash pulled the wagon slowly behind them. Rab continued to drive while Ehryn and Emrys kept a strict watch on the contents of the cart, wary of those who might snatch vegetables without paying.

Fringe paced nervously, his head held high and his ears pricked forward. The crowds and sounds of the town were fairly new to him; it was only his third journey into Almrahn.

Here and there Jeilin noticed a stranger eyeing Fringe with interest. Of course they would; he was a fine horse. She smiled and sat straighter in the saddle.

At last they found an empty corner and parked the cart. Shoppers began to make their way over, digging coins out of pouches and declaring their orders.

"Fringe and I are going to look around a bit," Jeilin said.

Rab nodded. "Don't go too far."

They squeezed through the crowd that was growing around their cart and stepped into the slightly more open center of the square. Jeilin looked along the wall to their left, where notice posters were always hung. The painted face of a criminal stared down at her; below it was a name as well as a reward offer for his capture. Another poster decreed a relatively minor and uninteresting law, and yet another offered a small cash reward for the left ear of any of the wolves that were encroaching on local farmers' property and livestock. Then, Jeilin spotted something that caused her heart to leap into her throat.

It was a large poster from the king—why hadn't she noticed it first? She read and reread it several times just to make sure that she wasn't imagining it. The poster announced a day three weeks in the future when new messengers would be recruited. The tryouts—a race among any willing competitors—would be held in Dresinva, the royal city!

Jeilin's mind began to spin. Dresinva was a full day's ride from the farm...she could make it; she could go and try out! She scanned the poster for more information. The competition was open to any serious rider and their horse, and would begin at dawn on October twentieth. October twentieth...the date was instantly burned into her mind; she wouldn't, couldn't forget.

Jeilin reached down and buried a hand in Fringe's pale mane, wanting to touch something warm and real that would keep her grounded in reality, for her mind was quickly leaving it. Visions of racing, of victory, and of golden stars streaked through her mind like comets, only to land and explode into more and more of the same kind of thoughts. "We're going to do it, boy," Jeilin whispered. "October twentieth...we'll be there."

Fringe neighed enthusiastically, though Jeilin suspected that he did so because he was trying to catch the attention of a nearby mare. The rest of the day seemed to pass in a blur, with Jeilin's mind working feverishly, contemplating the journey to Dresinva, the competition and...how she would tell her family that she was going to go compete. She let Fringe speed ahead of the wagon on the way home, excited and as eager to run as he, imagining that she was already racing to become a messenger.

****

Dinner that night was a welcome affair; everyone was ravenous after their long day in Almrahn. Even as she ate, Jeilin was unable to think of anything but the twentieth of October.

"What's on your mind?" Ehryn asked her.

Leave it to Ehryn to notice and bring it up before she had thought of a good way to tell everyone. She sighed. She might as well say it; the race was only three weeks away and she would need her family's support if she was going to be allowed extra time to practice her riding and some coin to make it to Dresinva and back. Or maybe *just* to Dresinva she thought, feeling the familiar, almost desperate, hope beginning to rise again.

25

"I saw an interesting poster in Almrahn today," she said, moving her food around on her plate.

"It wouldn't happen to be the one announcing that the king is seeking new messengers, would it?" Ehryn asked slyly.

Jeilin dropped her fork. He knew?

Everyone looked up from their plates to stare at Jeilin.

"I want to try out," she said finally. "Fringe and me."

For a moment, nobody said anything.

"There's going to be a race, and the winner, or winners—I don't know how many new messengers the king needs—will be inducted into the king's fleet of royal messengers. It's going to be held on the twentieth of October in Dresinva. It's open to anyone."

More silence. Jeilin didn't know what else to say.

"So three weeks from now, then?" Rab finally said as he buttered a roll.

Jeilin nodded, watching her mother out of the corner of her eye and waiting for her to say something.

"You're serious?" Almeda finally asked, her fork forgotten halfway between her plate and her mouth.

Jeilin nodded. "Yes, mother, I'm serious."

Almeda cast a bewildered glance at Rab, clearly asking for help.

"Come now Almeda," he said. "You shouldn't be surprised. Jeilin's dreamed of becoming a messenger ever since the first time she caught sight of one as a child."

"Yes, but…" Almeda frowned down at her plate. "A race in Dresinva, really?"

"Why not?" Rab asked. "It's her dream, and it won't hurt anything to let her try."

"I'll tell you why not!" Almeda said, swelling with indignation as she dropped her fork, which clattered against her plate. "Being a messenger is *dangerous*. It's no position for a young woman to put herself in!"

"It's not all that dangerous, mother," Jeilin said, earning herself a fierce glare.

"Oh, isn't it?" Almeda asked. "Tell me then, who carries the king's and officers' messages during wars?"

"The messengers, of course," Jeilin admitted, "but Alaishin hasn't seen war since well before I was born!"

"Be that as it may," Almeda countered, "you'd be out dashing across the kingdom alone and could even be set upon by one of your own countrymen!"

Jeilin opened her mouth to object, but Rab spoke first. "Everyone knows the penalty for harming or intercepting a royal messenger is harsh. There aren't many who would risk a painful death just to satisfy a curiosity over the royalty's correspondences."

For a brief moment, Almeda seemed at a loss for words. During that pause, Jeilin's heart soared. She hadn't expected her father to stand up for her like this.

"The harvest has been good this year," Rab continued. "We can spare some gold for the journey to Dresinva."

"You want to let her travel all the way to Dresinva *alone*?" Almeda asked, her voice pained.

"I was thinking that we could all go," Rab replied calmly. "The four of us can ride in the wagon while Jeilin rides Fringe."

Almeda became quiet again and Jeilin felt like her heart was glowing.

Chapter 3

The nineteenth of October was a glorious day, Jeilin thought. Fringe trotted rhythmically under her, his hooves eating up the Dusty Pass, drawing ever closer to the royal city. Even the sun seemed to know the day was the start of something special; it rose over the hills in a spectacular display of pink clouds with fiery, glowing linings.

"Slow down now," Rab called from where he sat next to her mother in the wooden cart's seat, a long set of driving reins resting in his lap. "You can't expect Ash to keep pace."

"Nor the rest of us!" Emrys added, walking beside the cart with Ehryn to give Ash a break.

Their long journey would take the better part of the day, and their plan was to arrive in Dresinva that evening and find lodging at an inn. They would rise early the next morning for the competition.

Jeilin forced herself to slow down. She carried a wonderful sense of hope and excitement in her heart that warmed her against autumn's chill all the way to Dresinva.

****

Dresinva was an explosion of turrets, towers, and flags. The royal city stood proudly against the dusky sky, impressive and welcoming, its open gates adorned with silk banners. Jeilin and her family were among a throng of other travelers who were pressed at the gate, eager to enter before they closed at dark. A pair of sentry stood watch, armed with swords, monitoring the flow of people and animals into the city.

Fringe neighed nervously as they stepped through the gates of the city that was new to him. Even Jeilin could count on one hand the number of times she'd visited the royal city. Moving forward through the crowded streets required patience for Jeilin and Fringe as her father led the way.

"I think I see an inn ahead," Rab finally said.

A wooden sign hung from a row of larger stone buildings, and as they drew closer Jeilin saw that it did indeed read "Inn."

Jeilin and her small entourage of family pulled over to the side of the street with some difficulty so that Rab could step inside to find the inn's owner.

After a moment, a short older man with a large white beard emerged from the inn with Rab at his side. "One room left," he said.

"And the stables?" Rab asked.

"Right next door," said the inn owner. "I think there are a few stalls left, but you should hurry—they're filling up fast—scores of people have come to the city to witness the start of the race tomorrow." There was no question about which race he meant.

A quarter of an hour later, Rab had also acquired two stalls and space for their wagon for the night.

Jeilin savored the feelings of immense happiness, nervousness, and excitement as she settled into the modest little room she and her family shared. A fire roared in the small stone fireplace as she splashed her face with water from a basin. There was one mattress, and the innkeeper had provided them with three wooden cots for Jeilin and her brothers.

Thoughts of the next day's competition raced through Jeilin's head as she crawled under her wool blanket, listening to her father snore. Fringe carried her over the blurred line separating consciousness from sleep and into her dreams, where crowds cheered as the king pinned a golden star to the front of her tunic.

Jeilin rose an hour before dawn the next morning, already dressed and eager to make her way to the stable.

"You need to eat something," Almeda said as Jeilin pulled on her boots.

Jeilin took the thick slice of bread and hunk of cheese that her mother had produced from a bag. She was too excited to feel hungry, but knew that she would need her energy for the race.

"I'm going to get Fringe ready," Jeilin said. "You four are going to meet me in the royal yard for the start, aren't you?"

"We'll be there," Rab said with a yawn.

Jeilin smiled nervously, then rushed from the room and out of the inn, eating the bread as she jogged toward the stable.

A warm rush of relief seemed to spread from her head to her toes when she heard Fringe neigh from his stall. Although two guards kept watch over the stable at all hours, Jeilin had still felt slightly uneasy about leaving him there for the night.

She eagerly slipped into the stall, drew a brush from the pocket of her tunic, and began to quickly groom Fringe. Fifteen minutes later she had saddled and mounted him, and had begun to make her way through the winding streets toward the castle that loomed in the distance. The streets weren't as full as they had been the previous evening, but they were unusually busy for such an early hour. Every time she caught sight of another horse and rider, she wondered if they were to be her competition.

Eventually she reached the castle gates. Two pairs of guards stood on either side, asking the occasional question, shouting the occasional admonition, and allowing people through—until it was her turn.

"Spectators are allowed in on foot only," one the guards barked when she arrived at the gates.

"I'm not a spectator," Jeilin heard herself say. "I'm a competitor."

Several of the surrounding people on foot scoffed, and Jeilin refused to act like she had heard. A very young man near her was on horseback too, but he didn't laugh. He looked nervous.

"Don't be wise with me, lass," the guard said, stepping forward.

"I'm not!" Jeilin insisted. She met the guard's eyes and forced herself to hold his scrutinizing gaze.

"You may enter," he finally said sourly.

Jeilin heard the guard snort as she passed under the archway.

A large and handsome lawn stretched out before the castle, and another guard stood a few yards from the gate, shouting commands. "Spectators to the left," he called to the entering crowds. "Competitors to the right!"

Jeilin directed Fringe to where a growing group of horses and riders waited. The young man who had been near her at the gate followed. Jeilin attracted a fair number of stares as she approached the group, stopping a couple of yards away from the nearest rider, a lean blond man on an even leaner grey horse. All of the present competitors were men, Jeilin noticed, unsurprised. Well, some of them were young enough that they were boys, really; but either way she looked at it, she was certainly the only female among them. Several of the men grunted or laughed when they saw Jeilin, while others seemed to be pretending not to notice her at all.

"Sneak your father's horse out while he was still asleep this morning?" asked a dark, burly man mounted on a stout bay.

Most of the group burst into laughter. Jeilin ignored him, looking instead to her left where thousands of observers were gathering. She could see them—men, women, and children—all ogling the group of riders, many of them pointing...probably at her, she realized.

Eventually Jeilin saw her family file in. Glad to see their familiar faces, she waved to them. When they caught sight of her and waved back, the group of riders burst into laughter once more. "Mama and papa come to watch their little girl?" the burly man asked loudly.

Jeilin continued to ignore them, choosing instead to take in the castle and stroke Fringe's golden neck. It was another awkward quarter of an hour before the gates closed and a horn was blown.

The crowd hushed and waited in expectant silence. The grand doors at the front of the castle were opened, and after several suspenseful minutes a man on a white horse galloped out over the lowered drawbridge. He was followed by an entourage of soldiers in striking red uniforms riding sleek black mounts, some of them bearing red silk flags stamped with the king's emblem, the silhouette of a soaring white falcon. The group of riders came to a synchronized halt as the crowd burst into cheers. Jeilin bent her neck to peer around another competitor for a better look at the white horse's rider. He had a build that hinted at lean muscle, a head of deep brown curls, and a beard with hints of grey. A gold crown gleamed on his head, set with stones. He was the king—King Darnasius!

The king graciously accepted the crowd's applause for several minutes before motioning for silence. When he spoke, his voice echoed over the grounds. "Welcome, citizens of Alaishin," he called. "I am pleased to see that people from all corners of the kingdom have come to watch and to compete in the race that will determine the best rider in the land to serve the fair and fierce kingdom we all call home, Alaishin."

The king paused to allow the crowd another moment of uproarious applause.

"The race will be long and hard, so let us not delay its start," he continued. "Will all competitors and their mounts please come forward."

The crowd of competitors that surrounded Jeilin began to click and nudge their horses' sides, and she did the same. Some two hundred pairs of horses and riders, including Jeilin, aligned themselves before the king. Jeilin felt a thrill of nervousness as the king scanned the large group of riders. She felt the thousands of observers' eyes upon her and her fellow competitors, but his gaze made her stomach do more summersaults than all of the rest combined.

"The race will begin and end here," the king said, and his strong voice carried across the expectant silence. "All competitors must ride out of the east gate and travel twelve miles due east across the Minor Plains until they reach the edge of the Grey Forest. There they will find guards waiting for them with sealed scrolls. The first riders to return with their scrolls, still sealed, will be inducted into my service as royal messengers."

The crowd burst into applause. The first riders to return? The king hadn't said how many of the first riders to return would be made messengers, Jeilin realized. Would it be the first two? The first three? The first ten? There was no way of knowing, Jeilin decided; she would simply have to return as quickly as possible. She cast a sizing glance at her competition, which was still completely male. Most of the men were young. There were a fair few who couldn't have been much older than Jeilin, mixed among many in their twenties and some others in their thirties. A smaller portion of older men were present, some with grey in their hair, and Jeilin caught sight of one man who appeared downright elderly. Most of the competitors who appeared to be around Jeilin's own age seemed slightly nervous and were mounted on horses of questionable quality. Jeilin wondered if she appeared as fretful. At least she knew that no one could mistake her horse for anything other than a quality animal, a thought that gave her some small measure of comfort.

Jeilin realized one thing as she looked around; she had an advantage that most of the other competitors did not. She was very small and light—by far the lightest. Plus, Fringe was a large, well-muscled, long-legged, and unusually fast horse. Carrying Jeilin was practically nothing for him. Some of the other horses were dwarfed by their large riders, and Jeilin doubted that they would be able to finish the race quickly, if at all.

"At the sound of the horn, the race will begin," the king announced. "I ask that those of you who are watching stay out of the way of our riders."

Jeilin's stomach was a nervous knot. Fringe pawed the ground impatiently. During the long seconds that stretched before the horn sounded, Jeilin contemplated the three weeks of vigorous endurance-training she had put herself and Fringe through. They'd ridden for hours each day, over the rolling plains, steep hills, and even on a rugged mountain trail. Of course, she'd been working him in such ways ever since the first time she'd climbed onto his back, but they had worked extra hard of late, and Fringe was in excellent shape for it. As a feral breed, Fringe was naturally hardy and strong anyway. They had a chance, Jeilin thought. They really had a chance.

The horn sounded and they were off. The pounding of nearly a thousand hooves was deafening. Jeilin knew that the ride was going to be long and hard and that they would need to pace themselves, but like the other horses and riders, she and Fringe were full of nervous energy and unable to resist showing off. The swarm of horses thundered past the watching, cheering crowd and out the open east gate. The Minor Plains, as they were called, stretched before them, flat and yellow.

Jeilin slowed Fringe to a trot and they moved along briskly, their breath fogging the cool early morning air. They were surrounded by scores of other riders, some trotting sensibly as they were, others thundering past them. They had twenty-four miles to go, Jeilin reminded herself. If they didn't pace themselves they'd expend all of their energy during the first half of the journey. She reminded herself of that fact each time another horse flew past her and Fringe.

The sun rose steadily as Jeilin and Fringe pressed on, still in great company but not as crowded as they had been at the beginning of the ride. Jeilin was grateful for the sun's warming rays.

Jeilin regularly checked the compass that she kept in a small saddlebag, making sure to travel due east. She noticed a few riders who seemed to be veering off course; perhaps they hadn't brought compasses.

They had traveled nearly eight miles, or so Jeilin estimated, when they approached a stream that wound its way through the plains like a blue silk ribbon. Jeilin slowed Fringe to a walk as they approached the water; she could see a dozen or so horses and riders stooped at its banks. She dismounted and led Fringe to the edge of the stream. He lowered his head and drank gratefully. Jeilin cupped her hands and brought the cool, refreshing water to her face. The other riders seemed to be too thirsty and too busy to say anything. Jeilin took their cue and remained silent. She waited until Fringe finished his drink and then mounted again hastily. She urged Fringe through the small stream, which hardly rose to his knees, and they were off again, riding eastward toward the Grey Forest.

For miles Fringe trotted obediently with his golden ears pricked forward, and Jeilin imagined that he understood the importance of the race. Occasionally, when another horse would speed past them, Fringe would snort and pull at the bit, not wanting to be passed. More often than not, though, they would see the same horse again later, sweaty, tired, and heaving as they pressed past, ahead once again.

Jeilin tried to estimate their progress and placing in the race. If she was right, and she hoped that she was, she and Fringe were doing very well. She wasn't sure how many horses were ahead of them, but she was sure that it couldn't be many. With his light load, Fringe seemed to be holding up noticeably better than most of the other horses.

Along the way, Jeilin even saw some riders who had dismounted and stopped, tending to horses that were either injured or uncooperative. She felt a twinge of pity for each of them at the sight, but at the same time she couldn't help but think that each was one less obstacle between herself and the life that she'd been dreaming of.

Jeilin's stomach seemed to do a cartwheel when she saw it—a thin grey band on the horizon—the Grey Forest! A thrill of success, of desperation, seemed to shoot through her veins as her heart started to beat faster. She let Fringe trot more briskly, inspired by the sight of the looming forest. She could see a horse and rider ahead of her and longed to surge forward, galloping past them. She held Fringe back. She would save that burst of speed for later.

As the forest drew closer and closer, Jeilin noticed something else—a tiny patch of red waving from the grey gloom. Eventually she was close enough to recognize it for what it really was: a royal flag. Jeilin squinted. The flag wasn't alone; stationed beside it were two sentries like the ones she had seen at the royal gates. Their stout black mounts stood beside them. They had to be the guards with the scrolls.

The horse and rider ahead of them, whom Jeilin and Fringe had been gaining on, sped forward. Able to bear it no longer, Jeilin did the same. Fringe surged ahead.

Jeilin saw a sudden movement out of the corner of her eye. Coming diagonally from the right was a sorrel horse and its rider. It was running hard, bits of foam flying from its mouth and flecking its cheeks. The rider must have veered off course, Jeilin realized, and was riding hard to make a comeback.

The other horse that had been ahead of Jeilin and Fringe for so long, a small and muscular bay, was drawing steadily nearer as Fringe plunged ahead. The sorrel to their right was still running hard, but was barely gaining on them. The red flag waved lazily in a slight breeze, and soon they were close enough that Jeilin could make out the white falcon embroidered on it.

The bay reached the guards first, with Jeilin and Fringe on his heels, barely behind. Both horses pulled up quickly, sliding and snorting. One guard handed a scroll to the bay's rider in silence, while another handed one to Jeilin. Jeilin took it and felt suddenly alive. In her own hand she held a scroll that she would deliver to the king, and if she got there quickly enough she would earn the privilege of carrying such messages again and again. She leaned forward and squeezed Fringe's sides tightly with her legs. He bolted forward and they were off, back across the Minor Plains and toward the waiting king and crowd of spectators. They thundered past the bay, and Jeilin laughed as Fringe's pale mane whipped in the wind, reflecting the sunshine.

Eventually, they had to slow down. When they did, Jeilin glanced over her shoulder. Behind them the hardy bay was clearly visible, trotting vigorously. Jeilin could just make out the shape of the sorrel in the distance, along with a couple of other unfamiliar horses. Ahead, there were no others visible. What did that mean, Jeilin wondered to herself. That there were others so far ahead that she couldn't even see them? Or that she was leading them all…that she was actually in first place? The thought was so exciting that it was almost too much to bear.

Jeilin's stomach plummeted when another horse and rider came into view. By the time Jeilin reached them, she realized that the horse was walking. The rider's head was bowed deeply and they seemed to be in no sort of hurry. Jeilin's eyes darted to the rider's hands—they were empty except for reins. Could that mean that he didn't have a scroll? Perhaps he had given up and turned around? The rider glanced up at Jeilin and Fringe as they hurried past. His dispirited gaze told Jeilin that her speculation had been correct. As she pressed on, she saw at least a dozen more riders who seemed to be in the same situation. Each time she approached one, her heart sped up frantically, and then slowed in relief as she passed them.

Jeilin became used to seeing these dejected riders making their way slowly back to Dresinva, and gave a stout, dark-haired man perched on a brown cob little thought when she first saw him. The man turned his head at the sound of Fringe's hooves and Jeilin saw his eyes come to rest on the end of the scroll that was protruding from one of her saddlebags. He dismounted from his horse and crouched at its side, lifting one of its hooves. He rummaged in a pocket as Jeilin and Fringe approached him, presumably looking for a hoof pick. The moment Fringe was beside the cob, the man jerked up and lunged at her side. So many things seemed to take place within one single second; Jeilin shouted as the man clung onto the saddle, groping for the end of the scroll. She tried desperately to kick at the man, but his weight was pressed against her leg, pinning it between his chest and Fringe's side. She struggled to cover the top of the saddlebag with her arm so that the man wouldn't be able to take the scroll. The man seized her slender arm in his large hand and began to pry.

Suddenly, there came a flash of brown coat and black mane, followed by a loud *thunk* as the man collapsed, relinquishing his hold on Jeilin's arm. The bay had passed fearlessly through the narrow gap between Fringe and the brown cob, and she realized its rider had delivered a sharp blow to the man's head as he rode by. Fringe panicked, rearing and veering off to the right at a hard run. The horn from the only saddle Jeilin's family owned caught Jeilin in the ribs, nearly knocking the wind out of her. For one terrifying moment, Jeilin thought that she was going to be thrown over Fringe's neck. She clung desperately to Fringe's mane and struggled to right herself. Fringe thundered on, straying farther off course and sending a fresh wave of sharp pain through her chest with every step.

Jeilin managed to stuff the scroll deep into the saddlebag. She seized the reins in her hands and struggled to correct Fringe. She slowed him with some difficultly and realigned him toward Dresinva. Her ribs ached and throbbed with every heavy breath, but the important thing was that she still had the scroll. She looked over her shoulder at the man who had tried to steal it from her; he had been knocked onto his haunches and was rising slowly. Jeilin hoped that he at least had a sizeable lump on his head from her rescuer's blow.

The bay that had been following so closely had passed her when Fringe panicked. Jeilin struggled to stay straight in the saddle as she urged Fringe to catch up with the bay and its rider. Finally, she was riding beside them. He was young, lean, and slight. His face was fair and proud, framed by short straw-colored hair. He appeared to be only slightly older than Jeilin, if he was really older at all. He did not return Jeilin's gaze but rather urged his horse forward, refusing to let Jeilin pass him.

"Thank you," Jeilin managed to call between pained breaths. Her ribs ached, but she willed herself to ignore the pain and ride forward. The fair-haired boy on the bay only nodded his acceptance.

Behind them, the sorrel pressed on.

By the time Dresinva came into view, Jeilin was sweating in the afternoon sun and her muscles ached. Fringe was tired, Jeilin could tell, but he maintained a quick trot nonetheless. Beside them, the bay did the same. Jeilin could see that the boy's white shirt was sticking to his sides, damp with sweat. The sorrel was the only distinctly visible horse behind them, and Jeilin noted with joy that it seemed to be falling farther behind.

Jeilin could hardly contain her excitement. She suspected strongly that she and the boy on the bay were vying for first place. If she was right…she was about to become a messenger! The thought was intoxicating.

Finally, the eastern gate they had departed through that morning became visible. It was wide open, with guards stationed at either side. The castle loomed behind it, and Jeilin thought she could just barely make out the crowd waiting inside the grounds. Somewhere amongst the throng was her family, waiting anxiously and about to be surprised when they saw her come speeding through the gates in what might be first...or second place. She and Fringe were neck and neck with the bay, cantering hard.

It seemed an eternity before Jeilin sensed that she was close enough to put on their final burst of speed. Fringe responded as soon as she leaned forward, ignoring how her ribs protested, and they rocketed ahead of the bay. Fringe's hooves pounded the earth and Jeilin gripped the saddle tightly between her knees, her eyes glued to the gate as they drew closer and closer. She heard the bay put on a burst of speed a moment later, and once again they found themselves neck and neck. Jeilin's side ached fiercely, and she struggled to keep pace with the bay, unable to ask Fringe for more speed. Each hoof beat sent an agonizing spike of pain up through her ribs, and she struggled to stay upright in the saddle.

They flew through the gates and onto the soft, mani-cured turf of the royal lawn. Ahead, the king rose to his feet, and the crowd broke into an uproar on the lawn where over two hundred horse-and-rider teams had been dismissed. Jeilin saw a group of mounted men gathered off to the side. Who were they? Had they already delivered their scrolls, or were they the riders who had quit and turned around? The bay inched ahead of her, but it was all she could do to endure Fringe's current speed.

She came to a sudden, jarring stop that sent a fresh wave of nauseating pain through her ribs and nearly unseated her a mere three yards from the king. He turned to face her and the boy on the bay, who had arrived a pace in front of her. They both held out their scrolls, and the king himself took them from their outstretched hands.

Chapter 4

J eilin thought she might be made deaf by the roaring crowd. Fringe pranced nervously. The king's gaze still rested on her and the boy, a fact that Jeilin was supremely aware of. Jeilin longed to scan the crowd for her family's faces, but dared not turn away from the king's attention. The crowd continued to cheer wildly…had they been the first to return with scrolls?

King Darnasius turned to the crowd and held up a single hand, silencing them. "The first to return with scrolls," he cried, making a sweeping gesture toward the boy and Jeilin with his right hand.

Jeilin's heart soared. The crowd burst into cheers again. She could hardly believe it; she had been the second, and very nearly the first, rider to return to the king with a scroll! Suddenly, nothing around her seemed real. The roaring crowd, the proud king, the many turrets and towers of Dresinva, the fierce red flags and banners flapping in the light breeze…this was surely all a dream. The roaring of the crowd seemed strangely distant; only Fringe, beneath her, seemed real. She buried her hand in his long mane, trusting the warmth to keep her grounded in reality. She squeezed her eyes shut. When she opened them again, the crowd was still there, as vast and loud as an army. The king beamed and raised his hand again.

"Riders, let the people see your faces," he said.

Jeilin applied her leg to Fringe's side, and they turned slowly to face the crowd, which seemed to have doubled in size since the departure that morning. The spectators roared again in unison, like a many-headed entity with their hundreds upon hundreds of eyes focused on Jeilin and the boy.

Jeilin became aware that she was being spoken to. "What are your names?" the king asked.

Being addressed by the king also seemed unreal, and Jeilin felt color creeping into her cheeks.

"Cai, Your Majesty," said the boy.

Jeilin heard herself give her own name, but it sounded as if someone else were saying it.

"I give you Cai and Jeilin," the king announced, "who will be inducted into my service and join the fleet of royal messengers this day."

The crowd went wild. Jeilin still felt strangely numb.

"The official ceremony will be held in two hours."

At the king's word, two attendants, dressed in livery that was more exquisite than any farm wife's finest dress, stepped forward. One assisted Jeilin down from Fringe while Cai dismounted on his own. They led their horses away, while two other servants appeared seemingly out of nowhere and led Jeilin and Cai into the castle.

The dreamlike sensation of unreality that had settled over Jeilin heightened as she stepped over the threshold, leaving the boisterous crowd behind. The stone walls muffled, but didn't quite silence, the sound of cheering. A young chamber maid with her hair neatly arranged in a long, dark braid appeared suddenly by Jeilin's side in the great entrance hall. "Follow me," she said with a curtsy. "You must prepare for the ceremony."

Another attendant led Cai in a different direction.

The girl led Jeilin up a flight of stairs and through several stone corridors until they arrived in front of a large set of ornately carved oaken double doors. She pushed them open, and Jeilin had to stop herself from gasping at what she saw.

The room was a bright, shining expanse of swirled white marble. At its center, the floor sunk down into a huge, pool-sized bath. Sunshine spilled in through a large, high window. Steam rose from the water, which was topped by a thick layer of bubbly foam. The fragrant scent of lavender filled the room.

"You may start your bath," the chambermaid said, pulling the doors shut behind them. "I'll be here to fetch you anything you may need."

Jeilin stepped behind a dressing screen next to the pool, eagerly stripped off her sweaty clothes, and left them on the stone floor next to her dirt-caked boots in a small pile. She spared a glance for her bruised ribs before she stepped out from behind the screen, eager to wash the dust of travel from her body.

She stood on the edge of the great tub and tested the water with her toe. It was hot, but not too hot—perfect. She lowered herself in and was surprised by how long it took her feet to find the bottom—the bathwater rose almost to her shoulders. Jeilin sighed. She could feel the soothing water washing away the sweat and dust that she had accumulated on her long ride. She splashed her face and removed the leather strip that restrained her hair before submerging herself completely under the water. When she rose above the surface again, the serving woman was there offering a thick, creamy shampoo that smelled strongly of honeysuckle. Jeilin accepted it and massaged it deep into her hair until it was more white with lather than it was deep brown.

When Jeilin finished her bath, she found that the old clothes she had left behind the dressing screen were gone. In their place was a stack of new garments, suitable for riding yet finer than anything she'd ever worn. A silver comb rested on top of the neatly folded stack. Jeilin picked it up and ran it through her hair. When she had picked out every knot, she admired the soft new breeches and felt the fabric of a new tunic in wonder. It was the softest, finest silk she had ever felt. The tunic was the same blazing red as the royal flags and banners. There were even woolen socks and polished leather boots, which fit perfectly. Jeilin felt as if she had received a lifetime of birthday gifts by the time she'd finished dressing.

The chambermaid was waiting patiently for her when she emerged from behind the dressing screen. She led Jeilin to another room. "You can rest here for now," she explained.

"Someone will come for you when it's time for the ceremony. Everything in the room is for your use."

The woman left and Jeilin was alone in the room. Across from a blazing fireplace, there was a sofa with luxuriously embroidered upholstery. In front of it was a low table covered in various dishes. There was a bowl of fruit, a platter of cheeses, another of breads, and one of cold meats. Jeilin's stomach growled and she realized for the first time how hungry she was.

She settled onto the comfortable couch with a sigh of relief. The day had been long and hard, and it was hardly over. She reached for a piece of meat; pheasant, she suspected. It was delicious. She poured herself a glass of water from a pitcher that rested on the table and drank thirstily. She continued to sample the offerings of the various trays until she was full. Then she reclined on the couch and closed her eyes. It seemed to Jeilin that she'd only drifted off a moment before when a knock at the door woke her.

She rose from the couch and hurried to the door. When she opened it, a handsomely dressed guard with a sword at his side was waiting. "I am to escort you to the ceremony."

Jeilin nodded nervously and followed him. She had never been to such an event and wondered what it would be like.

She was led out onto the grounds, where the royal stable was clearly visible. Cai and another guard were already there. Jeilin could see two men leading Fringe and Cai's bay gelding toward them. When they were reunited, Jeilin saw that Fringe had been thoroughly groomed, and that his mane had been expertly bound in tiny braids with red ribbon. Most surprisingly of all, he wore a handsome new saddle and matching bridle. Jeilin could tell that the saddle was made for riding quickly and over long distances. It looked very expensive, certainly not something that she would ever have had a chance to use back on her family's farm. "Your old tack is in the stable if you wish to retrieve it later," the groom informed Jeilin and Cai.

"Thank you..." Jeilin said, still in awe. Her old farm tack did not compare to what she had been given, but of course she would come back for it later; she knew that her parents still needed it for Ash.

Jeilin took Fringe's reins and stroked his smooth neck affectionately. He seemed happy; Jeilin knew that he must have been fed and watered.

"You'll ride from here to the front of the castle, where the ceremony will be held," one of the guards said. "Another messenger will lead you."

As if on cue, a horse and rider emerged from the stables, trotting toward them. The horse was a tall, lean grey whose body was smattered with dark spots. It looked to be built for speed. Its rider was a bearded man who appeared to be just short of his middle years. Golden stars flashed from the man's chest and his mount's bridle.

"Well, well," he said with a smile. "Congratulations, you two."

Jeilin murmured her thanks nervously while Cai said something similar. She couldn't believe that she was about to be put into the same league with the man in front of her. Could she ever look as confident in the saddle, as sure of herself as he was?

"Better mount then," he said. "They're waiting."

Jeilin climbed gingerly into the saddle, where she instantly felt more at home. She and Cai trotted behind the messenger and his horse as he led them to the front castle grounds where the crowd and the king waited.

The crowd burst into cheers for what seemed like the thousandth time that day as Jeilin and Cai continued to follow the messenger up an aisle of armed, flag-bearing guards. They stopped when they reached the end, where the king waited, standing regally.

"Dismount now," the messenger whispered to them. Jeilin slid stiffly back to the ground and stood at Fringe's head, holding his reins. Beside her, Cai did the same.

King Darnasius raised a hand and the crowd was silenced. "Today it is my pleasure to welcome two new riders into the elite ranks of Alaishin's Royal Messengers. Though they are young, they have proven themselves more worthy of this honor than the hundreds of others they competed against today. Cai, step forward."

Cai stepped forward at the king's command, still holding his horse's reins in one hand. The king pinned a shining golden star onto Cai's chest, and another just like it to his horse's bridle. "I, King Darnasius of Alaishin, appoint you as a Royal Messenger, bound by honor to my service, if you will swear to ride true and never betray my trust or the trust of your kingdom."

"I swear," Cai said.

The crowd roared.

"Jeilin, step forward."

Jeilin was almost surprised that she was able to make her legs move. Time seemed to stand still as King Darnasius reached out with another golden star and pinned it to her shirt. Surely she was imagining this...having the king's full attention. She watched in awe as he attached one just like it to Fringe's bridle. "I, King Darnasius of Alaishin, appoint you as a Royal Messenger, bound by honor to my service, if you will swear to ride true and never betray my trust or the trust of your kingdom."

"I swear," she said fervently.

The crowd roared again and Cai and Jeilin dropped to their knee, bowing before the king. The shouts and applause seemed to last for a small eternity. When Jeilin rose, she realized that evening had settled over the city.

"We have accommodations for both of you tonight in the castle," said King Darnasius. "A servant will show you to your quarters."

Two waiting grooms took Fringe and the bay by their reins and began to lead them toward the stables.

"You will both stay here tomorrow night as well, and leave on your first mission the next day."

The king turned and retreated toward the castle, followed by a small entourage of servants.

Her first mission? Jeilin wondered when the fact that she really was a messenger would settle in; it still seemed like a dream.

"Surely you two will stop by the Scarlet Banner this evening then?" the messenger who had escorted Jeilin and Cai to the ceremony asked.

"The Scarlet Banner?" Jeilin repeated.

"A local tavern," he explained. "A stone's throw from the common square, next to a tailor's shop."

Jeilin didn't know what to say. Why would she stop by a tavern?

"Of course," Cai said.

"Good!" the messenger said heartily. "A fair few messengers stopped in Dresinva to see who would be joining us today, and we'll all be at the Scarlet Banner this evening. It would almost be a crime if our newest messengers didn't join us."

"I suppose I'll be there too, then," Jeilin replied, trying to sound nonchalant, as if the idea of spending the evening in a tavern with a group of seasoned messengers—probably all men—didn't intimidate her.

"Farewell for now then," the man said with a grin. "By the way, my name is Eric." He and his dappled mount turned quickly and trotted toward the stables.

Jeilin turned to the mysterious, fair-haired youth beside her. It felt strange, having raced beside him all day and having gone through the ceremony together without ever being introduced.

"I'm Jeilin," she said, extending her hand.

He turned and faced her. "I'm Cai," he said, shaking her hand. He was only slightly taller than her, and his palm was rough with calluses. His expression was serious and unreadable. "Nice race," he said.

"And you," Jeilin replied with a smile.

"See you at the Scarlet Banner then," he said, and turned to walk away.

He probably had family he wanted to see too, Jeilin thought.

Jeilin turned toward the crowd and saw, with a rush of joy, that her family was waiting for her at the very front.

She hurried to them and when she reached them, she was immediately engulfed in a sea of open arms and shouts. Her bruised ribs throbbed, but she smiled anyway.

"I can't believe you won!" Ehryn shouted.

"I thought for a moment that I was seeing things when you came through the gate," Emrys added.

"You make it sound as if you expected me to come limping back in last place," Jeilin said, unable to stop herself from grinning.

"It's not that," Ehryn said. "It's just..." He stared at the golden star pinned to Jeilin's bright new tunic. "I just can't believe it. My little sister, of all people—a messenger!"

"To tell the truth, I can't believe it either," Jeilin confessed.

She felt her father's hand settle onto her shoulder. "Well done," he said with a grin. "I'm still in a state of shock as well."

Jeilin giggled.

Almeda looked as if she was unable to decide whether she should laugh or cry. "I can't believe it," she said with a dry sob. "My own daughter a...a messenger! Appointed by the king in front of the entire city!"

"We're not sure whether she's proud or devastated," Ehryn whispered to Jeilin.

"Both, probably," Emrys said. "She thought that this race would get the whole messenger thing out of your system, and that when we got home you'd realize that you wanted to marry Gadyn after all." He smirked. "We don't know what she's going to tell him now."

"Well...what's next?" Rab asked. His voice was hearty, but Jeilin could detect a trace of sadness. For the first time, she fully realized that she was going to be separated from her family.

"King Darnasius said that I'll be staying at the castle for the next two nights, and then I'll be leaving on my first mission."

Almeda let out another dry sob.

"Shall we go celebrate, then?" Rab asked. "Or do you...have another commitment?"

"I'm sort of supposed to meet some other riders at a, uh, tavern this evening," she said.

Almeda stopped sobbing suddenly and gasped instead.

"But I'd much rather eat with the family first and then go there later," Jeilin finished.

Rab, Ehryn, and Emrys beamed. Almeda tried to, but Jeilin could tell that the thought of her daughter spending the evening in a tavern full of strangers was heavy on her mind.

Jeilin left the royal grounds for the city streets, where she and her family walked back to the inn they'd stayed in the night before. Everywhere she went, people seemed to stare, to point, to whisper, and to shout. "I think you're drawing a bit of attention," Emrys said.

The inn's common room filled quickly after they entered. "We'll be busy this evening," the owner said with a grin as he took their orders. "A young maiden Alaishin's newest messenger...my, my...I never thought I'd see the day..." He hobbled back to the kitchen.

"Now don't take this personally, Jeilin, but I don't think anyone expected you to win," Emrys said.

The meal was hot and delicious, but Jeilin savored the time with her family more than the food. Now that she was staying at the castle and would leave on her first mission in two days' time, her days were numbered. She recounted her time inside the castle carefully, describing the food and the bath in lavish detail. Her family listened intently, and she felt a twinge of sadness when the time came for her to leave the restaurant and find the Scarlet Banner. She promised to meet her family at the inn the next morning before stepping out of the warm, chattering restaurant and into the lamp-lit city streets.

She knew that she was only a few minutes' walk from the common square, so the tavern must be nearby.

Ten minutes later she had found it, nestled between a tailor's shop and an apothecary, both closed. Half a dozen horses were tied to hitching posts out front. She pushed the door open nervously and stepped inside.

It was dimly lit compared to the inn, and less quiet. A score of men were inside, most seated at the bar, and a few gathered around wooden tables in small groups. Everywhere Jeilin looked, golden stars gleamed.

She spotted a familiar golden head of hair at the bar: Cai. There was an empty stool next to him. She started for it, strangely aware of how loudly the wooden floorboards were squeaking beneath her stiff new boots. She had made it almost halfway across the room before she was noticed.

"Our other new messenger has arrived!" one man called boisterously from a table, throwing down a hand of playing cards.

The tavern burst into cheers and applause. Jeilin hoped that the dim lighting would hide her flushed face.

"The new messenger? Where?" someone called from the bar. "Behind the little girl?"

The room burst into rowdy laughter.

Jeilin stopped in her tracks, suddenly wishing she hadn't come.

"Only joking!" The voice, which she saw belonged to a tall man clutching a mug of ale, called again. "Come have a seat! Drinks are on the house for our two new messengers tonight—isn't that right?"

The bartender nodded his consent as he filled two more mugs.

Jeilin took the empty stool next to Cai, feeling awkward.

"Hello," she said.

"Evening," Cai replied. A half-drained mug of ale sat before him on the bar.

"What can I get for you, miss?" the barkeeper asked her, casting an appraising look at her, his eyes eventually settling on the gold star pinned to her tunic.

"Just…a glass of wine, please," she said quietly.

The bartender poured her a glass of some dark wine and handed it to her.

Jeilin chanced a glance at the man on her other side. He was large and burly, with his bearded face hidden behind his mug of mead. He slammed it down on the counter abruptly and turned to address her. "Where's your mother?" he asked.

"What?" Jeilin said, taken aback.

"Good lord, do you mean to tell me that you didn't bring a parent?" he asked in mock surprise.

Jeilin scowled down at her wine glass. He continued to stare at her, and she took a small sip for something to do.

He laughed a rasping laugh and returned his attention to his mead.

"I did wonder whether you were going to show up." Jeilin spun on her bar stool and found herself facing Eric, the messenger from the ceremony.

"I had dinner with my family before I came here," she explained.

The burly man beside her laughed again, spraying mead onto the bar.

"Don't mind Vern," Eric said. "He's just angry at the world because he's getting too fat for his horse. His is the one standing tied outside, panting and swaybacked. You might have seen it on your way in."

Jeilin giggled.

"Always joking," Vern said bitterly. "One of these days I'll teach you a lesson."

Eric turned and stage-whispered to Jeilin. "He's all talk, of course; he could never catch me if he wanted to, on foot or on horseback."

Vern angrily mumbled into his mug.

The bar suddenly erupted into catcalls. Jeilin turned to see a woman emerging through the door. She was tall with long, lustrous brown hair that fell in loose waves almost to her elbows. She wore a short skirt of rough suede over brown leggings, a deep green silk blouse, and a long traveling cloak. Her tall riding boots were well worn but immaculate. Her skin was fair and her eyes were wide and brown. She was beautiful. Her cool, appraising expression did not match her delicate feminine appearance.

Then, Jeilin saw it—a golden star pinned to her green blouse, made visible when her cloak shifted as she stepped toward the bar. Jeilin gasped at the sight of another female messenger.

The woman stopped when she reached the bar—there were no seats left.

"Budge up," Vern grunted at Jeilin.

"You'd ask a lady to stand while *you* remain seated?" the woman asked, apparently annoyed. "I'll have your seat, Vern."

Vern glared at her and stood, mumbling. "Just this once, I suppose," he said to the woman while other riders laughed.

"The usual," the woman said to the barkeeper.

"Congratulations," she said, turning to Jeilin.

Jeilin hadn't expected the woman to address her. "Thank you," she replied.

"I didn't see you ride today, but I heard about it," the woman continued. "I hear you have a fine horse."

Jeilin nodded and allowed herself to smile slightly. "He's at the royal stables right now."

"My horse will be staying there for the night as well," the woman replied. "I'm Olwen," she said, extending a hand.

Jeilin shook her hand, noticing how slender and white her fingers were. "I'm Jeilin."

Olwen sipped her wine. She seemed kind enough; Jeilin was nervous, but felt encouraged enough to ask her more questions. She was relieved to know that she was not the only female messenger.

"Do all messengers stay at the castle when they're in the city?" she asked.

"Most do," Olwen replied. "We're always welcome to lodge at any royal palace, but it's not required. Most who choose to stay the night elsewhere are visiting with family or friends…or just in the mood for a night of revelry."

Jeilin suddenly realized how very little she actually knew about being a messenger.

Olwen smiled knowingly. "There's a lot to learn, and you pick up most of it as you go. Don't fret, though; your first assignment will be an easy one."

"Have you been a messenger for long?" Jeilin asked.

"For the past five years," Olwen replied. "And yes, I'm the only female messenger at this time—besides you, that is."

Jeilin was slightly disappointed; she had hoped that there were more. Still, she felt extremely fortunate to have met the only other one during her first day as part of the fleet.

"A drink for you, miss," the barkeeper said, shoving another glass of wine across the bar toward Olwen.

"I didn't order this; I've barely touched my first," Olwen said.

The barkeeper rolled his eyes. "A gentleman paid for it and requested that I deliver it to you," he said wearily.

"Idiot," Olwen said, loudly enough for the whole bar to hear. "Does he think that the king pays me less because I'm a woman? Does he think that I'm so destitute that I can't afford my own drink? Or perhaps he hopes that I will be so charmed by this precious gift that I shall leave the life I love to cook his meals and bear his children?"

"Or maybe," a man from the left end of the bar spoke up, "he just likes seeing you get worked up."

Everyone laughed.

"They're always trying to get the best of me," she said to Jeilin. "They'll give you a difficult time too, but you mustn't take them seriously."

For the next hour, Jeilin bombarded Olwen with questions. Olwen answered them all graciously. Two more mugs of wine appeared mysteriously in front of Olwen as they spoke. They remained beside the first one, untouched.

"Well, I'm exhausted," Olwen said finally, laying several coins down on the bar in front of her. "Walk back to the castle with me."

Jeilin was grateful beyond words at Olwen's invitation.

"Aww, the hen's leaving with her little chick," one of the men called out as they left the tavern.

Olwen ignored them.

Jeilin followed Olwen back to the castle, intensely glad for the company and direction. A waiting servant showed them to their separate rooms, which lay across the hall from one another. "Good night then," Olwen said as she disappeared into hers.

"Good night," Jeilin said, stepping into a beautiful room unlike any she could ever have imagined, dominated by a large four-poster bed and two high windows that showcased the starry sky outside.

Chapter 5

J eilin rose later than usual the next morning; the room
was so warm and comfortable that she slept past sunrise
without realizing it. By the time she rolled out of bed and
peered out the window, the sun had climbed high enough to
illuminate the castle grounds. Jeilin dressed hurriedly in the
clothing she had received the day before, fastened her gold
star carefully to her chest, and stepped tentatively into the
hallway. There was no one in sight.

She debated what to do. Olwen had probably already
risen, and, even if she hadn't, Jeilin didn't dare knock on
her door. What was she supposed to do today anyway? Was
there some sort of training she had to do, or was it to be a
day of leisure? Was there somewhere she could eat breakfast? There were so many questions in the palace, so unlike
her old life on the farm, where she could have gone through
the motions of any given day in her sleep.

At a loss, Jeilin started down the hall in a path that she
hoped would lead her outdoors and to the stables. A quarter
of an hour passed before she reached the large structure.
Breakfast would have to wait; seeing her family off was
more important.

After walking down several rows, she found Fringe stalled, contentedly eating a flake of hay. He peered over the stall door in greeting, still chewing. Jeilin patted his pale nose. A couple of grooms floated around the stable, wearing grooming aprons and flitting in and out of various stalls. Well, one thing was for sure; Jeilin needed to return the family's old saddle and bridle to her parents. After a little exploration, she found them in the tack room, next to her new saddle and bridle. She carried an assortment of tack back to Fringe's stall. She saddled him with the old saddle and hung the old bridle over the horn, then slid the new bridle with its golden star over his head.

Fringe cast a longing glance at his warm stall, where half a flake of hay still waited to be eaten, as Jeilin led him by the reins out into the sunshine. Once they were outdoors, Jeilin swung onto his back and they rode for the main gates.

The two guards opened the gates for her without a word, and she became a part of Dresinva's morning hustle and bustle.

For such small objects, it was amazing how much attention two golden stars attracted, Jeilin thought. As she rode through the city, people stared, whispered, pointed, and waved. At last, Jeilin found the inn where her family was staying. She secured Fringe to a hitching post and stepped over the threshold.

An assortment of travelers sat around a long, rough wooden table, enjoying their midday meal. Her family was among them. Ehryn, looking up from a plate of sausages and tomatoes, saw her first. She took the seat next to him, across from her father.

"I brought the saddle and bridle," she said after wishing them a good morning.

"That's right, you got a new set of tack," Emrys said. "There sure are a lot of perks to being a messenger, aren't there? Perhaps Ash and I should try out next time."

Ehryn and Jeilin snickered. "It'd be the death of him," Ehryn said.

"Yes, who'd pull the cart back home then?" Jeilin asked.

"Emrys would," Ehryn said. "It'd only be fair."

"Would you like something to eat, dear?" an elderly woman asked, approaching Jeilin with a pan of simmering sausages. Jeilin felt her salivary glands begin to work as the delicious scent of spiced meat wafted from the pan.

"Oh, well, I'm…not really staying here," Jeilin explained.

"No matter, dear. Anyone with a gold star on their chest deserves a hot meal," the old woman said, grinning toothlessly.

"Thank you," Jeilin replied as the woman set a plate before her and began doling generous portions onto it.

"See what I mean?" Emrys said. "There are a lot of *fringe* benefits…get it?"

Jeilin nearly choked on a sausage. "Your jokes are terrible, Emrys," she said.

"So how did last night go…at the tavern?" Almeda asked, attempting to sound nonchalant as she speared a sausage.

"Oh, it was fine," Jeilin said. "Guess what? I met the only other female messenger!"

"Well, I certainly hope she's a good role model," Almeda huffed.

"Oh…she is," Jeilin said absentmindedly, wondering what Olwen was up to that morning. Had she left on her next mission already?

"And how was your stay at the castle?" Rab asked.

"Fantastic," Jeilin said between mouthfuls. "You wouldn't believe the room I'm staying in…"

"So what have you got on your plate for the rest of the day?" Ehryn asked.

"I…don't know," Jeilin replied. "I got up and came straight here. I guess I'll find out when I get back." Jeilin hoped that Olwen, or at least a helpful servant, would be there to point her in the right direction.

"Well…" Rab said with a heavy sigh. "I guess this is goodbye for now, then."

"Oh…" Jeilin said. "You're leaving now?" A weight seemed to settle in Jeilin's stomach. What did she think was going to happen? She scolded herself. Of course her family would be leaving, and they wouldn't be arriving back at the farm until after dark, either. They had probably stayed later than they had intended to, hoping that she would show up. She would be leaving on her first mission the next day, so they probably wouldn't get to see her then even if they did stay another night. As for the rest of the current day, she had no idea what was going to happen, let alone when she would be able to see her family again.

"Yes," Rab said. "There's still a lot to harvest at home, and staying in Dresinva isn't exactly free, you know." He made an attempt at a light-hearted laugh, but Jeilin saw through it. "I have to admit," Rab continued. "I never really imagined that you wouldn't be coming back with us."

"Nor did I," Almeda said as she extended her small, pale hand across the table to cover Jeilin's.

Jeilin was taken aback by her mother's sudden and unusual show of affection. She struggled for something to say. "Well...I don't know where my next mission will take me, but if it leads me south of Almrahn, I'll be taking the Dusty Pass..."

"That would be nice," Rab said.

After breakfast, the family stepped outside and Jeilin removed the old saddle from Fringe's back, handing it to her father along with the bridle that she'd hung from the horn. There was an awkward moment of silence.

"I'll take it all into the cart," Jeilin said, taking the tack back from her father. When she had stored it away, she scanned the row of stalls until she saw Ash's familiar grey face peering out at her. She leaned on the door and patted his soft, whiskery nose. "I'll miss you, boy," she said. As a child, how many times had she urged Ash to canter across the fields, pretending to be the messenger that she now was? She gave him one last wistful pat, kissed his nose, and exited the stable.

Her father had untied Fringe and was waiting for her with the reins in one of his large hands. Jeilin embraced him and each of her family members in turn, ignoring the staring bystanders. When she'd finished, her father gave her a leg-up and she settled onto Fringe's smooth, bare back. There were many goodbyes, and, eventually, Jeilin directed Fringe down the busy street where her family was quickly crowded from her view.

The guards wordlessly allowed Jeilin to enter the castle grounds, just as they had allowed her to exit. Jeilin returned to the stables in low spirits.

"I wondered where you'd gone off to," a voice called, apparently from nowhere.

Olwen popped out of a stall into the aisle, holding a brush in her hand.

"I went to see my family off," Jeilin said.

Olwen smiled sympathetically. "Where do they live?"

"South of Almrahn, along the Dusty Path," Jeilin replied.

"Nice country. Do they farm?"

Jeilin nodded. "Crops." Silence followed as she swung open Fringe's stall door and led him in. She removed his bridle, leaving him to eat freely, and reemerged in the aisle.

"Is that your horse?" Jeilin asked, peering curiously in the stall Olwen had emerged from.

"Yes," Olwen said with obvious pride.

Like Olwen, the horse had a fair and delicate appearance. Its white coat, mane, and tail were spotless, its face refined, and its ears small and shapely.

"He's beautiful," Jeilin said.

"She," Olwen corrected her. "And thank you. Her name is Snow."

"How old is she?" Jeilin wondered aloud.

"Six. When I first entered the king's service I had a different horse, but he died. I've had Snow for nearly three years now."

Jeilin nodded. "So…how much longer are you going to be staying at the castle? Do we normally get breaks between assignments?"

"Sometimes we're dispatched again the next morning, and other times we might get to stay as long as a week," Olwen explained. "It all depends on what the royalty and military officers need, and you don't usually know what the case will be ahead of time. I'm leaving tomorrow, just like you."

"Do you know where you're going?"

Olwen nodded. "The Bay of Lights."

"The ocean?" Jeilin asked in awe. She had never seen the sea, and the thought excited her.

"Yes," Olwen replied. "It's five days' hard riding northwest of here, but worth every mile. It's beautiful, although given the choice I'd pick a warmer time of year to visit."

"Why are you being sent there?" Jeilin asked.

"I'm delivering a message from the king to his daughter, Princess Elin. She's been at the Bay of Lights since early this summer."

Jeilin finally voiced the question that she had been pondering all day. "Do you know…I mean, what am I supposed to…*do* today?"

"Well, I heard a *rumor* that you and the other new rider, Cai, are going to be treated to dinner with the king tonight."

"Dinner with the *king*?" Jeilin repeated incredulously.

"King Darnasius is surprisingly humble, as far as rulers go," Olwen answered.

A slightly familiar man walked into the stable and disappeared into the tack room. He reemerged carrying a saddle and disappeared promptly into a stall. When he came back out he was leading a handsome black stallion. A gold star flashed from the horse's bridle, and then Jeilin noticed its twin, which flashed from the man's chest, nearly obscured by his cloak.

"Off already, Rann?" Olwen asked.

"Only to Almrahn," he said. "What about you?"

"I'm to leave for the Bay of Lights tomorrow," Olwen said.

"I don't envy you," he replied. "A cruel wind blows off of the sea this time of year. Good luck."

"The same to you," Olwen said.

Rann nodded curtly at Jeilin and was gone.

"Well, I'm off to the palace for a bath...care to join me?" Olwen asked.

Jeilin still felt fresh from her bath the day before, but accepted anyway. After all, the palace baths were very inviting, and she would be dining with King Darnasius that evening. If ever there was an occasion for an extra bath in her life, it was now. Besides, she wasn't sure what she would do if left to her own devices for the rest of the day.

Olwen, apparently reasonably familiar with the castle, led Jeilin to the same room she had bathed in the day before.

A chambermaid with honey-colored hair that brushed her shoulders waited outside the oaken doors.

"We'll both be bathing," Olwen informed the girl, who then opened the doors for them and set a fresh pair of towels by the tub's edge.

"Ahh," Olwen said as she inhaled the sweetly scented, steamy air. "It should be a crime not to take advantage of the baths while you're here—remember that. The life of a messenger isn't always so luxurious...in fact, it's usually just the opposite. You'll be dreaming of these baths when you're riding frozen to your saddle through the middle of nowhere this winter. What happened to your ribs?" Olwen asked curiously as Jeilin slipped into the water.

"Oh..." Jeilin told her about how one of the other competitors had attempted to steal the scroll from her.

Olwen sighed disgustedly. "Even as a messenger you've got to be wary of people like that," she said. "Most of the messages we carry aren't the sort of thing that would attract people like that...personal letters, decrees, things of that sort...but we *are* sometimes entrusted with things of a very sensitive nature. Some messengers have been intercepted, and even killed."

Jeilin felt a little of the color drain out of her face.

Olwen must have noticed, because she laughed. "Don't look so serious! A life without risks isn't worth living...right?"

Jeilin shrugged and laughed herself. The dangers of winter and would-be thieves seemed far away from where she soaked in the warm and comforting bath.

"You must use this," Olwen said, reaching for an opaque, pale-yellow bottle that rested on the marble tile. She pulled out the cork and sniffed the bottle with a sigh of delight. "Shampoo made from the wildflowers that grow in the Callabrian Desert."

"Wildflowers grow in the desert?" Jeilin asked, puzzled.

"Once every seven years, if it rains enough," Olwen replied. "I've never seen it anywhere else; it makes your hair smell like wildflowers for a week."

Olwen plunged underwater and emerged a moment later looking very sodden. She began to lather the shampoo into her dark hair and passed the bottle to Jeilin. Jeilin mimicked her, feeling exotic and savoring the delicate scent of the foreign flowers that had come from a faraway land.

"Well, that ought to keep me from smelling like a man on the way to the Bay of Lights," Olwen said as she rung out her long hair.

After their bath was over, Jeilin continued to tag along with Olwen, who didn't seem to mind. Olwen led her to a small dining hall next to the kitchen. "Whenever you're at the castle, you can come here anytime to get something to eat," she explained as she popped her head into the kitchen. A round, ruddy-faced chef emerged.

"What would you like, madam?" he asked, and upon seeing Jeilin, nodded to indicate that she should order too.

"Something for our midday meal," Olwen said. "Whatever good things you've got around the kitchen will be fine."

A few minutes later Jeilin sat at the long table with Olwen, dining on cold game and hot soup. Jeilin thought silently to herself that it was too easy to get used to life at the castle.

"Is this where I should come to eat with King Darnasius?" Jeilin asked.

"Oh, no," said Olwen. "I'm sure he'll have the dinner in the formal dining area...you don't need to worry about finding it; he'll send a servant to fetch you."

"I wonder what Cai's doing?" Jeilin pondered out loud. "I mean, without someone like you to show him around and explain everything."

Olwen shrugged thoughtfully. "You don't know that he doesn't have someone. At least a dozen other riders stayed here last night, all men. Men stick together in their own way...we should too."

It was early in the evening, and Olwen was giving Jeilin a tour of the castle grounds when a servant found them. His brow, which had acquired a fine sheen of sweat, seemed to indicate that he had been searching for them for quite some time. He stopped and addressed Jeilin.

"His Royal Majesty King Darnasius warmly invites his newest messenger, Jeilin, to dine with him this evening. If she accepts, a servant will be sent to her quarters at six o'clock this evening to show her the way to the dining hall."

"Of course I accept," Jeilin responded quickly.

"Promptly at six this evening, then," the servant said, and whisked back to the castle looking relieved.

It was a quarter until six, and Jeilin was sitting alone in her room feeling more than a little nervous. Would it be just her and Cai at dinner, or would there be other guests as well? Would she be expected to speak with the king, and, if so, what on earth would she say? The only thing she knew for sure was what to wear—Olwen had told her to wear the riding uniform she'd been given. Her thoughts chased themselves in vicious circles until the much-anticipated knock came at the door.

Jeilin stepped out into the hallway, where the waiting servant guided her to the royal dining room.

The room was huge and immaculate, with rich wooden furniture gleaming everywhere. An ornate iron chandelier hung above the massive table, where Jeilin recognized more than one familiar face.

Cai was already seated, and Eric, the friendly messenger from the day before, was beside him. Across from him sat...Olwen! She turned in her seat and smiled merrily at Jeilin. An assortment of other messengers, some of whom Jeilin thought she recognized from the tavern, were also sitting at the table. She took the empty seat beside Olwen.

"As it turns out, all of the messengers lodging in the castle were invited," Olwen explained quietly as servants bustled about the table, setting out dishes, platters, and carafes of wine. "But they sent separate servants to invite us, and mine didn't find me until later."

There was a sudden hush, and then an immense scraping of chairs as everyone jumped up from their seats. Jeilin did the same and turned to follow everyone's gaze as King Darnasius entered the room. He strolled to the head of the table and took his seat. The others, including Jeilin, waited several moments before taking theirs. As soon as everyone had been seated, a dozen servants filed into the room, carrying silver platters and trays.

When an incredible feast of wild game, fresh vegetables, and decadent pies had been laid before them, the king spoke. "Welcome home, my faithful messengers. Tonight I welcome Cai and Jeilin into my service. Tomorrow they will embark on their first assignments, and I have purposely chosen routes for them that mirror those of two others. Cai, you will follow Eric to Ahnlin, and Jeilin, you will accompany Olwen to the Bay of Lights."

Jeilin rejoiced inwardly. She would be traveling with Olwen and she would see the sea! The world suddenly seemed a softer place. She dared a glance at Olwen, who was smiling. Had she already known?

"I am entrusting these two young riders to you, Eric and Olwen, and trust that you will help shape them into the excellent messengers they have committed to becoming. I ask that you do not take the assignment lightly."

"Of course not, Your Majesty," Olwen said, and Eric echoed her.

The king smiled. "Excellent. And I must remind the rest of you that although you have not been selected to bear the responsibility of taking them on their first mission, you will surely meet them at some point in the future, and I trust that you will also do everything within your power to help them, as others did for you in your early days. Now…let us eat."

****

A chambermaid knocked at the door the next morning to awaken Jeilin. Olwen filed into the room behind her, already dressed, her golden star peeking from underneath her traveling cloak. "Morning," she said breezily.

"Morning," Jeilin said as she rolled out of bed, too excited to feel groggy.

After dressing quickly, they stopped by the kitchen as they had the day before and ate a hearty breakfast. The scrolls that they had received from the king after the feast were tucked carefully into their tunics. "Do you think you could spare some food for the journey?" Olwen cheerily asked the cook. "We leave this very hour for the Bay of Lights." When they left the kitchen, they were weighed down with sacks of food: breads, cheeses, fruits, pastries, and dried meats.

"Now all we have to do is retrieve our horses, and we'll be off," Olwen said as they made their way to the stables. When they arrived, they found their horses already saddled and waiting. Like Snow, Fringe carried saddlebags, and a neat bundle had been tied behind his saddle's cantle. Olwen identified the bundle as a rolled-up tent. Jeilin peeked into the saddlebags and found several items, including a dagger with red enameling and a soaring falcon worked into the handle, and a couple changes of clothes just like the ones she wore, plus a thick cloak that she'd surely need during her journey north. "Looks like you have room for a few rolls in there," Olwen said, stuffing Jeilin's saddlebags to the brim.

The sun began to rise over Dresinva's skyline, a violent neon splinter against the misty grey sky, as they rode toward the main gate. After waving and shouting a quick greeting to the guards, they were off to the Bay of Lights and the magnificent, mysterious sea that Jeilin longed to see.

Chapter 6

T he first day of riding was productive, if uneventful. "A good day," Olwen described it that night as she sat cross-legged around a small fire with Jeilin. They had run the horses hard, but not ragged. Snow was amazingly light on her feet; Jeilin estimated that she would *almost* be able to keep pace with Fringe in a race. Olwen's riding was to be envied; she might as well have been born in the saddle, and she showed no signs of soreness as she made herself comfortable on the ground, rummaging through her saddle-bags and choosing her favorites from among the generous provisions the palace kitchen had supplied. Jeilin envied that too; her own thighs were twinging slightly on the inside, hinting at soreness that would come as surely as the sun the next morning.

The scent of wildflowers still clung as strongly to Jeilin's dark hair as it had when she had first emerged from the bath. The delicate scent that spoke of spring combined with the rich odor of autumn's decaying leaves, creating a pleasant paradox. Jeilin bit into a soft bun that she'd produced from her own saddlebag; it was almost as good as the buns her mother baked every day…almost. She failed to suppress a sigh as she imagined the little farmhouse where she had spent every night of her life until the present week.

"Homesick?" Olwen asked knowingly.

"A little," Jeilin confided. She didn't want to admit that her heart actually seemed to ache as she pictured the little house silhouetted against the rapidly darkening sky, smoke puffing from the chimney and light shining warmly from the windows as her family gathered around the table for dinner without her. Even Ash seemed lonely in her mind's eye, alone in the paddock without Fringe.

Olwen nodded as she sliced open a bright green apple with the small silver knife that she kept tucked behind her belt. "I was too, when I first left."

"Were you my age?" Jeilin asked, her curiosity suddenly piqued. She had been wondering about Olwen's history since she met her. She tried not to seem too eager, refusing to let her body lean forward like it seemed to want to.

Olwen shook her head. "I was twenty," she said. "A mere step away from old-maid-hood, in my mother's eyes."

Jeilin couldn't restrain a snorting laugh. Olwen smiled. "Ah, I see you know the type." She continued, gesturing with her knife.

"I was betrothed," she continued. "He was a fine young man...I did love him." For one fleeting moment, she sounded almost wistful. She rebounded quickly, her voice becoming almost boisterous. "But the thought of tending a hearth and mothering a flock of children nearly turned my stomach. The world seemed so big, and Mylin's Corner— that's the village where I grew up—was so small.

"Every day my mother pressured me with urges to marry, so that eventually I thought I might smother beneath them. Beynin was little better, eager to marry as he was. I became an expert at finding reasons to postpone the ceremony. Then came a day when I thought I was with child."

Jeilin nearly choked on her bite of bread. Hoping that Olwen would mistake her blushing for a simple lack of oxygen, she experienced a spectacular coughing fit. Olwen slapped her on the back and continued as if she had said nothing out of the ordinary; as if she had not mentioned...*that*!

"It nearly scared the life out of me. When I realized I had been mistaken, I was so relieved, and so terrified that it really would happen, that I left."

Jeilin focused intently on her bun, still blushing furiously.

"I was as surprised as anyone when I won the race to become a messenger," Olwen admitted. "I think it was the fear of marriage that chased me across those plains, to tell the truth."

"What about your horse?" Jeilin asked, eager to direct the conversation away from...*that*, lest her cheeks burn right off of her face.

"A gift from my father," Olwen replied. "As an only daughter, I was spoiled. I'd dreamed of having a white horse since I was a little girl, so my father bought me Mist for my seventeenth birthday. It just so happened that he was fast...a stroke of luck." Olwen frowned. "He broke his leg stepping in a hole while we were on our way to Hilan. Then I bought Snow."

Jeilin's shoulders dropped in sympathy.

"What about you?" Olwen asked.

Jeilin's cheeks were just beginning to cool down. "I found Fringe as a colt. His dam was from a feral herd that roamed near our farm. I've always wanted to be a messenger. One day I saw a notice hanging in a square in Almrahn…and now I'm here." She shook her head. "It still seems like a dream."

Olwen nodded in understanding. "You'll get used to it in time. Life becomes a blur of plains, mountains, cities, and palaces…all experienced from the saddle." She grinned suddenly. "It's not a bad life. Sure, you sleep on the ground more often than not, but the nights spent in the palaces make up for it."

Fringe nickered and stamped. Jeilin turned her gaze upon him and Snow; they both stood silhouetted against the dusky twilight several yards away, hobbled and tearing up mouthfuls of grass. Their pale coats gave them almost ghostly appearances.

****

When Jeilin rose the next morning, the sun was a fiery sliver on the horizon. She gave a small start of surprise when she poked her head out of her tent's flap and saw Olwen peeking out too. "And here I thought I might have to shake you awake after yesterday's riding," Olwen teased.

Jeilin shook her head. "You forget that I was a farm girl. I'm used to rising at dawn, and sleeping on the ground is more difficult than I'd thought." She frowned as she pressed a hand against the small of her back, attempting to rub some of the stiffness out of it.

Olwen smiled and stifled a yawn.

"You may have to strap me to my saddle, though," Jeilin said. "I'd be a liar if I said I wasn't sore."

"Stretching and breakfast might help," Olwen suggested. So, they brewed a pot of tea and made their selections from the saddlebags before saddling the horses. Jeilin frowned as she bent to touch her toes before inserting a foot into a stirrup and swinging stiffly into the saddle.

They walked the horses to a nearby stream. While the horses drank, Jeilin and Olwen filled water skins and tied them to their cantles.

Back in the saddle and facing the road once more, Jeilin heeled her mount in imitation of Olwen. The horses' hooves beat against the oft-trodden road, covering the seemingly endless expanse of bare dirt that wound through the planes and woods. The sun had just emerged completely from over distant treetops, and the morning air was cool and sweet. Jeilin sighed as Fringe settled into a canter. The golden star on her breast caught the fiery light, as did the one that shone from Fringe's bridle. She swelled with pride and urged Fringe into the day's first gallop, laughing as the breeze they created whipped through a few stray strands of her hair.

****

It was the morning of the fourth day of their journey to the Bay of Lights, and Jeilin was beginning to think that an entire season had passed overnight. "Did it suddenly turn to winter while I slept?" she asked, shivering in the saddle.

Olwen shook her head from her seat on Snow's back. "It's always this way close to the Bay of Lights. The cold air blows off of the Daiymihr Ocean. Even in the summer, there's a cool breeze, but it's quite pleasant then. The cold bites harder than a starving wolf during the winter, though," she said, adjusting her cloak.

Jeilin shivered harder and sighed, creating a cloud of frozen breath, wishing she had put on the extra coat that was rolled up in a bundle of clothes and secured to her saddle.

The breezes were even fiercer the next day. "They should have called it the Bay of Winds," Jeilin commented. "Or frostbite," she muttered under her breath.

"You'll forget about the cold when you catch your first sight of the city," Olwen replied, "and see why they have named it so. We'll arrive in the evening, which is for the best. One can't really appreciate it during daylight."

Jeilin shifted in the saddle. The cold couldn't curb her enthusiasm for seeing new places...she'd spent the past sixteen years in the tiniest corner of the world. Now it was time to see the rest.

****

Looking at the Bay of Lights was like peering into the world's largest, richest diamond mine during a flash of lightning. Brilliant white points of light spangled the twilight sky and stood out against the dark ocean; lanterns decorated each and every building, from the tiniest shanty to the royal palace. Jeilin stared wide-eyed, unable to decide whether the lighted city or the sea was more amazing. The waves crashing on the distant shore were still visible, if barely, in the dim evening light. Never before had she seen so much water…stretching as far as— no, *beyond* what her eye could see.

Fringe stepped higher and more quickly as the city on the water grew nearer. Snow's ears perked forward. Olwen laughed and patted her neck. "The horses can sense a warm stable and oats. For that matter, I'm rather excited about having a bath and a hot meal, myself."

Jeilin nodded. Suddenly, butterflies seemed to burst into flight in her stomach as the realization that she was about to deliver her first message dawned on her. For what must have been the hundredth time, she felt the sealed letter that she kept in a deep pocket beneath her cloak. The weight of it felt heavy as she anticipated actually handing it to a prince. Olwen had explained much to her over the past five days. She had made it very clear that a messenger was to *never* relinquish possession of the message they carried until they delivered it themselves to the recipient. No hand but hers was to touch the letter until it had been received. The penalty for a broken seal upon delivery was a trial for treason, which could possibly end in death if one was convicted… Jeilin swallowed as she remembered.

The air smelled strongly of salt as the horses' hooves left the dirt road behind for the city's cobblestone streets. The city's shop windows had been darkened, but warm light poured out from the windows and doorways of taverns, inns, and homes that were built mostly from small stones much like the ones that paved the streets. A few people walked the streets, but they seemed eager to arrive at their destinations and escape the cold winds. Strands of hair that had escaped Jeilin's ponytail whipped around her face as a particularly powerful gust swept through the streets, and Fringe's creamy mane fluttered.

The royal palace loomed in the center of the city, a tall stone structure capped with many white domes, each with a bright lantern shining at the very top.

"Time to make an entrance!" Olwen said, and urged Snow into a gallop. They met little resistance from the few subjects still out.

By the time they reached the palace grounds, Jeilin could feel the heat rising in waves from the muscles beneath Fringe's golden coat. She reined him in as Olwen did Snow. They slowed in front of a small archway built into the side of the castle adjacent to the stables. A large gold star hung on the wall above a door. "All of the royal palaces in Alaishin have an entrance for messengers," she explained as she swung out of the saddle. Jeilin nodded as she dismounted and removed her saddlebags. The cobble-stones felt strange beneath her feet after a day spent in the stirrups. Two grooms appeared to take the horses' reins and led them into the stable. "They'll be well taken care of," Olwen assured her.

Three men were waiting in the brightly lit hall that the messengers' entrance opened into. Two were helmeted and armed—guards. The third man wore red livery with a white falcon embroidered on the breast—a head-servant of some sort. At the sight of Olwen and Jeilin, he bowed deeply. "Who is it that you seek?" he asked.

Olwen had instructed Jeilin on how to announce herself during the fireside conversations they had shared during each of the past several evenings. In the event that more than one messenger arrived at the same time, the messenger delivering to the highest-ranked recipient spoke first. Prince Raihnin, the king's son, was elder brother to the Princess Elin, and was to succeed his father to the throne. So, Jeilin announced herself first.

"I bear a message for His Majesty Prince Raihnin," Jeilin said.

"I bear a message for Her Majesty Princess Elin," Olwen said.

The servant bowed again to each of them. He turned on his heel and proceeded down the hallway as quickly as possible without breaking into a trot. Jeilin and Olwen followed. They emerged from the hallway into another, and then another, and then took a flight of stairs. He never slowed his pace.

They halted in front of ornately carved doors that opened into a lavishly furnished reception room. Jeilin followed him inside as another waiting attendant bowed and disappeared behind a smaller set of carved doors. He emerged a few moments later, preceded by a tall, dark-haired young man who greatly resembled his father. His white coat was elaborately decorated with blue embroidery, and a sword hung at his hip. The servant who accompanied Jeilin announced her presence. "A royal messenger has come swiftly to deliver a letter to His Highness Prince Raihnin."

Jeilin's stomach was tying itself into a knot as Prince Raihnin turned his gaze from his attendant to her. His eyes were blue, startlingly so, against his nearly black hair that tried to curl despite the fact that it was cut quite short. For a moment, he appeared surprised, but he regained his composure quickly. "Let the royal messenger deliver the letter she has been charged with." Whether or not it was only her imagination, Jeilin wasn't sure, but she thought that the word "she" sounded strange in the prince's mouth. Her own mouth felt suddenly dry as she moved forward steadily, feeling as if someone else were controlling her body. She knelt when she reached the prince, as Olwen had instructed her to do. She pressed one knee into the lushly embroidered carpet, and extended her right hand, offering the sealed letter. At the same time, she stared up, into the prince's blue eyes, as was required. It was tradition that a messenger never looked down or away, lest someone other than the recipient take the letter, Olwen had explained. "A letter to his Royal Highness Prince Raihnin from His Majesty King Darnasius, ruler of Alaishin," she said. She forced herself to continue to meet the prince's stare, and prayed that her hand would not tremble. It seemed an eternity before she felt the thick parchment slide from between her fingers. The prince broke their eye contact, mercifully, when he held the letter up to the light to inspect the seal.

"You may rise," he said, meeting her eyes again.

Jeilin rose.

"You have served me and Alaishin well," he continued. "May neither your horse nor your luck ever falter." Olwen had taught her that that phrase was recognized as an official dismissal between a messenger and a recipient. Jeilin bowed deeply, glad to break eye contact again. When she stood, she couldn't help but meet the prince's eyes again as she was leaving. Before she knew it she was in the hall with Olwen again, barely able to stifle a sigh of relief. Olwen flashed her a small smile.

The chamberlain was eager to start moving again. Eventually he stopped abruptly in front of a tall pair of oaken doors. He knocked once and they swung open, the work of two chambermaids who waited inside. Jeilin hung back as the chamberlain stepped into the doorway with Olwen close behind. The servant spoke in a carrying voice that echoed throughout the high-ceilinged chamber where a small, slender young woman sat in an ornate chair, being entertained by a harpist and surrounded by maidservants. "A royal messenger has come swiftly to deliver a letter to Her Highness Princess Elin."

"Let the royal messenger deliver the letter she has been charged with," Princess Elin said, gazing upon Olwen. Olwen strode confidently across the room. When she reached Princess Elin, who Jeilin gauged to be several years younger than herself, despite the rouge on her cheeks and her elaborately curled dark hair, she dropped to one knee, her right hand extended, offering the letter.

"A letter to her Royal Highness Princess Elin from His Majesty King Darnasius, ruler of Alaishin," Olwen said.

Elin extended a small, delicate hand and took the letter. "You may rise," she said, and continued to recite words she must have memorized years ago. "You have served me and Alaishin well. May neither your horse nor your luck ever falter." Olwen bowed deeply, recognizing the classic dismissal, and left the room to rejoin Jeilin in the hallway.

The chamberlain led them downstairs and to the messengers' wing on the ground floor, where a chambermaid was waiting. "She shall show you to your rooms or to the baths, whichever is preferred."

"The baths," Jeilin and Olwen replied, almost in unison.

As she soaked in a deep marble tub, the hot water lapping over her shoulders, Jeilin finally allowed herself the sigh of relief she had been restraining since delivering her message to the prince. "I was so nervous," she admitted.

Olwen laughed. "You'll grow used to it in time, after a fashion. Speaking to royalty is always a little strange, but it gets easier."

"You seemed as calm as the princess herself," Jeilin said. "I fear I must have looked a fool in front of Prince Raihnin. It was all I could do to keep from trembling."

Olwen laughed again. "I wouldn't have minded delivering to him," she said. "He *is* handsome."

Jeilin blushed, hoping that Olwen wouldn't notice. She had tried not to think of how handsome the prince was when she had delivered the message to him; thinking about it had only increased her nervousness. Olwen snickered and Jeilin knew that she had noticed her blushes. She focused intensely on lathering her hair with the same wildflower-perfumed shampoo she'd used in Dresinva. Abruptly, Jeilin thought of something that made her forget about being embarrassed.

"Will I be on my own after this?" she asked. "I mean, when I deliver my next message?"

"I doubt it," Olwen replied. "I stayed with the messenger who trained me for several months."

Jeilin breathed another sigh of relief. "Who trained you?" she asked. "Was there another woman messenger then?"

Olwen shook her head, long tendrils of dark hair swirling in the soapy water. "A man named Merik."

"That must have been awkward."

Olwen shrugged, sending ripples over the surface of the deep bathing pool. "It was, a little...at first," she admitted. "But we got along quite well. Merik's the one who turned me on to the Callabrian wildflower shampoo."

Jeilin dropped the scrubbing brush she had been holding. To hide her reddening face, she plunged unnecessarily under the surface to retrieve it. She tried not to imagine the circumstances under which Merik might have suggested the shampoo to Olwen. Probably during an innocent conversation, Jeilin decided, like those she and Olwen had had over a fire on so many nights. Olwen was lounging as casually as ever when she emerged. "He only mentioned it to me one day after I commented on how pleasant his hair smelled," Olwen continued.

If she had supposed that that would reassure Jeilin, she had supposed wrongly. Jeilin only blushed more furiously. How pleasant *his hair* smelled? Men used wildflower shampoo? Olwen had actually *smelled* his hair? Jeilin was suddenly doubly glad that she had not been paired with a man for training.

****

After a hearty breakfast shared with Olwen in her room the next morning, Jeilin found herself back on horseback, but at a leisurely pace. The air was cool despite the bright morning sun that reflected off of the four golden stars that were displayed between her, Olwen, and their mounts. The cobblestone streets now bustled with activity, but everyone moved respectfully out of the way when they caught sight of those stars. Some of them did gape openly, though, perhaps seeing female messengers for the first time. Olwen was determined to show Jeilin places of interest in the Bay of Lights, which she had become familiar with over the years. They had had to sign a thick leather-bound log book before leaving the castle. As Olwen had explained, at least two messengers were required to be at the ready inside castle grounds at all times. There were three others at the castle, though they had seen none of them so far, and she and Olwen were the first to venture out of the castle that day. "Most men," Olwen had said, "would rather wait until evening so that they can gamble and carouse at taverns and inns. There's not much to interest them at this hour."

Olwen directed Snow down a winding cobblestone path that led away from the streets and to the nearby shore, where dark waves crashed against thousands of small, smooth stones like those that had been used to build the city and pave its streets, only smaller. Jeilin couldn't help but feel a sense of awe as the roaring sea filled her ears and the salty smell of the air grew stronger than ever. Soon, the horses' hooves trod carefully on the rounded stones.

Fringe snorted and backed up a few steps as a wave lapped at his hooves.

****

"This is *delicious*," Jeilin said at noon as she and Olwen rested on a bench at the edge of a small park, their horses tied to a nearby hitching post. They were eating a favorite lunchtime meal in the Bay of Lights: warm buns stuffed with sweetmeat and some sort of vegetable paste, which they had purchased from a street vendor.

Olwen nodded. "Some other cities sell them, or variants, at least, but none of them come close to how they make them in the Bay of Lights. There's a reason everyone eats them for lunch here."

"I'm going for a second," Jeilin said, wiping a drop of juice from the corner of her mouth with the back of her sleeve.

Olwen tossed her a silver coin. "Buy another for me too."

Jeilin caught it in her fist and ambled over to the cart. The buns weren't the only thing she could see herself growing accustomed to; having a leather purse full of coin at her belt was a new sensation. One she liked quite a lot. A messenger's pay was fairly generous, but not without reason, according to Olwen.

"One of the main reasons we're paid so well is because we need to have enough money on hand to buy a new horse," she had said. "Always make sure you keep at least that much set aside. It could be the difference between life and death."

Jeilin exchanged the two coins she carried for two more of the buns, and frowned. What Olwen said made a lot of sense, but the idea of having to buy a new horse because Fringe had fallen victim to something like a broken leg was unsettling. She had always imagined working as a team with Fringe to deliver messages…she silently resolved to set the money aside as Olwen had suggested, and to avoid thinking about the matter.

The sun had just begun its descent when Jeilin and Olwen returned to the palace grounds. With Fringe and Snow turned over to the care of grooms, the pair headed inside. "Shall we visit the royal kitchens together this evening?" Olwen asked. "I saw a large hunting party set out this morning, and I'll wager they'll have surrendered their game to the cooks by then."

Jeilin agreed.

****

Two days later, a slender maidservant in her middle years appeared unexpectedly in Jeilin's quarters. It was evening, and Jeilin had just finished her bath. She sat on the edge of her bed in breeches and a simple white blouse, toweling her damp hair.

"You are summoned by His Highness Prince Raihnin," the maid announced.

Jeilin dropped her towel, and then hastily seized it again and attempted to finish drying her hair. "Prince Raihnin?" she repeated.

The woman nodded. "We shan't keep him waiting," she said with a pointed look at the towel.

Jeilin tossed the towel to the floor. "Of course not," she said, shoving her feet into the pair of boots that had been waiting on the floor by the corner of her bed. Her stomach seemed to have contracted into a ball. For some reason, she hadn't considered that the prince she had delivered to would also be the one to send her on her way with a message again. She resolved not to make a fool out of herself as she followed the servant from her room.

Jeilin's hair dampened her cheeks as she waited at the door to Prince Raihnin's quarters. She wished she had had the forethought to at least tie it back before leaving her room. She hadn't, though, and flecks of water fell to the stone floor as the maidservant knocked.

The thick oaken doors were opened from the inside by two guards. The prince sat at a richly carved desk, dictating a letter to a secretary. "Enter, messenger, so that you may serve me and Alaishin," the prince said, exactly as his father had recited to her and Olwen less than a fortnight ago.

The prince looked up from his desk, and Jeilin found herself blushing once again under the directness of his gaze. She forced herself to meet his blue eyes and silently congratulated herself on not shaking, fidgeting, or doing anything more foolish than blushing. "I apologize if I have interrupted your bath," he said. Jeilin's face flushed even more furiously. Oh, how she wished she had tied her hair back.

"Please, don't worry, Your Majesty," she managed to say. "There is no need for an apology."

Prince Raihnin gave her the tiniest of smiles. "A gentleman must always regret imposing so upon a lady, even if she does serve her kingdom bravely alongside men."

Jeilin began to wonder whether the prince might mistake the color of her face, which had surely grown red enough to be mistaken so, for sunburn.

The prince turned and addressed his secretary. "That will be all, Medgean. I shall sign and seal it myself before surrendering it to Jeilin's excellent care."

Jeilin struggled to maintain a straight face. Prince Raihnin knew her name? Excellent? She wasn't sure whether her heart rate increased from pride or mortification.

The scrawl of the prince's quill was the only sound in the otherwise quiet room. Jeilin began to worry that the prince and his staff might detect the sound of her racing heart in such silence.

"This letter is to my cousin, Prince Stephen," he said, standing and extending his hand. "You will find him in the royal outpost in Sunlan, a little over one hundred miles northeast of here."

Jeilin recited the words she had practiced with Olwen so many times, but actually used only once before. "Nothing short of death shall prevent me from delivering your message with my own hand, and may death find me if it does."

"You hold my secrets and my trust, messenger. May neither your horse nor your luck ever falter."

Jeilin bowed and turned to leave.

Prince Raihnin's voice froze her in her tracks. "Jeilin," he said.

She turned quickly to face him again. "Yes, Your Majesty?"

"Will you share breakfast with me tomorrow morning, before you depart?"

First dinner with the king, and now an invitation to share breakfast with Prince Raihnin. Jeilin could hardly believe it. "Of course, Your Majesty," she said, hoping her voice sounded steady rather than shocked at the invitation.

He smiled. "Very well. I shall arrange for a servant to meet you in your chambers in the morning."

Jeilin wandered back to her room in a whirlwind of thought, almost colliding with a servant bearing trays as she turned a corner.

Olwen was waiting for her when she returned, sitting cross-legged on Jeilin's bed, absorbed in a book. She marked the page carefully with a ribbon and closed it when she looked up to see Jeilin. "There you are," she said. "I've been in the library...I brought you a book. I thought you might enjoy having something to read while we wait in the palace." She motioned toward a second leather-bound book that lay atop one of the pillows.

"Thank you," Jeilin said. "But I doubt I'll have time to read it...I depart tomorrow."

Olwen's eyes widened. "Whose message do you carry?"

"Prince Raihnin's."

Olwen's eyes grew even wider. "Is that where you've been, then?"

Jeilin nodded.

"I suppose I'll receive a summons this evening then too...unless...surely they haven't forgotten that you're to remain in my charge for a while longer?" Her forehead creased slightly, and she sounded disappointed at the prospect.

"I hope not," Jeilin said. Whatever worries Olwen had about the matter, they were nothing compared to her own.

"Where are you—where are *we* headed next?" Olwen asked.

"The royal outpost in Sunlan," Jeilin replied.

Olwen nodded. "Only two and a half days' ride from here," she said.

Jeilin collapsed onto the bed beside Olwen, suddenly realizing how drained her nervousness had left her. "I'm going to be sharing breakfast with Prince Raihnin tomorrow morning," she said flatly, staring up at the ceiling.

"Really?" Olwen sounded surprised, almost incredulous.

Jeilin nodded, feeling the familiar blush creeping across her cheeks once again.

"For what purpose?" Olwen asked.

"I have no idea, honestly," Jeilin said. "Before I left he extended the invitation, and, of course, I agreed."

Olwen flung her book aside, forgetting about the story she had been so absorbed in only moments ago. "This is intriguing!" she said, sounding uncharacteristically enthused.

Before she could say more, a servant knocked and entered the room. "You are summoned by Lieutenant Rhemley, Olwen," she announced. Olwen rose from the bed and strode across the room, not wasting any time. She turned and winked at Jeilin as she exited, and Jeilin was left on her own to contemplate her impending engagement with the prince.

Chapter 7

A s usual Jeilin rose with the sun the following morning. She dressed hurriedly in fresh breeches and one
of the red silk shirts that she had been given upon induction.
She brushed her hair, now mercifully dry, and secured it
neatly behind her head with the same strip of leather she'd
been using on her family's farm. She frowned. Who
breakfasted with a prince with a strip of old leather in their
hair? She cast her eyes around her room in search of a more
appropriate restraint. Her gaze fell upon Olwen's abandoned
book, from which protruded the end of the ribbon that she
had used to mark her page. She frowned even harder. She
would feel like a child with a bright red ribbon securing her
hair. There was nothing for it; the leather strip was her only
choice. She folded her hands on her lap and waited nervously for the promised servant to arrive.

She nearly jumped off of the edge of the bed when she
heard the awaited knock. The same fair-haired woman who
had escorted her to Prince Raihnin's quarters the previous
evening stood in the doorway. Jeilin followed her without a
word. The woman led Jeilin to an attractive blue decorated
dining room that opened into a spacious balcony overlook-

ing the distant countryside. A table was laden with silver trays and covered platters. It appeared enough to feed ten people, but other than the servants, she was alone. A servant silently pulled out a chair for her, and she seated herself, aware of every small scuff her boots made on the stone floor in the silent room.

Prince Raihnin arrived only a moment later. Upon seeing him, Jeilin stood hurriedly. He dismissed the servant who had accompanied him and approached the table.

"Good morning, Your Majesty," Jeilin said, hoping that she had done the proper thing by addressing the prince first.

If she hadn't, he gave no sign. "Good morning, Jeilin," he replied, while the servant pulled out her chair for her. Once she was seated, he found his place across from her at the table.

They were quite alone, other than the two servants who had remained, hovering dutifully a pace away from the breakfast table. Jeilin felt a start of surprise as she realized, when the servants began to fill their plates, that they were to remain that way. She hadn't anticipated being alone with the prince. What in the world would she say? *Should* she say anything?

The aromas of various fruits and hot, sweet cakes smelled heavenly. Prince Raihnin's dark hair shone in a beam of sunlight that fell across the balcony and the table.

"I see I've left you enough time to secure your hair this morning," he said, slicing a cake in half and topping it with a spoonful of fruit.

Jeilin didn't know what to say.

The prince continued. "It's almost a shame, because I liked it rather better yesterday evening."

Jeilin looked down at her plate and felt her face grow red again.

"Forgive me," he said. "I didn't mean to insult you. I only meant that your hair is very appealing when worn loose. It...flatters your face."

Jeilin looked up, resolving to meet the prince's blue eyes, and was surprised to find that he also had cast his gaze downward. She almost imagined that his face had grown pink as well. And had his speech faltered when he spoke of her hair flattering her face? She berated herself silently. Being invited to breakfast with Prince Raihnin had gone to her head, she decided. In the midst of mentally chastising herself for her pride, she suddenly remembered the old piece of leather that secured her hair. Should she remove it?

"It would be no trouble for me to free my hair, Your Majesty," Jeilin said.

"No, no," Prince Raihnin said. "Forget I said anything. I ought not to be giving women styling advice. My sister Elin would laugh at me if she knew, and give me the rough side of her tongue as well, likely as not."

Forgetting the prince's comments on her hair was highly unlikely, Jeilin thought to herself, but to him she said, "I'll pretend that you said nothing at all besides 'good morning,' Your Majesty."

He laughed as he buttered his roll, and Jeilin felt a surge of embarrassment when she realized that she was admiring his smile.

"Then I'll give you a little advice about your journey to Sunlan," he said. "Though it's northeast of here, it's actually considerably warmer, which I'm sure you'll be glad to know."

Jeilin nodded.

"Sunlan is a military outpost, as you're probably aware," he continued. "My cousin Prince Stephen is commanding there at present. He won't be difficult to locate—just look for a fair-haired, loudmouthed fool blabbering from atop the showiest warhorse you've ever seen in your life, and you'll have found him." Prince Raihnin's smile offset the harshness of his description.

"Though Sunlan borders the mountains that separate us from the kingdom of Ryeln, the outpost hasn't seen conflict for nearly a decade. It's always better to be safe than sorry, though, so be careful during your time there."

"Of course," Jeilin replied.

The rest of their breakfast passed in conversation involving Sunlan, the areas Jeilin would pass through on the journey there, and a few anecdotes involving the prince's cousin, which Jeilin thought quite amusing, though she doubted that Prince Stephen would appreciate how freely his cousin shared them.

"Well I won't delay you any further," Prince Raihnin eventually said, rising from the table. "I know that you and your companion would likely have left earlier if not for me."

Jeilin assured him that he shouldn't worry over it.

"Perhaps my cousin will send you straight back to me with a reply," he suggested with a small smile.

"Perhaps," Jeilin said, and left, realizing that she had forgotten to add "Your Majesty." She was almost too busy replaying the morning's conversation in her mind to think that the prince might be insulted.

****

"So?" Olwen said as soon as they'd ridden out of the royal gates and into the busy street. They heeled their horses into brisk trots as people dodged out of their way.

Jeilin was unable to restrain a tiny smile, and feared that she would begin to blush yet again as she remembered her recent hour with Prince Raihnin. "We had an excellent breakfast," she said. "And we talked...he told me about his cousin whose message I'm delivering." She tapped her chest to indicate the letter she'd stored in a pocket at her breast.

Olwen returned her slight smile and nodded. "A lieutenant who was lodging in the castle gave me a message for Prince Stephen as well," she said.

A moment's silence stretched between them.

"Look, look!" a small boy called out from a bakery's doorway. He had taken his even smaller sister by the hand and was pointing enthusiastically at Olwen and Jeilin. "They're *messengers*," he declared in what was perhaps the loudest whisper Jeilin had ever heard. His sister's eyes widened as she stared up at them in awe. Olwen beamed warmly at both of them and gave them a small wave. They both looked shocked, and then burst into giggles as the pair rode past them.

"I won't pester you," Olwen said. "Just give me the word and I'll shut up. But I'd be lying if I said I weren't curious about why Prince Raihnin invited you to dine with him this morning."

"I—" Jeilin started, and then sighed.

"He…complimented my hair." Jeilin was sure her cheeks were aflame as she and Olwen rode out of the east gate. Was she presuming too much?

Olwen smiled mischievously. "To Sunlan, then," she said, and urged Snow into the morning's first canter. The road stretched before them, and their horses' hooves ate it up as they left the sea air of the Bay of Lights behind.

****

The two and a half days Jeilin and Olwen spent traveling away from the Bay of Lights were more pleasant than those they had spent traveling to it. The farther they traveled from the sea, the warmer the climate became, just as the prince had foretold.

Sunlan was a village of middling size, nestled in the foothills of the Black Mountains. Children gathered at the outskirts of clusters of modest wooden homes and shops to watch and cheer as Olwen and Jeilin rode by. They had only a few miles to go before they reached the military encampment that was nestled between the high, jagged peaks of the Black Mountains on one side, and fields of wild grass on the other.

Jeilin knew from studying maps, which she did every evening by the campfire or in her room, that the Black Mountains were the northern border that separated Alaishin from the kingdom of Ryeln. The mountains were essentially a no man's land between the two kingdoms, and that was no wonder, as the mountains were as vast and harsh as they were tall. There had been peace between Alaishin and Ryeln for over a decade; the last conflict had been a relatively small skirmish some twelve years ago. The Black Mountains were widely considered by the citizens of Alaishin to be an effective barrier to protect against any Ryelnish ambitions, and Alaishin neither desired anything that lay in the harsh lands to the north, nor to cross the intimidating wilderness of the mountains.

The horses began to step more quickly as the outpost appeared, no doubt sensing stalls where they would be left to rest and feed. Rectangular barracks that had been built by soldiers from split logs lay parallel to a stable of similar construction. The outpost bustled with the activity of a few hundred soldiers and the craftsmen who accompanied them. The air rang with the sounds of a blacksmith's hammer and the sharp *clack clack* of men practicing swordsmanship with bundles of reeds.

Fringe and Snow galloped into the center of the camp, and half of the sparring men stopped to stare. One of them whistled, probably at Olwen, Jeilin thought. Still, she blushed. Olwen either hadn't heard or was pretending not to have. A fat officer on foot trotted toward them hurriedly and gave a hasty salute. Olwen returned his salute, as was customary, and Jeilin followed her example.

"We have come swiftly bearing letters to Prince Stephen," Olwen said.

The officer nodded and motioned for two nearby men to take their horses. "Right this way," he directed as the pair dismounted.

They followed the officer around one of the barracks to an open field that had been set up as an archery range. A golden-haired man sat atop a white horse; an impressive animal that had a neck like a stonemason's finest arch and legs as slender and graceful as a deer's. The animal never stirred as its rider pulled an arrow to his cheek, the bright red plumage that marked the end nearly brushing his face. A nearby group of men watched incredulously. The archer's aim seemed to be directed at a target so far in the distance that it appeared to be half the size of the others. There was a minute *twang* as he released the arrow. The small crowd seemed to hold its collective breath as the arrow flew. The horse remained so still and so beautiful that it might have been mistaken for a statue, were it not for a mild breeze that stirred its mane.

The arrow struck home, lodging itself in the red circle that had been painted in the center of the target. Half of the watching soldiers cheered, while the other half grumbled and dug begrudgingly into their purses. The archer atop the white horse absorbed the praise like a sponge. "I tell you, that arrow won't miss" he said. "It's as lucky as a soldier in a whorehouse. Not that I can't attribute its success to my admirable skills to a certain degree, mind you..." He turned his horse to face the cluster of observers, most of whom were now squabbling over the bets they'd placed on his archery skills.

A look of surprise flickered across the man's face for a fleeting second, and disappeared, swallowed up by a grin. "Well, well," he said smoothly. "To what do I owe the pleasure?" He seemed to be doing a very good job of dividing his considerable attentions between Olwen and Jeilin, hardly sparing a glance for the officer who had led them there. The soldiers who had been watching him stared too, and Jeilin felt surrounded by a wall of eyes.

The officer cleared his throat conspicuously. "Royal messengers have come swiftly to deliver letters to His Highness Prince Stephen," he said loudly.

"Let the royal messengers deliver the letters they have been charged with," Prince Stephen replied, still grinning and refusing to spare a glance for his officer. He swung down from the beautiful stallion as he spoke.

Jeilin and Olwen kneeled simultaneously. Jeilin spoke first—in the event that more than one messenger was delivering to the same person, the messenger with the letter from the person of highest rank spoke first. "A letter to his Royal Highness Prince Stephen from his Majesty Prince Raihnin," she said, meeting his gaze all the while, as was customary. He beamed down at her in a manner Jeilin found unnerving. Had he not been a prince, she might have even thought *annoying*.

"Well, well," he said again. "A message from my dear cousin Raihnin. Let's see what he has to say."

Mercifully, he turned his attention upon Olwen in order to receive her message before breaking the seal and reading the first. "A letter to his Royal Highness Prince Stephen from Lieutenant Rhemley," she said. He nodded, beaming all the while, and took the letter from her outstretched hand.

"You may rise," he said to them both. "You have served me and Alaishin well. May neither your horses nor your luck ever falter."

They rose.

Just as they turned and began to walk away, he added onto his statement. "And may you both join me for dinner this evening. Six o'clock. Mulney here will be glad to fetch you." He clapped a large hand on the shoulder of the officer who had brought them to him.

"Ah...thank you very much," Olwen said, her amusement nearly concealed under a practiced veneer of cordiality.

Jeilin mimicked Olwen's words.

"Wow," she said as soon as they were out of earshot of anyone she could see. "He's just like Prince Raihnin described him."

Olwen laughed. "What did he say about him? That you can see his ego a mile away?"

"You could put it that way," Jeilin said.

Jeilin and Olwen spent the rest of the afternoon sipping tea and reading (Olwen always kept a book or two in her saddlebags). Soldiers stood taller and stepped higher around them, and not, Jeilin knew, because they were messengers.

Officer Mulney found them promptly before six to escort them to dinner.

Prince Stephen entertained them in the small dining room located in his modest quarters, which, he boasted, were the most luxurious to be found at the outpost: a small split-log cabin situated next to one of the barracks. They ate venison, hunted down by the prince himself; an event that he related to the pair of them in glorified detail. "And that is how I determined that the arrow you came upon me testing this afternoon is lucky," he finished. He skewered a chunk of venison on a fork and motioned with it while grinning, as if to emphasize the fact that their delicious dinner was to be credited to his considerable luck and skill, both of which he was very fond of relating to others.

Olwen and Jeilin both nodded politely. Jeilin didn't dare meet Olwen's eye.

"But then, a pair of adventurous ladies like yourself aren't likely to be impressed by a hunt, thrilling as it was," he said, not sounding at all as if he believed what he had said, or as if he thought anyone else would. "You are brides of adventure!"

"You flatter us, Your Majesty" Olwen said, the corners of her mouth barely curving into a slight smile that Jeilin knew well. "What little adventure we encounter is nothing compared to the ventures of a prince."

Prince Stephen shook his head dramatically. "I'll hear nothing of the sort," he declared. "You are both surely brides of adventure, because if you weren't you would undoubtedly have each been claimed by men long ago." He leaned forward in a manner that suggested confidence. "Never have I seen such desirable women so...*free*." He placed a great emphasis on the word. "I'm beginning to regret that our royal fleet of messengers has been dominated by men for so long!"

Despite the fact that Prince Raihnin had related his cousin's mannerisms to her through anecdotes earlier that week, Jeilin found the force of his personality overwhelming. Her face felt as hot as the mug of tea she held in her hand. Olwen seemed to be faring much better; she knew worlds more about dealing with men than Jeilin, and seemed always to be either on the point of laughter or the point of unleashing a verbal lashing when in Prince Stephen's presence—Jeilin could never quite determine which.

The meal continued for over two hours, with Prince Stephen vacillating between relating dramatic tales to his own favor, and showering his two guests with compliments. Jeilin was unable to keep from laughing when he told one of the same tales Prince Raihnin had shared with her earlier that week, for Prince Stephen artfully omitted certain details, causing the tale to reflect much more positively upon him than the unabridged version.

He became more serious, if such a word could ever be applied to him, when the meal finally drew to a close. Dessert had been finished half an hour ago, and both Jeilin and Olwen had repeatedly declared that they were too full for more wine. "Well, I shall dictate a response to my dear cousin's message, and the lieutenant's, tomorrow," he said. "You will both of course take the day to rest before beginning the return journey the following morning. I'll give you charge of Prince Raihnin's letter, of course, Jeilin."

Jeilin's stomach seemed to want to cave in on itself, and her face felt suddenly hot...there was something *knowing* in the way Prince Stephen arched his left eyebrow. And why had he said "of course?" He paused, probably for dramatic effect, and then continued. "I know you are apprenticing under the lovely Olwen, so I won't separate you."

They both expressed their thanks.

"You shall both share an officer's cabin tonight," he said. "It's among the best we have to offer here, but I'm afraid it's quite modest nonetheless."

They both assured him that it would be more than suitable; sleeping arrangements, whether on cold ground or in a palace, were of no consequence in comparison to the importance of a messenger's mission.

"I hope you will both be comfortable," he finished. "If you're not, please come straight to me. Do not let the hour hinder you. I would be ashamed to let a lady suffer in silence because she was concerned for my convenience, and I shall be happy to remedy any problem or discomfort you might have." Ever smiling, he seemed to hope that they would find a reason to revisit his quarters in the night. Jeilin followed Olwen from his cabin, her face burning furiously.

Prince Stephen had sent one of his personal servants to escort them to their quarters, but it turned out to hardly be necessary, as the officer's cabin that had been vacated for their use was adjacent to his, no more than a few paces away.

"He's even worse than Prince Raihnin described," Jeilin said once she had settled with Olwen into the modest little cabin, her face still red in darkness as she recalled Prince Stephen's suggestions.

Olwen laughed. "He's nowhere near as refined as you'd expect a prince to be," she said.

"Not at all," Jeilin agreed. "I'm glad we're only staying here for a day."

"Of course you are," Olwen said, and Jeilin could hear the smile in her voice, though she was unable to see it. "And I expect that Prince Raihnin will be as well."

Jeilin was glad for the lightless night that kept Olwen from seeing her face. "I—I meant that I was glad we're not staying long because of Prince *Stephen*," she said, but the defense sounded weak, even to her. She *would* be glad to escape the attentions of the raucous Prince Stephen, but she couldn't deny that her heart beat a little faster when she thought of seeing Prince Raihnin again so soon. She berated herself silently when she realized that she was debating how she would wear her hair upon arrival at the Bay of Lights, and wishing that she had some of the wildflower shampoo to wash it with before beginning the return journey. She told herself not to be a fool, and drifted to sleep trying to obey.

****

The next morning, Jeilin and Olwen ate a breakfast of hotcakes with a handful of officers who had gathered around a fire. Jeilin relished the warmth; the morning was quite cool. "I wouldn't be surprised if it started snowing within a fortnight," one of the officers said matter-of-factly, surveying the sky that stretched over the country, pierced on one side by the jagged mountains. A couple of the others agreed, remembering that it was around the same time it had started snowing last year. They sounded dejected. Jeilin thought that it must be rather dull to be stationed in the wilderness in a northernmost corner of the country, especially during the winter. Prince Stephen had probably been providing most of their entertainment, she mused to herself.

"Here he comes," one of the officers declared under his breath, as if he had heard Jeilin's thoughts.

Prince Stephen was striding—no, strutting, Jeilin decided—across the grounds toward their fire. He wore a bright blue coat that made the sky look dull, with golden embroidery racing up the sleeves and flourishing around the collar. Matching golden buttons gleamed. His fair, wavy locks seemed to be a small light source of their own. Jeilin silently wondered how much time he spent preening his hair, and then, much to her chagrin, found that she was wishing she knew what made it shine so fiercely, so that she could try whatever it was on her own hair. She shoved Prince Raihnin's compliment out of her mind and took a deep drink from her mug of tea, as if it could wash away her embarrassment or dilute the foolish fancies that kept assaulting her mind. She was almost glad when Prince Stephen interrupted her unruly thoughts with an invitation.

"My ladies," he began. "I will be hawking today, and I would be honored to have you both as my companions." He beamed down at them. Even his teeth gleamed in the cold sunlight. She and Olwen both offered polite acceptances. After all, what else was there to do? Jeilin had never hunted with a bird, and truthfully, she thought it would be an interesting experience, if only she could keep her face from reddening with the prince's every other word.

An hour later, Jeilin and Olwen had mounted Fringe and Snow and joined Prince Stephen, who was astride his showy stallion as usual, at the edge of the outpost. "This way," he said, moving his horse forward at a leisurely walk. "I nearly always find rabbits in the fields east of here."

One of Prince Stephen's personal attendants followed with the falcon.

Their leisurely ride came to a halt in a field full of yellowing winter grasses, about a mile from the outpost. Prince Stephen offered to let one of the women release the hawk. Olwen declined and seemed amused when Jeilin accepted his offer.

The bird felt lighter on her arm than she had imagined. "Their bones are hollow," Prince Stephen said knowledgeably. Its talons felt almost heavy, though, even menacing. Jeilin was glad for the leather gauntlet she wore, but wondered how much protection it would provide if the falcon intended to harm her. The bird gazed at her with a round, glossy black eye. As Prince Stephen instructed her, his directions were surprisingly free of embarrassing remarks, though Jeilin thought that he touched her arm rather more than was strictly necessary.

Prince Stephen rejoiced boisterously when the hawk captured a rabbit. Jeilin hoped that he wouldn't decide that she was "lucky" like he had a particular arrow the day before.

"What's that?" Olwen said suddenly from atop Snow.

"Why, it's dinner!" Prince Stephen declared. "Excellent job, Jeilin. You're a natural!"

"No," Olwen said. "Not the rabbit—look!" She pointed toward the imposing, asymmetrical precipices of the Black Mountains.

Jeilin, Prince Stephen, and his hawk-handler all scrutinized the mountainside. At first, Jeilin saw nothing, but then...she noticed that the black of the mountain seemed to move. She continued to watch. Yes, the side of the mountain seemed to be undulating, almost like a pot of boiling, black water. And then there was sound. A distant alarm rang out from the direction of the camp. Prince Stephen's smile disappeared more quickly than the hawk had snatched the rabbit from the dry grass.

"The outpost!" he said, and wheeled his horse around in the direction from which they had come. The animal was nearly as fast as it was beautiful, but Fringe and Snow kept pace with the pale stallion without difficulty. The attendant galloped behind on his slower gelding, flogging its hindquarters with the end of his reins to keep up.

The outpost was in upheaval.

Everywhere, men seized weapons and swung into the saddles of horses that danced, absorbing the nervous energy from their environment and their riders. Officers barked orders and men scrambled into formation. The mountain was alive with a horde of dark soldiers, raining down on their horses, propelled by momentum as they poured onto the stretch of flat land that was all that lay between them and the outpost.

Chapter 8

J eilin's stomach contradicted itself, seeming to both flip and contract into a ball at once. The foreign riders appeared as devils as they galloped closer; Jeilin saw that their dark armor ended in the shapes of horns that crowned their heavy helmets. Half of the Alaishinian soldiers who surrounded her hadn't had time to don any armor at all. Everywhere, their coats and hair flapped in the cold breeze, unprotected, while the unexpected enemy drew nearer, a mass of dark armor, flying hooves, and weapons that she could just make out gleaming sinisterly in the early winter sun.

Olwen was beside her, reining in Snow, who kept side-stepping the chaos. Olwen caught Jeilin's eye; she looked strangely regretful.

Jeilin thought of Prince Raihnin's warning; "…the outpost hasn't seen conflict for nearly a decade…be careful during your time there." The descending troops must be from Ryeln, she thought. They must have crossed the rugged mountain range in the coolness of fall, escaping notice, like a phantom hand across the wilderness.

The Rylenish soldiers fell upon the outpost. A handful of their front line fell to well-aimed arrows and were promptly trampled by their own surging horde. More and more surged forward, replacing them; more than the outpost could hope to defend against.

Prince Stephen wheeled his fair, snorting mount to face Jeilin and Olwen. For once he wasn't laughing or smiling. The set of his jaw spoke of resolve, and his blue eyes of regret. "Ride to Raihnin at the Bay of Lights as quickly as you can. Tell him that Ryeln is upon us. May neither your horse nor your luck ever falter."

At his urging, the white stallion plunged forward, toward the strange soldiers who were ravaging the camp, before Jeilin or Olwen even had a chance to recite the return formality. In the short moment that it took Jeilin to begin to turn Fringe away, a Ryelnish soldier on his horse seemed to leap out of nowhere toward her. She opened her mouth to scream, but no sound came. The solider took the form of a large, horned mass of black armor, swinging a huge, curved blade overhead. Only half of his face was visible beneath his helmet; she saw that his small, dark eyes glared fiercely. In her shock, Jeilin noticed everything. There was a strange mark, a tapering slash of black, across his cheek, and the strange sword he wielded seemed to sing as it arced through the air. He seemed to bring with him a wave of heat; the cold of winter was suddenly gone as she was swallowed by his voracious, ferocious warmth. Suddenly, something—no, some*one*—crashed into her side, hard.

Prince Stephen. His horse's shoulder slammed into her leg with such force that she swayed in the saddle, nearly losing her seat and sliding off of Fringe's side. His arm brushed hers as she was forced to the left, nearly colliding with Olwen and Snow. The dark soldier's singing sword descended into Prince Stephen's unarmored shoulder, slicing through his blue and gold coat, cutting deeply into his body, and then deeper still. Fringe regained his balance and leapt away from what was turning into a scene from a nightmare. Jeilin saw red blossom on the prince's coat as he slumped in his saddle, spraying his snowy horse's coat with bright flecks of red.

Fringe and Snow were carrying their riders away from the violence at a breakneck speed as both horses' and riders' trained muscles and reactions took over. The soldier who had stilled Prince Stephen gave chase.

Fringe and Snow raced forward madly, unencumbered by the heavy armor that the Ryelnish soldiers wore, their riders almost as light as feathers in comparison. Jeilin cast a frantic glance over her shoulder and saw that another soldier had joined the chase. Their horned enemies demanded every bit of speed possible from their sweating mounts, but the space between them and the two messengers grew with every stride. Jeilin felt an almost sickening surge of relief when they and the outpost fell out of sight, but the urge to escape hardly lessened. Fringe didn't need encouragement to flee; he ran of his own free will.

Jeilin chanced a look at Olwen. Her face was as white as her horse; the corners of her mouth turned down, her eyes pained and worried. Jeilin thought she must look much the same. Olwen returned her stare and opened her mouth to say something, but closed it as if she had thought better of it. Instead, she stared straight ahead, riding hard as the village of Sunlan came into view.

Sunlan bustled with all the usual activity of a normal, undisturbed day. Villagers stared with their mouths open at Jeilin and Olwen, and at their horses, whose flanks were white with froth. "Enemies are upon us!" Olwen cried loudly without slowing. "Ryeln has come over the mountains!"

The village passed by almost instantly, in a great blur. Jeilin looked back over her shoulder at the townsfolk beginning to buzz and bustle with fear. She doubted that the foreign soldiers would leave the town untouched, and felt a pang of regret for the people who lived there, now without the protection of the military outpost.

They rode on into the night. It had been dark for some time when they finally stopped. They took shelter in a secluded place a fair distance from the road, settling in under pine boughs, with the horses hobbled nearby. They didn't dare build a fire, despite the cold. Instead, Jeilin and Olwen settled back-to-back under shared blankets, their heads resting on their softest saddlebags, the ones that contained clothing.

"We should beat them to the Bay of Lights as long as we don't waste any time," Olwen said. "By now they've probably sent lighter, faster riders than the ones we encountered, but we've got a good head start."

"And we're not royal messengers for nothing," Jeilin said, trying to maintain at least the appearance of bravery as the soldier's sword sang over and over in her mind, finally silencing itself in Prince Stephen's flesh.

"That's right," Olwen agreed as she punched her saddlebag pillow fiercely, presumably to shift it into a more comfortable position.

Soon they had both drifted off to sleep, exhausted, Jeilin with the prince's blood eternally raining down on his horse's snowy flanks in her mind's eye.

****

It was still dark when Olwen nudged Jeilin awake. She shoved a cold roll into Jeilin's hand before she had even completely thrown off her blankets. Jeilin ate it hastily, tasting nothing, and hurried to pack up the meager bedding they'd laid out a couple of hours before. Soon, they were both saddling their tired horses. Jeilin wondered how close the Ryelnish soldiers were as she swung into the saddle and pointed Fringe toward the too-distant Bay of Lights.

By early that night, the horses were exhausted, sweat soaked, and on their last wind. Jeilin and Olwen were sore and tired of rubbing away from their eyes the sleep that they couldn't allow. But finally they had reached the Bay of Lights.

They rode hard through the town, pausing for no one as the few people who had ventured out into the bitter cold leapt from their way. They couldn't reach the door beneath the golden star soon enough. "Take us to Prince Raihnin!"

Jeilin demanded as soon as they'd entered. The waiting guard leapt as if shocked, but something in her face commanded him to obey. He set off at a run, with Jeilin loping to keep up.

"See that the highest officers here all report to the prince, immediately!" Jeilin heard Olwen snap at the two other guards standing watch. Soon she was on Jeilin's heels.

By the time the guard stopped, Jeilin had acquired a horrible stitch in her left side and was unable to stop herself from panting. The guard shoved the heavy oaken doors opened unceremoniously, and Jeilin burst inside with Olwen close behind.

Prince Raihnin was inside, reclined on a bed that was resplendent in the finest silk sheets, absorbed in a book and wearing only a pair of breeches. Jeilin was too frantic to even think about blushing. "A royal messenger has come swiftly to deliver a message to His Highness Prince Raihnin!" the guard panted desperately from the doorway behind her.

The prince looked stunned; his book lay beside him on the bed, already forgotten. "How in the—" he began, but then he stopped himself. "Let the royal messenger deliver the message she has been charged with," he said, looking bewildered and expectant.

"I have no letter, Your Majesty, but a message from your cousin Prince Stephen," Jeilin breathed, struggling to speak as quickly as possible. She took a deep breath and plunged on. "Ryeln is upon us. They have come over the Black Mountains, and Prince Stephen is dead."

For a moment there was silence so acute that Jeilin could hear the prince breathe.

"You're sure you saw this with your own eyes?" he finally asked.

"Yes!" she declared emphatically.

His blue eyes seemed to bore into her.

Suddenly, there was a commotion as a handful of officers burst into the room. "Your Majesty!" one of them nearly shouted while managing a hasty salute. "Officer Helmihn reporting for duty! We were urged to come to you as quickly as possible."

"Enemies are upon us," Prince Raihnin said flatly. "These messengers have just brought me the news. Ryeln has come from over the Black Mountains; the outpost at Sunlan has been..."

He cast a demanding glance toward Jeilin.

"Destroyed," she said weakly.

The officers burst into a chorus over the unlikelihood of such an event. Prince Raihnin silenced them with a look. "Tell us what happened," he said to Jeilin. "And there will be no interruptions," he added, giving the officers a significant look. They were all silent as she related the events of the past couple days; how their time at Sunlan had been uneventful until the sudden attack. She finished by telling them about how Prince Stephen had sacrificed himself to save her from the Ryelnish soldier.

"Braggart and fool though he sometimes was," Prince Raihnin said, "he *was* brave. He'll be glad to have died in such a way. It'll give him something else to boast about in the next life." He smiled slightly at Jeilin. Was he trying to console her, she wondered?

He turned to the officers. "Send notice to my father and each city and outpost north and east of here first, save Sunlan," he commanded. "We'll need every messenger."

The officers each saluted and began to file out of the room hurriedly. One of them beckoned for Olwen to follow him, and another turned to Jeilin. Prince Raihnin held up an authoritative hand. "I need a word with her," he ordered. Soon, they were alone in the room. Jeilin's face burned as she remembered that he was still shirtless. He seemed to read her thoughts, and pulled a coat on rather hastily.

"You did an excellent job," he said. "You and your companion both; please tell her I said so."

Jeilin nodded. "Of course, Your Highness," she replied.

"I regret sending you out again so soon. I know you're exhausted, and rightly so, but I need you to carry a personal message to my father in Dresinva—you know as well as anyone how urgent it is. And, you'll be safest there, to tell the truth. You may have a fresh horse from the royal stables."

Jeilin had trouble with the thought of being separated from Fringe. "With all due respect, Your Highness, I'd rather keep my own mount."

He considered it for a moment and then nodded. "Very well."

The relief his agreement inspired was the only positive emotion Jeilin could muster. Her muscles ached in protest, but she knew that there was no reasonable alternative. Every available messenger would be dispatched promptly, and she was no exception.

"Your companion may accompany you," he said.

Jeilin breathed a sigh of relief, but then felt guilty. "I'll understand if Your Majesty cannot spare an extra messenger," she said. "I know the way to Dresinva well enough."

He shook his head. "The other messengers are all well-rested. The two of you will be able to keep each other awake and encouraged. The ride to Dresinva is not short."

Jeilin thanked him.

"No, I am in your debt, Jeilin," he said sincerely.

There was a silence that stretched too long for Jeilin's liking.

The doors burst open unceremoniously, again.

"A royal messenger has come swiftly to deliver a message to His Highness Prince Raihnin," an out-of-breath servant panted from the doorway as another messenger stumbled through it. The man was tall and unfamiliar, his hair short and brown. A tell-tale golden star gleamed on his heaving chest.

"Let the royal messenger deliver the letter he has been charged with," Prince Raihnin said starkly, looking as if he expected the worst.

"Avrin has fallen," he announced hurriedly. "Ryelnish soldiers came from over the Black Mountains."

Jeilin knew from her map studies that Avrin was a town near the border, much like Sunlan, but nearly forty miles farther eastward.

"There was not time for a letter to be written, Your Majesty," the messenger added.

"You were there when Avrin fell?" the prince asked.

The messenger nodded.

"And what do you think remains of Avrin now?" he asked.

"The Ryelnish soldiers outnumbered the Alaishinian troops by far," the man replied. "Surely anyone who picked up a weapon was cut down and destroyed. I...I don't know about the townspeople," he finished with a grimace.

Prince Raihnin addressed the panting servant who had led the messenger from Avrin to his quarters. "Take him to Officer Helming," he said. "Have him tell him everything."

Jeilin found herself alone with the prince again.

"I must oversee preparations to defend the Bay of Lights," he said to her. "See that you get a few hours of sleep. I'll prepare my message while you rest."

Jeilin nodded gratefully, thinking longingly of a soft bed in one of the palace's warm rooms.

"I'm sure one of my officers took your companion to give her a message. Please tell her to return it, and that she will be riding with you."

Jeilin nodded again.

Suddenly, Prince Raihnin smiled. It was small, brief, and perhaps rueful; but it was a smile. "You might as well know...I dismissed everyone as to steal a few moments alone with you." He turned to face her directly, and she felt numb under the full force of his blue eyes.

"Since the first time I laid eyes upon you, I've thought you're the most beautiful woman I've ever seen."

Jeilin couldn't hide her astonishment. Her mouth fell open slightly, and her eyes widened as they drank in the prince's image: his stunning blue eyes and his night-black hair. Suddenly, she remembered what he had said about her own hair and realized that she hadn't given it a single thought all day. She regretted the piece of leather that held it all back from her face. She reached up and untied it with fingers that were nearly numb. Her dark hair fell forward, brushing the sides of her face lightly.

Prince Raihnin grinned faintly. "I don't know whether I'll ever see you again," he said, his voice at odds with his somber words. "But if not, I shall always remember you as I'm seeing you now." He reached out to smooth down a lock of Jeilin's hair that stuck out rebelliously.

A shiver of excitement raced down her spine as he touched her. "I won't forget you either," she managed in a voice barely above a whisper. She turned away, battling mixed feelings of happiness and regret. A moment later she was descending a staircase on her way to bed, still looking and feeling startled.

She found Olwen, already asleep in her bed. She nudged her awake gently and related the prince's plan for them to travel to Dresinva together. Jeilin could tell she was glad, but only because she had grown used to her expressions; she fell back asleep promptly. Jeilin retired to the room next door.

One of the first things she noticed when she woke was a note that had been left on her bedside table. She had been so deeply asleep that she hadn't heard the servant who delivered it enter or exit the room. She read the elegant script eagerly:

My message to my father has been prepared. I am in a meeting with the officers in a room on the first floor, adjacent to the kitchens. Come when you wake. Raihnin

He had signed his name with no title, and Jeilin noted the detail with a sense of wonder.

She retrieved a silver comb from her saddlebags, which rested on the floor next to her bed. She ran it through her unrestrained hair and smoothed it hurriedly before pulling on her boots. She exchanged the wrinkled shirt she'd traveled and slept in for a new one and started on her way to the first floor.

A servant waiting at the door admitted her into the conference room. Prince Raihnin stood at the head of the table, staring down at a large map, with half a dozen officers hunched and poring over it with him. He looked up when he heard her enter.

Excusing himself from the heated study, he strode to the end of the room to meet her. He removed a sealed, folded piece of parchment from one of his pockets and gave it to Jeilin. The paper felt heavy and expensive in her hand, the best that gold could buy. Jeilin couldn't help but feel nervous and expectant after their last exchange. The officers were absorbed in their speculations and strategies and paid her no mind.

"Be careful," Prince Raihnin said. "I would very much like to see you again."

"I will," she replied, her voice coming out quieter than she had expected it to.

He paused for a moment, as if considering something. "Here," he said, and reached to his belt, unfastening a large dagger that hung there. He pressed it into Jeilin's hand along with the letter. She stared down at it, examining the finely tooled silver and marveling at its considerable weight. Silver vines and scrolls curled across the hilt in an intricate pattern, and startlingly large blue sapphires winked at her from among the flourishes. "It's not much," he said. "But it is something, should you need it."

"There's no need, Your Majesty—" Jeilin began, but the prince cut her off.

"It's just the two of us," he said, also aware that the officers weren't hearing a word of what was happening at their end of the room. "So call me Raihnin."

Jeilin knew that her shock must have registered on her face when Raihnin grinned.

"And I want you to have it," he continued. "It'll be something for you to remember me by if we don't meet again."

"Thank you, Raihnin," she said. His name sounded strange on her tongue.

He smiled and she realized for what seemed the thousandth time how beautiful he was. A sense of disbelief nearly overcame her.

"Nothing short of death shall prevent me from delivering your message with my own hand, and may death find me if it does," she whispered, reciting the formality that had suddenly taken on a more serious feel in light of the Ryelnish attack.

"You hold my secrets and my trust, Jeilin. May neither your horse nor your luck ever falter." He gazed down at her for one last moment before turning back to the discussion at the table.

Jeilin realized that she had been holding her breath when she began breathing again in the corridor outside the room where she had left Raihnin to agonize over maps with his officers. She clutched Raihnin's ornate dagger with both hands, as if physical contact with the gift would keep her grounded in reality.

Olwen was waiting for her in her room, holding both her own saddlebags and Jeilin's, all of which were nearly bursting with the food that she'd already collected from the kitchens. There were dark circles under her darker eyes. Jeilin had no way to hide Raihnin's gift; it flashed conspicuously at her side.

"A parting gift?" Olwen guessed.

"Yes," Jeilin admitted.

"We'd better get down to the stables then," Olwen said.

Jeilin was grateful that Olwen hadn't pressed the matter of the dagger further; Raihnin's affection still felt too unreal to speak of.

Their horses had already been saddled and were waiting when they reached the stables. It was still dark; they had arrived and were leaving in the same night. Fringe and Snow's coats were no longer matted with sweat; they had dried and been curried to a shine. No doubt they had had the finest care possible, but there was no dodging the fact that their rest had been sparse any way you looked at it, just like their riders'.

The saddle felt painfully familiar as Jeilin settled into it, her muscles suddenly remembering all of the night's earlier aches and sending painful spikes of protest throughout her body. A slight frown on Olwen's face said that she was feeling the same. They urged their horses forward.

The sun cracked over the horizon, a violently orange slit that cut the dark winter night in half as they rode through the city. A minority of the city's inhabitants braved the cold, stirring in the streets. Did their faces look unusually worried and their movements strangely wary, or had Jeilin's imagination and the dim light conspired against her? She shook her head and clutched the front of her cloak so that it hugged her body, refusing to think about the bloody events at Sunlan more than she could help. A sudden image of Raihnin suffering the same fate as his cousin set a spasm of fear throughout her consciousness, and for a second she longed to turn her leg into Fringe's side and send him galloping back to the palace where she could see the prince again, even if only for a second. Her hand that held the reigns twitched. She rode on beside Olwen and Snow, out through the southern gate, and told herself that her eyes watered because of the cold, biting wind that rolled off of the ocean. Soon, the sound of waves crashing on the rocky beaches had faded, and even the city's bright namesake lights had winked out, absorbed by distance and the greater light of the breaking morning.

Jeilin and Olwen had resolved to make the journey to Dresinva, which normally took five days, in four—a taxing decision. Extreme fatigue forced Jeilin to have to fight slumping in the saddle, but fear of being beaten to the capital by Ryeln kept her feet in the stirrups and her eyes on the horizon. The only mercy was that the air seemed much warmer once they outran the cruel gusts that poured off of the ocean. But even that had its dark side; each mile they put between themselves and the sea seemed to make it that much more unlikely that Jeilin would ever be reunited with Raihnin.

Chapter 9

J eilin unsheathed the dagger Raihnin had given her when she and Olwen finally stopped to make camp on the first evening of their journey. The small fire they'd hurried to build warded off the cold winter air for a few feet, and Jeilin sat as close to it as she could bear. Fringe and Snow stood hobbled nearby, clipping the deadening grass that grew at the edge of the forest. They'd selected their location, which was invisible from the road, for safety reasons. The night was too cold to forego the fire.

The dagger was surprisingly difficult to remove from its sheath, which was the last thing Jeilin had expected from something of such remarkably high quality. After a few tugs, it was finally freed. Though it was dark, Jeilin's eyes didn't miss a small object that fluttered to the ground. She reached down and picked it up; it was a very small, thin rectangular piece of parchment that had been folded in half. Her heart nearly leapt out of her chest—or at least that's how it felt—when she unfolded it and recognized Prince Raihnin's neat script. The bit of paper that had kept the dagger from unsheathing smoothly had only afforded room for a few sentences; sentences that Jeilin knew she would find herself reading over and over again.

By now you have left for Dresinva, and I am organizing the troops in the bay. How I longed to keep you here with me, or even to ride with you to the capital! I dared not voice these desires while you were here, lest I give into temptation and endanger the kingdom. Still, I want to make my feelings known. I am thinking of you, just as I said I would be.

Truly,

Raihnin

Jeilin's face felt suddenly hot. She stared at Raihnin's note in astonishment, reading it several times over again before she finally refolded it and tucked it into a small pocket that had been sewn inside her tunic. Olwen was gazing at her curiously from across the fire.

"A note from Prince Raihnin," Jeilin explained. Even to her own ears, her voice sounded weak. That a prince—never mind a prince as stunningly handsome as Prince Raihnin—should ever be thinking of her, a farm girl turned messenger, seemed almost unbelievable.

Olwen only smiled. "We'd better turn in then."

Jeilin nodded her agreement. They would only allow themselves a few hours' rest before riding again, and they needed every minute. She held her hands up to the fire one last time and then balled them quickly into fists as she turned away to crawl into her tent, hoping to make the warmth last. Exhausted, she was asleep before the heat left her palms.

****

Frost covered the ground the next morning, a thin layer of translucent ice crystals that stretched as far as the eye could see. The sun began its ascent, a fiery sphere peeking over the horizon, causing the frost to sparkle in a million different places, dazzling.

"It's beautiful," Jeilin said as she stretched, gratefully absorbing the heat of the waning fire.

Olwen nodded and yawned.

They shared a hastily eaten breakfast around the fire. The food the palace kitchens had supplied them with was cold, but still good, and the hot tea that Olwen brewed was welcome. Jeilin regretted having to pack away the mug that had warmed her hands, but lingering at the campsite was out of the question. They packed away their scant belongings, put the fire out, saddled and watered the horses, and were off, the cold wind whipping through manes, tails, and hair alike.

****

By the third day of their journey, they were on schedule. "It looks as if we'll arrive tomorrow as planned," Olwen said. Jeilin nodded her approval wearily; they had been traveling hard.

That morning, they shared the road with unexpectedly large numbers as a band of Alaishinian soldiers marched past them. Jeilin thought longingly of Prince Raihnin when she saw them. The officer leading the regiment nodded respectfully to them as they passed. Jeilin didn't know whether seeing the army on the move was good or bad news, but she hoped it was good.

****

With a final wind and burst of speed, they reached Dresinva just before evening on the fourth day. The large city was a welcome sight, with its familiar spirals and turrets that stretched majestically into the sky. Jeilin fondly remembered the time she had spent with her family in the city, and it seemed almost homelike. They cantered eagerly to the western gate.

The two guards who stood watch there surveyed them from under their helmets. Their eyes flicked casually toward the golden stars on their horses' bridles, and then the ones on their chests. They nodded curtly, stepping aside to make enough room for two horses to move through comfortably.

But they were already halfway through the gate when Jeilin noticed something with a start.

"Olwen, wait! I—" she began nervously.

The two guards leapt forward more quickly than Jeilin would have thought possible, abandoning any pretense of nonchalance, and thrust their steel-pointed spears at them. The points stopped just short of Jeilin and Olwen's sides. Fringe snorted and tossed his head. Jeilin reined him in,

137

urging him to be still, lest he propel her into the spearhead. Only a spear's length away, Jeilin could clearly see what had caused her to object. Each of the guards' faces were marked distinctly with the same tapering, black slash across one cheekbone. There was only one other face Jeilin had ever seen that bore that mark, and that was the face of the Ryelnish soldier who had slaughtered Prince Stephen.

The guards' eyes were dark and cruel. "Proceed through the gates," one of them growled in an unfamiliar accent. He pressed his spear point against Jeilin's side for emphasis. She glanced frantically at Olwen. Olwen gazed back at her, pale and silent. The spearhead pressed harder, surely drawing blood. Olwen winced faintly and Jeilin knew that she had felt the same thing.

Jeilin squeezed lightly, sending Fringe forward at a careful walk. The guard let his spear catch painfully in Jeilin's flesh, carving a furrow in her skin as it fell away.

As soon as they were inside, a dozen more tattooed Ryelnish soldiers who had clearly been waiting at the sides of the gate converged around them. "Messengers," said the man atop the grey stallion as he eyed the stars that shone from their bridles and chests. "Relinquish your messages," he said, a dangerous edge to his voice.

Jeilin drew her cloak around herself instinctively as she remembered the words she had recited before leaving, and horror filled her. *Nothing short of death shall prevent me from delivering your message with my own hand, and may death find me if it does...* The words she had sworn to Prince Raihnin.

A spear was at her side again. A gasp announced that Olwen too had yet to give up her message. "Relinquish your messages," the man demanded again.

A wave of nausea washed over Jeilin as the spear point pressed harder, sending a jolt of pain through her side like forked lightning. The cobblestone street seemed to sway beneath her; a death grip on the pommel was the only thing that kept her in the saddle. Fringe pranced uneasily beneath her, a movement that nearly sent her toppling onto the street below. Suddenly, Jeilin's cloak was torn from her, and a large hand found the pocket inside where she had stowed Prince Raihnin's message to his father, King Darnasius.

The man emitted a cruel bark of a laugh as he tore it open and scanned the contents. He seized Olwen's too and shoved them both deep into his own pocket. Jeilin dared to meet Olwen's eyes; she looked like Jeilin felt: angry, ashamed, and on the verge of sickness.

"You will follow me," said the soldier who appeared to be in charge, from atop his hefty grey warhorse. "You will die if you resist." He spun and urged his horse forward at a trot. Jeilin and Olwen did the same, maintaining a close but careful distance behind him. Several of the other soldiers fell in behind them. Jeilin broke into a nervous sweat that dampened her brow despite the cold.

The streets were strangely empty. A stray dog, marked by its clearly visible ribs, trotted out of their way, taking refuge in an alley. Here and there, soldiers stood guard, all with the same black mark across their faces. How long had they been here, Jeilin wondered. And if they'd infiltrated the capital, what might they have done to the rest of the country? Panic seized Jeilin as she thought of her family, and Fringe danced uneasily beneath her, picking up on her alarm. Snow was doing the same, whether because of Fringe or because Olwen was feeling the same, Jeilin didn't know. As they moved on, fear for her mother, father, and brothers writhed in the pit of her stomach.

Jeilin and Olwen were escorted by the hostile Ryelnish soldiers to a large square very near the castle. Here, the bustle of activity contrasted sharply with the nearly lifeless streets. Ryelnish soldiers stood gathered in small groups, some eating their midday meals while others gave orders or appeared to be on some sort of guard duty. They all wore the black mark, and Jeilin noticed that a few of them had strange red halos surrounding theirs. The most obvious thing, though, was a body that hung from a very tall gallows in the center of the square. Jeilin noticed it with distaste and hastily averted her eyes.

Their small procession came to a stop. "Look," the leader commanded, thrusting a pointing finger skyward toward the body. Jeilin could feel her shirt clinging to her side, damp with blood where the spear had pierced her skin. She raised her gaze reluctantly. The corpse, a man's body, hung perfectly still. His clothing was white and scarlet, and his face obscured by dark waves of hair.

"King Darnasius," the soldier leading them said. "Is dead. No message you brought can help him now, though it *will* be of use to Ryeln."

Jeilin's stomach plummeted onto the cobblestones; she felt nauseas again, and not just because she was observing the results of a hanging. Raihnin resembled his father greatly; the realization hit Jeilin like an iron wall as she gazed dizzily up at King Darnasius' lifeless body. Really, the only differences in their appearances were hair length and a couple of decades...Jeilin dropped her gaze, allowing it to follow her stomach to the street below.

"This city has been seized by Ryeln," he said. "You will be given a choice to join the victorious, or die."

Jeilin's head spun as they continued on, eventually stopping on the castle grounds where a large encampment sprawled across the royal lawn. Ryelnish flags peeked above the tops of tents, mimicking the large one that flew flamboyantly at the top of the castle's highest tower, where Alaishin's banner had been. Jeilin cursed herself for not noticing it when she had approached the city. Ryeln's flag featured a simple tapering, triangular, bone-white slash on a stark black field. Jeilin recognized the shape on the flag; she had seen it reversed on the face of every Ryelnish soldier, a black stripe that stood out boldly against fair skin.

Jeilin and Olwen were instructed to dismount when they reached a section of the camp where several men had gathered around a fire to sit, looking dejected. They were Alaishinian, as was evidenced by their lack of the Ryelnish mark and their subdued manner. They were unrestrained, but under the watchful eye of several Ryelnish guards who held spears like the one that had pierced Jeilin's side. Any attempt at escape would have been suicide. Jeilin emerged from the nauseas fog that had clouded her mind enough to notice that each of the captured men she sat among wore a small golden star on his chest. The next thing she noticed was that Fringe was being led away by a Ryelnish soldier, as was Snow. Bitter bile and fury rose in her throat and she curled her hands into fists, her fingernails biting into the flesh of her palms and branding angry red crescents into them. Somehow the fact that Fringe was being taken from her was even more infuriating than being captured, more infuriating than…anything! Jeilin decided as she realized that she was shaking with anger.

Olwen misinterpreted her quivering. "They haven't killed us," Olwen whispered, "That's a good sign."

Jeilin's neck didn't seem to want to move. She shook her head stiffly. She only had eyes for Fringe, who was being led farther and farther away by the wretched black-clad soldier. Olwen's grip on her shoulder grew stronger when she understood. Jeilin forced herself to tear her gaze away from her horse and meet Olwen's eyes. Hers were angry too. Very angry.

"There's. Nothing. We. Can. Do," Olwen bit off each bitter word as if Jeilin wasn't the only one she needed to convince.

Jeilin snorted angrily and tried to crush the thoughts of reaching for her dagger that kept popping up in her mind. One of the guards was eyeing her deliberately and seemed to know what she was thinking; he hefted his spear in warning. Jeilin was forced to settle for staring in anger at nothing, looking as dejected as the rest of the group. In her silent, brooding rage she lost track of time. At some point, they were joined by three more messengers. Jeilin recognized two of them as Cai and Eric. Jeilin wondered if they had ridden up to the city gates and into the trap just as she and Olwen had. Their arrival brought the number of captive messengers up to about twenty. Apparently, Raihnin hadn't been the only one to attempt to send news of the invasion to the king in Dresinva.

The sun had barely begun its descent when the same looming soldier who had escorted Jeilin and Olwen reappeared, his dark eyes squinting in a permanent glare above the strange marking that he shared with the rest of the Ryelnish army. He had arrived with a small entourage, making him appear important.

"Alaishin is conquered," he addressed the dispirited group, and his flat accent seemed to chop each word into a strange new sound. "You can die with it, or you can join Ryeln. We value your knowledge and skills. Join us and you will keep your status and your life, only you will be serving a new, stronger master." Jeilin's stomach contracted and she fought the urge to vomit as she heard the way his voice swelled with pride. "You will be in the service and under the protection of Ryeln, the greatest military power the world has ever seen. Choose wisely. You have half an hour."

He turned on his heel and walked away, flanked by his loyal escort of lesser men.

As the ground spun, Jeilin tucked her head between her knees.

A worried buzzing swept through the group, and she caught words like "treason," "hopeless," and "dead." A hand rested lightly on her shoulder, surely Olwen's. Jeilin looked up reluctantly to meet her gaze.

"What will we do?" she asked, desperate to hear the woman she looked up to more than anyone say something that would assuage her frantic grief. Olwen frowned down at her, and the same sadness seemed to be tugging at the corners of her brown eyes, causing her to appear sadder, older…

"I can't answer that for you," Olwen whispered, barely audible. "But I choose life."

Jeilin nodded, mortified when she realized that she was suddenly choking back tears. Silence fell over the pair like a thick blanket of fog; Jeilin was sure that she couldn't speak, and Olwen seemed to be lost in unhappy thought.

The proud soldier—a general, Jeilin overheard as one of his subordinates addressed him—returned within the shortest half of an hour Jeilin had ever experienced. He unsheathed his sword unexpectedly, with lightning speed. Jeilin flinched. He took several regal strides forward before planting the tip of his blade in the earth. With one long stroke, he carved a line. "Those who will join Ryeln shall gather on my right," he said. "Others…to my left."

Jeilin was already on the general's right side, a fact for which she was grateful, as her legs felt too weak to move her body. Her heart accelerated, beating wildly as others joined them on the right, shifting uneasily away from the line as if afraid they'd be cast over to the left if they stood too close to it. Eventually, there were only four men on the left side of the line. One of them was Eric. He stood as still as a stone, his face expressionless. Jeilin felt infinitely more frightened than he looked; the absurdity of that fact and the weight of his bravery were shaming.

So this was who she was, she thought to herself. A traitor who valued her own life more than the oath she had sworn. She couldn't serve Ryeln. No, she *wouldn't* serve Ryeln. Her field of vision seemed to shrink until she saw only the terrible line, an ugly scar marring the earth, dividing the cowards from the loyal. She didn't move.

"All right," the general barked. "It's done. Follow me, *servants of Ryeln.*" He said the title with an obvious pleasure, and shoulders hunched everywhere as thirty-two eyes examined the ground.

The other four, the *loyal* four, Jeilin thought, stayed behind. Jeilin felt a stab of pity and admiration, a double-edged sword that cut down her sense of self-worth. Their shuffling procession came to halt in front of a large tent of gleaming black silk.

A man emerged, a man who brought with him a sense of self-importance even greater than the general's. He was tall and imposing in his immaculate night-black uniform. Two hard, dark eyes were set deep in a face that might have been carved from stone, and his mouth was a tight line under a black moustache that curved downward on each side like a boar's tusks. Jeilin was unsurprised to see that the familiar black mark curved across his protruding cheekbone. Silver pins crafted in the same shape as the mark stood out against his dark collar, polished so that they shone even in the dull evening light.

"Commander Hsat," the burly general said with a salute, his voice nearly reverent.

Commander Hsat returned the formality, his expression never wavering. "These are the latest messengers who wish to join us?" he asked.

"Yes, sir," the general replied.

The commander gave a quick, stiff nod of approval and addressed them. "You will each swear the oath that will deliver you into Ryeln's service individually before me," he said. "When it is done, you will be one of us." He nodded again at one of the messengers who stood at the front of the group. "To your knee," he commanded. The man obeyed. Jeilin could see a sheen of sweat shining on his forehead, despite the cool air. He looked very much as if he wished that he hadn't been chosen first.

"Repeat after me," Commander Hsat instructed in a voice that was used to being obeyed. "I hereby relinquish my citizenship and service to the kingdom of Alaishin."

The man repeated Commander Hsat's words, though they sounded sour in his mouth.

"I swear my life and my services to Ryeln. May death find me if my loyalty ever wavers."

Commander Hsat nodded his approval when the man finished the brief oath. "I hereby appoint you as an official messenger of Ryeln." He reached forward and wrenched the golden star from the man's chest. He threw it to the ground and stepped on it, grinding it into the dirt with the toe of his boot.

The small ceremony repeated itself.

Jeilin was one of the last to be sworn into Ryeln's service. She repeated the oath mindlessly, thinking of Raihnin, who looked too much like his father who hung in the square. Each word was a lie. When Commander Hsat ripped from her chest the golden star she had worn with such pride, she resisted the urge to hit his hand away.

When she rose, she drifted aimlessly to the side with those who had already sworn the oath and waited for Olwen, whose face was a perfect mask, betraying no emotion as she swore.

When everyone had finished, a soldier led the group to a small clearing nearby in the camp and told them that they were to set up camp there. They were informed that they would find their horses and their belongings, including their tents, in the stables. Jeilin felt relief for the first time since they had been stopped at the city gates. At least she still had Fringe and her personal belongings. It was a small comfort, but it was something.

She found Fringe stabled safely a few stalls down from Snow. She slipped inside the stall and wound her fingers through his cream-colored mane, willing herself not to think about what would have happened to Fringe if she had stood on the left side of the line…imagining her closest companion, who she had raised from a foal, being given to another rider, especially a Ryelnish soldier, was maddening.

She stroked his neck, which was thick and fuzzy with winter hair, speaking softly as if he were the one who needed to be comforted. After a few minutes, when she had reassured herself that Fringe would be fine, she reemerged from the stall and found her saddle and bags. She walked alongside Olwen, hefting her belongings to the camping area they had been assigned.

Conversation in the small encampment was dull and forced. Nobody really wanted to rehash their capture, their failure. Jeilin decided to go for a walk. She wandered aimlessly throughout the camp, marveling at the fact that she was permitted to do so. Apparently, the Ryelnish took the oaths very seriously...they truly considered her one of them. She shuddered at the thought, refusing to think of herself that way. She had already resolved to ride for the good of Alaishin instead of Ryeln if she ever had the opportunity...if Alaishin wasn't totally crushed by Ryeln's massive army. She bit into the flesh of her lower lip, thinking of Raihnin, and knew that she could never truly abandon her loyalties to Alaishin while he was still alive. She would never be able to serve Ryeln loyally if they killed Raihnin either, she realized. The thought sent another shiver down her spine as she remembered his father's defeated body, hanging lifelessly against the winter sky.

Lost in thought as she was, Jeilin nearly tripped when she collided with a man who was hurrying around the side of another large tent, a man who she recognized as...Eric. Jeilin winced; her shin throbbed painfully where it had collided with his. His dark eyes were wide, his motions hurried…was he trying to escape? Jeilin opened her mouth to speak, but nothing came out. Where were the other three men who had chosen the left side of the general's line? A loud scream, which cut off abruptly, unnaturally, answered her question. Their executions had begun. Jeilin felt the familiar wave of nausea that had unsteadied her in the square wash over her again. Suddenly, she realized that Eric had a knife in his hand.

Jeilin froze. She met his eyes for a second that seemed an eternity as understanding dawned on her like a cruel sun. Eric was going to kill her. Her panicked brain urged her to reach for her own dagger, but its desperate signals never reached her fingers, which felt suddenly numb. She deserved it, another part of her mind declared. She'd committed treason, and now death had found her. Eric's blade flashed and she cried out as her body reacted automatically, her hand reaching forward stupidly, uselessly toward the dagger.

Something warm seeped over her hand. It took her a moment to realize that she wasn't in pain. She looked down and saw that she was clinging pointlessly to Eric's hand, which was wrapped around the knife's handle. The blood that sprayed over her hand was his; he had plunged the dagger into his own chest. He spoke and his speech was too staggered, too tight with pain, for Jeilin to make out his words completely. She thought she caught the words "may death find me if it does." Eric crumpled to the ground, bleeding profusely. Jeilin watched in horror as he shuddered and died.

"No!" Jeilin crouched and lunged forward automatically, scrabbling uselessly at the knife's hilt, bloodying her fingers further. She heard the rush of footsteps a moment before someone emerged around the side of the tent.

It was the general. Jeilin cringed.

The general cursed, but then was suddenly silent. He kneeled down and examined Eric's face. When he rose, Jeilin was shocked to see a broad, if cruel, smile break the hardened plane of his features.

He clapped a huge hand on Jeilin's comparatively tiny shoulder. "Got him!" he roared. "Stop the search!"

More feet rushed around the tent, following the sound of the general's voice. Half a dozen soldiers gathered at the blood-soaked scene. "What happened?" one of them demanded.

The general was still grinning, and Jeilin's shoulder was still sagging under the weight of his hand. "One of our new messengers found him before we did," he said with an unmistakable note of pride in his voice. "Killed him."

Jeilin listened in shock. The six newcomers stared at her incredulously. "*Her?*" one of them asked. The general nodded. "Her hand was still wrapped around the hilt when I came upon her."

The soldiers surveyed her, nodding in surprised approval. Did they really think that the oath had had such an effect on her? That a few words had altered her loyalty so radically, had made her a *monster*?

She wiped her hand on the grass, desperate to rid herself of Eric's blood. Most of it came off, but her skin was still stained red, from her fingertips to her wrist. She rose slowly, and the general's hand felt like the weight of the world on her shoulder. Apparently they did think she was mad with loyalty, she realized as the general steered her back to the same tent that Commander Hsat had emerged from earlier. "Wait here," he said, and disappeared inside.

When he emerged, he wasn't alone. Commander Hsat strutted alongside him, a curious expression on his face. "Her?" he finally asked, just as the soldier had a few minutes before. The general assured him that it had indeed been her.

"Mmmm…" Commander Hsat was eyeing the knife as well, but he seemed pleased. "Such loyalty," he finally said. "Not many would have killed him…most are too weak, too *emotional*," he spat the word out like it was something indecent. "Most would have allowed him to escape." He sounded bitter by the time he finished. "You'll make an excellent example for the others." He actually smiled at her.

An example? Jeilin wondered what exactly that meant. She suppressed a shudder at the thought of the others finding out what she had done. Well, what they *thought* she had done.

Her fear manifested within minutes. Her face burned crimson as she stood by Commander Hsat's side, unable to meet the other messengers' curious gazes. She didn't dare to look up, but she imagined their curiosity turning to horror as the commander related her supposed exploit to them, his hard voice glowing with rare approval and pride. "She will be the first to be honored with the mark of Ryeln," he finished.

Jeilin's stomach clenched. What did that mean?

A soldier stepped forward from the commander's entourage, clutching a leather pouch under his arm.

"The rest of you form a line," Commander Hsat instructed.

They obeyed.

Understanding crashed down around Jeilin when the needle pierced her skin for the first time. She suppressed a horrified scream and forced herself to remain still. The needle ducked under the surface of her skin again, pressing against the hard bone that lay under the skin that met her hairline on the left side of her face. She winced as it surfaced and plunged under again and again, guided carefully by the man's hand. Jeilin wanted to beat his hand away, to weep, and not just because of the pain. The needle migrated slowly and excruciatingly across her cheek bone, and by the time it stopped she felt like she had shoved her head into a hornets' nest.

She scrambled to her tent under the cover of darkness, refusing to meet the eyes of those who still waited in line. She curled up with a saddlebag for a pillow, laying only on her right side to protect her inflamed left cheek. She finally allowed herself to cry, silently and bitterly.

Chapter 10

A t some unknown point, Jeilin's tears dried as sleep swallowed her, exhaustion from her breakneck journey triumphing over bone-deep grief. Waking seemed like surfacing from a deep lake; it took several moments before Jeilin realized that someone had entered her tiny tent.

"It's me," Olwen whispered, crouching over her in the cramped quarters.

Jeilin recognized her voice, though it was much too dark to see her. Gratitude pierced her sorrow; she didn't want to see Olwen's beautiful face marred by the "mark of Ryeln." Tears welled in her eyes once again as her imagination rose against her, showing her exactly what Olwen's face would look like with the addition of the disfiguring tattoo. She tried not to imagine her own.

Abruptly, Jeilin remembered that she had more pressing matters to discuss with Olwen than their matching disgraces. "Olwen, I…"

She didn't get far before Olwen intervened in a tone so quiet that it was barely discernable. "I know you didn't kill Eric," she whispered hurriedly.

She felt a surge of gratitude again. Of course Olwen would know she hadn't done it. Of course.

"He killed himself," Jeilin whispered, still in shock. "I tried to stop him." Despair cracked her voice. "And then the general found me...they thought I did it because I was *angry* at Eric for not joining Ryeln and for trying to escape..." For a moment, she was lost in disbelief. "They're...insane," she finished.

"I know this isn't what you want to hear," Olwen said carefully. "But you've got to look at the bright side. Eric was going to take his own life anyway—you being in the wrong place at the wrong time...well, it's curried favor for you. And that will help our mission more than you can understand right now."

Jeilin's heart skipped a beat. "Our mission?" she whispered, breathless.

Though the darkness blinded her, Jeilin was sure that she sensed Olwen's smile.

"You didn't think I'd abandon Alaishin so easily, did you?" she asked. "My loyalties haven't changed. Eric gave his life for Alaishin in one way...we'll give ours in another."

Jeilin breathed a sigh of relief that was half-sob.

"I've got to go to my own tent," Olwen said. "I don't want anyone to get suspicious. I'll see you in the morning."

Jeilin bid her goodnight and settled back into her blankets. Falling asleep for a second time was more difficult;

her mind raced with questions, speculations, and half-formed plans.

****

The morning was cold, and not just in regards to the temperature. Several small fires had been built in the messengers' area of the camp; Jeilin and Olwen shared one alone. "They're serving breakfast," Olwen said, though it was obvious; Ryelnish soldiers strode about as a subdued dawn broke over the foggy grey horizon, most carrying bowls of something that was being distributed somewhere near the center of the sprawling camp.

Jeilin was silent. She didn't look up at Olwen. The tapering black stripe that stood out on her cheek was shocking, offensive…worst of all, it reminded her of her own. Her cheek stung fiercely, and she finally understood the red halos that had circled the marks on a few of the men she'd seen in the square the day before. If Jeilin hadn't been so absorbed in her own silence, she wouldn't have heard Olwen's whisper.

"If you continue to sulk so, you may compromise your new reputation," she said.

Olwen's words stung. Her *reputation*? Jeilin scowled at the fire; suddenly, it seemed unnecessary as anger warmed her.

"Let's go," she said bitterly, standing abruptly and dusting off her breeches with more effort than was necessary.

155

Breakfast was a bowl of some sort of Ryelnish porridge and a biscuit. Jeilin and Olwen stood in a line of hulking men for a few minutes before being served theirs and returning to their fire. Each time Jeilin lowered her head to take a bite, she could feel the gazes of her fellow Alaishinian converts boring into her. "They're all staring," she said under her breath to Olwen. "Do they…?"

She didn't need to finish her question. Olwen too spoke into her bowl. "Some of them don't believe that you killed Eric," she replied. "Others are unsure…some may believe Commander Hsat's story. I overheard some of them talking about it last night."

Jeilin glared into her empty bowl.

"How could they *think* that?" she whispered.

Olwen gave her a sympathetic look.

There was a collective rustle of cloaks and shifting of gazes as a Ryelnish officer strutted into their little corner of the camp. He was tall and more slender than most of the Ryelnish, with a thick black mustache that he had trimmed to neat points. "You'll all be inducted into Ryeln's messaging system today," he announced matter-of-factly. "Each of you will consult with General Mhin. I'll take the first of you to him now." He motioned abruptly at the nearest man, a messenger whom Jeilin didn't recognize. He followed wordlessly.

Jeilin and Olwen exchanged worried glances. "Do you think they'll keep us together?" Jeilin whispered hurriedly.

"I don't know," Olwen said. "But after…yesterday…it wouldn't hurt for you to explain our situation if you're given a chance. You may have curried enough favor to be granted such a request."

Jeilin nodded, resolving to make an opportunity to ask, even if one wasn't offered.

****

It was late morning when the mustached officer escorted Jeilin to her appointment. She was glad that she would go before Olwen; hopefully they would agree to her request before they had a chance to dispatch her.

General Mhin turned out to be the same general who had first escorted Jeilin and Olwen to the camp, the same general who had discovered Jeilin at the scene of Eric's suicide. His foreboding face cracked with the same smile that he had bared at her the day before. Jeilin stood stiffly in the open flap of his tent, unsure of what Ryelnish protocol demanded. She finally decided on a simple "Good morning, General Mhin."

Her greeting must have been acceptable, for his smile remained unwavering for a few more moments as he directed her to sit. She sat in a simple wooden chair across from the writing desk that the general loomed over.

Mercifully, General Mhin wasted no time recounting the previous day's events. "How long did you serve Alaishin before you decided—most wisely—to join Ryeln?" he asked in a tone that seemed to indicate that he had asked the question many times before, and would ask it many times again.

"One month," Jeilin replied.

157

A flash of surprise crossed the general's face, lasting only a second before a look of understanding replaced it.

"Ah," he replied. "It's almost as if you never served any other kingdom at all...your actions have already proven that your new loyalties are strong." He smiled again as he bent over an open journal of some sort, scrawling something onto a blank page.

Jeilin's stomach clenched. How wrong he was. How very wrong, she thought. She held her secret rebellion close in her heart, as if treasuring it could erase General Mhin's assumptions. Outwardly, she forced herself to nod.

"General Mhin," she spoke, taking advantage of as good an opportunity as would likely present itself. "I was traveling with another, more experienced, messenger at the time of my...conversion. She was helping me learn the lay of the land. She has sworn loyalty to Ryeln too—I think it would benefit Ryeln if I were to continue my training with her."

The general peered up from his journal, his expression unreadable. "She," he said simply. "The other female..." There was a pause in his speech during which Jeilin steeled herself for disappointment; her heart seemed to sink into her toes. "I suppose that it would benefit Ryeln," he finished simply.

Suddenly, Jeilin's heart felt as if it had soared back to its proper place, or somewhere near it. The fog of gloom she had been thrust into would seem thinner, less foreboding, with Olwen at her side. In a way, it would be like before. Like yesterday, only yesterday.

"You'll both wait here until someone dispatches you," General Mhin continued. "See that you're rested and on the ready. We have many messages to send and we need our messengers at their best, their fastest—quick communication is vital to the successful completion of our conquest."

Jeilin nodded. "I will, General Mhin."

"You are permitted to leave camp for food or exercise. You may not leave the city."

Jeilin nodded her understanding again.

General Mhin motioned for her to rise.

"Thank you, General Mhin," she said as she prepared to leave.

"I'm expecting only the best from you, Jeilin," he said.

Jeilin didn't know what to say. General Mhin's eyes met hers, and she could see her reflection in the deep black of his irises. She dared not look away. Several seconds passed before General Mhin broke eye contact. His gaze did not leave her, however—instead it traveled below her chin, lingering disconcertingly around her chest and hips. A chill raced down Jeilin's spine and she had to force herself not to shudder, longing to seize the sides of her woolen cloak and wrap them around her front, hiding herself from his stare. Instead, she settled for a quick nod and ducked out of the tent, stumbling slightly, her stomach tied in uneasy knots.

Olwen waited for her by the little fire they'd built. Her gaze was half hopeful and half worried when Jeilin hurried into view. "Good news!" Jeilin said, unable to suppress a small smile as she settled on the hard ground by Olwen. "General Mhin agreed to let us continue my training," she lowered her voice with the last few words, realizing how loudly she had spoken.

Olwen smiled back at her. "I'm glad."

The mustached officer was back, beckoning for Olwen to follow him. She stood and flashed Jeilin another tiny smile as she departed.

Jeilin situated herself closer to the fire and held her hands to the flames, absorbing the heat. The assurance of Olwen's continued companionship seemed to glow from the inside of her, a warm flame that brightened her perception of their grim circumstances.

Olwen returned shortly. "What do you say we head out for a ride?" she suggested.

Jeilin agreed. Languishing around the fires was dull, and constantly feeling the stares of the others on her back was beginning to wear her down. Together they stepped out of the small ring of warmth that surrounded the fire, into the unheated winter air.

"I hope they've treated the horses well," Jeilin thought aloud. "Agh!"

Silver stars blossomed like miniature fireworks in front of Jeilin's eyes, and she suddenly realized that she was on the ground. She tried to reason how she had come to be there, but a nauseating pain in the side of her head fogged her thoughts. She heard an angry exclamation, and the fact that it had come from Olwen registered vaguely in her mind. There came an answering cry, angrier. Jeilin realized that she wasn't breathing; her lungs seemed to have frozen as she lay confused, curled on the frigid earth. Someone thumped to the ground beside her, jostling her left arm and triggering a shooting pain from elbow to shoulder. Finally, she gasped in pain, gulping frosty air.

"What?" was all Jeilin was able to articulate as someone seized her carefully by the shoulders and helped her to her feet. "Olwen, what happened?"

Olwen sighed and shook her head, wiping her brow with the back of her hand as if she expected sweat to have formed there; the thought was absurd given the temperature. "He...lunged at you," Olwen said, gesturing with her free hand at Jeilin's attacker.

Jeilin recognized his fair hair and slight build with a shock of surprise. "Cai?" The young man who she had raced to the finish line only weeks ago—it seemed so much longer than that—lay crumpled on the ground with one arm curled protectively over his ribs, his breathing ragged. She thought she saw him grimace when she said his name. Jeilin twitched as if she had been shocked when she realized that Olwen held a small knife in her hand, its short silver blade gleaming coldly in the December sun. For a moment, she only moved her mouth wordlessly. "You took that from him?" she finally managed to ask.

Olwen nodded, her expression grim.

A Ryelnish soldier snatched Cai roughly by the arm and jerked him to his feet. Another was behind him, pressing a spear point into the small of his back. Cai stumbled up on unsteady legs and winced as it pressed further into his skin. He glared murderously at Jeilin. "We saw everything," the soldier growled as he twisted Cai's arm behind his back, rendering him motionless.

A hulking figure marched angrily into the middle of the clearing where every eye was now trained on the cluster that contained Jeilin, Olwen, Cai, and the two soldiers. It was General Mhin. A thin soldier hurried behind him with an air of self importance, probably the one who had informed him of the commotion.

"What's going on?" the general demanded brusquely.

"This messenger attacked the other with a knife, without provocation," said the soldier who held Cai tightly by his arm.

General Mhin frowned, affronted by the attack on his new favorite. "Our code demands that she decide his punishment," he said, turning to Jeilin. "Anything, including death."

Jeilin barely restrained a gasp of horror. She opened her mouth, intending an attempt to excuse Cai from any punishment, but wondered with a thrill of disgust what effect such a thing would have on her "reputation." She swallowed her objections and said in the steadiest voice she could manage, "a flogging." The punishment seemed cruel to Jeilin; she hoped that it seemed serious enough for the general.

General Mhin nodded, surveying her with an expression she could not read. "Very well."

The general turned in the direction of his tent and strode purposefully away as the two soldiers who had captured Cai forced him to his knees. He struggled weakly, barely able to even inconvenience his punishers as they secured him. Judging by his movements and what she knew of Olwen's kicks, Jeilin strongly suspected that several of his ribs were cracked. The sound of tearing fabric rent the air as his shirt was ripped from his body and cast aside, exposing his flesh to the cold winter air. His back was slender, almost child-like, Jeilin observed. A nasty bruise had blossomed on his side, and his pale skin had pebbled instantly in the cold. A third soldier was approaching, carrying what appeared to be a very nasty whip; Jeilin thought that she saw bits of bone at the tips. She turned away in shame and horror. Cai's screams filled the camp as Jeilin hurried for the stables, and followed her into the city streets as she galloped saddleless-ly away.

She stopped only when she'd reached the gates. "Are you carrying a message?" one of the guards called to her. She shook her head wordlessly, wheeling Fringe around. It was only then that she realized that Olwen had followed her. She too had foregone her saddle in her haste. Snow's grey nostrils flared, showing pink, and Olwen looked nearly as winded. As she pulled alongside Fringe, she silently motioned for Jeilin to follow her.

Not knowing what else to do, she did.

They ended up riding the paved, angular trails of a city park, abandoned that cold winter day. "You did the right thing," Olwen said.

"He didn't deserve a flogging," Jeilin replied.

Olwen frowned. "I don't know if they would have let it go."

Jeilin looked at her friend's face and was overcome with the offensiveness, the ugliness, of the mark. "What are we going to do?" she asked.

"What we spoke about doing," Olwen said firmly. "Whatever we can to help."

Some time later, they shared a subdued ride back to the camp. General Mhin, perhaps the last person Jeilin wanted to see, noted her arrival. "A fine horse," he said, surveying Fringe. "How did you come to own him?"

"I found him as a colt," Jeilin replied, surprised by the question. "His mother was from a local feral heard and had died. I raised him." She wrapped her fingers possessively in Fringe's long mane.

General Mhin appeared surprised; Jeilin might have even thought impressed. He straightened, apparently finished with his inspection. "You missed the midday meal; the cooks have already scrubbed the kettles clean. But I'll send one of my servants to your tents with food for both of you."

Jeilin and Olwen thanked him politely and rode forward at his dismissal.

"He must be even more impressed with you than I first realized," Olwen said quietly as they hung their bridles on pegs in the tack room.

Jeilin shook her head. "He might be impressed," she said. "But personally, I'm disgusted. I can't wait to be dispatched."

A servant was waiting beside Jeilin's tent when she and Olwen returned, holding a tray veiled by a cloth. Jeilin could see steam escaping from under the edges. The servant proffered the tray. Jeilin hesitated. Olwen swooped in and took it.

Curls of steam billowed skywards when she whipped the cloth away from the tray. Jeilin felt guilty when her stomach growled. She and Olwen settled by the nearest fire, which they shared with two other messengers who appeared to be doing nothing in particular, other than staying warm. Jeilin pretended not to notice their speculating looks as she ate the meal the general had sent. The tray held bowls of some sort of Ryelnish dish: a spicy mixture of rice, chicken, peppers, and peas. Jeilin experienced a fresh wave of guilt as the delicious food warmed her. There was also a pitcher of hot wine and bowls full of plump, purplish berries that Jeilin didn't recognize. Jeilin marveled at the novelty of eating berries in winter; she doubted that anyone but the officers had been served them. An idea occurred to Jeilin as she cradled the fruit dish in her cupped hands.

She hurried over to a particular tent that had been drawing her eye ever since the furious ride through the streets of Dresinva. Her speculations were confirmed when she stooped down, as far inside as the little one-person tent allowed. Cai lay face-down on a sparse pile of blankets, easily discernable by his slight build, fair hair, and the wide bandages that covered his otherwise bare back. Jeilin winced at the sight of them; blood had blossomed through, soaking the bandages until they were more red than white. Cai stirred as she knelt in the entrance, no doubt feeling the gust of icy air that had rushed in with her, but he was unable to turn his head far enough to see her or to rise.

"Who is it?" he asked.

Jeilin hesitated. "I brought you something to eat," she said quickly, leaning forward and extending her arm to place the cup of berries by his hand where he would be able to reach it.

"You brought me *something to eat*?" Cai asked incredulously.

"Look. I'm sorry. I didn't really kill Eric."

"Then why is this the first time you've said so?" Cai asked.

Jeilin didn't know what to say. How could she explain that she'd allowed the Ryelnish to go on believing the lie on purpose? She ducked back out of the tent, leaving the dish of berries behind. She hoped that Cai would come to believe her.

Olwen and the two men around the fire were watching Jeilin curiously when she reemerged, but none of the Ryelnish seemed to have seen. Olwen breathed a sigh of relief.

Olwen didn't question Jeilin at the fire, but rather continued her meal as if there had been no interruption. Jeilin drank from her cup, savoring the slightly spicy wine, and wiped her bowl clean with a slice of bread that had accompanied the meal. A soldier strode toward the fire just as she was finishing the last crumbs.

"You're both to report to General Mhin's tent at dawn tomorrow," he said. "He has an assignment for you."

Chapter 11

D arkness still blanketed the camp when Jeilin rose the next morning. Firelight cast a dim circle around a large pot where a man was already stirring and distributing porridge to several other early risers. Jeilin stood in the breakfast line with Olwen, pondering her impending assignment, wondering if it would present the opportunity to be manipulated for the good of Alaishin. Her stomach felt twisted and knotted by the time her bowl had been filled.

After a trip to the stables, Jeilin and Olwen led their horses to General Mhin's tent, where an assembly of soldiers was gathered. General Mhin wasted no time in explaining the day's work. "We're recruiting for the army," he said. Then, turning to Jeilin and Olwen: "A recruiting party is always accompanied by a messenger."

The news discouraged Jeilin, who had been expecting to be sent away with a message, not assigned to a day trip. Still, she was glad that she hadn't had to speak with General Mhin alone again—with all the organized bustle of a small band of soldiers preparing to march, he thankfully didn't seem to have time to eye Jeilin again as he had the day before.

The band of soldiers, led by General Mhin and accompanied by Jeilin and Olwen, moved out of the camp within a quarter of an hour. Dresinva's citizens stared from the safety of home and shop windows as they proceeded through the streets. By the time they reached the gates, a sense of curiosity had nearly overshadowed Jeilin's disappointment. What did the world outside of the city look like now? Ravaged and burned? Desolate and lonely as people cowered inside their homes?

Evidence of a battle greeted everyone who exited through the gate they used; telltale furrows in the earth, and large, fresh patches of freshly churned dirt where casualties had mercifully been buried. A few dead horses remained, stripped of their tack. Scavenger birds circled overhead while laborers with shovels struggled to beat them away when they landed. If only she and Olwen had approached the city from this side, Jeilin thought, they never would have ridden into the trap.

The journey away from the city was slow, even leisurely, for Jeilin, Olwen, and the others who were mounted as they kept their horses' paces slow enough to match the foot soldiers' speed. That, combined with the fact that there was no visible damage at the homes and farms they began to pass, made the ride almost relaxing. They had traveled about a mile and a half past previously visited properties when General Hsat ordered the procession to halt at a small stone farmhouse surrounded by fields that surely would have been bursting with crops had it been summer. The steady ribbon of smoke that rose from the home's single chimney reminded Jeilin of home. Suddenly, the full implications of Ryeln's recruiting campaign struck Jeilin, along with horror. Had her family's little cabin already been visited by a band like the one she was now a part of? Or were they waiting in confusion, their fears being fed by rumors coming down the Dusty Pass from the city?

The little house's front door creaked open partially, revealing a pale, round face framed by wisps of wheat-colored hair. General Mhin was at the door. "We are Ryeln, the world's greatest military power, and we are procuring able-bodied men for our army," he said, his voice swelling with that fierce pride that Jeilin had come to dread hearing.

An infant's wails were clearly audible from within the dwelling. The woman had dark circles under her eyes; she appeared exhausted and frightened. "My husband is dead," she said in a tight voice. "And my sons are too young to walk. You'll find no one here."

"How did he die?" General Mhin asked impassively.

The woman's grip on the doorframe tightened. She nodded at the path they had traveled, toward the city. "In the battle at Dresinva," she almost whispered.

"We must search your home," General Mhin said.

The woman frowned and stepped backward, retreating from the door as two soldiers stepped forward. They returned within a few minutes, empty-handed, and the procession moved on to the next dwelling.

There they found a farmer in his middle years and his family. The farmer himself was dismissed as ineligible due to a severe limp, but his three sons caught the general's eye.

Just as he opened his mouth to speak, their mother interrupted frantically. "Please don't take my boys!" she begged. "They're too young for the army! And we need them here on the farm!"

"How old?" the general asked.

"Twelve, fourteen, and fifteen," she said, her brown eyes wide with fear.

"Take the oldest," the general instructed his subordinates.

The mother burst into tears. "Please!" she shouted. "Please, don't!"

The boy's eyes were wide as he stared at the band of soldiers, mostly hulking men, all with the menacing mark across their hardened faces. His expression was disbelieving as one of the soldiers took him by the arm and directed him to stand among them.

"His service will bring honor to your family," General Mhin said.

The mother wailed. Her husband's eyes, dark blue and winged with wrinkles from his years in the sunny fields, looked sad. "Please," he said. "Is there anything we can do? Perhaps gold...we don't have much, but we'll pay whatever we can!"

General Mhin shook his head. "My decision is final. You and your family should be rejoicing."

The mother only cried harder.

The youngest of the boys looked on the verge of weeping too. His eyes, as blue as his father's, were slick with unshed tears. He stared up at Jeilin, who was mounted at the general's side and towered above the soldiers who had traveled on foot. She could feel his eyes on the mark that marred her face, and felt ashamed at the fear she saw in them. She was one of them—Ryelnish. As far as anyone else knew she had poured across the Black Mountains with the rest, aiding the slaughter that poured over the border. Departure from the little farm was bittersweet—Jeilin was glad to be out from under the fearful gaze of the devastated family, but she carried a part of their sadness with her as Fringe ambled down the winding dirt road, keeping slightly behind the general's fearsome warhorse.

Expansion efforts at the next home proved to be a disaster. The farmer who owned it was one of the few who had survived and escaped from the battle at the gates of Dresinva. With a bandage wrapped around his head, concealing a wound that must have just begun to heal, he rushed the general with a sword and was cut down by a Ryelnish soldier before coming within a yard of him. The Ryelnish band moved on, leaving the farmer's family to see to his body.

The day stretched on, and by its end the band had arrived back at the camp in Dresinva with a dozen new soldiers for the army. Many were Jeilin's age, or even younger. Jeilin had dismounted and was leading Fringe to the stable with Olwen and Snow at her side when she saw a familiar man with a leather pouch tucked under his arm approaching the group. She knew that they would be up most of the night, waiting in line for their turn to have the mark forced into their skin.

The next day was much the same, and the next week. Eventually the band began traveling far enough away from Dresinva that they camped on barren plains and farmers' fields along the way, no longer returning to the city at night. Each day was more worrying than the last for Jeilin as they traveled the Dusty Pass toward her family's farm. A couple weeks ago, she would have been thrilled to learn that she would be traveling past her home. Now, she dreaded the day they would reach it. She constantly struggled to shove away images of her brothers being captured and branded with the mark; the idea of Ehryn or Emrys serving in Ryeln's army seemed absurd, horrifying.

By the time the familiar little cabin became visible on the horizon, Jeilin felt like a mess of nerves. She turned to Olwen, whom she had confided in several days ago, and gave a minute nod, signaling that they had reached her home. Olwen nodded back her understanding. Jeilin longed to dig her heels into Fringe's sides and send him flying to the cabin to warn her family, to somehow save them from Ryeln's martial greed. Each slow step felt like the hand of a clock inching slowly forward toward a disaster.

Jeilin was fighting nausea by the time the band stopped in front of the cabin. Ash whinnied from his paddock behind the house. What would her family think? What would they say when they saw her wearing the mark of the enemy, riding beside the general who had come to tear their family apart?

A pale face peered from one of the windows—Ehryn or Emrys, Jeilin couldn't quite tell. The door opened slowly, and Jeilin's father stepped out. A sword hung at his belt, one that Jeilin had never seen him wear before, one that she knew must have been a souvenir of the distant military training of his youth. His face was firm and his expression determined as he met the general's gaze.

"We are Ryeln, the world's greatest military power, and we are procuring able-bodied men to join our army," General Mhin recited.

Rab opened his mouth to speak, but whatever he had been about to say was lost as his wife burst out from the door behind him. "And what if no one here desires to join your army?" she demanded, making it sound more of a command than a question. Her cheeks were flushed and her eyes were fierce with a glint that Jeilin had seldom seen. "What if— *Jeilin!*" her voice, wild with shock and horror, seemed to echo across the plains, perhaps even permeating the forest, alerting the wild beasts to Jeilin's treason. Her mother instinctively lurched forward, but the soldiers drew their swords.

At the sound of her name, Ehryn and Emrys came dashing out the door to stare in disbelief. Though they had been apart only months, Jeilin could already mark differences in their appearances that had not been there before. They looked older than they had in October. October seemed so long ago.

"You know them?" General Mhin asked.

"Yes, General Mhin," she replied. "They are my family."

Jeilin's family seemed to be just as shocked by the sound of her voice as they had been to see her. Rab's expression had gone from determination to disbelief.

"I see," said General Mhin, his eyes flickering toward her, forcing her to resist the urge to squirm in the saddle as she remembered the way they'd lingered the day before. "Then you may have the honor of choosing who will join us."

Jeilin struggled not to wilt in the saddle, trying to determine whether she should feel relieved or terrified. She gazed down at her brothers, father, and mother. Meeting their stares wasn't easy. Finally, she resolved to dismount. Her legs felt weak as she stood after hours of riding, but she forbade them to wobble. She stepped forward toward her family, her right hand curled tightly around the ends of Fringe's reins.

"Jeilin," her father said. "Choose me."

"No!" Ehryn and Emrys said in unison. "I'll go!"

Almeda's gaze darted back and forth between each of her children and her husband. She looked frantic.

Rab shook his head. "I'm the head of this family," he declared. "I've served in the military before, and I can do it again."

"Father," Emrys said. "One of us should go. You shouldn't be considering it."

"Your face!" Almeda burst out.

Jeilin tried to speak in a calm voice that wouldn't reveal her shame. "I'm a messenger for Ryeln now," she said.

"Everyone who serves Ryeln bears this mark." She hoped that she had managed to sound matter-of-fact.

Still fighting to conceal her inner turmoil, Jeilin thought furiously. Her father was older and more experienced, but perhaps *too* old—reflexes slowed by age could be the difference between life and death on the battlefield. On the other hand, so could inexperience. She resisted the urge to chew her lip, to cry tears of frustration. "Ehryn," she finally said. He was the oldest of the twins, if only by a few minutes. It was a stupid reason to choose him, perhaps, but a reason all the same.

Ehryn nodded and stepped forward bravely. The rest of the family opened their mouths, presumably to protest, but Jeilin spoke first. "You've served your time in the military, father, and mother needs you here. Ehryn is..." her voice trailed as she wondered what exactly she had been intending to say. 'The oldest by a quarter of an hour,' she scoffed at herself silently. "...Ehryn is my decision," she finished. "I'm sorry if any of you are unhappy with it."

"You'll still have your husband and your other son to tend the farm," General Mhin spoke to Almeda, who looked as if she was struggling fantastically to keep herself from another outburst. Almeda only frowned as she stared at her two children who had been claimed by Ryeln—stared as if she could somehow reclaim them as her own with her eyes.

Ehryn placed a hand on Jeilin's shoulder. "I'm glad that she chose me," he said. "You needn't worry that I'll drag my feet the whole way. Father fought when he was my age, and there's no reason why I shouldn't."

Almeda's eyes bulged incredulously, and Jeilin knew that if she could speak freely, she would have declared that there was *quite* a difference between serving in Alaishin's military and serving in the strange and fearsome foreigners' war machine. Surprisingly, she only rushed forward wordlessly, seizing Jeilin and Ehryn in a fierce embrace. Rab and Emrys joined in as well, and for a brief moment the family was reunited. Then came sad goodbyes.

"Goodbye, Mother, Father, Emrys," Jeilin said as she climbed reluctantly into the saddle, steeling herself for the inevitable heartbreak that departure would bring.

"Goodbye," Ehryn said.

One by one they echoed their goodbyes to her and Ehryn.

Jeilin kept her eyes on her family and their home, trying to absorb all of the memories and familiar sights that she could. Her family wore tight expressions, worried and sad. Behind them, the front door hung halfway open, spilling heat and warm yellow light out into the winter afternoon. Jeilin could just see part of the fireplace, and one of the little wooden figures that her father had whittled resting on the mantle above it. A delicious aroma announced that her family had been just about to enjoy dinner when the army had interrupted. Suddenly, Almeda dashed inside. Rab and Emrys frowned, and Jeilin mirrored them without realizing it. Was her mother so disgusted, or so furious with her, that she didn't even want to watch her leave?

Her mother's reappearance soon soothed her worries; the small woman bustled over the frosty ground to Fringe's side. She reached up, unwrapping something from her apron and pressing it into Jeilin's hands. Jeilin could feel the warmth seeping through her gloves, and the heavenly smell confirmed that the small package contained some of her mother's cooking. Jeilin smiled down at her mother, trying not to think of how the motion would contort her tattoo. "Thank you," she said.

Almeda nodded and hurried to Ehryn's side, pressing a similar bundle into his hands. Jeilin dared a glance at General Mhin and saw that he was sitting impassively on top of his charger. His gaze shifted to her almost at once, as if he'd sensed her eyes upon him. Jeilin looked down at Fringe's neck and smoothed his mane, though it didn't need it.

As the band moved again, leaving the little cabin behind, Jeilin clutched the package of food to her stomach. It felt so warm, while the rest of her felt chilled down to her toes.

She resisted turning again to scan the band of soldiers for Ehryn's face; the sight of it only made her think of how his was soon to be ruined like hers. Still, she knew he was there, only a few yards behind her. His presence sent thrills of excitement through her heart, though she hated to admit it to herself. Bringing him back to Dresinva was like bringing a piece of home into her new, foreign life.

****

By the time General Mhin's band returned to Dresinva it was days later and they had acquired several more young men, including Gadyn, Jeilin's would-be fiancé from her old life. Jeilin remembered with chagrin the day he had been taken from his home; he'd looked sick when he recognized her, and Jeilin had felt his disbelieving eyes on her back throughout the rest of that day's march. A cold shoulder and large amounts of time spent exercising Fringe had been enough to keep him at bay; Jeilin dreaded the thought of his inevitable questions, of hearing him exclaim over her desecrated face.

Fringe's ears pricked forward as they entered the camp on the royal grounds, and his step livened as the stables came into sight. Jeilin patted his neck. No doubt he was looking forward to an easy night spent in a warm stable with plenty of oats. Snow kept stride with him, her dark eyes gleaming.

"A bath in the palace will be perfect after all of this traveling," Olwen said with a smile. Though they slept in the camp where they were at General Mhin's disposal, bathing in the palace at will was a privilege that messengers had been granted. Outwardly, Jeilin returned her smile. Inwardly, she was not yet quite used to the tapering black mark that negated her friend's pleasant expression.

As she rode Fringe toward the stable, Jeilin heard General Mhin commanding the new recruits. She knew they would be spending the evening and likely half the night in line, waiting for their turn to be marked by Ryeln. She turned in the saddle for one last look at her brother's face. To her surprise, it was Gadyn's eye she caught, not Ehryn's. She looked away in shame, resisting the urge to touch her cheek.

Jeilin and Olwen relinquished their mounts' reins to grooms and retreated to the castle. The stone corridors were barely warmer than the outdoors, but the bathing room was warmed by a large fire. After days of riding and camping in fields, Jeilin felt as if she were thawing in water that was almost, but not quite, too hot to bear. Her hair felt slightly stiff as she unwound the old leather cord that bound it and let it brush the surface of the water. Jeilin breathed a sigh of relief as she relaxed for what seemed like the first time in at least a week. Olwen was also relaxed, but silent. She had often been quiet during the expansion campaign through the Dusty Pass, and Jeilin suspected that she had been keeping silent in order to avoid prying about Jeilin's feelings and family. Not that Jeilin minded talking about it to her; in fact, Olwen always had been an excellent listener.

"You know that tall fellow we picked up about a mile down the Dusty Pass from my family's home?" Jeilin asked.

"The handsome one?" Olwen replied with a smile.

"I suppose," Jeilin said, rolling her eyes.

Olwen grinned. "I noticed he hasn't taken his eyes off you since he's been recruited. Though I suppose he doesn't hold a candle to—" Olwen stopped, suddenly serious. "To you know who," she finished. Jeilin grimaced. Even the most casual conversation became tricky when you had to remember to leave names out. The last thing Jeilin needed was to face the gallows because a servant overheard her mention her relationship with Prince Raihnin.

"No, not at all," Jeilin said, unable to suppress a grin. "His name's Gadyn," she continued. "And he's the one my mother wanted me to marry. Well, he wanted me to marry him too."

Olwen arched an eyebrow. "And you didn't want to?" she asked knowingly.

Jeilin shook her head. "I'm like you. I just want to be a messenger. I didn't want to get *married*," she said, sinking a little lower into the water.

Olwen laughed. "So you wouldn't be interested in marrying *anyone*?" she asked slyly.

Jeilin's face warmed. "Well," she said. "It's not like...maybe someday in the future...hypothetically of course..." The thought of marrying Raihnin made her knees wobble in a way that Gadyn's offer certainly never had. It was ridiculous, though, she told herself; imagining that a prince would want to marry a farm girl turned messenger. But men didn't just go around leaving love letters in begemmed daggers for sport, did they? Jeilin frowned and shook her head as if to clear it. With a ruthless conquering army sweeping across the kingdom, it was hardly the time to be fantasizing about an improbable marriage. She didn't even know if Raihnin was still alive.

"Sorry," Olwen said. "I was just trying to have a bit of fun. I didn't mean to be tactless."

"It's all right," Jeilin said. "Fun seems to be few and far between these days; you might as well have it when you can."

Olwen nodded thoughtfully while massaging a frothy shampoo into her long hair. She didn't say it, but Jeilin knew what she was thinking; that she missed the old days and couldn't wait to have the opportunity to do something to try to bring them back, to try to save Alaishin. That Ryeln could be defeated and driven out of the kingdom seemed a great unlikelihood in the subdued city of Dresinva, but hope of it was what drove Jeilin to persevere nonetheless. Perhaps Dresinva was the worst of it, she thought; perhaps Prince Raihnin was rallying troops at the bay, preparing to strike back. Perhaps one day the only thing left from the nightmare would be the black mark etched into her face. Perhaps.

Chapter 12

T he next morning dawned cold and bright, and the sparkling frost was soon muddied beneath the trampling of soldiers' boots. Jeilin rose from her blankets, which, like her freshly washed hair, smelled of a floral sweetness. She had noted where the newly acquired soldiers had set up tents and headed in that direction with her bowl of morning porridge and a biscuit.

She found Ehryn seated on a log at the edge of one of the many small fires that dotted the camp. By the time he noticed her, she had already taken a seat beside him. An angry red halo surrounded the fresh tattoo that sliced across his cheekbone. When he turned his bloodshot eyes toward her, Jeilin thought bitterly that no one would ever have difficulty telling him from his twin again, if they were ever reunited.

"I didn't know who to choose," Jeilin said quietly. "I hope you can forgive me."

Ehryn shook his head dismissively. "I would have chosen me if the decision had been mine," he said. "There's nothing to forgive."

He paused for a moment and then asked, "How in the world did you go from being an Alaishinian messenger to this?" he asked, gesturing toward his cheek.

"Olwen and I—she's the messenger who's been training me—were delivering messages to the royal outpost in Sunlan when Ryeln attacked. As far as I know, we were the only ones to escape. We carried news of the attack to Prince Raihnin in the Bay of Lights, and then he sent us here. We didn't realize that Ryeln had taken the city until we reached the gates, and by then it was too late. Death or Ryeln…they let us choose."

Ehryn nodded. "We begin training today."

It was Jeilin's turn to nod.

"I suppose it won't be so bad, learning to use the sword…" Ehryn said.

"I suppose," Jeilin said with a frown. It wasn't learning to use the sword that she feared for him; it was actually *having* to use it.

An officer approached the middle of the recruits' camp. "I'll see you later," Jeilin said, slipping away quickly.

She found Olwen wandering among the messengers' tents. "I've been looking for you!" she exclaimed. "We've just been summoned by General Mhin."

"Are we being dispatched?" Jeilin asked breathlessly.

"I'm not sure," Olwen said, but she too sounded nervous, even hopeful.

They made their way to General Mhin's tent together and were admitted by a guard. The general was at his writing desk, surrounded by a stack of papers, a pot of ink, and various quills. "I have a message for you," he said, sparing a quick glance at the two of them. "I'm sending you both together to an outpost we've established in Tela-narahn—that's a large village by the sea, about a day's ride south of the Bay of Lights. Do you know it?"

"I do," Olwen said. Jeilin marveled at how calm her voice was—her heart was suddenly racing at the thought of riding toward the bay.

"You'll be delivering this to General Tehn," he said, handing over a sealed piece of heavy parchment.

Jeilin reached out and took the message, tucking it into a pocket under her cloak.

"Ride quickly, but be on guard," General Mhin said. "We have a lot of soldiers going between here and Tela-narahn heading toward one of Alaishin's last footholds, the Bay of Lights."

Jeilin's heart soared, and she had to resist shouting for joy. The Bay of Lights was still resisting the Ryelnish army. Surely Raihnin was alive and well! The news and the assignment was what she had hoped for every night as she curled up in her tent, running her fingers over the dagger Raihnin had given her, taking comfort in the fact that his hand had rested there too.

"Yes, General Mhin," Jeilin and Olwen said together. And with a quick dismissal and a salute, they were exiting the tent. Jeilin could feel General Mhin's eyes on her back as she moved, and rounded the corner hastily, eager to escape from his sight.

Once they'd returned to the messengers' camp area, Jeilin and Olwen collected their sparse belongings and rolled up their tents as quickly as they could before hurrying to the stables. Their horses had already been saddled and were waiting, clean and well rested. Jeilin's heart would have been light as she swung into the saddle, except for one thing; she would not be able to bid Ehryn goodbye. They quickly left the bleak city behind, riding toward the coast.

****

"Can you believe our good fortune?" Jeilin asked that evening as she and Olwen sat around the little campfire they had built in a secluded field. They were finally alone again, and both felt it was a relief not to be crowded by hundreds of milling soldiers. The horses had been hobbled and were clipping at what sparse winter grass they could find.

"If we can find a way to turn this for the good of Alaishin instead of helping Ryeln conquer what resistance is left," Olwen responded.

Jeilin nodded. "There's got to be a way. Something's got to come up. Anyway, it's a relief to know that there still *is* a resistance."

Olwen nodded. "There's still hope," she said, sounding unsure.

"We could keep on riding to the bay," Jeilin said wistfully.

Olwen frowned. "I wish we could too, but we'd be throwing away any chance we have to help save Alaishin. These marks would likely as not get us killed if we tried to carry messages for the prince, and we don't even have any valuable information to take to him yet."

"We have this," Jeilin said, indicating the message from General Mhin that she'd stowed on her person.

"True," said Olwen, "but we've no idea what it says, and we'd have no choice but to flee to Raihnin if we opened it, even if we found that it was useless."

"I suppose you're right," Jeilin said. "Maybe a better opportunity will present itself in Telanarahn." A better opportunity *had* to present itself in Telanarahn.

****

The outpost at Telanarahn was a mass of tents dotted with quickly assembled stables and towers, bustling with the activity of busy officers and even more soldiers than there had been in Dresinva. Clearly, they felt that a confrontation with the resistance growing in the bay was imminent. The message that Jeilin and Olwen had brought was received eagerly by General Tehn, a man who seemed to differ little from General Mhin.

After leaving their horses with grooms in a large stable, Jeilin and Olwen assembled their tents in the area that General Tehn had instructed them to. Nearly a dozen other messengers had already set up there, but unlike Dresinva, their accents revealed that most of them had come across the border with Ryeln. The black tattoos allowed Jeilin and Olwen to slip into their ranks without questions or division, and Jeilin marveled once again at how a simple oath and mark seemed to buy blind and complete trust. Jeilin and

Olwen did everything as a pair, but the crowds left them unable to discuss the matters that consumed both their minds.

Jeilin rose with the sun the next morning, expecting a dull day, void of what distraction a city like Dresinva had provided, thinking that she would spend it in anxious thought and speculation. As it turned out, she had barely combed her hair and secured it with the familiar leather cord when a soldier appeared among the messengers' tents in search of her and Olwen. "You're needed by General Tehn," he said, and escorted them to the general's tent. At first she was surprised, as there had been a dozen other messengers present the night before. Would she and Olwen really be dispatched again so quickly? But as she crossed the camp on her way to General Tehn's tent, she saw that most of the other messengers were gone.

General Tehn stood when they arrived, clutching a folded and sealed piece of parchment in his right hand. "I've prepared a reply message for General Mhin. I am sending you both back to Dresinva today."

"Yes, General Tehn," Jeilin and Olwen said together. Jeilin made her best attempt at sounding like the news was no surprise to her, but in truth she hadn't expected such a prompt dispatch. Rest was hardly her concern though; she had been counting on her time in Telanarahn to provide an opportunity to return to Raihnin with valuable information of some sort.

"Deliver this to General Mhin," General Tehn said, relinquishing the letter. Jeilin took it from his hand.

"Yes, General Tehn," she said again, and with a salute she and Olwen exited the tent.

They scarcely spoke while they gathered their supplies and secured them to their saddles, and they left the outpost in an eager but silent canter. Fringe's gait was smooth as the bustle and noise of the outpost faded into the empty silence of the winter plains, but Jeilin's mind was in turmoil. "What do we do?" she finally burst out when she was sure that only the deadened grass would hear.

"Ride to Dresinva," Olwen said.

"We could take the message to the bay instead," Jeilin said.

"We could," Olwen said judiciously. "But I don't think that we should."

"Why?" Jeilin asked. Each hoof beat carried them farther from Prince Raihnin and what was left of the kingdom of Alaishin. She longed to urge Fringe into gallop toward the bay, to leave the Ryelnish nightmare behind.

"I hate this too," Olwen replied, casting a sympathetic look toward Jeilin as she sat perfectly straight in Snow's saddle. "I want to ride to the bay and put this outlandish façade behind us just as badly as you do. Well, almost as badly." She smiled knowingly. "I may not have the same feelings for the prince that you do, but serving the royal family and the kingdom is the one thing I've loved above all others; it's who I am."

"Oh," Jeilin said, frowning.

"But things are really brewing in Telanarahn," Olwen explained. "I have a feeling we'll be sent back as plans for

188

Ryeln's confrontation with the resistance at the bay are refined and finalized between generals. We might be shortchanging Alaishin by delivering this letter—the closer Ryeln gets to the confrontation, the more valuable and timely the information contained in the letters will be."

Jeilin nodded as she slowed Fringe to a trot. "You're right," she said. "We should wait."

Olwen smiled. "Look on the bright side. You'll get to see your brother."

Jeilin smiled too, for a moment. "Yes," she said. "I do want to see him again before disappearing. It may be the last time…it looks like he'll probably be marching against Prince Raihnin's men."

"I'm sorry," Olwen said simply.

The somber ride ate up the rest of the day, and the pair made camp in deserted places that evening and the next.

****

King Darnasius' body still hung in the square; Jeilin cringed inwardly and cast her eyes to the pavement when she and Olwen rode quickly by it. Despite the longing she had experienced to ride to the bay instead of to Dresinva, Jeilin felt a strange sense of relief upon entering the camp sprawled across the royal lawns. The place had become rather familiar, and the new presence of her brother made it seem more so.

General Mhin received his message with a brief smile. "I hoped you would return to me," he said. "You both have done well." His dismissal revealed no more than his greeting, though Jeilin did feel his eyes upon her again as she left his tent.

"Do you think he'll dispatch us to Telanarahn again soon?" Jeilin asked Olwen quietly.

"Yes," Olwen said. "He'll have a reply to General Tehn's message, and he obviously prefers using you."

Jeilin frowned. She was all too aware that General Mhin preferred her a little *too* much. The way he looked at her made her uncomfortable. His gaze was different than how she'd seen other men look at her before. The light that she remembered seeing in the flirtatious Prince Stephen's eyes had never touched General Mhin's. And there was none of the tenderness or admiration that made her heart beat a little faster when she looked into Raihnin's. The General's gaze was hungry, sly, almost predatory…

"I'm going to find Ehryn," Jeilin said, doing her best to shove thoughts of General Mhin's black eyes from her mind.

The sky had begun to grow dusky as those who hadn't eaten yet queued up around the great iron cook pots—Jeilin hoped that whatever training her brother was undergoing wasn't engaging him at the moment. She proceeded to the area of camp where she'd found him before and began her search around the cook pots, stopping to take some food for herself.

She spotted him on his way to a fire with a bowl of soup and bread. "I've been hoping you'd show up," he said, grinning at the sight of her.

"I was dispatched several days ago," she informed him. "I've just returned."

"It seems your journey was safe," Ehryn noted with relief in his voice.

"I think I may be sent back soon, though."

Ehryn nodded. "It seems there's a lot going on now...there's talk that a resistance is alive somewhere, talk of confrontation."

"I know," Jeilin said, meeting her brother's eyes. They held sadness, and Jeilin knew him well enough to detect unasked questions as well. "I want to say goodbye now," she said. "In case I don't have a chance to later."

"Me too," Ehryn said.

There was a moment of silence as Jeilin pondered the possibility of a deeper meaning in Ehryn's words. "I want to thank you for being so understanding about *all* of this; for not resenting me for choosing you," she finally said.

"I'd be a fool to resent you," he said. "To tell the truth, I admire you."

Jeilin blushed and became suddenly and intensely interested in her bread. "There's nothing to admire. Anyway, I never imagined I'd hear *that* from the brother who once convinced me that mud cakes would taste like real cakes if left out in the sun to bake long enough."

Ehryn laughed. "Well consider this repayment for that mouthful of dirt."

The dusky evening had faded to night by the time Jeilin left her brother for her tent. Knowing that their hour together might have been their last caused her heart to ache, but she felt grateful that the hour had been happy, and that she had had a last chance to remember home with him. She stole another glance of him scraping his bowl clean by firelight, and walked away.

****

The camp was busier and louder than usual the following morning. Jeilin watched as scores of soldiers marched in strict formation out of the camp and into the city streets. They were a mass of blackness; their dark uniform and armor gave the impression that night was reclaiming the morning. Their fair faces stood out, highlighting the black marks that slashed across all of their cheekbones, silently announcing who they were from beneath the horned helmets that Jeilin remembered from Sunlan. Here and there flags flew above the winding ribbon of marching men, bearing bone-white slashes across night-black fields, rippling in the cold wind, the reverse of each soldier's face.

The air seemed to grow colder as Jeilin remembered Sunlan, as the image that she struggled to push from her mind each night loomed ominously, a seemingly endless circle of fear and blood and death. She scanned the passing soldiers nervously, searching for Ehryn's face, hoping that she would still be able to tell the difference between her brother and the rest of the soldiers, any of which might have been the one who plagued her nightmares, slaughtering Prince Stephen nightly. They all looked the same in their armor, and they moved too quickly for her to see most of their faces. With a frustrated sigh she turned on her heel and strode quickly toward where Ehryn's tent was, or had been.

She released her breath, never having realized that she had been holding it, when she caught sight of Ehryn working a sword drill with another trainee.

"You there," a voice called from behind her.

Jeilin spun around, facing an armorless soldier.

"General Mhin wants you at his tent, and the other one who travels with you," the soldier said.

Jeilin nodded. "I'll find her."

She cast one last wistful look at her brother. At least she'd been able to say goodbye this time.

Olwen was near her tent, running a silver comb through her long brown hair as she sat in front of a fire. "General Mhin wants us," Jeilin said.

Olwen stood and smiled, tucking the comb into a pocket. "I told you," she said quietly as they walked together to the general's tent.

Jeilin nodded. "Do you think those soldiers are leaving for the bay?" she asked, motioning toward the last of the many who had filed out of the camp into the streets.

"It's likely. I imagine that General Mhin will be sending troops to support General Tehn's."

"This could be it then," Jeilin whispered.

Olwen cast her a serious look and gave a barely discernable nod.

Jeilin's heart raced as they were admitted into the general's tent.

General Mhin had clearly been waiting. "I have an important message for you," he said to them both. "You will carry this to General Tehn. I'm counting on you to arrive in at least half the time the troops I'm sending will. It is of the utmost importance…I trust you both not to disappoint me."

"You know you can rely on me, General Mhin," Jeilin said. The lie came naturally and only added to her excitement; she suppressed a smile as her hand closed around the heavy parchment.

"I know," General Mhin said, his dark eyes meeting hers. "I'll have a word with you alone before you depart." Jeilin's stomach clenched as Olwen gave her a pained look before she slipped out of the tent. She was eager to depart, to leave General Mhin and the Ryelnish army behind forever. What did he want?

"A woman with courage such as yours is a rare jewel," General Mhin said, his gaze unwavering. "I never expected to find one in this weak kingdom. I am fortunate to have your pledge and your service in my army, and yet…" Jeilin held her breath as his eyes swept over her from her head to her toes. "I am not satisfied."

Jeilin swallowed as her heart sped. "I'm afraid I don't understand," she said, hoping that her voice sounded steadier to his ears than it did to hers. "Has…has my performance not been satisfactory?" Jeilin wondered. Did he suspect her treacherous motives? Or, worse…did this have something to do with the way he'd been looking at her?

"Your performance has been completely satisfactory," General Mhin said. "My dissatisfaction lies in another area." Jeilin's relief was almost immediately swallowed up by an even deeper sense of dread as he continued. "When I think of the bravery and tenacity that a woman like you would surely pass on to my sons...well, the thought of sending you away from my tent day after day seems unwise. So I will have you as my wife, Jeilin. I would have you bear my sons, and they would become Ryeln's fiercest warriors."

Jeilin mustered all of her strength to remain standing. General Mhin's *wife*? The idea was absolutely absurd! His gaze weighed on her heavily, to the point that she feared she would collapse. "I..."

"I am one of Ryeln's foremost generals," General Mhin said. "And I can say with confidence that you are Ryeln's most courageous woman—and a great beauty as well. Surely you see that our union would be a perfect match that would bring glory to our kingdom." He reached out and placed a large hand on Jeilin's shoulder. She wanted to pull away, but didn't dare move for fear that she'd fall over. "Ride for me one last time," he said. "And then I will make you one of Ryeln's most revered women."

Jeilin didn't have the power to speak. Instead, she nodded, hoping that the general would mistake her stare of horror as one of admiration as she mustered a salute and left his tent.

Fringe and Snow quickly outpaced General Mhin's troops, who were mostly on foot. Despite the sore muscles she had earned over the past week and never having had much of a chance to catch up on sleep, Jeilin sat straight in the saddle, urging Fringe to maintain a lively gate. She could hardly wait to reach Raihnin, and was also eager to put as much distance as possible between herself and General Mhin. After his talk with her, she'd hurried to mount Fringe, and hadn't spoken a word until she and Olwen had ridden out of the city. Then she'd related her horror as they rode past the war-turned earth outside the city walls, pushing Fringe into a ground-eating run. By the time she and Olwen stopped to make camp, her enthusiasm hadn't wavered.

Jeilin pulled General Mhin's message out from a pocket under the layers of clothing she wore to keep the cold at bay, resisting the urge to cringe as she remembered the last words he'd spoken to her. If she returned to Dresinva, General Mhin would expect her to… Never mind, she thought, she *wouldn't* be returning to Dresinva. "What do you think it says?" she asked, running her thumb over the thick wax seal.

"Probably where the troops that left Dresinva this morning are headed," Olwen replied.

Jeilin held the parchment up to the firelight, which revealed nothing. She ran her thumb over the seal again.

"Best not to open it yet," Olwen said from her side of the fire.

"When?" Jeilin asked. "I'd like to know whether we'll be doing Prince Raihnin any good with this message when we finally reach him."

"When we're past Telanarahn," Olwen said. "We'll be safe on our way there as long as we've got the sealed message. After we pass Telanarahn…well, capture would mean only one thing whether or not the message is intact, so we might as well know what we're risking our necks for."

"Right," Jeilin agreed, tucking the message away.

****

The rest of the journey toward Telanarahn passed without incident. Once, Jeilin and Olwen encountered a battalion of Ryelnish troops. Where they had come from, Jeilin was unsure, but they too were marching toward Telanarahn. They rode past the soldiers quickly, receiving a few salutes and nods.

"We'd reach the outpost by early evening at this rate," Olwen said from the saddle later.

"But we'll be riding past," Jeilin said, remembering the plans they had laid the last couple of nights by firelight.

"Right," Olwen said. "We'll begin to bear eastward in a few miles. At first we'll be following the border of the Great Ridge Forest to the north, but eventually we'll find an old trading road that is seldom traveled. I doubt that any officers would choose our route over the newer and more direct roads…we'll just have to pray that we don't encounter anyone."

By evening they had officially abandoned the route to Telanarahn. Jeilin almost expected the air to crackle with the excitement she felt, but they rode mostly in silence, trying to make themselves invisible against the trees at the outskirts of the Great Ridge Forest.

"We need to stop and make camp," Olwen said a while after the day had settled into night. "If a horse breaks a leg tripping in the dark now, we'll have lost everything, for ourselves and for Alaishin."

Jeilin agreed. "There's not even a moon," she observed. Above, the sky was as black as a Ryelnish banner, but unrelieved by even a sliver of white.

Within a few minutes, they had selected a nook in the forest edge where a few pines would hopefully hide their camp from view if anyone else crossed the plains that bordered the forest. After removing tack from, rubbing down, and hobbling their horses, Jeilin and Olwen began the routine of assembling their small camp, gathering firewood and erecting tents.

When the fire was blazing and a small stack of extra wood had been set aside, Jeilin and Olwen gathered together around it and prepared to open General Mhin's message. Jeilin withdrew it from her pocket and felt the perfect seal one last time. Apprehension tied her stomach in knots as she contemplated breaking the seal with the blade of the dagger Raihnin had given her. Not long ago, she never would have considered opening a message she'd been entrusted with. But now… She pulled out her dagger and destroyed the seal with a quick slice of her blade. She and Olwen each read the letter at once in silence, their heads pressed together as they held it as close to the flames as they dared.

General Tehn,

I have received your request for troops and am sending a large battalion of my men. You may expect them to arrive east of the bay as we discussed within five days of receiving this message, a couple of days after the arrival of the battalion I understand that General Shi has deployed to the same location. May Ryeln crush the resistance and be victorious,

General Mhin

Jeilin was the first to speak. "What do you think?" she asked. "Will this information be worth anything to Prince Raihnin?"

"I'm no general," Olwen replied. "But I think it will be, if we deliver it in time."

Jeilin folded the sheet of parchment and tucked it away again. Exhausted as she was, thoughts of soon being reunited with Raihnin kept her awake later than usual. Her mind vacillated between daydreams centered around the prince using words like "beautiful" and "truly," and doubt—doubt that Raihnin had ever been as enthusiastic as she imagined, and worse, that he would reject her when he saw her marred face. She reached into her smallest pocket and restlessly fingered the folded piece of parchment that had fallen out of the dagger—Raihnin's letter to her—and worried herself to sleep.

Jeilin awoke a little while later to pressure on her arm and warm breath on her cheek. Someone was leaning over her. She opened her eyes warily—it was still dark; she couldn't see anything, but she caught the familiar scent of flower-scented shampoo as something soft brushed her face. "Shhh," Olwen breathed. "It's me. Listen—someone's out there, creeping around."

They both held their breath. Somewhere, a twig snapped. The quiet night magnified the small sound. A horse nickered.

A dozen possibilities raced through Jeilin's mind, each worse than the last. "A horse thief?" Jeilin whispered suddenly, reaching for Raihnin's dagger. Horse thieves had not been the first possibility to occur to her, but it was the only one that she could bring herself to say aloud.

"I don't know," Olwen replied. "But we'll be lucky if that's all it is."

Chapter 13

O lwen ducked silently out of the tent, and faint moonlight illuminated her just enough for Jeilin to see that she had unsheathed her dagger. Jeilin followed her as quietly as she could, her knuckles white as she nervously gripped the hilt of her own weapon. She tried not to think of what it would feel like to have to use it. A slight rustle came from the horses' direction, and Olwen froze in her tracks, nearly causing Jeilin to trip over her. Jeilin's eyes were still adjusting to the dim light, but she almost thought that she could make out a shape a few yards away that was slightly darker than the night. Her heart raced while her breathing slowed to a stop, and she prayed that their flight hadn't been discovered by Ryelnish soldiers. And then she saw it, as a cloud shifted from in front of the winter moon: a white face, save for one black slash that crossed a cheek. She heard Olwen breathe in deeply, and then saw her leap forward wildly toward the figure.

There came a muffled cry as they collided, and then both thumped to the ground. The brief struggle that ensued subsided suddenly, by which time Jeilin's eyes had adjusted enough for her to see that Olwen was on top. "Don't!" a frantic voice cried. Jeilin was relieved to hear that it was male. She rushed to where Olwen had pinned the intruder to the ground.

"Are there more of you?" Olwen asked. Jeilin could see that she had her dagger pressed to his throat.

"No," he said quickly, struggling to speak clearly against the blade that threatened to silence him permanently. "There's only me and my horse."

Jeilin gasped as she recognized the young face, framed by fair hair and as white as the moon with terror. "Cai!" she said.

"If you've come to seek revenge against Jeilin again—" Olwen began.

"No!" Cai protested. "I know now that she didn't kill Eric!" His words tumbled out in a rush.

Olwen removed her dagger from his throat, but continued to hold him against the cold earth, making sure to keep the blade where it was still visible to Cai.

"Why are you here, then?" Olwen asked.

Cai breathed a sigh of relief as he began to explain himself. "I was dispatched from Dresinva too," he said. "Just a little later than you two were. I saw when you both began to veer eastward, away from Telanarahn, and I followed you from a distance. I lost sight of you for a while and had to wait until dark to ride toward the light of your campfire. I just now found you."

"Why did you follow us?" Olwen pressed.

"It's obvious that you're riding to the bay, where the resistance is. I want to go too, of course "

Olwen sat up, releasing Cai. He rose to his knees slowly, massaging a shoulder. He moved stiffly—clearly, the wounds across his back still pained him. "Look," he said, reaching beneath his coat and pulling out a sealed piece of parchment. He broke the seal with his thumb. "I can't go back now, see? I've no choice but to ride to the Bay of Lights. Besides, I think this message is very important—I overheard the general saying that he was sending me because I was the lightest, the fastest."

Olwen was silent for a moment. "All right," she finally said. Snatching the message from his grasp, she knelt by the fire pit, where the flames had been reduced to glowing embers. She took a piece of firewood from a nearby pile and stirred the smoldering ashes until they grew red hot, then threw a handful of dried pine needles on top. Soon small flames were licking the darkness. Jeilin knelt beside her by the fire's edge, peering down at the letter, which had been penned in a familiar hand.

General Tehn,

I have just received word that General Shi's men were delayed in a small town east of the bay called Maiyin. The enemy was lying in wait; I regret to report that General Shi was surprised by the ambush and forced into retreat. Shi and his men are now marching on toward the bay with half of their original number, and many of those who remain have been injured. The enemy troops seem to be on their way back to the Bay of Lights. They suffered fewer casualties, but their leader, the dead king's heir, fell in battle. Whether he lives, and what the extent of his injuries are if he does, we do not know. May he be an example to the rest of the rebels, and may they fear Ryeln's arrival at the bay.

General Mhin

Olwen folded the letter up quickly. "I'm sorry," she whispered to Jeilin.

Jeilin retreated to her tent, glad that the night hid her face as she slipped inside. She barely heard Cai's voice, asking to see the message. She felt as if she had fallen through ice and plunged into frigid water. Ever since she'd left the Bay of Lights, she'd been imagining Raihnin inside the castle, putting pins in maps and discussing strategy with his generals—safe, at least until the impending conflict at the bay itself, by which time she would be there with him. Why had he led an ambush miles away from the bay? Why?

****

"We'll reach the Bay of Lights this evening, if all goes well," Olwen announced the next morning. Cai had joined Jeilin and Olwen around the fire for breakfast. His bay gelding stood hobbled beside Fringe and Snow.

"I'm sorry," Cai said.

Jeilin's heart jumped. He knew about her…her and Raihnin…the time they'd spent together and the letter he'd given her? She cast a searching glance at Olwen. Why would she have told him? Olwen shook her head.

"For attacking you," Cai continued. "For thinking that you killed Eric."

"Oh," Jeilin said, relieved and distracted. "Don't worry about it. It's nothing."

Cai frowned. "I really am—"

"I know," Jeilin interrupted. It really was nothing, she thought, compared to the news about Raihnin. "I'm sorry too," she said after a moment of silence. "For ordering you whipped. I thought I had to order something to…to keep in General Mhin's good graces, so that I could get away to the bay."

"I deserved it," Cai said.

"No, you didn't," Jeilin replied. "We'd better saddle up. We need to get going."

Steam clouds formed around the horses' noses as their breath froze in the cold morning air. Jeilin saddled Fringe quickly, tying her tent behind the cantle and checking the girth. She couldn't swing her leg over the saddle quickly enough. Fringe plunged ahead across the frosty plains at her urging with Snow and Cai's bay close behind.

It wasn't long before they came to the nearly forgotten trading road Olwen had spoken of. It wound through the prairie grass like a great dirt snake, well established but old and seldom traveled. Jeilin listened hard for the sound of marching men or horses' hooves in the distance, and Fringe picked up on her nervousness, dancing beneath her.

"It looks as if we're all clear," Olwen said. "If we follow this road northwest, it will take us straight to the Bay of Lights."

Jeilin heeled Fringe forward, leading again.

Olwen stopped them at midday, pulling a map out of a saddlebag. She studied it briefly. "Here," she said, dismounting and leading Snow into the edge of the forest, which began only a few yards from the road. "There's a spring where we can water the horses," she explained.

Jeilin dismounted and led Fringe by the reins while Cai did the same, bringing his bay behind her. Olwen led them through tall trees, all of which, except for the evergreens, were winter-bare. Beneath the green boughs of an especially large pine, a small spring bubbled over a rocky bank and ended in a small pool at the bottom. They each took turns allowing their horses to drink and refilling their water skins. Fringe drank deeply as Jeilin knelt beside him, careful to keep her fingers out of the icy water. She stroked his golden neck absentmindedly; ever since she had read the message Cai had brought, she'd found it difficult to concentrate on anything. Images of Raihnin kept flashing through her mind: Raihnin dead, Raihnin dying, and Raihnin atop a snowy war stallion, being cleaved in half by a Ryelnish soldier like his cousin Prince Stephen had been, his blood falling like rain…

"Are you all right, Jeilin?" The sound of Olwen's voice pulled Jeilin out of her despairing visions. Her water skin was full, overflowing even, and Fringe had finished his drink; droplets of icy water were dripping from his chin.

"Yes," Jeilin replied, rising hurriedly and backing Fringe away from the edge of the spring so that Cai's horse could drink.

Olwen shot Jeilin a worried look when Cai stooped by the water to fill his skin.

Jeilin flashed her a feeble smile, but her stomach was in knots and her mind already panicking over what news she would hear when she reached the bay. Surely the troops would have returned…she could only hope that they'd returned with Raihnin alive rather than dead. She winced at the thought, knowing she probably wouldn't even be allowed to see his beautiful body one last time if the latter was the case. Her, a former farm girl with an ugly mark on her face that declared her a traitor…she would be laughed at, maybe worse if she suggested that Raihnin had ever…

A shout erupted.

Jeilin tensed and spun instinctively, but not before Cai slumped forward into the shallow pool with a splash, and not before she saw blood blossom beneath its surface. There was no one behind her. She peered anxiously past the pool, where a man had emerged from among the trees. He was tall with hair the color of Olwen's and a beard to match—and poised to throw another blade. Jeilin threw herself to the ground and scrambled forward toward Cai. A knife sliced the air above her head as she seized one of his boots and began to drag him backwards, freeing his face from the water. The knife that had flown above her came to rest in a tree trunk beside the man. Jeilin turned to see Olwen scrambling at her belt for another blade to throw.

The man dropped the blade he had been holding and raised his empty hands into the air. "I have no desire to harm a woman," he said. "But if you force me to, I shall."

Olwen muttered a curse before dropping to her knees beside Jeilin. Together they rolled Cai onto his back. The hilt of a knife stuck from his chest, just below his collarbone on the left side. His blue eyes sprung open, accompanied by a sputter that sprayed spring water onto the forest floor. The violent force of coughing up the water he had swallowed caused his body to spasm in agony; blood seeped across his coat.

"Why would you do this?" Olwen demanded, sparing the stranger a vicious glance as she knelt beside Cai, brushing muddy leaves from his hair and face.

The man leered and yanked his coat aside, revealing a small golden star that gleamed from his chest.

Olwen cursed again.

"I see you know what that means," the man said. "But you needn't fear; I shan't harm you two ladies if you agree not to resist capture. I'm sure that—"

Olwen interrupted him. "You fool," she said. "Don't you have a message to deliver? Go and leave us be."

The man glared. "Go and leave three enemy spies *be*?" he said dangerously. "I think not." His right hand moved toward his belt again.

"We're not the enemy, and we're not spies," Olwen said. "We are Olwen, Jeilin, and Cai, and we ride for Alaishin."

Surprise flickered across the man's face, quickly replaced by anger.

"Ah, you recognize my name, don't you?" Olwen said.

"That means nothing," he said. "I have heard of the lady-messenger Olwen, but she is dead and you are a fool to think I'd believe such a claim. Alaishin? Look at your faces!"

"You don't know what you're talking about," Olwen said, biting off each word. "I'm not dead. I was captured by the enemy when I arrived with a message in Dresinva, along with Jeilin. We're carrying Ryelnish messages to Prince Raihnin in the Bay of Lights!"

Jeilin tried desperately to read some answer from the man's face when Raihnin's name was mentioned, but all she could see was a mixture of confusion and fury.

"You certainly *look* like the enemy," the man said in a cool tone that worried Jeilin.

"Surely you can tell from my voice that I have lived here all of my life," Olwen said. "I don't have that wretched Ryelnish accent."

The man continued to eye them all suspiciously, but said nothing.

"We had the option of either entering Ryeln's service or dying," Olwen said flatly. "We figured that we might still be able to do some good for Alaishin if we stayed alive."

The man frowned. "Who's he?" he asked, waving a hand toward Cai, who lay wet and bloody, shivering on the ground.

"Another messenger who is still loyal to Alaishin," Olwen said coldly. "I rather think you should have asked that question before you stuck a knife in him."

"Why should I believe you?" the man asked, ignoring Olwen's jab.

"Because I have the letters to prove what I'm saying," Olwen replied. She reached into Cai's coat pocket and delicately removed a folded piece of parchment with the broken seal. One corner was soaked with blood, and Cai gasped despite her carefulness.

Jeilin fished the other letter out of her own clothing and handed it to Olwen.

With both of the messages in hand, Olwen advanced around the pool to the man, eyeing him warily.

After studying the letters and their broken seals, he grunted. Olwen drew back her arm and hit him hard across the face with an open hand. With a curse, he stumbled and grabbed at his face. "A grunt? That's it? How about an apology?" Olwen demanded.

The man breathed and muttered something uncomplimentary under his breath. "I am sorry about your friend," he said. "But surely you can see why I thought…"

Olwen sighed. "I suppose I can," she admitted after a moment of silence, and trudged around the pool back to Cai's side. She knelt beside him. "Brace yourself," she instructed, and grasped the knife hilt. Cai's eyes rolled upward into his skull and he screamed as she pulled it free. Immediately, Olwen pressed the edge of her cloak over the wound. "Undo his buttons," she instructed Jeilin as she leaned forward to apply pressure. "He'll freeze to death if we don't get him into a dry shirt and coat."

Jeilin's numb fingers flew over Cai's coat buttons, fumbling a couple times. Olwen helped her pull his arms free of the sleeves, and the coat was cast aside. Jeilin used Raihnin's dagger to cut him free of his shirt while Olwen rooted through his gelding's saddlebags in search of another. She returned with one and with some bandages from one of her own bags.

"I have a spare cloak," the man volunteered. "By the way, my name is Mehlren," he added as he joined Olwen and Jeilin, holding Cai's head as the other two worked to wrap bandages across his chest. Jeilin felt a pang of guilt when she caught a glimpse of the fresh scars, still a vivid pink, that striped Cai's back. She was sweating by the time they had finished and bundled him into the dry shirt and cloak.

Mehlren helped Cai to his feet, apologizing. Cai looked too green to reply. "Do you think you can sit in the saddle?" Olwen asked.

"I must," Cai replied.

Jeilin led Fringe by his reins with one hand, and Snow with the other, picking her way through the trees and out of the woods. Mehlren and Olwen supported Cai on either side as they walked toward the road. A handsome sorrel gelding, obviously Mehlren's, stood tied to a branch. How had he managed to sneak up on them so quietly, Jeilin wondered. She frowned. Worrying about Raihnin had made her careless; she'd been too absorbed in her thoughts of him to pay attention to her surroundings.

Together Mehlren and Olwen boosted Cai into the saddle, where he swayed but did not fall.

"Are you riding to the bay?" Olwen asked.

Mehlren nodded. Together, the trio and their mounts continued down the road at a walk.

Hours passed and the day faded into evening. Jeilin guided Fringe with her leg so that she rode close beside Olwen. "What time do you think we'll arrive, at this rate?"

Olwen frowned. "If we rode all night, it'd be nearly morning by the time we reached the bay."

Jeilin tried not to let her face reveal her agony. She longed to break out of the torturous walk, to urge Fringe toward the bay and Raihnin, who could be dying as they crept along.

Olwen sensed her pain anyway. "I know that this is difficult for you," she said. "Time is of the essence...I think it would be best if you took the two messages and rode ahead."

Jeilin's jaw dropped in shock. "I can't just leave you," she protested.

"You need to," Olwen said. "How quickly these messages are delivered could make all the difference for

Alaishin, and it just doesn't make sense for all of us to lag behind. I'll stay with Cai—you go."

Jeilin's heart was racing, and Fringe had begun to step in a more lively fashion, picking up on her excitement, as Olwen turned to address Cai and Mehlren. "I think that Jeilin should ride ahead," she said. "Time is of the essence; all of us continuing at this pace might seal Alaishin's doom." She reached beneath her cloak and handed Jeilin the message that she'd fished from Cai's pocket earlier that day. Jeilin tucked the bloodstained piece of parchment away with the other in her own pocket.

Cai nodded his agreement wordlessly from the saddle, but Mehlren frowned. "If it comes to that," he said. "I really should be riding ahead as well."

"You're responsible for this," Olwen reminded him, motioning toward Cai. "You could give your message to Jeilin and stay to help me with Cai."

"That goes against the creed!" Mehlren declared incredulously.

"This situation is bigger than the creed!" Olwen replied with equal spirit.

Mehlren eyed Jeilin silently, and she felt his eyes linger on her mark. "You can trust her," Olwen said. "She's sacrificed more for Alaishin than you know; that mark is just another sign of that."

Mehlren shook his head. "I'm sorry, I can't," he said, and heeled his mount to a gallop.

Tears welled in Jeilin's eyes, a product of anger and disappointment, threatening to spill over. Olwen muttered something angrily at Mehlren's back, which had all but disappeared in the dusky evening light. "Go, Jeilin," she said.

Jeilin shook her head. "I can't leave you alone to care for Cai."

"The fate of the kingdom depends on it," Olwen replied. "You swore an oath to Alaishin, not to me! We'll make camp in a while—I'll see you tomorrow. Now, go!"

Jeilin reached out and took one of Olwen's hands in her own, squeezing it hard. "Tomorrow," she said. "Goodbye, Olwen, Cai." Fringe exploded into a mile-eating gallop; in a short time, Jeilin had overtaken Mehlren and his sorrel and left them far behind. She rode into the night, praying that Fringe wouldn't stumble as they flew down the road with only a half moon to light their way.

The cold sea winds greeted Jeilin before the city became visible. When she finally saw the many pinpricks of white light in the distance, she wept tears that froze on her cheeks. "Raihnin," she said. She wanted to practice saying it before she saw him, she wanted to be able to say his name without blushing and stumbling over her own words, but no matter how many times she said it, her heart fluttered like a caged bird and the night could hardly hide her pink face. "Raihnin, Raihnin, Raihnin," she chanted as she rode toward the luminous city, willing him to be alive.

The gates were heavily guarded. Jeilin approached cautiously with her hands raised into the air, dreading the moment when the guards would see her face. "I ride for Alaishin!" she declared as she rode forward, her reins abandoned, directing only with her legs. "I carry messages for His Majesty Prince Raihnin!" One of the guards shouted when he caught sight of her face, and several of them surrounded her, spears and swords at the ready. "Please," she said. "I left here for Dresinva carrying Prince Raihnin's message to his father. When I arrived, King Darnasius was dead, and I was captured by Ryeln. My time with them was spent plotting to ride back to the bay with messages stolen from Ryeln. I have them here!" She held the messages high in one fist. One of the guards advanced with a lantern.

"Let's see them," he said cautiously. Jeilin dismounted and unfurled the first message in the lantern light, taking special care to show the seal. The guard seemed to take a lifetime to read it; each second was an agonizing eternity. "And the other," he finally said. Jeilin unfolded the second message hurriedly. "Surrender all of your weapons," he said firmly.

Jeilin scrambled through her saddlebags, finding and handing over the dagger with Alaishin's symbol that she had been given when she had first become a messenger. Then, she unfastened Raihnin's dagger from her belt and relinquished it. The guards' eyebrows shot up their foreheads when they saw Raihnin's ornate weapon. "A gift," Jeilin explained.

"I'll have to ride with you—you won't make it through the doors alive without an escort," one of the guards replied.

"Thank you," Jeilin's knees felt weak as she breathed a sigh of relief. She climbed back into the saddle and waited anxiously as the guard procured a horse and mounted. As soon as he was seated, she urged Fringe through the open gate. The city streets were empty; a cold winter night in the midst of a war didn't encourage people to be out and about after dark. Fringe plunged ahead at Jeilin's urging, and the guard's mount labored to keep pace with him. The roar of crashing waves echoed the froth of thoughts and worries that raged inside Jeilin's mind. By the time the door under the golden star was in sight, she had broken into a nervous sweat despite the icy winds.

She fell when she dismounted, catching herself with her wrist and scraping it on the cobblestones. In her panic, the pain never touched her. The guard struggled to stay on her heels as she handed over Fringe's reins and sprinted for the door. "I bear a message for Prince Raihnin," Jeilin gasped between labored breaths. The guards at the door appeared startled, and the servant absolutely shocked. The guards stood in front of her and prepared to protest, but the one who had accompanied her from the city gates intervened.

"She speaks the truth," he said, also panting.

The guards eyed her warily, but stepped aside.

"I need to see Prince Raihnin!" Jeilin spoke urgently to the servant.

But instead of moving, he just eyed her nervously.

Chapter 14

"Come with me," the servant finally complied. Jeilin breathed a sigh of relief. He was alive. He had to be alive. She followed the attendant anxiously through corridors and up staircases. Each hall seemed another mile, and her breathing was labored as she kept pace with the frail-looking man, who seemed eager to be rid of her. Finally, they arrived at the set of beautifully carved oaken doors that Jeilin recognized. Raihnin's bedchamber. She was finally here again, after all of her dreaming and hoping… Her heart seemed ready to pound out of her chest as she stood before the doors, and the servant knocked. "A royal messenger has come swiftly to deliver a letter to His Highness Prince Raihnin," the servant announced.

A feeling of surrealism overcame Jeilin as she stepped inside the room. She lost her breath when she saw Raihnin, lying propped in bed with a bandaged shoulder. His voice seemed a favorite song she had been waiting ages to hear when he spoke. "Let the royal messenger deliver the letter she has been charged with," he said. "And let everyone else leave." Several servants and a woman who might have been a nurse swept around Jeilin and out of the room in a quiet rush. Jeilin walked slowly to his bedside on unsteady legs and fell to her knees. Extending her hand, which held both of the letters, she said; "Letters for His Majesty Prince Raihnin's use, taken from Ryeln."

Electricity seemed to shoot down Jeilin's arm when Raihnin's fingers brushed hers. "You may rise," he said after he'd taken the letters; but he never gave her a chance to. His hand cradled her head, and his fingers entwined in her hair as he drew her closer to the edge of his bed.

Jeilin leaned on the edge of his bed. "What happened to you?"

"I was struck by an arrow and fell from my horse. Other than the arrow wound, it's only bumps and bruises. I'll be fine. And you—what happened after I sent you away." Jeilin thought that she detected guilt in Raihnin's voice as he finished the question.

"Olwen and I rode to Dresinva without incident," she began. "We were halfway through the gates by the time we realized that the city had been taken. It was too late then— we were captured. They let us choose between joining Ryeln or death. Olwen and I chose Ryeln, but we intended all along to help Alaishin."

Raihnin reached out and traced the tattoo across Jeilin's cheek with his finger. "Everyone—all of the soldiers and messengers—who serve Ryeln bear the mark," she explained. He studied her face in silence. Jeilin frowned. "I know it's terrible," she finally said. "I don't expect you to think…that I'm beautiful anymore." Jeilin fought hard to keep tears from welling in her eyes again and hoped that

Raihnin wouldn't notice. She tried to be reasonable, diplomatic, as if the thought of Raihnin losing interest in her didn't break her heart.

"Of course you're still beautiful," he said.

"What are you talking about?" Jeilin demanded, hiding the mark with her hand. "This mark, it's—"

"It shows how brave you are," Raihnin said, taking her hand and gently pulling it away. "And that makes you more beautiful."

Jeilin was too shocked to speak. Raihnin didn't let go of her hand. "Tell me about what happened in Dresinva," he said softly, continuing to hold her hand.

"A general named Mhin, the one who wrote the letters I brought you…" she began. Their conversation was interrupted only once when Raihnin summoned servants to carry to his generals the messages Jeilin had brought him; otherwise, they talked all night.

****

"I suppose you'd better get some rest," Raihnin said when the sun broke over the horizon, splintering the darkness with streaks of orange light.

"What about you?" Jeilin asked.

"I need to discuss things with my generals," he replied, pushing himself up and out of his bed with a grimace. Jeilin frowned; there were dark circles under his eyes, and it was obvious that the movement caused him pain. "I'll have a chambermaid show you to a room and the baths, if you'd like." Before she knew it, Jeilin was being ushered down the halls while Raihnin left in the opposite direction.

Jeilin finally had a chance to mull over her night with Raihnin when she settled into a bath, breathing a sigh of relief as the hot water washed over her tired muscles. Suds streamed down her arm and to her elbow, dripping onto the water's surface as she traced her cheek with her own hand. Raihnin still thought that she was beautiful. Jeilin pushed aside bubbles that had gathered atop the bathwater to peer down at her reflection in wonder. Beautiful? She touched her face again. It seemed almost like a dream. Blushing as she remembered how Raihnin had touched her face and held her hand, Jeilin set to work on scrubbing the dirt and stiffness of travel out of her hair. By the time she had finished and donned a clean set of clothing, she couldn't help but feel more prepared to meet Raihnin again. She combed her hair carefully, allowing it to hang straight and loose, as she wondered when their next meeting might be. She was still wondering when she lay down, grateful for the first bed she'd slept in in quite a while.

The sun had climbed high into the sky by the time she woke. Olwen! she thought, throwing her blankets aside. She ran a comb hastily through her hair as she glanced around the room for signs of her friend's arrival. Everything seemed just as it had been when she'd fallen asleep, and no books had been left on her bedside table. She dressed quickly and stepped out into the corridor, just in time to find a serving woman bustling down the hall with an armful of linens. "Excuse me," Jeilin said. "But has another woman messenger arrived today?" The woman gave a little squeak of surprise, and adjusted her stack of linens as she peered over them with wide eyes. "A woman with a mark like this," Jeilin added, motioning toward her face.

"No mistress," the woman replied. "Not to my knowledge, and I'm sure I'd have remembered that." The woman hurried down the hall, gripping her burden in one arm and using her free hand to lift her skirts so that she wouldn't trip. Jeilin frowned in disappointment. It was already afternoon, and she had expected Olwen and Cai to arrive by late morning. She ambled down the corridor, absorbed in worries and thinking vaguely of visiting Fringe in the stables, where she would be sure to know as soon as Olwen and Cai arrived.

Jeilin realized that she had neared the kitchen when the delicious scents of soup, freshly baked bread and a myriad of other dishes drifted toward her, causing her to realize how hungry she was. When had she last eaten? Sometime during the journey when she, Olwen, and Cai had still been together, she remembered. Sighing with concern over the thought of the pair, she slipped into the kitchens. She wound her way through a large room filled with wooden tables where a few people, mostly servants, were enjoying meals. "Excuse me," Jeilin said as she approached a round, matronly cook who was stooped over a large pot that smelled of something delicious. The cook turned slowly, a jar of spices in hand.

"Oh!" she exclaimed when she saw Jeilin, giving a little start. The corners of Jeilin's mouth pulled down against her will. She would have to get used to approaching people more subtly, she decided. By the time Jeilin politely requested something to eat, the woman had begun to eye her with a decidedly different expression. The sort of expression one would expect to see on a cat, Jeilin thought; an expression that said she knew the beginning of a secret, and was curious to know the rest. "Of course, dear," the cook said.

A minute later the woman presented her with a bowl of stew and a plate of crumbly cheese and thick bread. Jeilin thanked her, took the bowl, and couldn't help but notice that the woman watched her turn away with a raised eyebrow. What was that supposed to mean, she wondered as she left the steamy kitchen and found a seat at an empty table.

Although she made it a point as she stared down at her food not to make eye contact with anyone, Jeilin also couldn't help but notice that many of the other diners were eyeing her with interest as well. Some with a hint of fear too. Jeilin sighed. She had never imagined that anyone would find her frightening. But then, she had never really imagined that a prince would find her beautiful, either. Nor brave, she thought as she remembered her most recent conversations with Raihnin and Ehryn.

A group of serving girls that had gathered around one of the tables in a corner of the dining room giggled when Jeilin rose. She left, too absorbed in daydreams involving Raihnin and nightmares concerning Olwen and Cai to wonder much about it. She jumped when she turned a corner and nearly collided with a man in livery. He appeared equally alarmed.

"Pardon me, mistress Jeilin," he said, dabbing at his brow with a handkerchief as if he had been walking as quickly as possible, if not actually running, through the corridors. "His Highness Prince Raihnin has sent me to deliver a message to you."

"What is it?" Jeilin asked as her heart suddenly began to beat faster.

"He wishes you to dine with him this evening at six," the attendant replied. "If it pleases you, I'll meet you at your room at a quarter till to escort you."

Jeilin nodded. "That will be fine."

"Very well, just before six," the man replied, as he bowed and headed back down the corridor.

Jeilin continued down the hall, feeling a little guilty over her full stomach. Olwen and Cai might still be out there, eating cold lumps of hardened bread and cheese.

Wishing she had worn a cloak, Jeilin stepped outdoors into the icy winds. She crossed a courtyard briskly, hurrying toward the stables. She breathed a sigh of relief as she stepped inside, where heat from the bodies of men and horses warmed the air. A quick walk up the aisle of stalls revealed Fringe, who peered at Jeilin over a mouthful of hay. She lifted the latch of his stall door and slipped inside. He nuzzled her with his soft, pink-striped nose as she slipped her hands beneath his blanket, pressing them against his warm body. "I don't suppose you've seen your friend Snow?" Jeilin asked. Fringe peered back at her with dark, bright eyes and ripped away another mouthful of hay. "I suppose you haven't," Jeilin said with a sigh.

"Do you need him saddled, miss?" a young groom asked, peering anxiously over the stall door, apparently afraid that he had delayed Jeilin's departure by missing her when she first arrived.

"No, I'm only visiting," Jeilin replied. The groom looked relieved. "Tell me, though," Jeilin said. "Have you seen a woman on a white mare arrive lately with a fair-haired young man on a bay gelding?"

The groom shook his head. "No, but I've only just come back from my meal."

Jeilin felt a tiny surge of hope. "I'll look myself then," she said, stepping out into the aisle, closing and latching the door behind herself. She strode down the aisle, inspecting each horse as she passed. Once she came upon a white horse, but its neck was too arched, and it was a bit too tall...a stallion. There were many bays, but Jeilin remembered that Cai's had a Roman nose. She turned and walked the other way, checking the horses on the other side. She left the stable with a hollow feeling in her stomach, despite her recent meal. She paused to scan the castle yard before returning indoors; there was no sign of a woman on a white horse, or her companion. Jeilin glanced at the sun—the servant would be waiting outside her quarters soon. She stepped into the comparative warmth of the castle halls and hurried to her room.

Once inside, she sat in front of the mirror that hung on one of the walls and picked up her silver comb. She re-placed it on a stand when she was sure that her hair was perfectly smooth. Then, she surveyed her reflection. Her eyes were as large as she had remembered them. Her fair face looked strange to her, surrounded by her almost black hair. She still hadn't grown used to the mark, which cut across her cheek and drew her eye, making it difficult to focus on her other features. She had her mother's small nose, she realized. What would her mother think if she knew what seemed to be growing between her and Raihnin? She laughed aloud at the thought. No doubt she would stuff her into a fancy dress and drag them both to an altar herself. Jeilin laughed again. Marriage—to a prince no less? She was being foolish. She picked up her silver comb again and gave her hair one last run-through just as a knock came at the door.

Jeilin jumped up, nearly overturning the carved wooden chair she had been sitting in. She smoothed her best breeches and shirt, took one last look at the mirror, and answered the door.

The same attendant she'd encountered in the hall was waiting. "I'll show you the way, if you please," he said with a dignified bow. Jeilin followed him through a maze of halls and up a flight of stairs, trying unsuccessfully not to feel nervous. The room that the servant led her to was the same one that she had first shared breakfast with Raihnin in, the one with the balcony that gave a scenic view. Jeilin could see snowflakes falling beyond its railing. With a pang of guilt, she imagined Olwen and Cai out in the snow somewhere, hopefully alive.

"Jeilin," Raihnin said as soon as the servant had departed, leaving them alone. His hand cradled her head again but

225

this time he leaned forward and pressed his lips to hers. There were so many feelings rushing through her, she couldn't help but stand frozen. "What's wrong?" he asked when the kiss ended, his face troubled as he studied hers. "I'm sorry," he said. "I shouldn't have—"

"No," Jeilin said. "It's not that. That was…wonderful. It's Olwen and Cai. They still haven't returned, and I…"

Raihnin frowned. "Jeilin," he said, guiding her to a chair at a table that was loaded with beautiful dishes and platters displaying a variety of delicious smelling foods. "I've recently received some bad news."

Jeilin's heart leapt in fear, and then seemed to stop. "What is it?" she asked.

"A band of Ryelnish soldiers is marching toward the Bay of Lights, along the road that you traveled yesterday." Jeilin gripped the edge of the table. "I'm sorry," Raihnin added.

"I—I didn't realize that there were any so close," Jeilin said. "After reading the messages, I thought…"

"They're what's left of General Shi's men, the ones we fought a few days ago. They're moving faster than we expected them to."

"They must be very close to the bay, then."

"They are. We're riding out to meet them tomorrow morning. We think it will be a couple of days before the rest of the Ryelnish battalions who are coming arrive—our plan is to crush the rest of Shi's men before the rest arrive, so that we reduce their numbers."

"We ride out tomorrow morning?" Jeilin asked.

Raihnin covered her hand with his. "Not you, of course," he said. "But a battalion of our soldiers, General Mara, and I—"

"What?" Jeilin interrupted. "You'll need messengers!"

"Yes," Raihnin said. "But I'll take others. You've done quite enough for Alaishin—for me—already."

Jeilin jumped to her feet. "I want to come!"

"Jeilin," Raihnin protested.

"I won't stay here," Jeilin said. "Ever since I left for Dresinva I've been going mad wondering what was happening to you and if you were safe. And now you're going to ride off to war again, still bleeding from the last battle! I won't wait here alone and go through that again. I can't. Whatever happens, I want to be there."

Raihnin sighed. "I felt the same way, and had the same worries about you. I would feel better if I knew you were safe here."

"I won't be safe here if you lose, Raihnin."

He sighed. "All right," he finally said. "You can ride with us, but you must promise to obey me."

"Of course," Jeilin said. "I've already sworn to obey you."

"No matter what," Raihnin said firmly.

"No matter what," Jeilin repeated.

Raihnin stepped closer to her with a sigh and wrapped his arm around her waist again. "Now," he said. "Let's try not to think of all that is happening and enjoy this evening together." He pulled her into an embrace where his lips paused above hers. This time, she fully leaned into him, and

227

he kissed her gently before releasing her to take his place across from her at the table.

Jeilin tasted from the bowl of soup that sat in front of her. She could tell that it would have been delicious any other time, but nerves and her already full stomach dulled her taste buds. "Is something the matter?" Raihnin asked.

"Well, to tell the truth," Jeilin said, resting her spoon beside her bowl. "I ate a short while ago, right before your attendant found me and extended your dinner invitation."

Raihnin grinned across the table from her. "So did I," he admitted. "But I thought that dinner would be the perfect excuse to steal some time alone with you." Jeilin blushed. "Let's just skip straight to dessert," Raihnin suggested. He pushed aside his soup bowl and Jeilin imitated him as he lifted the lid off of a silver tray, revealing an artfully iced cake. He carefully cut her a slice and slid the plate across the wooden surface of the table before taking one for himself.

The cake was sweet and moist. "Raihnin..." Jeilin said.

"Yes?" he replied.

"This could be our last evening together," she said.

He laid his fork down by his plate and stared across the table at her. "It could," he said levelly.

Jeilin hesitated. "I want to know," she finally said. "Why. Why me?"

"What?" Raihnin asked.

"I don't understand why you're so fond of me." Jeilin said, trying to maintain eye contact.

Raihnin frowned. "What do you mean? I told you, you're the most beautiful woman I've ever seen."

Jeilin frowned too. "That's difficult for me to believe."

Raihnin pushed away his chair and stood. "Well it shouldn't be." He strode around the table to her. "Surely you know."

"Know what?"

"How beautiful you are."

"No." Jeilin shook her head.

"I can't believe that no one's ever told you," Raihnin said, stroking her face.

"Even if I was," Jeilin said. "You're a prince—well, you'll be a king now. I'm just a farmer's daughter who won a race."

"And why does that matter?" Raihnin asked.

"Well, I'm not…" Jeilin paused as she searched for the right words.

"Not what?" Raihnin asked. "You're brave and loyal," he said. "In fact, you don't seem to be afraid of anything. I don't know many women who I can say that about. And you're more beautiful than any princess."

Jeilin stared back at Raihnin in wonder. "But my face," she said. "No princess would ever have this face."

"Perhaps not," Raihnin said, leaning closer to her. "But a queen might."

Jeilin gasped.

"I don't want to hear any more about the mark," Raihnin said. "I've already told you that it only makes you more beautiful. Every time I see it I think about what you've endured for me, and I love you more."

Jeilin pressed her face against Raihnin's good shoulder. She couldn't bring herself to look him in the eye anymore, but she knew how she felt too. "I love you, Raihnin," she whispered, and for once his name didn't seem so strange on her lips. She could feel him smile as he kissed her. The uneaten cake and full glasses of wine sat on the table, forgotten.

****

Jeilin awoke before dawn the next morning, as she always did. She lay still for a moment with her eyes closed, remembering a wonderful dream. No, it wasn't a dream, she thought; it only seemed like one. Then she remembered what the day had in store, and she leapt out of bed, dressing quickly. She slipped into her boots and ran her silver comb quickly through her hair before tucking it into a leather bag with the rest of her belongings. She was relieved to see that her two daggers laid returned on her bedside stand. She packed one away, while the other—the one Raihnin had given her—she fastened to her belt. Jeilin slung the bag over her shoulder and hurried out of the room, stopping only to grab a piece of bread for breakfast as she hurried to the stables.

Jeilin allowed a groom to saddle Fringe for her as she walked quickly down the long row of stalls and back. Still no sign of Snow or, as far as she could tell, Cai's bay. She tried not to think of Olwen and Cai laying cold and dead in the snow somewhere as she led Fringe out of the stable and swung into the saddle. She could see large formations of men waiting neatly on the snow-dusted lawn while others, some on foot and some on horseback, darted to and fro, counting, double-checking, and shouting commands. She could see a tall figure sitting impressively atop a grey warhorse—Raihnin.

She rode to him. He smiled when she brought Fringe to a stop beside his horse. "Good morning," he said. Jeilin smiled back. "We're almost ready to march," Raihnin said. "My officers are attending to a few last-minute preparations." The sun began to rise, casting a glow over the horizon.

Jeilin rode at the front of the battalion, beside Raihnin as they marched out of the city and began their journey. A group of seasoned soldiers rode in a cluster around the prince, their sharp eyes scanning the landscape for any sign of danger. Cruelly cold winds gusted off of the sea and caused the banners and flags to snap loudly. Jeilin drew her cloak closer around her body. "You must ride back with the other messengers when I say so," Raihnin said, casting a sharp look in her direction.

"I will," she promised.

They rode on, limiting their horses to a steady walk that the men on foot could keep up with. "How many Ryelnish soldiers will there be?" Jeilin asked.

"Half our number," Raihnin replied. "And some of those wounded."

Jeilin reached out to touch Raihnin's shoulder, her fingers brushing chain mail that was as cold as the air that blew off of the ocean. "You will be careful, won't you?" she asked.

"I won't take any unnecessary risks," Raihnin replied.

Jeilin didn't stop frowning. What did that mean? She didn't even think that it was necessary for Raihnin to go with the battalion to meet the Ryelnish soldiers that morning, but there they were, and she realized just how brave Raihnin truly was.

Suddenly, a horn sounded with a single urgent note that cut through the cold wind. The men behind Jeilin roared. "Ride back with the other messengers!" Raihnin said sharply. Jeilin lingered for half a moment, admiring the face of the man she loved before turning Fringe and heeling him toward the back of the formation. There she found her place with the other messengers and rode in the human circle that soldiers had created around them. Leaning forward in the saddle, she could see the silhouettes of the enemy beginning to take shape on the horizon.

Chapter 15

The very air that surrounded Jeilin and the Alaishinian troops seemed to thicken as they moved forward, and it was soon filled with a black rain of arrows that streaked over the gap between the two armies. Jeilin saw men fall on the frontlines of both sides, while others deflected the arrows with their shields. She prayed that Raihnin had been among the latter. She found herself breathing a little faster as Fringe picked up on the mood and began to dance. The open field between the two armies seemed to take both a very long time and a very short time to close, and then everything was chaos. The men on the frontlines of either side clashed with a roar and the sounds of many weapons meeting. Jeilin began to sweat as she worked to keep Fringe under control. The subtle flexing of leg muscles and pulling of reins surrounded her as many of the other messengers did the same. The ring of soldiers around them remained, alert and poised to fight.

Jeilin lost sight of Raihnin in the mass of men that danced and fought and fell before her. She watched nervously as the two armies melded together into one violent mass. The horned helmet worn by many of the Ryelnish soldiers was the only distinguishing feature that Jeilin could recognize in all of the confusion, save for when she caught sight of a soldier's face long enough to see or miss Ryeln's mark. Horses screamed, collapsed, and struggled to rise again, often losing their riders. Jeilin stiffened in the saddle as she remembered that Raihnin had been one of those lost riders in the last battle; she hoped desperately that he would not be one again. Jeilin rocked in the saddle as another horse stumbled and collided with Fringe's hindquarters. The sound of steel on steel rung in her ears. She wasn't sure how long the battle had been raging when she suddenly realized that it was surrounding her.

The two sides became obvious again to Jeilin, and she could see the tattoos on the faces of several men who were cutting through the Alaishinian ranks with deadly fury. She thought she saw a spark of surprise in the eyes of one Ryelnish soldier when his gaze fell upon her face, but all expression died when an Alaishinian man ran him through with his sword. The ring of soldiers around the messengers was still intact, but Jeilin couldn't help but feel nervous as a group of Ryelnish troops attacked those who were protecting her. Fringe tossed his head, and she shifted nervously in the saddle, gripping the dagger she wore at her belt.

It was a relief when the last of the tattooed men who'd tried to break the circle was cut down. When he was, Jeilin realized that the battlefield seemed to have quieted. The ground was dark with bodies, and Jeilin uttered a prayer of thanks each time she saw the familiar mark, relieved that she hadn't found Raihnin among the casualties. Sickening waves of worry ebbed and flowed, wrestling for dominance with brief sensations of morbid relief as Jeilin continued to scan the battlefield. Steel still clashed as the battle subsided, and Jeilin began to wonder again about Olwen and Cai as the threat of immediate danger seemed to lessen. Had they been captured by the Ryelnish army as they marched toward the bay? Were they alive, and if so were they being held captive somewhere just out of sight? The urge to know overtook her.

Jeilin steeled herself and squeezed Fringe's sides. He charged forward, anxious to move, breaking out of the circle. Jeilin heard cries from behind that she thought might be directed at her, but she rode on, directing Fringe to skirt around the edge of the battle, circling it as she moved toward the enemy's side, praying that the tattoo on her face would prove to be good for something. Her hair whipped in the breeze as she rode, and she hoped that it would give any Alaishinian men who might mistake her for one of the enemy pause before they struck at her. Once, an arrow flew close enough by her that she heard it as it sped past. She hoped that it hadn't been aimed for her, and rejoiced at her good luck if it had.

Her luck seemed to hold out as she galloped past those Ryelnish men who were still standing; no one attempted to stop her and none of their blades flashed in her direction. Relief and a desperate sense of urgency surged through Jeilin as she finally slowed Fringe's gait. She'd made it—she'd circled around and ended behind most of the Ryelnish troops. Some of them looked her way, but most didn't look long once they'd seen her face. She paced Fringe to and fro, scanning for any sign of prisoners.

She halted Fringe when something promising caught her eye: a string of people kneeling side to side, apparently bound together by rope that secured their wrists and ankles. Her heart leapt when she saw a woman's head of long, brown hair, and beside her, a captive with a shock of fair hair. Half a dozen other people, all men of varying ages, knelt at either side of the pair, and Jeilin scarcely had time to wonder who they were or why they were there. She urged Fringe in their direction, and, at the same time, a Ryelnish soldier approached the string of prisoners on foot. Jeilin's heart beat faster when she saw that he wielded a cruel-looking dagger with a curved blade that reflected the sun, which had climbed higher and higher into the sky as the battle raged. She recoiled in shock as the soldier seized the first prisoner by his hair, yanked his head back, and unceremoniously slit his throat. He relinquished his hold on the dying man's curls as blood sprayed in an arc on the grass and began to flow onto his shirt, staining and soaking it deep red.

The other prisoners began to stir, struggling against their bonds and protesting. Olwen shook aside her hair, revealing her face. Jeilin flinched—Olwen's face was bruised, and she didn't look well. There were dark circles under her eyes, and she must have been cold, for she wore no coat or cloak. The second man screamed as the soldier seized him by the hair. A sickening realization struck Jeilin: the Ryelnish were losing badly and didn't want their prisoners to survive them. Blood poured from the gaping slash in the second man's throat and only one man remained between him and Olwen. "Stop!" Jeilin cried.

The soldier stood and turned at a greater speed than Jeilin would have thought a man his size would have been capable of. He was large and muscled, with a hard face and long black mustaches. She watched as his eyes scanned her face and his dark brows plunged, carving angry furrows into his forehead. Jeilin steeled herself and tried to sound as calm and authoritative as possible. "General Shi wishes to see to these prisoners himself," she said. "By killing them you are incurring his anger." The man paused and twirled his dagger. Jeilin labored to breathe evenly, grateful that she had remembered the general's name from the letters, and hoping that the soldier would believe that he had sent her.

"I am General Shi," the man said.

The winter air seemed to freeze in Jeilin's lungs, and she felt just as frozen in the saddle as General Shi advanced toward her.

"Jeilin!" a voice cried, and she twisted in the saddle in the direction of the battlefield.

"Raihnin!" she gasped, stunned to see him pulling his mount to a stop beside her. Sweat had dampened the grey warhorse's flanks, and the animal's nostrils flared pink as it gulped air. Other than a few nicks, both horse and rider appeared unharmed, if worn.

The sleek sound of metal sliding against metal brought Jeilin to her senses again. General Shi had unsheathed his sworn and had wasted no time in approaching Raihnin. Jeilin watched in horror as Raihnin brandished his own. Shi darted forward and swung at the horse's legs with a skilled blade stroke. The animal reared, evaded the blade, and screamed as it lashed out with sharp, steel-shod hooves and shook its dark mane. The horse came down with his teeth flashing, and General Shi grunted as one of the stallion's feet clipped his shoulder, momentarily throwing him off balance. Raihnin seized the opportunity and swung deftly, his blade cleaving into Shi's neck. The general crumpled to the ground.

Jeilin dismounted and swallowed the bile that rose in her throat, scrambling toward the prisoners with her own dagger in hand. Except for Olwen and Cai, who appeared too shocked to speak, they all wrestled against their bonds and cried out when they saw her. Jeilin ignored the others and knelt first behind Olwen. She inflicted a minor cut on her wrist as she cut her bonds, but Olwen showed no sign of pain, only relief and gratitude. She embraced Jeilin, but only for a moment, before Jeilin set to work on the rope that bound Cai. Then she set to work on the others. She was freeing the last prisoner, a man in his middle years who still appeared terrified, when she heard something that nearly stopped her heart.

"Raihnin!" she screamed, for she had heard him cry out in pain. A Ryelnish soldier wielding a sword had appeared beside Raihnin's horse, and a cruel leer twisted his tattooed face. Jeilin noted with horror that the tip of the soldier's sword was red and gleaming. Raihnin reeled in the saddle, his face blood covered. The soldier raised his sword again, but was cut down quickly by the first in a group of

Alaishinian men Jeilin recognized as those who had ridden with Raihnin at the front of the battalion.

Raihnin, bleeding onto his neck and armor and horse, was like a scene from a nightmare. The body-strewn battlefield seemed like a fitting backdrop; here and there skirmishes were concluding and most of the Ryelnish lay dead. One of Raihnin's men took his horse's reins while two others lifted the prince from the saddle and eased him to the ground. Jeilin tossed Fringe's reins to Olwen and scrambled to his side. One of the men called loudly across the field, waving his arms as Jeilin knelt and forced her fingers between Raihnin's dark locks and the cold ground, cradling his head. Blood poured over his cheeks and ears, wetting Jeilin's hands and staining her sleeves.

"Hold his head steady," said a man with a leather pouch tucked under his arm as he settled to the ground beside Jeilin. He opened his bag and began sorting rapidly through the contents with an air of experience. A large hand thrust through the circle of people who had gathered to surround Raihnin, offering a rag that looked to have once been someone's shirt. One of the soldiers seized it and began dabbing Raihnin's face with it, mopping up blood, as the man with the pouch held a needle up to the sun and forced a thread through its eye. Jeilin saw Raihnin's eyelids flutter, but the blood that had seeped into his eyes clouded them, reddening their whites.

The rag was tossed aside, blood soaked, revealing a long gash that cut diagonally across Raihnin's face, from beneath his right eye to the corner of his mouth, where it cut across the edge of his lips and down into his chin. For an instant, the whiteness of bone was visible before the wound began to seep more blood. The laceration had already filled with it, like a trough, by the time the needle made its first insertion. The man pushed it through Raihnin's flesh, bridging the gap with thread and piercing again, then pulling it tight. Raihnin groaned and shuddered as the man repeated the motion. The last thing Jeilin saw was the thread pulling Raihnin's flesh together, forcing it to meet, and then she knew nothing.

****

The first thought that Jeilin had upon waking was that she must have overslept, for her room was flooded with bright sunlight. The second was that she was lying on her back on a battlefield, staring up toward the afternoon sun. "Raihnin!" she said, pushing herself upright.

A pair of hands pressed against her shoulders, restraining her. "Wait," Olwen said. "They're finishing the stitching—I think you should wait until it's done."

Jeilin could see the group of men, still gathered around Raihnin, a few yards to her left. Someone else held his head now, a soldier with a long reddish beard and a scrape across his forehead. She caught a glimpse of the needle flashing in the sunlight through a gap between the soldiers' arms, and shuddered, nodding weakly. Olwen embraced her.

"Thank you for rescuing us," she said. "Thank you."

"Yes, thank you," Cai said, appearing behind Olwen. "I owe you my life."

Jeilin sighed. "I was afraid that you both were dead," she said. "I was so glad when I saw you both alive…and so scared."

"You were brave," Olwen said.

Jeilin shook her head. "I was shaking inside," she said, and then added, "Raihnin's the brave one, riding across the enemy's side without a mark to hide behind." She bit her lip, blinking back tears. "I'm afraid I'm responsible for this," she said, waving a hand at Raihnin and the men who surrounded him.

Olwen squeezed her hand. "Don't think that way," she said. "A battle is a battle…injuries happen, and after all, he's still alive."

The group around Raihnin began to disband as the man with the leather bag tucked away his needle. The prince lay still, as pale as the snow that clung to the ground in small patches here and there. Jeilin rushed to him. His skin was cold to the touch, but Jeilin pressed her hand to his neck and felt the steady beat of his pulse. Blood was drying around his wound, a long line of mounded flesh bound by black thread. It pulled the right corner of his mouth into a half-frown. The tears that Jeilin had been struggling to suppress leaked silently from her eyes, trickling down her cheeks as the winter air chilled them. "We'll have to fashion a stretcher," Jeilin heard one of the men say from behind her. Jeilin wound her fingers in Raihnin's hair, pressing her hands against his skull, and stayed there while it was prepared.

A short while later, two men lifted Raihnin carefully onto a stretcher, and another two carried it between them. Jeilin remounted Fringe reluctantly and rode as closely beside him as she could, removing her gaze from Raihnin's face for only moments at a time, and only to give Fringe the most basic directions she could get by with. Olwen, Cai, and a handful of Alaishinian soldiers followed on foot, picking their way over the corpses that were the only remnant of General Shi's troops.

Halfway across the battlefield, Olwen gasped. Jeilin turned in the saddle and saw her mentor staring down at one of the many fallen horses. The one that had caused Olwen to pause was white, with dainty legs and a delicate face. Snow. An arrow protruded from Snow's chest, and her dark eyes stared sightlessly up at the afternoon sun. Beside her a rider—a Ryelnish soldier—lay, also pierced by arrows. Olwen knelt and unsheathed her dagger. Jeilin watched as she cut away a long lock of pale hair from her horse's mane and tucked it away into her clothing. Jeilin had never seen Olwen cry, but she looked closer to doing so than she ever had as she turned sadly away from her dead mare. Jeilin stroked her own mount's neck, feeling grateful that he had sustained no harm during her exploits.

Cai frowned too. Where was his horse, the bay gelding with the Roman nose, Jeilin wondered. Was it too among the many horses that lay dead on the battlefield, their legs bent at impossible angles?

The battalion marched back toward the city, victorious but grim. Jeilin worried constantly that the blankets that had been layered over Raihnin—mostly taken from under the saddles of the battle's equestrian casualties—would not be enough protection against the Daiymihr Ocean's cruel gusts. Several times she thought she saw him shiver, but whether he really had or whether his carriers had simply hit a bump in the road, she couldn't be sure. When they finally reached the city and the castle under the dusky sky, Jeilin couldn't have been more relieved.

Jeilin followed the men who carried Raihnin to his quarters, ready to fight anyone who might try to stop her or send her away. An assortment of soldiers, servants, and nurses hurried to settle the still sleeping prince into his bed, and to Jeilin's relief, none of them questioned the necessity of her presence.

A physician was summoned to examine the wound and Raihnin's condition, and he stood at the edge of the bed speaking with Raihnin's nurses and his younger sister, the Princess Elin, who had been waiting anxiously when the war party returned. The physician spoke of blood loss, and of possible infections and the fevers that might accompany the wound. The nurses nodded grimly as the physician gave instructions on caring for Raihnin while the princess listened sadly. Princess Elin swept after the physician and the nurses after the conversation ended, but she paused at the oaken doors to meet eyes with Jeilin. Jeilin thought that she saw curiosity and perhaps even sympathy in her eyes, and then she was gone. At last, Jeilin was alone with Raihnin.

She knelt at the side of his bed as she had only two nights ago—it seemed a very long time ago. She studied his face for what seemed the thousandth time since the battle, still struggling with the way that it looked sad. She reached under the blankets and took his hand. It felt colder than it should have, despite the layers of linens and quilts and the fire blazing in the grate. Evening had passed well into night, and Jeilin's knees were aching by the time Raihnin's eyes finally fluttered open. He turned to see who was holding his hand, and as he saw Jeilin, she realized that despite the wound, his face could still express a sense of happiness.

Chapter 16

"Y ou're safe." As Raihnin spoke, Jeilin could see that doing so caused him obvious difficulty and pain; the stitches that held the wound on the right side of his face together also held the right corner of his mouth shut, and moving his jaw tugged at them, causing little beads of fresh blood to appear at the seams.

"I'm sorry," Jeilin said. "I didn't know that you'd followed me. I'm the one to blame for this."

Raihnin shook his head slightly. "Do I still have your love?"

Jeilin smiled. "Of course."

More droplets pooled at the stitches as he tried briefly to smile, trickling down his cheek, staining his pillow. "I'd follow you a thousand times again if I could," he said. "What's a wound compared to losing you? It's nothing."

"You have to stop talking," Jeilin said. "You're hurting yourself."

He squeezed her hand. She leaned forward and, very carefully, kissed the unhurt side of his face.

****

"I think he'll recover as long as the wound doesn't become infected," Jeilin said the next morning at breakfast. Olwen and Cai sat across from her at one of the wooden tables in the dining hall by the kitchens. Their faces were still bruised, but the dark circles were gone from beneath their eyes. Jeilin had eventually retired to her own room the night before after Raihnin had woken, leaving him in the care of the physician and the nurses.

"That's a relief," Olwen said with a smile. Cai nodded his agreement.

"What about the war?" Jeilin asked. "I mean, the next battle, with General Mhin's troops and all of the rest. Have you heard any news?"

Olwen set her glass down on the table, and Jeilin noticed for the first time that she wore a band of white, braided hair around her wrist. "Well, nothing really official," Olwen replied. "But there's been a lot of talk going around. Rumor has it that the Ryelnish troops are getting close…very close."

"A battle is expected within the next couple days," Cai said.

****

It was scarcely past midday by the time Jeilin slipped back into Raihnin's room, but she had been longing to return since she had last left. It seemed to her as if days had passed. To her surprise, she found Raihnin sitting upright against a stack of pillows, listening to a report from an officer. She attempted to back quietly through the door she had just entered, but Raihnin had already noticed her. He dismissed the officer curtly, promising to resume the conversation later.

"I stayed away as long as I could," Jeilin said. "Because the physician said that you needed rest. And here you are behaving as if nothing happened." She frowned.

"I have to," Raihnin replied. "Ryeln is approaching. The war is nearly upon us." Jeilin was relieved to see that his wound remained dry as he spoke, though she could still see that it pained him. "I'd been wondering what took you so long to return," he added.

Jeilin crossed the room and embraced him. "Do you know when we'll ride out?"

"The day after tomorrow," he replied.

"How is your wound," Jeilin asked after enjoying the embrace for a few moments. "Does it hurt badly?"

"It is painful," he admitted. "But it will heal. In the end it will look worse than it feels." Jeilin wrapped her arms more tightly around his neck. "Does that bother you?" Raihnin asked.

"Does what bother me?" Jeilin replied.

"The wound. The way I look now."

"No," she said, and meant it.

"Then you won't ever worry again about your mark? Since when people see us together in the future, they'll pity you—a stunning beauty with such an ugly husband." He attempted to smile playfully, but the stitches prevented it.

Husband? Jeilin could hardly believe what she had heard—her heart leapt. "Not ugly," she corrected him. "Handsome and brave."

"So are you," he said.

Raihnin leaned down and Jeilin tilted back her head so that their lips met. They barely brushed, but Jeilin felt weak as Raihnin tightened his arms around her waist so that she was pressed against his chest. "Promise me something," he said.

"What?"

"Promise me that you really will obey me and won't run off again during the battle."

"I will."

"Good," he said. "I couldn't bear to lose you because you decided to do something heroic again."

****

The days left before the war with Ryeln seemed to evaporate like drops of water thrown onto a hot pan. The entire castle buzzed with activity, nerves, and excitement on the morning of the battle as the troops prepared to march. Raihnin sat tall on his proud grey warhorse again, between two of his generals. Jeilin was beside him on Fringe, and Olwen and Cai were there too; Olwen on a sleek black mount borrowed from the royal stables, and Cai on a handsome sorrel. Before them, thousands of troops stood ready to march into battle.

They were still outnumbered, though; Raihnin and his generals estimated that they would be facing twice their number in Ryelnish troops. Strategies had been laid with the help of the messages Jeilin had carried—they knew that Ryelnish troops would be attacking from the south and the east, so they planned to have one battalion march north and around to flank the Ryelnish that would come from the east. The rest of Alaishin's troops would stay to defend the city from the south and the east, and Raihnin would remain with those who would defend the city. She hoped desperately that the plans would be enough to save the bay, and ultimately Alaishin.

The first battalion had already marched northward as Jeilin rode forward with Raihnin to the fields outside of the city. She prayed that they would be successful as she watched from behind the thousands of troops who waited for the enemy to appear in the distance. Raihnin's fingers brushed the back of her hand. "Remember," he said. "If the battle comes this far, you must ride back through the gates, behind the city walls and to the castle." Jeilin nodded. In addition to the first promise, Raihnin had made her agree that morning that she would ride to safety if the battle came close to their viewing point behind it. The city and the castle would not be safe for long, though, Jeilin knew, if the Ryelnish troops pushed that far.

Jeilin's stomach fluttered spectacularly, as if it were full of the ravens that circled overhead. When the Ryelnish troops became visible on the horizon, the air felt suddenly colder. She cast a nervous glance at the birds overhead, which waited eagerly for the feast that always followed battle. Raihnin's hand brushed hers again. The all too familiar horned helmets became discernable as the Ryelnish troops marched forward, giving the impression that a hoard of monsters was advancing across the earth. An especially cold wind gusted from behind, sending Jeilin's cloak flapping in the air around her. Fringe shifted his weight under her. Jeilin could make out the enemy's banners flapping in the wind, and though they weren't close enough for her to see the insignia they bore, she knew that as they drew closer she would see the bone-white slash on the black field.

Jeilin tensed, and thought she could feel everyone around her do the same when the distance between the two armies became small enough to send arrows over. The Alaishinian archers released a great volley that temporarily darkened the sky as they arced overhead. Vacant spaces appeared, especially at the front lines, in the Ryelnish army's ranks, as the arrows found homes and those who still stood marched over their fallen companions. Jeilin could hear a distant din of growls and barks, and she knew that it came from the dogs, which smelled blood and snarled with their teeth bared and hackles raised as their handlers waited for the command to release them. The dogs were one of the few advantages that Alaishin had over its enemy, and Jeilin hoped that they would make a difference. Large and fearless, the dogs sprinted across the closing gap between the two armies. Some fell as victims of the Ryelnish archers and others were cut down as they charged into the front-lines, but others seized throats and tore them out, barely pausing to taste the blood before latching onto another. Ryeln discharged an answering wave of arrows, and empty spaces began to dot the Alaishinian ranks as well.

The two armies met with a roar like thunder, and the sun flashed off of their whirling blades like lightning. Here and there surviving dogs still leapt and seized great mouthfuls of flesh. Jeilin watched as the armies melded together in a great death dance; there were more of the Ryelnish men, but the Alaishinian men fought well. "The battalion that left from the northern gate should be here soon," Raihnin commanded. "If all goes as planned, they'll arrive before we lose too many of our men."

A black mass became visible in the distance, creeping across the winter-bare landscape behind the Ryelnish troops—it was the northern battalion, arriving at the battle scene as if Raihnin's words had summoned them. There was a slight slowing in the mayhem as the fighting men felt the ground tremble beneath their feet, shaken by the northern battalion's cavalry as they raced forward, their horses' hooves tearing up the ground that stretched between them and the backlines of the Ryelnish army. The Ryelnish soldiers surely cursed the arrival that would seal them solidly in the center of a mass of their enemies, and the Alaishinian men fought harder, their morale buoyed by the sight.

Soon, the Ryelnish soldiers were sandwiched between the two battalions. The cavalry plunged forward through the mass of tattooed swordsmen, their blades flashing while their mounts struck out with hooves, crushed men under their weight, and tore flesh with jaws stronger than even the war dogs'. The Ryelnish men began to diminish, pressed in on one another, cut down like weeds as the Alaishinian army closed tighter around them like a noose. A gap in the Alaishinian line at the southern end of the field allowed some opportunity for escape, and as many Ryelnish soldiers as could, poured out of it, though many of them died before ever reaching it. Jeilin's hopes soared—Alaishin had a real chance at victory, she thought. Beside her, Raihnin appeared pleased.

Eventually those Ryelnish soldiers who had been unable to escape were reduced to piles of corpses, most of which would become food for the ravens and vultures before there was time to bury them. Those who had escaped had joined the Ryelnish battalions that had closed around the southern end of the city, where a smaller Alaishinian battalion fought hard to keep them at bay. "We need to join the southern battalion," Raihnin said. "They won't be able to hold out much longer without reinforcements." Generals and officers jogged about on their horses, shouting orders as Raihnin's words flowed down the chain of command. Soon, the battalion began to move southward, a sea of humanity ebbing on a bloody shore.

A short march brought the soldiers to where the southern battalion was defending the city against the rest of the Ryelnish army. Alaishin was noticeably outnumbered, and Ryeln was pushing them backward, foot by foot, toward the city. The two sides were too intermixed to shoot a rain of arrows so Raihnin's men marched forward as one, flanking the Ryelnish from the eastern side. Time passed, and though the reinforcements fought hard, Ryeln bore down upon them, pressing further toward the city. "Jeilin, it's time for you to return to the castle," Raihnin said with a sober voice.

The battle had drawn closer to their watching spot, and enemy soldiers and the occasional arrow had begun to come too close for comfort.

"You'll come with me?" Jeilin asked.

Raihnin opened his mouth to protest.

"Please," Jeilin said. "You can watch the battle for a while from the castle. Your injuries will slow you, and all of the Ryelnish soldiers will be targeting you anyway."

"I can enforce our plans here, Your Majesty," one of the generals who watched with them said, "so that you may accompany your lady to the safety of the castle."

Eventually Raihnin nodded his agreement. Jeilin couldn't tell if he was frowning because he was reluctant to leave the battlefield, or because of his wound.

"Come on," Jeilin said, turning to Olwen and Cai. It had been agreed that they needn't stay on the battlefield, as Cai was still recovering from his knife wound and both of them from the bumps, bruises, and other small wounds they'd sustained as prisoners.

"We must ride quickly," Raihnin said.

The four horses—Raihnin's fierce grey, Jeilin's golden Fringe, Olwen's leggy black, and Cai's sorrel—took off at a sprint and dashed for the gate. They pulled up their mounts in a sudden stop, only to find that the gate was a hotbed of violence. A handful of Ryelnish soldiers had managed to fight their way through to the gate, and were engaged in heated combat with the Alaishinian men who guarded it.

"The eastern gate!" Raihnin declared, wheeling his stallion about and urging him in the direction that they had just come from.

Jeilin imitated him, leaning forward slightly in the saddle, asking Fringe for speed. She glanced over her shoulder, where Cai was riding his sorrel hard and Olwen... "Olwen!" Jeilin shouted.

Somehow Olwen had been the last to convince her mount to turn, and before she could urge him into a run, the Ryelnish soldiers had converged upon her. Her horse tossed his head and screamed as the soldiers hacked at him, his great dark eyes rimmed with white, until they rolled upward into his skull. Olwen was struck across the chest by a blade, and Jeilin watched in horror, pulling backward on her reins, as Olwen's body folded around it and she toppled from the saddle, disappearing under the heads of the Ryelnish men.

Jeilin screamed. "We have to keep going!" Raihnin said, his voice fraught with urgency. "Jeilin!" he had seized Fringe's bridle and attempted to pull him forward. The soldiers who had killed Olwen surged forward with a cry, recognizing the prince. "Jeilin!" Cai drew back his arm and hit Fringe across the hindquarters as hard as he could. Fringe sprung forward, returning eagerly to a gallop. As they sped away, Jeilin couldn't help but look over her shoulder. Their pursuers met resistance from Alaishinian men, and one by one they dropped away, engaged in battle. The horses' coats were slick with sweat by the time they stopped at the eastern gate. The men who guarded it recognized Raihnin at once and opened the gate with haste.

The sounds of the battle were muffled by the thick city wall once the gates closed behind them. Jeilin stopped Fringe, struggling to smooth her ragged breathing.

"I'm sorry, Jeilin," Raihnin said. Jeilin panted, and in her mind's eye she saw Olwen folding around the blade that had taken her life, again and again. What horror and pain Olwen must have felt as the soldiers separated her from the rest and attacked her! And she, her friend, had only ridden away, only saved herself... "There was nothing you could do, nothing *any* of us could have done," Raihnin said as if he knew her thoughts.

"Come on." Jeilin urged Fringe halfheartedly into a canter over the cobblestone streets, as she and Cai rode behind Raihnin. Terrified citizens peered down at them from their windows, their faces pale with worry and fear.

Once inside, Jeilin watched the battle from a window high in the castle with Raihnin. "We're losing, aren't we?" she asked. The black mass of Ryelnish soldiers had pushed the Alaishinians, who were scarcely over half the other army's number, ever further toward the city. Soon, they would be fighting with their backs to the city wall.

Raihnin surveyed the scene with a tight expression. Finally, he nodded. "I'm sorry, Jeilin," he said softly. "I did everything I knew to do."

"It's not your—" Jeilin began.

"No," Raihnin interrupted her. "My father is dead—that leaves me in charge." Jeilin reached out to hold his hand, and he took it, folding it into his as he continued. "I was so happy when you returned...I couldn't believe my good fortune. These past few days, I'd built myself up for a victory, and imagined us with years to spend together loving each other. Now I see that the remainder of our time together is numbered not in years, or even days, but in hours. You don't know how sorry I am."

Jeilin didn't resist as he drew her away from the window into an embrace. She was careful when he kissed her, allowing her lips to touch his with only the slightest pressure. She was surprised when he pressed his mouth hard on hers—she could feel the threads that held the right corner of his mouth together, could taste his blood in her own mouth, but he didn't flinch or lessen his passion.

"Raihnin," she said, pulling breathlessly away.

"What is it?" he asked, his lips brushing her ear.

"It doesn't have to be this way," she said. "I think there's still a chance—I think there's something I can do if—"

He silenced her with another kiss, and looking into her eyes when their lips parted said, "No."

Chapter 17

"Please, Raihnin," Jeilin said. "You have to listen—I have a plan."

"Does it involve you leaving the castle?" Raihnin asked.

"Yes."

"Then no," he said firmly.

"I think it could make a real difference!" she insisted.

"You're not going out there," Raihnin said.

She touched her tattoo. "But I'm the only one who can do it, now that Olwen's—"

"You'll end up just like her if you go out there!" For the first time, Jeilin heard real anger in Raihnin's voice. "You're mad if you think that I'm going to let you charge out into the middle of a raging battle, trying to save the kingdom while I wait here, left to imagine how they'll kill you!"

"Maybe they won't!" Jeilin said. "Maybe my plan will work! I look like one of them, they'll think—"

"Send the boy," Raihnin said. "Cai. He has the mark too."

"I already need him for my plan," Jeilin said. "Both of us have to go."

Raihnin cursed. "Jeilin, please, can't we just enjoy this last little scrap of time together before both of our lives are over?"

"I don't want this to be our last hour together."

"Well, it is," Raihnin said. "Please just savor it."

Jeilin seized both of his hands and said, "I could divide them. The Ryelnish army—I could tell them that another Alaishinian battalion is marching from the north. They'll turn some of their troops from the battle here to confront them. Then our men will have a chance to defeat the ones left behind instead of facing the whole army at once. After they've done that, they can pursue the rest of the Ryelnish soldiers, and that will move the battle farther away from the city."

Jeilin glanced down through the window to the battle below; the Alaishinian men were being pushed further, fighting for every inch.

"Why couldn't Cai do that instead of you?" Raihnin asked.

Jeilin shook her head. "We're both going to do it," she said. "We'll both ride in as if we haven't met and find different officers. I don't think that one messenger making the claim would be enough for them to act upon it, but if there were two…"

Raihnin groaned. "There are too many 'ifs' Jeilin. What if it doesn't work at all? What if they seize you as a traitor and kill you? What if a stray arrow, or a wanton blade stroke for that matter, finds you?"

"In a couple of hours or less, the Ryelnish will fight through to the city and gain access to the castle," Jeilin said. "We know that the enemy will find us then, but if I go through with my plan, there's still a chance!"

"But if it doesn't work, you'll die alone while I wait, away from you, and the enemy won't be able to find me and kill me quickly enough."

"I don't want to leave you, Raihnin. There's a part of me that says that my plan is foolishness, and tells me to stay here and wait in your arms for death, to enjoy our last hour or two together. But there's another part of me that says that I swore allegiance to Alaishin, and that I owe it to the kingdom, and to you, to try. I can't just give up when I know there's still a chance that this can be turned around, and that we could have those years together."

"You promised to stay by my side during the battle, Jeilin."

"I know. I won't go unless you agree. But I know that you want a chance too. Please, let me try."

****

Jeilin's stomach felt full of ravens again as she and Cai stopped their mounts at the inside of the eastern city gate. Raihnin was there too; he had escorted Jeilin to the gates on his grey warhorse. He dismounted, handed his reins to Cai, and lifted Jeilin down from her saddle. The bitter taste of blood filled their last kiss. "I love you, Jeilin. Come back to me," he said.

The gates shut behind Jeilin and Cai, the sound of their closing lost in the roar of warfare. The pair dashed forward together with as much speed as they could muster, and then separated so that it would appear as if they hadn't met. Circling the fighting, they both scanned the mass of toiling soldiers for the sight of generals or other officers, and an entry point through which to enter as safely as could be expected. Jeilin prayed that all of the Ryelnish soldiers who had seen her and Cai with Raihnin were dead.

Jeilin's hands shook, holding the reins, when she saw him: a fierce-looking man on horseback, surveying the activity of the Ryelnish men with an air of obvious authority. She heeled Fringe forward, winding through the fighting men as if through a maze. Once, a man stumbled backward into Fringe in an attempt to avoid a blade thrust, causing Fringe to trip and snort in fear. Jeilin regained control quickly, though, urging him on toward the officer on horseback. "Sir!" she called when she rode within earshot. "Sir!" The man turned, reining his horse, to face her. Jeilin's mouth went dry under his piercing stare. "There's another Alaishinian battalion marching in from the north," she said. There was no need for Jeilin to fake the signs of having just stopped a hard ride; she was breathing rapidly, and Fringe's thick coat was damp with sweat from the effort to reach the officer.

"What?" the man snorted, sending his nostrils flaring as his thick, dark eyebrows plunged downward.

"There's an Alaishinian battalion we didn't know about marching in from the north as we speak," she repeated. "I'm helping the scouts spread the word."

The officer snorted angrily again, and his horse danced to avoid two men as they whirled by, locked in battle. "Come with me," he said, and Jeilin had no choice but to ride after him as he charged across the battlefield. They stopped to speak to another officer, who also looked angry when the first officer related the news. He glared at Jeilin. "How far away are they?" he asked.

"About a mile and a quarter to the north," Jeilin replied, reciting the answer that she and Cai had agreed upon. She scanned the field quickly, searching for a sign of Cai's fair head among the helmeted troops. She saw none, and could only hope that he was carrying the message to other officers, unhurt.

The two officers exchanged a few more words that were lost to Jeilin in the din of the battle. "Go tell General Zhu," the first officer said, waving to his left. Jeilin looked and saw another man on horseback, engaged in combat with an Alaishinian soldier. She rode toward him, hoping that he was General Zhu. He finished his opponent just before Jeilin reached him, removing his head with a single sweep of his blade. Jeilin pretended not to be fazed as the soldier's head toppled from his body to the ground, where men and horses would trample it underfoot.

"General Zhu!" she called, and the man must have been General Zhu, for he turned to face her without any expression of surprise. "I've been sent to tell you that there's an Alaishinian battalion marching toward us, about a mile and a quarter to the north of here." General Zhu frowned, and Jeilin gasped as he whirled his blade in her direction; she was too stunned to move. A metallic *shing* ended abruptly in a soft *thud* as the general's blade found home in human flesh. Jeilin stared in astonishment as blood sprayed onto her coat sleeve, fanning out from an Alaishinian soldier's neck. The dead man brushed her leg as he fell to the ground—Jeilin hadn't so much as heard him approaching from behind her.

"A second one?" General Zhu asked. "You're sure?"

Jeilin nodded. "I'm helping the scouts spread the word," she said. Her stomach felt tied in knots.

"Who's been informed?"

"I'm not sure," Jeilin replied. "I just gave the news to two officers, and they sent me to you. There are others spreading the word as well."

General Zhu nodded, though what that meant, Jeilin couldn't tell. "Come with me, messenger," he said. Once again, Jeilin found herself riding across the battlefield, trying not to flinch each time a blade swung too close. General Zhu led her to a place away from the center of the battle, behind where most of the men fought. Jeilin felt a pang of longing and fear as she glanced toward the castle where Raihnin was surely watching, too far away to make her out, and wondering whether or not she was alive. How would she escape the general and the other officers who had gathered there? How would she make it back to Raihnin without arousing suspicion? Her heart hammered away, and it felt as if it were caught in her throat as she swallowed.

"If we wait here for them to arrive," Jeilin heard one of the officers say. "It'll be like at the eastern gate—they'll trap us like fish in a net and cut down our men at their leisure!"

"We could divide the troops and send some northward to meet them," one of the officers suggested. Jeilin's heart soared as she tried to appear as if she hadn't heard anything particularly interesting, as if she were hardly listening at all.

"And weaken our presence here when it's clear that we'll prevail within the next hour?" another officer countered.

"All of their plans have centered on surprising and surrounding us here," the other man said. "We can destroy their expectations and their hope by meeting them with a large battalion and defeating them before they reach the battlefield. Their number can't be very large—they don't have enough men to spare for that. After we take care of that battalion, we'll return here to the battlefield and finish what remains of the Alaishinian army."

Jeilin dared to glance at General Zhu, who seemed to be in charge and had been listening thoughtfully throughout the exchange. He turned unexpectedly to speak to Jeilin. "Find General Talsun and tell him to report to me immediately," he said. "You'll find him near the southern gate, overseeing the men who are fighting to break through there."

"Yes, sir," Jeilin replied. She was immensely relieved as she navigated the battlefield once again, hoping desperately that her mission would afford her a chance to escape to the east gate without notice. She made considerable headway, covering over half the battlefield without incident. She tried to stick to areas where there were heavier concentrations of Ryelnish soldiers; the mark made her feel safer there. General Zhu's rescue had proven that there were Alaishinian men who would not hesitate to cut her down just because she was a woman. She had just begun to truly hope that escape was imminent when an Alaishinian man leapt toward her from out of the chaos. She noted with horror that he was followed by at least half a dozen more men, all of whom seemed intent upon attacking her.

She shrieked as the first man seized her right leg and pulled hard, tearing her halfway out of the saddle. She struggled to stay upright, clinging to Fringe's mane and heeling him as hard as she could with her uninjured leg. Fringe didn't move forward—one of the men had grabbed his reins just below his chin and stood in his way. Rather, he bucked, which sent Jeilin reeling off of his back as white-hot pain shot down her right leg and up her side. The fact that she was vomiting barely registered as she hit the ground, where she was immediately seized, seemingly by several different men, all of whom, it felt, were pulling her in opposite directions. "I'm not—" she began, but another wave of pain turned her protest into a scream; her hip felt like it had been wrenched away from her body. The last thing she heard was a shrill neigh from Fringe, and then a blow to her head plunged her into unconsciousness.

264

****

Jeilin didn't feel so much like a person when she woke as she felt like a semi-conscious mass of bone-deep aches and fiery pains. She seemed to be floating in a dark mist, and then she realized that she hadn't opened her eyes, but she thought that she could hear sounds. Not just sounds, she realized, but voices. One of them was familiar, she thought, but she couldn't quite make it out, or fathom who it might belong to.

"I think she tried to open her eyes!" Jeilin heard the familiar voice say. Then she realized that one of the aches wasn't really an ache, but a warm, even pleasant pressure— someone was holding one of her hands. That she was lying down was her next realization. Her eyes opened slowly, seemingly of their own accord, and then it all came back to her. Raihnin, the battle, and the attack! Where was she? Raihnin!

"Jeilin?" Raihnin was there, leaning over her, surrounded by stone walls—she was inside the castle. But how? "Jeilin! She's awake!" A second face, summoned by Raihnin's words and vaguely familiar, loomed over her. He was the physician who had attended Raihnin, she realized.

"Raihnin," Jeilin said, and he smiled when he heard his name. "How did I get here?"

"Some of my men carried you in from the battlefield," he replied.

"No," she protested. "I was attacked by Alaishinian men."

Raihnin stroked her face. "They weren't attacking you, love. I sent them. They were to bring you back to me, and make it look to the Ryelnish as if they were taking you prisoner."

Jeilin contemplated Raihnin's explanation for a few moments. Her hip throbbed as if it had been struck by a hammer—no, a battering ram, and her head felt as if there were a dent in it. "They did a fine job," she finally replied.

"I'm sorry," Raihnin replied. "One of your horse's hooves struck your head when you fell. It was an accident; you were never supposed to be hurt."

"Never mind," Jeilin said. "I'm grateful to be here. I didn't know if I'd be able to make it away from the battlefield."

"You've no idea how grateful I am." His lips brushed her forehead lightly.

Jeilin steeled herself to ask the inevitable question. "What about the plan...did it work?"

"Let me show you," Raihnin said, and with that he knelt, offering Jeilin his uninjured shoulder. He slipped his arm under hers, supporting her as she climbed stiffly out of bed. He guided her carefully across the room to a window.

"What am I supposed to be seeing?" Jeilin asked.

"The battlefield," Raihnin replied.

Jeilin gasped. "Where is everyone?" The field outside of her window certainly didn't look like the battlefield—there were corpses, but no signs of fighting, or even life, for that matter. She might have been looking to the east, where the battlefield there had been abandoned in favor of that south of the city.

"Gone," Raihnin said. "Your plan worked yesterday."

"Yesterday?" Jeilin repeated in wonder.

"Yes, you've been asleep," Raihnin replied.

"What happened?"

"The Ryelnish troops split, like you predicted. By the time the ones who had marched to the north returned, we'd finished those they'd left behind. Our archers took even more as the remainder marched back from the north, and the rest perished in combat."

"It worked," Jeilin said, glad she was being supported by Raihnin, for her knees were weak with relief and wonder.

"Yes," Raihnin said. "Now all that's left to do is drive out the small battalion in the capital."

"Will that be hard?" Jeilin asked.

"No," Raihnin replied. "Alaishin is safe."

"What about Cai?"

"He played his part well," Raihnin said softly. "But he never returned."

"Oh." Suddenly, hot tears were pressing against the backs of Jeilin's eyes, threatening to spill over. She fought to hold them back as she remembered beautiful, fearless Olwen, her mentor and closest friend, who had sat with her around so many campfires, and Cai, who had agreed to aid her with her risky plan without hesitation. "My brother is at the capital," Jeilin said, remembering Ehryn.

"I've already sent a small army to Dresinva to reclaim the city," Raihnin said. "Your brother should still be there. Most of the troops who remain in the capital were still being trained. They sent their more experienced men to handle the resistance here at the bay.

Jeilin nodded, comforted by the thought of Ehryn returning home to rejoin her family.

"My men managed to rescue your horse as well," Raihnin said. "I know he means a lot to you."

Jeilin smiled, still blinking back tears. "Thank you."

"There's still one problem, though," Raihnin said.

"What is it?" Jeilin asked, bracing herself for another emotional blow.

"I'm king now," Raihnin said.

"How is that a problem?" Jeilin asked.

"You haven't agreed to be my queen yet."

Jeilin's heart skipped a beat. "What?"

She gazed up at him breathlessly as he cupped her face in his hands. "Jeilin, will you be my queen?"

Looking at Raihnin's still-handsome face, she answered with ease. "Yes," she said, and as their lips met, she thought that she had never known sorrow half as deep as her joy.

Acknowledgments

First of all, thank you to my parents for supporting my love of horses so that when I grew up, I knew enough about them to write the stories I dreamed of writing as a kid.

I'd also like to thank my parents, as well as Jamie, Jake, and Bryar for being *The Messenger*'s first readers and encouraging me to seek a publisher for the book.

Last but certainly not least, I'm grateful to Lisa Paul for being as passionate about Jeilin's story as I am. Also many thanks to Sheila Ashdown and everyone at Lands Atlantic for working so hard to bring it to life.

Panda Books

Snuff-Bottles and Other Stories

Deng Youmei was born into a poor family in Tianjin in 1931. When his father lost his job, he and his family moved to Deng Village in Shandong, where his forefathers had lived. After the Japanese invaded North China in 1937, he became a messenger in the Eighth Route Army. Being too small, however, he was sent back to Tianjin, where he led an itinerant life doing odd jobs until he was forced to go to Japan as a labourer, experiencing all kinds of hardships. In 1945, before the Japanese surrender, he returned to China and joined the New Fourth Army as a journalist. He took part in the War of Liberation and wrote a number of short stories based on army life and his life in Japan.

In the 1950s he was wrongly criticized for writing *On the Precipice*, a vivid, simple and much read story about the troubled lives of intellectuals, and sent to do manual work for over a decade. With the end of the "cultural revolution" in 1976, Deng's energy returned and he started writing again, producing several novellas and stories on modern themes and folklore, which were well received.

Deng Youmei is now a council member of the Chinese Writers' Association.

Panda Books
First edition 1986
Copyright 1986 by CHINESE LITERATURE
ISBN 0-8351-1607-7

Published by CHINESE LITERATURE, Beijing (37), China
Distributed by China International Book Trading Corporation
(GUOJI SHUDIAN), P.O. Box 399, Beijing, China
Printed in the People's Republic of China

Snuff-Bottles
and Other Stories

Deng Youmei

Translated by Gladys Yang

Panda Books

CONTENTS

Preface

Deng Youmei, the son of a poor peasant, was born in Pingyuan County, Shandong in 1931. As a child he lived in Tianjin, in the same compound as the destitute yet arrogant concubine of a Manchu noble, and his interest in Manchu Bannermen dates from that time. He had little formal education but a very chequered career, caught up while a boy in the resistance to Japanese aggression. At eleven he delivered messages for the 8th Route Army. In his early teens he was carried off to Japan to work in a factory; then he joined a cultural troupe in the New 4th Army and was a reporter attached to the People's Liberation Army.

After Liberation Deng came to Beijing. In 1951 he started writing. He received encouragement from Zhao Shuli, the popular author of *Rhymes of Li Youcai* who used traditional forms and colloquial language enjoyed by illiterate peasants. Zhao's advocacy of popular literature had a strong influence on him. Another important mentor was the writer Zhang Tianyi, his tutor in '52 when he studied in the Literary Institute of the Writers' Association. In '57 his story *On the Cliff* won an award. But Deng considers his early writings too simple and stereotyped with their contrived happy endings. "My stories had a tiger's head and snake's tail," he says.

After he was made a Rightist in '57 Deng worked for twenty years as a manual labourer in Beijing and the provinces. In '62 he went to the Northeast to work in a clock factory. As it had no dormitory he bought a shelter which he shared for six years with a Manchu. From this man and a Manchu actor he learned a great deal about old Beijing and the life of Manchus there.

After the fall of the Gang of Four he went on writing. *Our Army Commander*, which deals with Marshal Chen Yi, won an award in '78.

In 1979 Deng tried his hand at fiction with more local colour. The Gang had tried to stamp out old customs, an intrinsic part of the cultural heritage, but some of these were reappearing and Deng believed that young people should learn about them. His *Taoran Pavilion Park,* set in Beijing, won a short story prize, increasing his confidence. He followed it up with *Black Cat, White Cat, Han the Forger, Na Wu, Snuff-Bottles* and other tales about life in Beijing past and present with obscure townsfolk as the main characters. This illustrates a new trend in Chinese writing. For years writers here were fettered, required to write about workers, peasants and soldiers. Intellectuals were not eligible as heroes, let alone effete Bannermen at the turn of the century. In the fifties even Lao She's superb play *Teahouse,* dealing with the lives of ordinary citizens in three historical periods in Beijing, was criticized in some quarters as unhealthy. Now writers can face up to reality and tackle any theme — provided they make no attack on the socialist system.

There has been an upsurge of popular literature, both indigenous and imported, with translations ranging from Jules Verne and Dumas to Agatha Christie and Arthur

Haley. Deng's Beijing stories have the best qualities of popular literature, as they are compulsive reading with unforgettable characters and packed with information. Indeed, one of his reasons for writing about old Beijing is to fill in a gap in young people's general knowledge. Ironically, for a country with such a long history which has produced brilliant historians, history teaching in Chinese schools tends to be excessively dull. For generations most Chinese learned their history from classical novels, the theatre or story-tellers, and few novelists in recent years have tackled historical themes. Deng's work is thus much to be welcomed. And he was bold to enter this field, inevitably inviting comparison with one of the greatest writers of this century — Lao She, Beijing born and bred.

Deng recalls that after the Gang of Four was toppled new fiction appeared like mushrooms after rain, and he wondered how best he could make his contribution. Comparing his qualifications with those of other writers, he decided that many ex-Rightists could write about their painful experiences, and he was less skilled than Wang Meng or Liu Binyan in highlighting social problems. His forte was an extensive knowledge of Beijing and its history, people of all walks of life there and their social customs. During the "cultural revolution" when there was a dearth of novels, he had bought some works on antiques and Buddhism, and the knowledge so acquired became grist to his mill, as did the anecdotes he picked up from actors, bird-fanciers and old Beijing residents who went each morning with him to Taoran Pavilion Park to practise Chinese boxing.

Deng's wife in her article introducing *Snuff-Bottles* explains her misgivings when he chose this new line. She was reassured by the glowing reviews he received. He has been compared with Balzac because he writes the history that many historians omit, the history of social conventions and everyday life. Others have compared his work with genre paintings, for he covers a broad canvas, achieves a rich texture, and graphically conjures up bygone times researched in detail.

Many Chinese writers today are drawing on Western techniques. Deng, however, has developed traditional story-telling. *Snuff-Bottles* has a lead-in about snuff-bottles before the action starts, a practice dating back to the stories told in market-places in 11th-century China. Similarly, it ends with a hint that there is more to come. Deng also has the old story-tellers' mastery of thumbnail sketches and dramatic dialogue. His characters come to life, each one unique, each completely convincing, and their setting is unmistakably old Beijing, arousing nostalgia in senior citizens.

The complex characters created by Deng are a far cry from the stereotyped heroes and villains common in the first thirty years after Liberation. They are more reminiscent of those drawn by Lu Xun, some being failures or outcasts with few redeeming features. Na Wu, the incompetent son of a bankrupt Manchu family, is arrogant, dishonest and easily fooled. His decadence is tragic. Like him affable, timid Wu Shibao, descended from martial Bannermen, has been brought up with no trade to live on his pension. He sets great store by "face". When his pension stops he is willing to work for a living only if he cannot be seen demeaning himself in this way. He fails to take up arms to resist the imperialist troops, but refuses to disgrace China by painting foreign invaders inside his snuff-bottles. He is lucky to be taken in hand by the potter's strong-minded daughter.

Not long after Liberation Zhou Enlai warned the children of high-ranking cadres to learn a lesson from the degeneracy of the descendants of Manchu Bannermen, and not to live as parasites cashing in on the achievements of their parents. Deng's message to the younger generation today is somewhat similar. He wants them to understand that China had reached a dead end, could only be revitalized by revolution; to realize how New China has evolved from the old, and work hard to build up the country.

Deng decided to write about snuff-bottles after reading an account of Wang Xisan, a painter of snuff-bottle interiors, and his trials during the "cultural revolution". Wang painted bottles for his brigade to sell to finance their water conservancy project. He was training apprentices and doing well till the Red Guards attacked him for his "decadence". Deng then read up on snuff-bottles and made friends with old craftsmen, including Wang Xisan. While collecting material he was struck by the patriotism and strong sense of self-respect of Chinese craftsmen. In a temple in Foshan he saw a bronze incense-burner cast during the Boxer Uprising, with four legs planted on four foreign aggressors. The man who made that did so at the risk of his life. This helped Deng to visualize an honest, high-minded craftsman who would never stoop to flattery or deceit, and so he created the memorable potter Xie.

We look forward to reading more of these characters' adventures. Unfortunately Deng's output has been slowed down by his duties in the secretariat of the Writers'

Association. However, he plans to write a sequel describing the fate of snuff-bottle painters from the founding
of the Republic in 1911 to the invasion of China by Japan.
A further sequel is planned to deal with the post-Libe-
ration period.

1985

Gladys Yang

Snuff-Bottles

OF late the huge tobacco industry has produced cigarettes for people of all walks of life the whole world over, superseding the traditional taste for snuff. Too bad, but there it is. Snuff is much better for your health than cigarettes or cigars. Sniffed for its pungent odour, it serves as a stimulant or prophylactic, and you don't poison yourself by inhaling smoke. You can sniff it for your own enjoyment without affecting anyone next to you. And by covering your mouth with a handkerchief when you sneeze, you avoid polluting the environment. Snuff was brought to China in 1582 during the Ming dynasty by Matteo Ricci.* The Kang Xi and Qian Long reigns (1662-1795) were its golden age, when nobles and commoners alike took snuff. Then those who couldn't abide snuff must have seemed like the old fogeys today who can't dance disco. When Kang Xi went to Nanjing, western missionaries offered him many presents. He declined them all but the snuff. And readers of *A Dream of Red Mansions*** will remember that when one of the serving-maids had a stuffed-up nose, the young master made her sniff some Western snuff, so that a few sneezes cured her. Cigarettes in all their long history have never attained such a high reputation.

---

* Matteo Ricci (1552-1610), an Italian Jesuit, was sent to China by Portugal in the tenth year of Wan Li.

** A very popular 18th-century novel.

Another confirmation of the superiority of snuff is that from the end of the Ming dynasty, when it came into vogue, our craftsmen used their traditional skills to improve on the manufacture of snuff-bottles. Though too small to hold wine or rice, these bottles embody the arts of jade-polishing, gold-inlaying, carving, ceramics, lacquer, painting and cloisonné in a unique Chinese craft. In the course of the last few centuries many fine bottles have been lost or destroyed, but some superb examples still remain. They may be made of metal, stone, jade, glass, pottery, porcelain, bamboo, wood, mother-of-pearl, horn, ivory, coconut or gourds. There are subdivisions too. Thus porcelain bottles can be classified according to the kilns where they were fired. . . . In a word, these little bottles exemplify the level of Chinese craftsmanship and the characteristics of specific periods. Hence the best fetch very high prices on the world market. At an auction in Germany in 1976, within a few minutes a Chinese snuff-bottle was sold for two million marks. After the death of the well-known American connoisseur Mr Stevenson, his collection of Chinese snuff-bottles fetched U.S. $1,400,000. He had remained a bachelor all his life, devoting himself to the study of snuff-bottles; and experts in this field compare his researches with those of Mme Curie. In the West there are two international associations to study snuff-bottles, the members of which are increasing every year. So it is no empty boast to claim that our snuff-bottles have blazed a new trail in art.

It is true that for thousands of years millions of people have studied, worked, fallen in love, married and raised families without setting eyes on a single snuff-bottle. But it would be wrong to underestimate snuff-bottles, in view of the high tribute paid to them in China and abroad. Countless craftsmen racked their brains and strained every nerve to breathe life into these inanimate materials. So whether or not you take snuff or use snuff-bottles, you must acknowledge that this craft embodies our people's industry and skill and is a fine contribution we have made to world civilization. But I have strayed from my subject which was the superiority, hygienically speaking, of snuff over cigarettes.

It is said that one school of novelists in the West opposes drafting a plot before starting to write. Instead they pick on a subject, then follow their own stream of consciousness. So let me adopt this method to tell the story of some snuff-bottles.

2

Certain snuff-bottles contain "interior paintings". Transparent bottles of crystal or glass lend themselves to this technique. The craftsmen paint landscapes, figures, flowers or birds on the inside surface, appending an inscription. Whether the style is romantic or realistic, seen from outside the painting is exquisite. But this is an extremely difficult art, as the bottle-neck is too small to insert a bean — sometimes a hairpin is all that will fit in. Most people used ear-picks to extract the snuff, and even then couldn't always get any out. So imagine how hard it must have been to paint the interior. Especially as these miniature paintings and inscriptions had to be done back to front. Some said the best way was to lie on your back on the ground, holding the bottle up, otherwise you couldn't see your strokes clearly. Others claimed that it took half a year to paint one bottle with a hair dipped in enamel. Yet others maintained that none but immortals could execute these paintings. Because at that time the *famille verte* enamelled pieces known as "Guyuexuan" were in fashion, the characters *gu* （古）and *yue* （月）gave rise to the rumour that they were the work of certain immortals named *Hu* （胡）. As these immortals liked to play tricks and could take the form of alluring girls or produce magnificent porcelain, it stood to reason that they could also paint a few snuffbottles to bamboozle mere mortals. But as more and more of these bottles with interior paintings appeared this theory broke down. To paint a few for fun was one thing, but to paint whole sets for sale to make a living was something to which no immortal would stoop.

Later, painters with distinctive styles made a name, and by the start of the twentieth century Beijing had four of these. Beijingers in their polls have never followed the practice in the Olympic Games or the awarding of literary prizes: instead of selecting the best three or five they always list four names, whether "The Four Famous Doctors", "The Four Best Actors" or "The Four Happiness Pills". So they listed the four best painters of snuff-bottles: Ma Shaoxuan, Ye Zhongsan, Zhou Leyuan and Wu Changan.

This story of ours is about Wu Changan.

3

Wu Changan, first known as Wu Shibao, was a Manchu of the White Banner serving in the arsenal. His grandfather's military prowess had resulted in his being made a cavalry officer, and his title had been inherited by Wu's uncle. Wu himself lived idly at home on the small patrimony left to him with a few chests of antiques. Far from being a horseman, if he rode a donkey to White Cloud Temple he shook with fear. Still he took pride in his descent from a martial family, and when in good spirits liked to dwell on it.

Wu Shibao, now in his thirties, lived contentedly at home. He whiled away his time playing with crickets, airing his thrush, taking snuff or sipping wine. Though not well off he had enough to live on. The Beijing gentry had five status symbols: a reed-matting awning, a goldfish tub, a pomegranate tree, a sleek dog and a plump slavegirl. Wu couldn't afford an awning and had had to sell his last slavegirl; still he had the three other symbols. His dog, though not sleek, was a genuine Pekingese. He was content with his lot, and sometimes enjoyed going to a private opera performance to sing an aria or two.

One day he went to a birthday feast in Prince Duan's palace to sing *Eight Immortals Offer Birthday Greetings*. Suddenly a eunuch whispered in his ear, "See here, His Highness wants to take command of the Righteous and Harmonious Society,* so if you make up a few lines praising that society it's sure to please him."

Though Wu had no inclination to do this, since this was a birthday feast he felt he should please his host and take this chance to shine. Especially as Prince Duan was then in favour, his son Pujun having been made the heir apparent by the Empress Dowager and taken into the palace, so that the prince might later well become the emperor's father. Accordingly Wu Shibao sang these impromptu lines:

---

* Known in the West as the Boxers.

The Eight Immortals wish Prince Duan long life
And have brought all the denizens of Paradise:
First, Tripitaka and Pigsy,
Close behind them Sandy and Monkey. . . .
All the heroes of old fly to the palace on clouds
To greet His Royal Highness, the Commander. . . .

At this the prince roared with laughter and asked, "Who is that little monkey?"

The eunuch told him, "He's from the White Bannerman family of Wu. His forbears were military men, but he has no posting."

"So he's from a martial family," said the prince. "Let's send him to the Tiger Spirit Battalion."

This Tiger Spirit Battalion was a shock force set up to crush the foreign devils. So Wu Shibao was appalled. Hastily kowtowing he said, "Thank you, sir, for this gracious favour, but not being able to fight I daren't accept it."

The prince retorted, "You won't have to fire a rifle. They need a secretary. That's a job you can do. With my backing they'll pay you handsomely."

Afraid to hold out, Wu kowtowed and withdrew, frantically wishing that he had kept quiet so as to be spared this favour. The man who accompanied him on the fiddle, Shou Ming, was a poor bannerman wise in the ways of the world. Seeing Wu's panic he persuaded him to bribe the eunuch to ask for sick leave for him; and as the prince's proposal had been made on the spur of the moment, since Wu was adamant he didn't insist. A year later, in 1900, Beijing was occupied by the allied army of eight imperialist powers. In their peace negotiations with the Manchu government, they demanded the punishment of the Boxer ringleaders. So Prince Duan, instead of becoming the father of the emperor, lost his princely rank and was banished to Xinjiang for life, while the Tiger Spirit Battalion was disbanded.

Beijing's occupation by the allied army involved Wu in trouble too. His peke ran away. While looking for it he was seized by foreign troops and made to bury corpses for a whole day. When he saw the number of dead he recalled with a shudder his assignment to the Tiger Spirit Battalion.

A year later a peace agreement was signed and life returned to normal in Beijing. To celebrate his narrow escape, on the Double Ninth Wu invited Shou Ming and one or two other friends to burn incense in the Temple of Heavenly Peace.

Since Beijing lies south of a desert, in spring sandstorms darken the sky, in summer the sun is fiery. The best season is autumn, which is why climbing some height on the Double Ninth Festival is more popular than spring outings.

4

In those days, as Bei Hai and Coal Hill lay inside the Forbidden City, commoners had to go elsewhere for their outings. Their favourite choices were Anglers' Terrace in the west, Earth City in the north, and Fa Zang Temple or the Temple of Heavenly Peace in the south. Why were these places so popular? Earth City had plenty of open ground suitable for barbecues; Anglers' Terrace had a track for horse-racing; Fa Zang Temple's high pagoda afforded a good view; and the road to the Temple of Heavenly Peace west of Pearl Market was lined with good restaurants. Wu had selected the Temple of Heavenly Peace so that on the way back, in North Half Lane, they could have a meal at Guangheju, famed throughout the city for its kidney and steamed fish dishes.

Shou Ming, who had persuaded Wu to apply for sick leave, had once held a small official post, but had since turned his back on officialdom for some reason. Admired for his fine accompaniments on the fiddle and his imitations of famous opera singers, he was invited to most celebrations in different princely mansions. Though poor he had won respect because he never went in for shady deals. It was not, however, sociability or love of fiddling for its own sake that took him to so many parties. He used them to earn commissions from dealers in antiques by finding customers for them. This was not as easy as it sounds, calling for discrimination and the ability to satisfy both salesman and customer. They had to have confidence in him, and the price he asked had to be acceptable to both parties. So he had acquired certain characteristics: his friends found him warm-hearted and reliable, but he set rather too much store by face. For should his "prestige" be undermined, this side-line would be closed to him.

On their way back from the Temple of Heavenly Peace they had a slap-up meal in Guangheju, till other customers started arriving for dinner. Wu Shibao got a waiter to wrap both of them up a take-away dish in a lotus leaf. Then, coming out, they walked to the end of the lane just as a black carriage was driven out of Vegetable Market. Shou Ming, caught off guard, bumped into it and staggered. At once down jumped an attendant in a tasselled cap, who grabbed him by the collar and slapped his face.

Wu swore at him, "You swine! Knocking into someone and then roughing him up."

The carriage curtain was raised then. An official poked his head out and yelled, "What insolent wretch is holding up my carriage? Beat him!"

Wu recognized that voice. Looking up he saw that it was his family's slave Xu Huanzhang, son of Xu Dazhu of East Village. His forbears, bringing land with them, had asked the White Banner to accept them as slaves and had been registered with the Wu family. Unlike domestic slaves, apart from delivering rent and grain each year and paying their respects at festivals, they tilled their own land and did no work for their masters. Some were landlords themselves with tenants, hired hands and servants, living in luxury. But if their masters sent for them for some "Red or White Occasion" — a wedding or funeral — they had to come sounding gongs or wearing mourning, bowing low as they entered and withdrawing backwards, acknowledging themselves as their masters' slaves. They could lord it at home, but coming out as slaves they had to know their place. Indeed, they took pride in this. They would lecture their own domestics, "Call yourselves slaves? You should see how *we* behave in our master's house. If he coughs we pass over a spittoon without waiting to be told. At an order from him we jump to it. We know exactly when to bow or withdraw — there's nothing slack about *us*!"

Recent years had seen changes. Many masters were growing too poor to keep even domestic slaves, and had let them redeem themselves for a few taels of silver. Some had even been reduced to working as coolies.

Some of the bannermen slaves on the other hand had become officials or merchants and grown rich. So their masters started putting the squeeze on them. One master was so poor that he worked as a porter while his former slave was an official in charge of horses in the army. When the master had no money he toted his load to the official's yamen and waited at the door for the arrival of his slave's carriage. Then he shouted, "Get down, you wretch, and take over my load for me." As a dignitary couldn't stoop to do this, he had to kneel down and offer his master money to hire someone else in his place. For after a slave's manumission and even if he held office, the laws of the Manchu dynasty decreed that he must still obey his master's orders; and the latter could beat him to death yet get off with only one grade's demotion in rank. No slave dared risk this.

Though Xu Huanzhang's parents had redeemed themselves, he still had to acknowledge the Wu family as his masters. He had nothing but contempt for Wu Shibao. How could he let such a pauper bully him? But he had no objection to being a slave so long as it paid off. That meant finding a new master outmatching his old one. As nowadays even the Empress Dowager was afraid of foreigners, his best course was to find himself foreign backing. So he became a Catholic, and a Catholic priest introduced him to the Foreign Languages College, where he learned Japanese and French. During the uprising of the Righteous and Harmonious Society he panicked for several months, lying low in the foreign hospital in Jiaominxiang as a volunteer orderly. He did not venture home until four days after the occupation of Beijing by foreign troops, because they spent the first three days killing and looting. Xu knowing this sat tight. Since Wu Shibao was a White Bannerman, Xu as his slave lived in their garrison area north of Chaoyang Gate and east of Dongsi Street. This district was now under Japanese occupation. Xu walking home noticed that over the gates of several princely mansions were white flags with the inscription "Submissive Subjects of Japan". But the white flag over his own gate had no inscription on it. At once he asked what this meant. He was told that there was an unwritten rule: All families which did not hang out flags could be massacred by the Japanese as Boxers. Some princely mansions had taken the lead in hanging out white flags, and the small fry who hadn't fled had been forced to follow suit. But some of them couldn't write, others were unwilling to call themselves submissive. To save a little face they had just put up white flags. On hearing this Xu shook his head and ordered his wife to take the flag down at once.

His father intervened, saying, "Don't do that. The Empress Dowager has fled, all our Manchu troops have retreated, and even Prince Su has put up a white flag. Do you want us to be shot by the foreign devils?"

"I'm not taking it down," Xu explained. "I'm going to write something on it."

His wife protested, "The Japs will let it pass without writing. Why should we call ourselves traitors?"

"Shut your mouth!" snapped Xu. "Who are you to butt in on discussions of state affairs?"

"For shame!" retorted his wife. But she went out to take down the flag and tossed it on the desk. Xu had learned Japanese. He ground ink, dipped in his brush, spread out the flag and wrote in neat Japanese, "Submissive Xu Family". Then he hung the flag up again.

This inscription proved most efficacious. The very next afternoon a Japanese sergeant escorted by four Japanese infantrymen came to call on Xu. At that time in Beijing, Japanese-speaking Chinese were harder to find than frozen pears in mid-summer. The Japanese, who needed interpreters for their puppet Pacification Bureau, naturally sought out the man who had written Japanese on his flag. The following day Xu sported on his left arm an armband with an official chop and the title Pacification Bureau of the Imperial Japanese Army. He started swaggering out with Japanese patrols to make arrests, kill rebels and find local gentry willing to organize a committee to preserve public order for the invaders. He lorded it over the northeast part of Beijing.

The Japanese knew that these collaborators cut no ice with the local people. They might keep order in the streets for a while, but in the long run they would be quite useless; they therefore asked about the princes and high officials in this district, hoping to find some big shot willing to work for them. For Xu this was a stroke of luck. It so happened that in this district lived a certain black hatted former Han army official named Shan Qi, now minister of Civil Affairs. One of his guards was Xu's neighbour, and Xu, passing this man's gate on his way home, saw him sitting by a low table in the yard eating cucumber which he washed down with liquor. At first Xu paid no attention and walked on. Then the slamming of the gate behind him alerted him. He thought, "Didn't that fellow go with Prince Su in the Empress Dowager's escort when she fled to Shaanxi? Why has he popped up again?" So he marched straight back and hammered on the gate. "Second Master Shan, open up!"

The previous summer this guard's wife had been cursed by Mrs Xu for dumping melon rinds and emptying slops by her gate, and he had stormed to Xu's house and slapped his father's face. On his return recently the news that Xu had gone up in the world and become an interpreter made him rather uneasy. In his cups he had forgotten to close his gate, and being spotted by Xu had made him more nervous; so he had bolted the gate and started indoors. Then, in his anxiety, he went back to peer out through a crack. As he did this, Xu hammered on the gate, scaring him out of his wits. When he opened up and saw Xu's crafty grin he tried to appease him by coming clean, forgetting the prince's rule of secrecy. He told Xu that Prince Su had come back to Beijing for peace negotiations.

The next day Xu presented a confidential report to the Japanese, informing them that since Shan Qi's return from the west he had been lying low at home smoking opium. For this he received a reward of ten taels of silver. Shan Qi seemed an ideal recruit, high-ranking, in favour of learning from foreigners and specially well disposed to the Japanese, being friends with a well-known ronin. The occupation forces lost no time in contacting this ronin, and sent the head of the Pacification Bureau to call on Prince Su, so that for many years his family worked faithfully for the Japanese Empire. The first service he performed for them was to organize a patrol of three hundred infantrymen and Green Battalion soldiers. The Japanese appointed Xu Huanzhang as the clerk of this patrol. After the allied army was disbanded, this puppet force was reorganized to form the basis of China's earliest police force.

During the occupation when Wu Shibao was conscripted to bury corpses, he had spotted Xu Huanzhang. Xu, wearing a sun-helmet, a grey cloth gown and white armband, was whipping the Chinese carrying corpses and digging mass graves for them. Wu's first impulse was to greet him and ask Xu to get him off; but he thought better of it and, turning his face away, pulled down his hat so that Xu shouldn't see him. He mustn't lose face like that! Better stick it out than let everyone know that this collaborator was his slave. So he gritted his teeth and bore it. But today this swine had nearly knocked over his friend. Raising his voice he said superciliously:

"Just look who it is — that cur Xu! Who do you think you are?"

Xu gasped, thinking, "Now I'm in for it." This wasn't in his yamen but in the street, where the laws of the Manchu Empire still prevailed. If he let Wu abuse him, how could he order people around in future? He must make the best of it, and settle scores with him later. He forced a smile.

"Why, sir, greetings!" He jumped down from his carriage and bowed. "Your slave was blind, made a bad blunder!"

The coachman who had slapped Shou Ming promptly scuttled away with all the other attendants. When Shou Ming saw that Xu was his friend's slave and that he was apologizing, he calmed down. "It doesn't matter," he said. "I wasn't hurt. You may go."

But some of the crowd which had gathered knew and hated Xu Huanzhang, and had been longing to get even with him. Seizing this chance they all chimed in together:

"The idea, a slave beating his master!"

"With a foreign boss, what does he care for his old master?"

"When a son misbehaves, it's the father's responsibility, for a slave to abuse his master is because the master is too soft!"

"Quite right."

"See the way this slave is dressed and what his job is? His master isn't even as smart as his groom. They've turned things upside down!"

"It's against the rules of the Manchu Empire. Twenty years ago, when Shi Songjun was a cabinet minister and his master died, he put on mourning and marched as a musician in front of the coffin."

All travellers by road from the south had to pass Vegetable Market on their way into Beijing, and as pleasure-seekers too were coming back from their outings, soon a large crowd had gathered. They were a mixed lot. Some shouted, "Beat him up!" "Hell, his bannerman master wants this slave to get him in with the foreigners!"

This was more than Wu, who had been drinking, could take. He hurled his lotus-leaf package at Xu, swearing, "Damn you! Now you've become an official and made a name, you refuse to acknowledge your master! I'll give you a public lesson to teach you your place."

The crowd gloated to see a smartly dressed official get offal thrown all over his face by a shabby bannerman. They cheered and egged Wu on, some joining in, till Vegetable Market seethed with excitement.

Xu knew that if he resisted he might be trampled to death. Red in the face, he stood with his arms at his sides, repeating, "You're right, sir. Thank you for teaching your slave a lesson."

Wu Shibao, a decent, easygoing fellow, didn't want to go too far. When Xu admitted his fault he cooled down. And though Shou Ming had lost his temper he was clear-headed. When he heard the comments of the crowd and saw Xu's equipage and evident power, he suspected that if they went any further Wu would suffer the consequences. He at once tried to smooth things over. And by now Wu was sobering up.

"I did this for your own good," he told Xu. "You're young with all your future ahead of you. You must keep control of yourself and not forget who you are. Be off now!"

The disappointed onlookers sighed, then scattered.

On going home Wu slept. That evening, thinking back to what had happened he felt he had gone too far but didn't give the matter much further thought. A day or two later when word of this had spread and friends praised his sense of justice and discipline, it struck him that he had certain hitherto unknown heroic qualities. He was wondering how to develop these when suddenly the Ministry of Punishments sent men to drag him off in chains. Questioned about his performance on Prince Duan's birthday and his appointment to the Tiger Spirit Battalion, he realized that he was suspected of being a Boxer. He protested his innocence.

The magistrate said, "If you feel unjustly treated, go and complain to the foreigners in Jiaominxiang. The Japanese Embassy brought this charge against you. It's in their hands." Then, bound with chains weighing forty pounds, Wu was dragged off to the condemned cell.

Wu's wife was the daughter of a Blue Banner officer at the foot of the Fragrant Hills. The daughters of bannermen had a privileged position at home, addressed as "young mistress" and not obliged to kneel to their elders during festivals, for later they might be selected to serve as ladies-in-waiting in the palace. This preferential treatment influenced their characters. A goodhearted Manchu girl was self-confident, self-respecting, bold, open and broad-minded; a disagreeable one was self-willed, unreasonable, conceited and troublesome.

Not long after Wu Shibao's imprisonment, Xu Huanzhang went unexpectedly to his house with gifts large and small for his master. He explained that he had come to apologize for the way his groom had offended Wu that day. Told tearfully by Mrs Wu of her husband's arrest, he expressed great indignation and, slapping his chest, swore to find out his whereabouts and rescue him. Mrs Wu in her desperation believed him. She begged this loyal retainer to save her husband.

Xu took her to see the officers in charge of Wu's case in the Ministry of Punishments. They confirmed that the charge against him had been brought by the Japanese who wanted him beheaded, so the case would be hard to settle. Only when Xu pleaded with them did they consent to approach someone influential, but asked an exorbitant price. Still, as her husband's life was at stake, Mrs Wu didn't count the cost. She called in the money owed them then sold her trinkets, handing in a bribe of over a thousand taels — but all to no effect. She was starting to have her doubts about Xu Huanzhang when he brought her some good news: "The master's death sentence has been revoked. Tomorrow, ma'am, you can go to the prison to see him."

Mrs Wu was extremely nervous, never having been inside a gaol before. However, Xu had bribed the prison guards for her beforehand, so that she was admitted to see Wu without much ado. Although they had never been too close, at the sight of each other they wept. Asked about his trial, he told her that the magistrate had ordered him to confess that he was a Boxer who had set fire to churches and killed foreigners. When he denied this he had been locked in a condemned cell and left there. Later Xu Huanzhang had come to tell him in secret that he had bribed the magistrate, and the next time he was examined he should say nothing, just sob for his mother — then he would get off more lightly. Though Wu didn't trust Xu, he had clutched at this straw. And weeping in court several times had proved effective. Yesterday he had been moved into this good cell, where the food was better, the warders more polite, and all said he would be granted a remission though no sentence had yet been passed.

His wife sighed, "You don't listen to me, just take your Nanny Liu's word as holy gospel. Aren't I the one who's saved your life? I'd have you know I bought your reprieve for you. It was I who sent Xu Huanzhang to you. So just figure out which of us you should put first in future."

Never mind why Mrs Wu and Nanny Liu had fallen out, Wu now felt most indebted to his wife. He swore that once free he would do whatever she said.

On Mrs Wu's return, she thanked Xu profusely, then asked him when her husband would be released.

"That first sum bought the master's life," said Xu. "To get him out of prison you must raise more."

"I've sold everything I had," was her reply. "Where is more money to come from?"

"We farm 120 *mu* of your family's land, ma'am.

They've yielded next to nothing these last few years what with flood, drought and insect pests. Better make over the title-deeds to me to get the master out."

Mrs Wu had never regarded land as property, and had no idea what this estate was worth. Since she had sold her precious jewels, what did she care about title-deeds? She made them over to Xu. Only when she knew that her husband would soon be out did she wonder how to justify this to him.

In fact, from the start this whole business had been engineered by Xu and his accomplices in the Ministry of Punishments. Xu had drawn up the indictment from the Japanese Embassy to intimidate the ministry. When Wu, on Xu's advice, just cried for his mother in court and would answer no questions, that placed the magistrate in a dilemma. Since the Manchus based their rule on filial piety, not even a magistrate could stop a son from weeping for his dead parents. But if he kept this up, how could they square matters with the foreigners? Then one officer secretly proposed reporting that the prisoner had gone mad, and his case would have to be shelved until he recovered his senses. As foreigners had the same rule themselves, he said, they couldn't raise any objections. The magistrate acted on his advice. Word had already been spread that Wu was bound to be sentenced to death as he had been imprisoned in a condemned cell — this was also the work of Xu's accomplices. Not only was Wu taken in, but the magistrate too.

Wu spent only two days in comfort before being thrown into a common cell. The food there was lousy, the warders a rough lot.

5

This cell, not a large one, already had two occupants. One was a tall, thin elderly man, diffident and sparing of speech, forever brooding. The other, a rough, boisterous strapping fellow, had on the uniform of a treasury guard. The elder called the younger Brother Bao; the younger called the elder Master Nie. Bao kept a copy of *The Romance of the Three Kingdoms* tucked under his pallet, and every day after their airing would ask Master Nie to read him another instalment. Nie would nod and sit by the door where the light was better, to read a couple of chapters with a fluency which showed that he was a man of some education. The warders treated him with consideration, bringing him three meals a day with large helpings and good food. While Wu ate cornmeal muffins and salted turnips, Nie had steamed rolls of white flour with one meat and one vegetable dish. In indignation Wu asked why they received such different treatment.

The warder sneered, "His board and lodging are paid for; yours aren't."

Though puzzled Wu didn't like to ask more questions. As for the treasury guard, his meals brought in from outside by his colleagues included not simply chicken and meat but rice wine masquerading as chicken soup under a layer of oil. When he ate, Wu turned away from that tempting aroma, for fear they might despise him for his greed. And antagonized by their preferential treatment, he huddled in one corner not talking to them.

Bao not only ate and drank heartily, he inhaled snuff heartily too. Most snuff-bottles are short and narrow, but his jade bottle was the size of a wine gourd. He would pour a small heap of snuff on to a saucer and smear it with his thumb up both his nostrils, giving himself a butterfly moustache. Wu watched him with revulsion mixed with envy, being a snuff addict himself. Now that he was cut off from news, too worried to eat or sleep, he longed more than ever for snuff. His own was finished, and no new prisoners had moved in, yet he wouldn't stoop to ask Bao for a pinch. He poked frantically with his ear-pick in his empty bottle, scraping around to find the least little scrap and carefully poking it up his nose, but it seemed to have no flavour.

The guard put on a big show each time he took snuff, snorting and clearing his throat before he loosed off a tremendous sneeze. Inhaling snuff is as contagious as yawning. When Bao sniffed it Wu's nose itched. So he scraped his bottle till he could get no more out, refusing to believe that it was empty and holding it up to the light to examine it.

Wu's bottle was of yellow crystal, and where there was snuff inside it appeared dark brown. One day after holding it up to the light he discovered a blob of snuff about the size of a pea in the lower left corner. As he bent the end of his ear-pick and gingerly poked it in, Master Nie, usually so taciturn, reached out to stop him.

"Don't scrape any more," he said, "or you'll spoil the picture."

Wu froze and stared blankly at him. "What did you say?"

Nie indicated the bottle. "Look and see."

Wu held it up once more to the light while burly Bao leaned over to have a look too. "Ha!" he exclaimed. "Fine. A bamboo and orchid design. I didn't know you were such a dab at painting snuff-bottles!" He and Nie both laughed.

Wu saw then that by poking about with his ear-pick he had inadvertently produced a picture: the lower left side was like a clump of orchids, the right side like bamboos. In spite of himself he smiled. Master Nie cheerfully reached for the bottle, bent the tip of his own ear-pick and with a few sure, deft strokes produced a design in the style of Zheng Banqiao.* He appended a line of old poetry too and the signature "A Man of Changbai".

With a bow Wu said, "You must excuse me, sir. I had no idea that you were such a fine artist."

Master Nie returned his bow. "I learned this little skill to make a living. But you, sir, have a natural flair — admirable."

Meanwhile the guard passed over his snuff saucer. "If you want some snuff, try this," he said. "Don't go on scraping your bottle or you'll spoil that picture."

Wu scooped up some snuff between his thumb and first finger, stuffed it into his nostrils and gave two hearty sneezes. He remarked with a smile, "For days I've been longing for a good sneeze."

Bao replied, "For days I've been waiting for you to ask me, but you never did. Is it because you can't read and were afraid I'd ask you to read *The Romance of the Three Kingdoms* to me?"

"Not knowing you I didn't like to ask," Wu explained. "If you'd offered me some I'd have taken it like a shot."

"How could I take liberties with a bannerman?" countered Bao.

---

* Zheng Banqiao (1693-1765) was a well-known artist.

By chatting like this the ice between them was broken. Wu asked the guard what the charge against him was. Stealing silver from the treasury, Bao told him.

"I heard that you have to strip naked before going in there, put on a uniform inside, then strip again before leaving. How can you bring silver out?" Wu wanted to know.

"The body has its orifices," said Bao. "You hide it up the biggest. Not in your mouth, though, because each time you leave you have to call out to the officer in charge."

Wu flushed and muttered, "Then surely you can't take much. Why should you be jailed for such petty pilfering?"

"Well, it's not easy," said Bao. "The most I ever smuggled out was four ingots weighing ten ounces, but passing the officer I had to fart, so one of them shot out. This is an old, old racket, so an officer with any sense would turn a blind eye; but I came up against someone new to the job. He made a big issue of it and had me locked up."

"Were you sentenced?"

"To execution."

"Heavens!"

"Don't worry, I shall get off. It costs several thousands to replace a guard, more than a prefectural post! If we couldn't smuggle out silver up our arses, who'd take the job? Most officers know that."

Master Nie's case, it turned out, was even stranger. He wasn't a prisoner, just lodging in prison. A craftsman who made pictures inside snuff-bottles in the style of Guyuexuan, some time earlier he had made a set of eighteen with realistically painted designs. This set had been bought by Ninth Master Zai, who liked it so much that he had sent for Nie. As Nie reached his mansion just as he had to go out, he ordered his servants to put him up somewhere. And in conclusion he said, "Find a safe place where no one else can get at him to order another set of these snuff-bottles. Otherwise mine won't be worth much."

A safe place? What could be a safer place than prison? Ninth Master had friends in the Ministry of Punishments, so his servants installed Master Nie there. Already two months had passed, yet Ninth Master hadn't found the time to see him.

Wu asked, "At this rate when will you get out?"

"Whenever Ninth Master remembers me," said Nie.

After that Wu made friends with them both. When time dragged he asked Nie to teach him how to paint the inside of snuff-bottles. As Nie knew that no bannerman would rely on this for a living or spoil his own trade, he gladly taught him some of the basic techniques. Wu proved to have a natural aptitude. He filled his bottle with earth to colour it brown, then emptied out the earth and drew designs with his ear-pick, showing each to Master Nie for his criticism. He repeated this process until by degrees he mastered the art and was eager to perfect it. But then because of the weight on his mind and his poor diet he suddenly fell ill. Bao gave the warder money to fetch a doctor and Nie brewed his medicine for him. When he vomited or had diarrhoea, the two of them washed and nursed him without a sign of disgust. Despite his pampered life Wu couldn't but feel touched by their devotion, one of them condemned to death, the other the victim of a great injustice. When over the worst he said, "You two have saved my life, how am I to thank you?"

"We're friends in adversity, why talk of thanks?" asked Nie. "Doing you a good turn I've forgotten my own troubles and don't feel so bad."

"I'm the one who should be thanking *you*, sir!" declared Bao. "A few days ago I kept thinking: If I'm really snuffed out and the King of Hell asks what good deeds I've done, I won't be able to answer. First I slaved like an ox for my master stealing silver, and then stole for myself. When I die I'll have no one to mourn me — I've done nothing for anyone else. But doing a bit for Master Wu has cheered me up, because now when I die someone will remember me — right? This is something money won't buy." He burst into tears.

Nie hastily put in, "Stop blubbering. What's got into you? You're usually so jolly."

"I used to crack jokes to keep my spirits up. Now that I've not joked for a few days my heart feels lighter."

Wu said, "Your colleagues treat you so well, you shouldn't feel isolated."

"They're afraid I'll inform on them," retorted Bao. "Trying to shut my mouth to save their own skins, not out of genuine feeling. If I get out I shall quit this damn job. I'll be Master Nie's assistant or your gateman, Master Wu, to keep you company. It won't cost you a cent, I've plenty of silver. I just want you to treat me as your younger brother."

This was so unlike Bao's usual way of talking, the others questioned him about his past. They learned that most treasury guards were bought as beggar orphans under ten, and trained to hide silver in their anuses.

First his owner stuffed a greased egg up a boy's arse, then a stone or iron ball, gradually increasing the weight and the amount. If any boy resisted he was beaten. It was as cruel as training a cormorant to catch fish. When the boy was old enough to join the guards and his master had got him a place, in the daytime he had to carry loads of silver; in the evening his master waited for him at the gate to chain him and cart him home, not unchaining him till it was time to go back the next day. In 1900 Bao's master had been killed by the soldiery while he lay low in the treasury, and so he had won his freedom. Being homeless he had rented a couple of rooms in an incense shop where he kept his stolen silver. The shopkeeper, Ma, a decent man, had promised Bao that when he had saved enough he would help him find a wife. But a few months later Bao had landed in trouble.

"You ought to have been more careful," remarked Wu.

"We often get caught out," replied Bao. "But the others have families or bosses to pull strings to get them off. I have only my mates, who won't put themselves out too much. So I still don't know where I am."

After that the three of them were on closer terms.

Some days later the warder suddenly announced that Wu had a visitor. He felt both pleased and alarmed. Pleased to have contact at last with outside, afraid that during his absence of six months or more some trouble had happened at home. He was startled to find that his visitor was neither his wife nor Nanny Liu but Shou Ming.

"Why have you taken the trouble to come, friend?" he asked.

"Isn't that what friends are for?"

"Why hasn't my wife been? Has something happened at home?"

"Nothing." The silence that followed convinced Wu that something was wrong. Before he could ask, Shou Ming went on, "I'm here to apologize. I've found out that this lawsuit of yours was cooked up by that scoundrel Xu Huanzhang. Since you offended him because of me, I can't let it go at that. Don't worry, I'll find a way to get you out. There's a new magistrate now in the Ministry of Punishments, and those men in cahoots with Xu have left. I'm working on it. Before long you'll hear something. Take my advice and tell the truth next time you're cross-examined. Say yes, Prince Duan wanted you to join the Tiger Spirit Battalion, but you refused. As for those lines you made up on the spur of the moment, you later forgot all about them because you'd never had anything to do with the Righteous and Harmonious Society. Just deny all the charges, I'll see to everything else."

When Wu, back in his cell, told his friends they congratulated him. That evening, as it happened, Bao was sent wine, and the three of them drank together. Then Nie sat up straight and drew the two others closer. "We were fated to come together like this," he said. "Once Master Wu goes, who knows when we'll meet again. I'm getting on in years, not long for this world, and I've something to ask you both."

He sounded so solemn that they listened intently.

Nie told them that while he could paint the inside of snuff-bottles, his chief skill lay in firing Guyuexuan wares. This technique had been invented by Hu Xuezhou, a Suzhou scholar of the Qian Long reign, several of whose ancestors had served as officials and amassed an excellent collection of porcelain. After repeated failures in the examinations, Hu gave up all thought of fame and diverted himself by studying ceramics. From appreciating the work of other men he went on to making new wares of his own, combining Western enamel with Chinese techniques to produce an eggshell porcelain as bright as a mirror. He called this Guyuexuan. Qian Long on one of his tours south, presented with some of this porcelain by Suzhou officials, admired it so much that he ordered Hu to the capital to serve the Imperial House. Since the emperor conferred these wares on his princes and chief ministers, some reached the hands of the people of Beijing. They caused a sensation in the capital and fetched enormous prices. Many potters tried in vain to counterfeit them, for their secrets were closely guarded. Hu's family had passed this art on to only one male descendant in each subsequent generation. They employed assistants but only for the rough work, dismissing them at crucial moments when they worked behind locked doors.

Hu's descendant in the seventh generation, Hu Shushi, had one son and one daughter. By this time the family was fairly rich. When his son was six a tutor was engaged for him and his orphaned cousin Nie Xiaoxuan, partly to keep the boy company and partly as an act of charity. Little Nie was an intelligent lad. Apart from his classwork he studied calligraphy and painting, revealing a natural aptitude and making better progress than his cousin. When Hu Shushi had time he would instruct him, so that by the age of twelve the lad could paint the inside of snuff-bottles and was assured of a livelihood in future. After the tutor left he stayed on to help out with odd jobs in repayment for his board for the last few years.

In the tenth year of Xian Feng (1860), Hu's son was twenty and his father was about to initiate him into the art of making Guyuexuan when Anglo-French forces attacked Beijing. Young Hu, who had gone to Tianjin on business, was trampled by the horses of these undisciplined troops. Less than a month after his return home he vomited blood and died. As for Hu's daughter, pockmarked since her childhood she was now in her late twenties but not yet betrothed. She kept house for her father. Hu Shushi would soon be sixty and these blows aged him prematurely. Worried because his time was running out and his daughter had no husband to rely on, and not wanting the family skill to die out, he invited Nie Xiaoxuan to become his apprentice and son-in-law at the same time. Nie was fascinated by Guyuexuan, but had never dreamed of learning its mysteries. As for his girl cousin he had nothing against her, since they had been brought up together. He accepted gratefully. Then elders of their clan were invited and a lucky day was chosen for Nie to bow to his master and marry into his house. For fear, however, that his son-in-law might have a change of heart, Hu showed Nie only how to mix materials and paint, and taught his daughter how to fire the kiln, so as to ensure their continuous co-operation since each would be indispensable to the other.

Having told them this, Master Nie took Wu's hand and said, "Little did I think that over thirty years later my wife too would be killed by foreign troops. Luckily she'd already passed on her skill to our daughter. It was with my daughter's help that I made that set of eighteen snuff-bottles. Now my life hangs by a thread, and what if I die? I'd thought of doing as my master did and choosing a young apprentice and son-in-law, to teach him my craft. But I doubt if I'll have the chance."

The guard said, "Doesn't sound as if Ninth Master has it in for you. So why lock on the dark side?"

"You never know," replied Nie. "And it would be criminal to let this skill die out with me. I must find someone to take over from me; then I shan't care even if it comes to the worst. In the whole wide world you're the only two I can ask. If one of you will agree, I shall be able to close my eyes in peace."

"I'm too crude for this," said Bao. "I could do donkey-work or help with money, but I can't read or write, can't draw a straight line — I couldn't for the life of me learn to paint."

Nie's eyes turned to Wu Shibao.

Wu thought it over then said, "This is too big a thing for me to take on. All my life I've fooled about and never taken anything seriously. I don't think I'm up to it. It's too great a responsibility to accept."

Nie countered, "I know you're a man of property and look down on earning a living. But are you content to live out your life like that, taking and giving nothing in return?"

"I've never thought about it."

"Suppose we compare this world of ours to an inn where all of us must put up. If we simply use what's left there by other travellers, not contributing anything, in the long run we'll leave nothing to those coming after us but a heap of rubble. On the other hand if each of us does his bit, if you plant a tree, I plant a flower, this inn will grow more prosperous. And those coming after will look up to us. If everybody does this, wouldn't this world become a better place?"

"Right!" exclaimed Bao. "Even I can see that. Don't you get it, Master Wu?"

Wu demurred, "It would take a long time to learn such a wonderful skill."

"You can write and paint, you know my style, so that's no problem," Nie assured him. "All you need to learn is how to produce the different colours. This is the precious secret we've passed on from generation to generation. And this is where other potters have failed when they try to imitate our Guyuexuan. We've produced thirty different colours, but they at most manage seven. This skill is my whole life to me. I'm passing it on to you and entrusting my daughter to you at the same time. Since I'm asking a favour of you, I wouldn't dream of setting up as your master. We're friends, and I don't believe you'll let me down."

Nie was obviously dead serious. Wu, recalling how he had nursed him through his illness, felt it would be too heartless to refuse. He sprang to his feet, smoothed his clothes and bowed. Nie hastily protested, "This won't do."

"Since this is a serious business, let's go about it properly," Wu replied.

"I'm passing on an art," objected Nie, "not setting up as your teacher, Master Wu." They went ahead in earnest then, one teaching and one learning Guyuexuan techniques.

In less than a month Wu Shibao was summoned to court. Shou Ming had pulled certain strings, and the new minister going through the old files had decided to make a start with Wu Shibao's case. The charge against him was refusal to join the Tiger Spirit Battalion. The minister said, "That Tiger Spirit Battalion was partly responsible for the atrocities of the allied army. Since Wu didn't join it, he's in no way involved." He sent for Wu. Acting on Shou Ming's advice, Wu refrained this time from invoking his dead parents. He protested his innocence and gave truthful answers to all the questions put him. The new minister, also a Manchu, sighed, "How could a bannerman be imprisoned on such a flimsy pretext? This is really beyond me. Release him!" He ordered his secretary to summarize the case, so that he could indict his predecessor.

Wu kowtowed resoundingly three times, and so ended his year and eight months behind bars.

As he was about to leave gaol, Nie produced a package wrapped in tissue paper from which he took two gold bracelets. He told Wu to take these to his daughter Willow, for she would recognize these tokens and trust him.

6

On leaving prison Wu was struck by the width of the streets, the vastness of the sky, the smartness of the passers-by and the cheerful bustle all around which contrasted so strongly with his unkempt hair, pale face and ragged clothes. Pedestrians eyed him superciliously and knowing that he cut a poor figure he slunk along at the side of the road, head bent, afraid of meeting some acquaintance. In the time of Kang Xi it had been decreed that the Eight Banners should garrison different districts. Since then the number of bannermen had increased and certain houses had changed hands, but the Wu family still lived in Liquor Lane. When Wu entered the lane, however, he couldn't find his house. He paced up and down several times, finally stopping at the gate of his neighbour Gu. The Gus, captains in the White Banner, had been the Wus' neighbours for several generations. Wu Shibao had attended the same school as their eldest son. There was no mistaking their house. He stepped forward and knocked. The gate was opened a crack by their gateman Zhou Cheng; but after a single look he shut it again.

"Clear off! No beggars allowed here."

"Old Zhou, it's me!" called Wu. "Don't you recognize me?"

"Who?" Zhou re-opened the gate and stared at him, then muttered to himself, "Can it be Master Wu?" He bent one knee in greeting. "How are you, sir? Over your trouble?"

"I'm all right, but how is it I can't find my house? Is that it with the new awning, freshly painted door posts, and plastered walls? . . ."

Zhou was wondering how to answer when out came a middle-aged man in a silk suit, his hair loosely plaited, holding a folding fan. "Who are you talking to, Zhou Cheng?" he demanded.

Wu stepped forward and bent one knee. "It's me, Second Uncle. Greetings!"

"Wu Shibao! What a scarecrow you look! I heard you'd gone to Shandong to make your fortune with some Mongol prince. Why do you look so down and out?"

"Second Uncle, I've just. . . ."

Gu scowled. "After being jailed as a Boxer you still

dare show your face here? Shame on you! You! You're
no neighbour of mine. Zhou Cheng, shut the gate."

The gate shut with a bang.

Wu was trembling with rage, unable to move, his
head in a whirl, when the gate opened again.

"Clear out, Master Wu," Zhou Cheng whispered.
"Your house was sold long ago to the Huang family of
Taipingcang."

"Where's my family then?"

"Your wife died last winter. Nanny Liu took the
young master off with her."

"You. . . ."

Zhou Cheng's master called to him then, and having
dropped a string of cash at Wu's feet he quietly shut
the gate and bolted it.

Everything was dark before Wu's eyes. He seemed
to be choking. All sense of direction lost, he blundered
along to the north end of South Small Street. A horseman approached from the east with two guards and behind them a big sedan-chair with felt covering. At sight
of it people yelled, "Make way! Master Ma is going
back to Beansprout Lane." They scurried out of the way
but Wu kept going, staring blankly ahead, as if he were
blind and deaf. Luckily a bailiff came over for fear he
might make trouble. He pushed him into a corner and
slapped his cheeks. That brought Wu to his senses. He
burst out sobbing and after that felt better. But where
should he go?

He realized that with his ragged clothes, matted hair
and grimy face he couldn't call on anyone. Besides, it
was growing dark, his legs ached and his stomach was
empty. He must find somewhere to spend the night,
and decide what to do tomorrow. He wasn't far from

Chaoyang Gate. Better try one of the inns for carters there. This string of cash should be enough for two bowls of noodles and a place on the *kang*.

He limped over to an inn and a waiter welcomed him at the gate.

"What do you want?"

"To spend the night."

"Come on in."

Just then a middle-aged man in slippers, holding a water-pipe, came out and barred Wu's way.

"Where are you going?"

"I'm staying here."

"Staying here?" The man eyed him from head to foot, then said grimly, "We're full up."

"I don't want a single room, I'll share a *kang*."

"Our big *kang* is full up too. They still haven't closed the city gates, go and have a look outside."

As Wu turned to leave he heard this innkeeper fume, "Have you no eyes in your head? If you let in a man like that you'd frighten all our customers away. Starving for opium by the look of him, he'd filch whatever he could."

Wu shivered as he made off. He reflected that since grain carts passed through Chaoyang Gate the inns, being big, were choosy. Better head north to find a smaller inn which would be more obliging. It was nearly lighting-up time when he found a little inn outside the city with some earthen tables in front of it and a few tree stumps as stools. He sat down and ordered four ounces of buckwheat noodles. Having eaten this he asked the innkeeper, "Can I stay for the night — it's too late to go into town."

The innkeeper saw that his clothes though old looked

respectable, he hadn't bolted his food and had tipped the waiter. So he answered with a smile, "You're welcome. We've a big *kang* in the east room with only one carter there, you'll be company for him." He told the waiter to show the guest in, brew a pot of good tea and take him a basin of water.

The carter, sitting cross-legged on the *kang*, was eating donkey meat to go with his liquor. He nodded to the newcomer and said, "Good evening. Like a drink?"

Since leaving gaol that day this was the first man who had treated Wu civilly, although they were complete strangers. He bent one knee and said, "That's very good of you!"

The carter's greeting had been quite perfunctory, but Wu's sincere thanks made him spring up and take his arm. "Fate must have brought us together," he said. "Please give me the pleasure of drinking with me." Tempted by the smell of the liquor Wu replied, "Then I won't stand on ceremony." He sat down on the other side of the low *kang* table while the waiter went off to fetch chopsticks and report this to his boss. The innkeeper was fond of company and countrified old-world ways, so he fried two sliced towel gourds and took this in to them saying, "I hear you hit it off as soon as you met, bringing good luck to my small inn. Politeness pays, so I'm treating you both to a dish."

Urged by the carter to join them, after demurring politely he sat on the edge of the *kang*. He had been rather puzzled by Wu. So when a few cups had made Wu more animated, he tried to draw him out. Wu, who had been bursting to confide in someone, described how he had been framed, imprisoned, released, unable to find his house, and finally turned away from the inn in town.

Liquor loosens a man's tongue and makes him reckless. At the end of Wu's account the carter swore that if he met Xu Huanzhang he'd horsewhip him, if he met Gu he'd curse his ancestors. He pounded the table in his indignation.

"Well, sir," the innkeeper asked Wu, "what do you plan to do now?"

"As soon as it's light I'll go to look up a friend."

The innkeeper shook his head. "First you should shave your temples and plait your queue, then have a bath and shave and change into clean clothes — you can borrow or hire some. The way you are now, no one in town is going to let you in — you may even be arrested as a vagrant. Don't take offence at my frankness, but even beggars look a sight better than you."

Wu nodded then shook his head. "You're quite right, but I haven't a cent."

"Have you nothing you can sell?" asked the innkeeper.

"After a year and more in gaol with nobody even sending me food, I've nothing."

"Just now when you paid for your meal, I saw you take out a snuff-bottle, a dark crystal bottle with a design and inscription inside it. Right?"

Wu fingered his pocket, exclaiming, "Seems I've given myself away!"

"In my line of business we learn to use our eyes," the innkeeper explained. "When good customers bring valuables here, I have to keep an eye on them. I also have to see what strangers bring in, because I don't want to be involved in a lawsuit. If not for that bottle

I wouldn't have dared take you in. I'm a rough fellow and don't understand antiques, but living in the capital I've seen enough to tell that yours is something special. In fact, the way you look now, this snuff-bottle can only land you in trouble. People itching to get hold of it will accuse you of stealing it. There are all sorts of rascals about, and weasels go for lame ducks. Suppose some of them started a fight with you and snatched your bottle, what could you do about it? Take my advice and sell it. A family like yours must have plenty more. After you've found your son you can enjoy life again; so why not use this now to tide you over?"

Wu was convinced. Besides, he wanted to see what connoisseurs thought of his skill. He nodded. "Tomorrow, then, I'll take it to a curio shop to show them."

The innkeeper laughed. "That wouldn't do. A big shop would swindle you. Seeing you so hard up they'd offer you next to nothing."

"What's your advice then?"

"I'll show it to some of my friends. If they want it, fine. Otherwise I'll go with you to the Ghosts' Market.* But I warn you, if we sell it I shall expect a commission."

The innkeeper often made a bit on the side like this.

In those days the Grand Canal was used by travellers going south by boat, and the area outside Dongzhi Gate was deserted. The innkeepers here had to put up thieves and smugglers and help them to get rid of stolen goods. Since this innkeeper's best contacts were pawnshop

---

* So called because the salesmen took their wares there after dark and dispersed at dawn. Since many of them sold stolen goods it was also known as the Thieves' Market.

assistants or men in the Thieves' Market, he didn't advise Wu to go to a curio shop. When Wu agreed he asked to have a closer look at the snuff-bottle.

"What a beauty!" exclaimed the carter, grabbing the bottle from Wu to have a look. "How could you paint those branches and leaves inside? Half a years' carting wouldn't earn me enough to buy this bottle."

"Then be careful not to drop it, or you'll have to sell your horse and cart to replace it," joked the innkeeper as he took the bottle away to examine it. Though no connoisseur, he had often sold snuff-bottles for other people, and in the process acquired some discrimination. As this type of interior painting now had a history of seventy or eighty years, he was familiar with it and knew the names of many snuff-bottle painters. He had sold one painted by Zhou Yueyuan and it seemed to him that Wu's bottle was similar. So he kept a tight grip on it. But after a close look he shook his head.

"What's wrong with it?" Wu asked.

"There's no name."

"Yes there is — the man from Changbai."*

"No seal."

Wu thought to himself, "It was hard enough getting hold of ink in gaol, where would I get vermilion for a seal?" He answered, "Ma Shaoxuan's bottles don't usually have a seal."

The innkeeper objected, "Other bottles are opaque or dark. Why is this of yours transparent?"

"Most bottles painted in Dao Guang's reign are transparent. This proves the age of mine."

---

* The Changbai Mountains in the north were where the Manchus came from.

The carter was worn out, and they were talking over his head. He said, "Why the hell argue about it here? Go to the market tomorrow to see what price it'll fetch. I'll be off in the small hours to Yellow Temple. If you want a lift you'd better turn in early."

7

By the fourth watch the carter was ready with his big iron-hooped cart. He headed north beside the moat till he reached Desheng Gate.

Outside Desheng Gate before dawn there were two markets: the Labour Market and the Thieves' Market. Because they were adjacent, people often lumped them together and would say, "Let's go to the dawn market at Desheng Gate." In fact the two markets had nothing in common. The Labour Market was where carpenters, masons or coolies went before daybreak to find work. And if you wanted to build a house, put up a stove or have a wedding suite made — in those days they didn't have wine cabinets or sofas but were just as keen as we are today on wedding furniture — you went to this market too. You stood by the road and called, "I want two masons and an odd-job man." At once men flocked round to ask "What pay?" And so an agreement was reached. There weren't many clocks or watches in those days, nor was there an eight-hour working day. The rule was to start work at sunrise and knock off at sunset. So men had to be hired at five or six in the morning. Hence they were called "five o'clock workmen".

The Thieves' Market was quite different. It had no stalls in fixed places, nor were goods displayed according to categories. They covered the whole gamut from luxury articles to the cudgels used by beggars to beat dogs. And you could place orders too. You slung your money-bag over your left shoulder, rested your chin on your right hand and took up your stand in a conspicuous place. Then you would be accosted.

"Looking for something?"

"A small jade pendant — with blood red marks on it."

"I can get you one. It'll be pricey."

"Well, let me see it first."

Certain transactions involved many taels of silver. But there were cheap goods too.

"What do you want, sir?"

"I've lost one of the five brass buttons on my jacket."

"It so happens that I have one!"

"How much?"

"Just give me those two dumplings and we'll call it quits."

That was another deal. People here had to be good-tempered. You mustn't flare up however high the price asked, or lose your temper however little was offered.

"How much is this tin candlestick?"

"Tin? Look again! It's copper-nickel."

"How much?"

"Ten taels."

"Nothing doing."

"What's your offer?"

"One tael."

"Up that a bit."

"No more!"

"Done."

Why sell it so cheap? The candlestick was stolen and

the thief wanted to play safe by getting rid of it quickly. For this reason, however valuable a thing you couldn't ask where it came from. And for the same reason you really could find bargains: a precious blue and white jade bottle for the price of a bottle of vinegar, or a bronze Shang cup for the price of a brass spittoon. On the other hand you might buy a root of coriander passed off as ginseng, or Mongol boots with paper soles passed off as brocade buskins. But in those days Beijingers were less sophisticated and liked to boast of their bargains to show how smart they were. Most who were bamboozled kept quiet about it for fear of being laughed at. So one heard only about the bargains in the Thieves' Market, and more and more bargain-hunters went there at the crack of dawn. Then sharpsters bought cheap glass bottles, polished them and coloured them to look like antiques, and craftily passed them off as stolen goods, standing in some dark corner to tout these wares. If a bannerman or noble came along they would pretend to be reluctant to sell, but in the end would ask — and get — the price of agate or nephrite. By the time it was light enough for the customer to catch on to this swindle, the Thieves' Market had broken up. Then to save face he would keep it a secret.

It was after the fourth watch by the time the carter had driven Wu Shibao and the innkeeper to the Yellow Temple. In those days it was already derelict because the Lama centre in Beijing had moved to the Yonghe Palace.

The innkeeper led Wu about a *li* to the west. Turning south they saw lights glimmering in the distance and shadowy figures moving about the Thieves' Market, raising a din. They made their way there quickly. The market seemed a shambles. Some stalls had hung up oxhorn lanterns, others paper lanterns, yet others aristocratic but ramshackle festive lanterns. The colours of the goods were hard to make out, although their shapes could be seen. There were pans and crockery, tables, chairs and stools, lutes, chess sets, scrolls of painting, swords and spears, fishing rods, opium lamps, porcelain, glass, bronze, lacquerware and women's clothing. . . . Some men were leading bear cubs, some carrying owls. The place was a jumble of everything you could imagine.

Wu asked, "How can we sell anything when we haven't brought a lantern?"

The innkeeper laughed. "The less you say here the better. Just keep an eye on me and don't get lost."

He stopped in front of a small stall and squatted down for a look. On a piece of the blue cloth were two dishes for washing brushes, a square inkstone, a few wine cups and four porcelain snuff-bottles. He picked up a coloured bottle with a dragon design.

"How much?"

The stall-holder held up four fingers. The innkeeper put the bottle down and stood up.

"How much will you give?" asked the other.

"A dragon with only three claws isn't worth anything."

"I've better ones." The salesman produced a purse and gingerly took out two snuff-bottles wrapped in cotton-wool and paper.

Wu craned forward to have a look, and saw that one had an obscene painting by Ma Shaoxuan. The innkeeper asked its price.

"I can't sell it for less than twenty taels," said the

stallkeeper. "And that's because it's synthetic jade. If it were crystal I'd ask twice that price."

"Will you sell it for two taels?"

"All right. 'If your first sale's a give-away, you'll have luck the whole day.' "

The innkeeper beckoned Wu to follow him, and they went to several more stalls to price snuff-bottles, after which they stopped by a big stall under a street light.

"Now we have an idea of the market price," the innkeeper said. "This bottle of ours will fetch at most fifteen taels."

Wu pretended to sigh, though inwardly delighted. Because this bottle of his had cost ten taels, and never in his life had he sold anything at a profit.

This large stall had on it knick-knacks of various kinds including a few snuff-bottles. Two had interior paintings of Western girls, and these were being examined by a tall, thin, round-shouldered man squatting on the ground. The price asked was fifty taels; he offered three taels apiece. When the stall-holder came down to forty, he raised his offer to seven for the pair. Finally he bought them for fifteen, wrapped them up in a handkerchief and walked away. The innkeeper followed him closely for some distance, then stepped up to him and said:

"I can see you're a connoisseur, sir. I've something else to show you." Without waiting for an answer, he produced Wu's snuff-bottle from his girdle and held it out. The other man rubbed it with his thumb, glanced at it casually and said, "Not bad. How much?"

"Let's not haggle. You can have it for twenty taels."

"It's worth it. Show it to someone else. You shouldn't

have any trouble selling it." He returned the bottle and went on his way. The innkeeper followed him.

"Have another look at it, even if you don't want it. Make an offer."

The other man stopped and took the bottle again. He held it up to a lantern by the roadside and asked seriously, "How much?"

"I said twenty taels and no haggling."

"If it had a seal it would be worth it. There's no seal."

"Eighteen."

The man held the bottle up again and gave an exclamation of surprise. "Where did you get this?" he asked eagerly.

"Where did I get it? Don't you know the rule here?"

The other gripped the bottle tightly. "You don't understand. Just tell me where it came from."

"Never mind that, it's not stolen."

"I didn't say it was. I asked where it's from. This bottle has been through my hands, in fact I sold it. I want to find the man who bought it from me."

Wu sprang out from the shadows then and seized his arm. "Brother Shou Ming!" he cried. "It looked like you but I couldn't be sure, so I've been waiting, watching."

"Is it you, Master Wu? Why didn't you let me know you were out? If I hadn't found you today I meant to go to the Ministry of Punishments to ask. . . ."

Wu pulled out a handkerchief to wipe his eyes. "I wanted to call on you. But how could I show myself outside like this? I decided to sell this bottle to buy some new clothes."

Shou Ming's question about the snuff-bottle had made

the innkeeper suspect that Wu had stolen it. He was about to slip away when he saw this wasn't the case. He came over again. "So you two know each other. What a lucky meeting!"

Wu lost no time in introducing the innkeeper to his friend. Shou Ming asked, "Have you left anything in the inn?"

"Nothing," Wu answered.

Then Shou Ming offered the innkeeper a large string of cash. "We two haven't seen each other for so long, I'm taking my brother to stay with me for a few days," he said. "You've been a great help to him, so allow me to treat you to a bowl of tea."

Though thanking him the innkeeper felt disgruntled. He suspected Shou Ming of taking Wu away to make a profit out of his snuff-bottle, depriving him of his commission.

Wu asked, "What brought you to the Thieves' Market today?"

"I often come here."

"You must have time on your hands."

"If I don't do a little business how am I to eat? You've been out of circulation for over a year and don't know the situation. I must put you in the picture. As the state has to pay the foreigners a 'Boxer Indemnity', our bannermen's allowances have been cut. And in troubled times like these, who gives private opera shows? So there's no opening for fiddlers. A bannerman has to live, like everyone else."

"Can you tell me what's become of my family?"

"I know the whole story, but this is no place to talk. Come home with me and I'll tell you."

8

The morning after Wu Shibao's release two of Ninth Master's servants, one carrying a lantern, the other leading a mule, went to the prison to fetch Nie Xiaoxuan. When a warder went in to call him, he and Bao were sound asleep. The warder kicked him saying, "Get up, get up. Congratulations!"

Nie shook with fear. For in those days if a warder came before dawn to offer congratulations, it usually meant big trouble. He nudged Bao and said, "Brother, this may be the end of me. . . . If you get out, please take my family word. Remember the date, so that they don't get it wrong. . . ."

The warder slapped him on the back, exclaiming, "You've got it wrong. Ninth Master has sent for you." The two servants outside, tired of waiting, urged them to hurry. The warder bundled Nie out and locked the door before Bao, still half asleep, had grasped what was happening. When he did he went to the door and shouted, "Don't worry, I shan't forget."

Nie turned back to call, "Tell my daughter I can't bear to think of our family's craft dying out. Tell her to find Master Wu. . . ."

A servant dragged him off before he could finish, fuming, "Stop dawdling. Ninth Master's waiting. If he loses patience he'll raise hell. Get a move on!"

Out of the prison they helped Nie on to the mule and hurried to the south of Qianmen. . . . Hey, you may say, surely all the princes lived in the Inner City. Why should Ninth Master live outside Qianmen?

Ninth Master, the eldest son of a prince, had at twelve been made a general of the second rank. He should have been further promoted, but when Pujun, whom he had always disliked, had been made the heir apparent he had sworn and raged in his cups. Word of this reached the Empress Dowager and so she refused to promote him. As a result, Ninth Master put on a show of leading a fast life but actually kept close to Prince Su and made up to foreigners. He redeemed a celebrated prostitute and bought a mansion for her outside Qianmen, where he spent most of his time, neglecting his proper business. In fact he wanted to avoid being spied on in the palace, and to ingratiate himself with foreigners. He wore foreign material, sported a foreign watch, smoked foreign cigarettes and listened to foreign music — to him everything foreign was superior. And this paid off. Especially after the Boxer Uprising when the Manchu government had to send an envoy to Tokyo to apologize to the Japanese government. The court appointed Na Tong as its envoy, and Prince Su told him that to smooth his way he should take Ninth Master with him. Na Tong reported this to the Empress Dowager, saying that it was the foreigners' wish. So she dared not refuse, though she never liked Ninth Master. Preparing to go abroad, he had forgotten Nie. But today, while selecting gifts for the Mikado and Japanese ministers, he had taken another look at Nie's snuffbottles and remembered that the potter was still in prison. He had therefore sent for him. Ninth Master smoked opium all night and slept in the morning. He had sent for Nie after midnight, but it was morning by the time he arrived and Ninth Master was asleep. The steward put Nie in the stable to wait till his master woke up in the afternoon.

Ninth Master had taken such a fancy to those eighteen

snuff-bottles that he had had Nie locked up so that he couldn't make another set, in which case his would no longer be unique. However, now that several months had passed he felt less strongly about it. Besides, if he gave these bottles to the Japanese they would no longer be his. He had therefore intended to give Nie some silver and let him go. Had Nie arrived punctually at dawn or Ninth Master stayed awake a little longer, that is what would have happened. But when Ninth Master woke that afternoon he was told that Liao Qian, a monk from Haiguang Temple, and Nie were both waiting and he was asked which he would see first.

This Liao Qian had come from Hengshan in Hunan with a golden dish containing his right hand, which he had chopped off and fried in order to ask princes and ministers for alms to build a new chapel. This had caused quite a stir in the capital. Ninth Master, who loved anything sensational, naturally sent for him first and, without troubling to change his clothes, went to the hall by the second gate to receive him. The monk greeted him and was offered a seat. They chatted politely until he asked for alms.

"Wait a bit!" said Ninth Master. "You're said to have cut off a hand to raise alms to build a chapel. I want value for my money. So far I haven't even seen that hand of yours, so how can you ask for alms? Take off that red cloth and let me have a look."

The monk hastily bowed. "Amida Buddha!" he cried. "I didn't want to offend Your Highness' eyes."

"Stop talking tripe! Off with it."

The monk knelt to remove the red cloth, then held up the charred hand black as a bird's talon. Ninth Master, bending forward to look, nearly bumped his nose on it, making him start. He pounded the table and swore, "You swine! This isn't a human hand, you've fried up some claw and brought it to Beijing to cheat us."

The monk protested, "Never! I've set my heart on building up our poor temple, how could I cheat Heaven or our benefactors?"

"If you're really in earnest, cut off your other hand now. Then you can stop begging and I'll pay for the building of your new chapel — how about it?"

Pouring with sweat, the monk kowtowed repeatedly.

"Here!" Ninth Master called to his men. "Press his hand down on the threshold and chop it off for me."

With a shout two guardsmen dragged the monk to the gate, rolled up his sleeve and pressed his left wrist down. Then swish! they unsheathed their swords. The terrified monk passed out. At a sign from Ninth Master the guardsmen sheathed their swords.

"Bring him to with a basin of water!" he ordered.

Two basins of cold water were fetched to douse the monk, who came to, shivering. When he saw his hand still intact he made haste to kowtow.

Ninth Master bellowed with laughter. "Well, how about it?"

The monk pulled a long face. "You frightened me out of my wits."

"When you yanked up that stinking claw of yours you nearly bumped my nose. You gave me a fright — why shouldn't I pay you back? All right, go and tell my steward I'm donating five hundred taels."

The monk went off in a daze, leaving Ninth Master in a high good humour. He sent for Nie Xiaoxuan, who stopped outside the gate, kneeling down there to kowtow. His ragged clothes amused Ninth Master, as did his abject terror. He chortled, "Show me your hands."

In bewilderment Nie fearfully held out his hands, ashamed that they were so dirty after those months in prison. But this didn't trouble Ninth Master. First he inspected the palms, then told him to turn his hands over. He then said to the servants, "Look at them. These are hands too. The monk's can only beat a wooden fish* or be chopped off to raise alms; these can fire Guyuexuan porcelain and paint beauties — that's worth a lot more. I'll buy them. Name your price."

Nie said, "You've already paid me, sir, for that set of snuff-bottles."

"He's not buying snuff-bottles," put in one of the servants. "Ninth Master wants to buy the hands that made them."

Nie told him, "Tell your master my hands can only work when they're part of me. If you cut them off they won't be worth anything."

He had said this in a pique, but Ninth Master thought it a smart answer. "Right," he said. "You can sell me just your hands, or your whole body. Let's draw up a contract. If you sell all your Guyuexuan to me, and to no one else, I'll pay for you in silver. If you sell just your hands, all right, you won't be able to work and I'll support you."

Nie was too flabbergasted to reply.

Ninth Master went on, "Steward, take Nie Xiaoxuan to the stable and see that he's well looked after. I'll

_____

* A percussion instrument used by Buddhist priests to beat the rhythm when chanting sutras.

give him time to make up his mind. If he hasn't by this evening, he'll have to do as I say."

"Have a heart, Ninth Master!" cried Nie as two guardsmen lugged him out. Ninth Master laughed for a while, then ordered his steward to weigh out ten taels of silver for Nie the next day, and give him some old clothes before letting him go. Today he would first play this trick on him.

Seeing his master's good mood, to please him the steward said, "Sir, I've got the hundred goats you wanted. We pay that mutton shop opposite three taels a day for the use of them. When do you want to use them? Just give the word."

Ninth Master roared with laughter. "I want them now. Have them herded to Yi Shun Teahouse to wait for me there."

This teahouse outside Xuanwu Gate, not far from Hufang Bridge, was patronized by actors and curio dealers, but few nobles ever went there. Ninth Master sometimes amused himself by dressing in cotton like a commoner and going for a stroll outside Qianmen. The other day he had gone out again incognito and in Liulichang met a man with a performing monkey. He had a small cart drawn by a goat and was making the monkey drive it round in circles. The sight intrigued Ninth Master, who bought the cart and goat for a dozen taels. When he wanted the monkey, the owner wouldn't sell. He told the owner to bring the monkey on his back while he himself led the goat, to put on a performance in his mansion. Reaching Yi Shun Teahouse he ordered the man to wait outside while he went in for some tea with the goat. But no sooner had he found a seat than a waiter came over to tell him, "Sir, we don't allow goats in here."

"I'll go as soon as I've rested," said Ninth Master. "My goat isn't occupying a seat, so why can't it come in?"

The young manager behind the counter, new to his job, announced, "The goat can stay if you pay for it."

"Very well."

After drinking his tea Ninth Master paid for two bowls. The waiter hesitated to take this money, but the young manager snapped at him, "Go on. Take it."

This had annoyed Ninth Master. On his return home he had ordered his steward to borrow or to buy a hundred goats.

So now, after a few puffs of opium and some snacks, Ninth Master called for his horse and rode straight to Yi Shun Teahouse. At the gate he handed his reins to a groom and walked in. That afternoon a storyteller had been invited to tell an extract from the romance *The Three Heroes and Five Gallants*, so seven tenths of the tables were full. As he hadn't yet started his story all the customers were staring out of the window at the two men in red-tasselled caps and the flock of goats standing stockstill there, blocking the road. They couldn't guess what this meant. Ninth Master marched up to the counter, behind which today a man with a beard was seated. He asked, "Where's that young manager?"

The young manager in the counting-house at the back stuck his head out to ask, "What is it?"

"I came here the other day to drink some tea. You

charged me for two bowls, one for me, one for my goat
— right?"

The manager stared at him and recalled what had
happened. An overbearing money-bags who felt the
whole city was too small to hold him, he stepped forward and answered, "Yes I did, what of it? You got
off cheap; the price has gone up today. Twice as much
for a goat! A man has two legs, a goat four, it takes
up more space."

Ninth Master nodded and threw down a piece of
silver. "Four cash per goat, four hundred for a hundred goats," he declared. "Weigh this silver. If it's too
much, you can keep the change." Then he shouted to
his men outside, "Bring 'em in!"

At once a guardsman raised the door curtain, while
others whipped the goats so that they surged in. The
customers cried out in dismay and jostled each other to
get out, but the doorway was blocked by goats. Unable
to squeeze through they had to jump out of the windows.
Soon the whole street heard this uproar and came to
look. The goats were running amok. Being goats, not
sheep, they climbed upstairs and even upset the shrine
of the Kitchen God. Teapots and bowls were smashed
to smithereens. The young manager wanted to storm,
but the man with the beard restrained him. "Don't lay
a finger on him. Hurry up and kowtow. Haven't you
seen the yellow girdle he's wearing?"*

Ninth Master had a good laugh over this bedlam.
Then he went out and galloped off to Prince Su's mansion to discuss what gifts to take the Japanese.

---

* The colour yellow was reserved for the Imperial House.

9

When Shou Ming had taken Wu Shibao home he told him what had happened in his family during his imprisonment.

At home Wu did nothing but fritter away the time. His wife liked to call on friends to gossip and chew betel nuts or gamble. Resenting the fact that her husband had no post, she naturally did not look after the household for him. This was left to his old nanny.

Nanny Liu came from Three Rivers County. Widowed in her thirties, she had one son who had now married and kept a little restaurant in Three Rivers. He had urged his mother to go and live with him in comfort, but as Wu's father was half paralysed and needed someone to look after him she refused to go. After the old man's death Wu had a son, and since they couldn't afford to hire a nurse he persuaded her to stay on for a couple of years. In a bannerman's household a wetnurse was treated better than ordinary servants. If the child she cared for grew up to head the house, she had a special status. Nanny Liu had no patience with Mrs Wu's flighty ways and, having Wu's interests at heart, would nag at her for her extravagance. So Mrs Wu made cutting remarks about her, and often lost her temper with her husband. But he refused to dismiss her, knowing that if Nanny Liu left the household would very soon be upside down.

After he went to gaol the trouble started.

Nanny Liu and Xu Huanzhang's father had both worked at one time for the Wu family. She knew what Xu was like. When he came now, giving himself airs, he pretended not to recognize her. She urged Mrs Wu not to be taken in by him, but Mrs Wu turned a deaf ear. And when she told Nanny Liu to collect the silver lent out to settle the lawsuit, Nanny Liu was unwilling. Then Mrs Wu made a scene, sobbing and storming, complaining to the neighbours that Nanny Liu was stopping her from getting her husband out of gaol so that when he died she could grab their property. Nanny Liu had to ask their neighbour Master Gu to check her accounts for her, then back she went to Three Rivers.

Mrs Wu could not even cook, let alone mind a child. She hired as her maid-servant He, the wife of a paper-hanger at the end of the lane. Since this woman was out for what she could get, she fell in with all Mrs Wu's wishes. Mrs Wu liked to gamble, but since her husband's arrest her former gaming-partners had stopped inviting her, and she was fearfully bored. She asked Amah He where she could find a lottery.

"You needn't go yourself, ma'am. I can get someone to come and take your stake. The next day she'll bring you your winnings. If you win, just give her a tip. If you don't, she won't expect anything."

So Mrs Wu tried her luck. Soon she became addicted. Sometimes she won, sometimes she lost, but her losses exceeded her winnings. Before long she was heavily in debt. And when she could no longer pay Amah He wages the woman left.

After spending a few months at home with her son, Nanny Liu started worrying about little Master Wu. On the Double Fifth Festival, taking some sweetmeats, toys and glutinous rice cakes, she went to visit him. The sorry state of affairs that she discovered nearly reduced her to tears.

"I thought you'd do better on your own without me

to vex you," she told Mrs Wu. "But in just a few months you're in such a bad way!"

Unwilling to admit her gambling losses, Mrs Wu alleged that she had been ill and forced to spend money in the yamen. She still had money owed to her, but no time to collect it. Nanny Liu thought: I know how badly off you are. Why boast like that? Though tempted to wash her hands of her, she felt that would be letting Master Wu down. She gave her a few taels of silver. "I didn't know you'd been poorly, ma'am," she said. "So I didn't bring you anything. Take this to buy yourself something you fancy. My son's building a house now, and that keeps me busy. When it's finished I'll come back to see you. And if the master still isn't home and you are not well, I'll take the young master to look after him."

"How long will the building take?" demanded Mrs Wu. "I've lost my appetite and can't sleep, I just can't cope with a child. If you want to show your gratitude to us, take the boy off with you now. Bring him back for New Year when the master should be home."

Nanny Liu was sorry for the little boy. She packed some of his clothes and bedding and took him home with her in a cart which had come to deliver local products.

After the child had gone, Mrs Wu's life was emptier than ever. She locked up the house and went to stay in her old home. Since her parents' death her brother had headed the household. He had inherited the rank of a captain and the tradition of letting his wife run the house. When he first married her, his sister had antagonized her by constantly running her down to her mother-in-law. Now that Mrs Wu had turned up in this beggarly state, she wanted an eye for an eye, a tooth for a tooth. For being a bannerman's daughter herself she had learnt to boast and bully other people. Mrs Wu had not been there long before her brother slipped her forty taels and urged her to go back home.

On her return Mrs Wu found out what it was like to be penniless and unwanted. She regretted having squandered their property, and worried for the first time how she would account for this later to her husband. She hoped the interest on her forty taels would set her on her feet. But she didn't know how to do business, and was afraid of losing face; nor was she content to make a tiny profit. The simplest solution, it seemed to her, was winning a lottery. After all, some people did make a fortune by gambling. The way to do this, so Amah He had told her, was to sleep in a graveyard until you dreamed what to stake your money on.

So on the first of the tenth lunar month, the day when ghosts wanted padded clothes, she prepared some paper offerings and decided to go out of town before the gates closed to solicit a dream in the graveyard northwest of Eight *Li* Village. Those forty taels of silver were her last hope, and for fear they'd be stolen if she left them at home she tucked them into her girdle under her padded gown. As she locked her gate her neighbour's gateman Zhou Cheng was sweeping the street outside their house. He asked where she was going.

"I'm going out of town to burn offerings and make a vow. There's no one at home, please keep an eye on things for me."

"Will you be back tonight?" he asked. "It's not safe out of town after dark."

"Don't worry," she said. "The bastard's not yet born who'd dare touch a bannerman's wife."

Every household closed its gate and minded its own business; Zhou Cheng wasn't one to gossip, so no one else in the lane knew that she had left.

In those days *kangs* were heated with coal. She had neglected to put out the fire. By dawn the next day it had made the *kang* red-hot, scorching the matting and the piles of bedding so that they started smoking and giving off acrid fumes. By midday the neighbours examined their own bedding to see if something was burning, but not a spark could they find. Still the fumes grew stronger. When some of them went into the lane in the afternoon to look, they saw smoke pouring from the Wus' roof. When they found the gate locked they flared up. "We must look into this! It's all very well for her to burn her own place, but there's no knowing where the fire will spread." Her next-door neighbour Gu had the gate kicked open, and everyone rushed in. Smoke was billowing out of the hall, so they tugged open the door. At once flames spurted out, singeing the queues and eyebrows of those in front. It took some time to put out the fire, but at least they stopped it from spreading. However, the Wus' house was a charred mass of rubble, its roof had fallen in. A neighbour reported this to the Daxing County authorities and sent to the Blue Banner for someone from Mrs Wu's family. The elder who came was horrified when he inspected the damage. He asked where Mrs Wu was.

Only then did Zhou Cheng tell them that she had left the previous afternoon with some paper offerings to make a vow.

"Gracious Buddha!" the elder exclaimed. "She's

lucky to have escaped — I thought she must have been burned."

By now an inspector had arrived from Daxing County. In amazement he told them, "What a coincidence! This morning a woman's corpse was fished out of a pond northwest of Eight *Li* Village, dressed in Manchu costume. We haven't yet figured out whether she drowned herself or was pushed in."

"What was she wearing?" asked Zhou Cheng.

"A purple brocade padded gown and black shoes."

"That's her," he declared. He urged her clan elder to go to identify her.

On the third of the twelfth month Nanny Liu brought the young master to Beijing. By then the elder had carted away the charred timber and water vats, leaving nothing but black rubble. Zhou Cheng asked her in to his gatehouse and gave her a bowl of hot water, then described what had happened.

"Such a fine family snuffed out!" exclaimed Nanny Liu. "All parted, ruined or dead."

"It is not to be wondered at. Even princes' families were done for when the foreign troops marched in. Now, what's to become of your young master?"

"I'll take care of him till Master Wu comes out. He can't be locked up for life. And I'll trouble you, when he comes back, to tell him that the little master's with me."

Master Gu had it in for Wu Shibao because he had disgraced the Banner, and the fire had threatened his own house. He therefore proposed that Wu's name should be struck off the bannermen's register. That was why he had treated Wu so callously when he came back. Luckily when Shou Ming went to find Mrs Wu, goodhearted Zhou Cheng had told him all this; otherwise Wu might never have learned the truth.

10

When Wu had heard this account, he rolled his eyes, foamed at the mouth and fell down unconscious. Shou Ming needled him with a pin for picking up opium pellets, and with a cry he spat out a mouthful of phlegm. Reassured, his friend wrung out a towel for him and said, "Wipe your face, have a drink of water and rest a while." Dizzy, parched and exhausted, Wu dried his tears, wiped his face and drank some tea.

He was about to ask where he could stay when he heard Mrs Shou outside calling to her daughter, "Go at once and pawn this gown, then buy twenty cents of mincemeat and three cents of spinach. We'll make noodles with meat sauce for Master Wu."

At once Wu stood up to take his leave.

Shou Ming, flushing, said softly, "Let's go out together. I'll treat you to a meal in Door Frame Lane."

"No," said Wu. "I can't have you spending money on me."

"Don't listen to my old woman," answered Shou Ming. "She likes to shoo guests away, she's so close-fisted. Let's steer clear of her. Why can't she go out of town too in search of a dream?"

"They say you shouldn't speak ill of the dead," said Wu. "If only my wife had listened just once to Nanny Liu, she wouldn't have come to such a sad end. She was the bane of my life!"

They walked along, chatting, to south of Qianmen,

where Shou Ming treated Wu to a dish of tripe, then took him to have a bath and shave, after which they drank a pot of tea in the bath-house while the attendant washed Wu's clothes and Shou Ming helped him to map out his future.

Wu had given the matter no thought while in prison. Asked his plans he could not answer. Shou Ming had been poor for so long that he knew how to manage. He said, "If you've no ideas then listen to me. But mind you do just as I say."

"I will," replied Wu. "My son's with his nanny, I'm not worried about him. But I promised a friend in prison to look after his family. He was good to me, so I must keep my word."

"Quite right. But as things are there's nothing you can do. Find a lodging first and some way to earn enough to build up your strength and fit yourself out."

"That makes sense, but what work can I find?"

"That's up to you, but you'll have to get off your high horse."

"Want me to be a professional ballad-singer?"

"That's one possibility, but there's no need yet."

"Set up a stall in the street and sell my calligraphy?"

"Well, how about it?"

"No. Hard work I don't mind, but that would make me lose face."

Shou Ming laughed. "I knew it. All right, you won't have to appear in public. Those snuff-bottles you paint are marketable. I'll find you a small lodging-place and buy you some bottles and pigments. I'll see to selling them and buying the materials. You don't have to use your own name, you can choose a pseudonym."

Wu looked up and sighed. "I never dreamed I'd be reduced to this, to earning a living with my hands!"

"When you've painted a few you'll stop feeling that way. A skill's worth more than a thousand *mu* of good land. You and I are better off than most bankrupt bannermen. There are plenty in a worse way than us."

Shou Ming proposed finding him a lodging near Hademen, where craftsmen of every kind lived. He could rent a room to paint in privately. All traders from the provinces had to pass through that gate and the street was flanked with eating-houses and tea-houses, so that meals would be no problem. Besides, food and lodging in this district were cheap. Wu might think the place beneath him, but beggars couldn't be choosers.

Wu nodded. On leaving the bath-house Shou Ming took him to a small inn near Garlic Market. The innkeeper Du, who knew him, accepted him as guarantor and let Wu move in on the understanding that he would pay for his lodging two weeks later. His room, in the east courtyard, was empty except for an earthen *kang* with a mat. It looked to Wu little better than the prison. He sucked his teeth.

"Don't worry." Shou Ming smiled. "Now we'll get you bedding."

"I've never been in an inn like this before — just four bare walls."

"You can hire bedding and a mosquito net by the day, but since you'll be here some time that isn't worth it. I'll buy you some secondhand. And once you have things of your own here, the innkeeper won't worry if you're a bit slow in settling your score. Won't be afraid you'll decamp. If you rented his bedding but didn't pay, he'd take a dim view of it."

Just then the waiter brought in a grimy little *kang* table, a teapot with a cracked spout, and two chipped bowls. Standing to attention he asked, "The manager wants to know if this gentleman will be eating here or outside?"

Shou Ming said, "He'll eat here this month, and longer if the food's good. Otherwise we'll find somewhere else."

The waiter boasted, "You should know, Master Shou, that customers come here because of our food. The whole of Beijing knows that this inn has good food, warm rooms, warm *kangs* and new quilts."

"You've grown smart since last I saw you," joked Shou Ming. "Don't give me that talk. Master Wu is my good friend. If you don't look after him well you'll answer for it, you wretch!"

When the waiter had left Shou Ming said, "Their food is lousy, but now you can eat for the rest of this month without paying. In the morning you can get soya milk and fritters in that shop opposite. I'll leave you a few taels for odd expenses. We'll see what's to be done later on."

"No, I can't take your silver," protested Wu. "I've put you to too much trouble."

"Do as I say. I'm not giving you this or the money for your bedding. I can't afford to. Aren't we partners in business? I'll buy materials and sell snuff-bottles for you, and deduct my commission afterwards from your earnings. So I shall get back my capital plus interest. Friendship is one thing, business is another. You're new to this so I'm putting you in the picture."

Wu nodded his agreement.

11

The bearded manager of Yi Shun Teahouse was no fool. When he knew who Ninth Master was he roared with laughter. "Iron-mouth Liu is really a good fortune-teller. He predicted that this year I'd be honoured by a visit from a great noble." He ordered the waiters to spread tables for Ninth Master's servants in the back yard, to serve them first tea then wine. "I've nothing else to offer to show my respect but tea," he said. "I'll give each of you gentlemen a bamboo tally, so that you can always drink tea here on the house."

As they were leaving he presented each with a packet of good jasmine tea, and even gave the shepherds four strings of cash apiece.

When Ninth Master returned home that evening he asked what had finally happened in the teahouse. His servants exaggerated, saying the goats had run completely amok, smashing all the teapots and bowls, wrecking tables and chairs and even trampling down the stove in the kitchen. But when the manager heard that Ninth Master had sent them he had faced north to kowtow his gratitude for being taught this lesson. Hearing this, Ninth Master threw out his chest and took two big pinches of snuff.

"All right then, we'll let him off. If he hadn't apologized I'd have sent two hundred goats there three days running, to teach the wretch a good lesson."

His men pointed out, "It'll be ten days before he can reopen."

Ninth Master chuckled. One of his men suggested, "You let off steam, sir, the manager ate humble pie, and you had your fun. Now I suppose you'll make up for the damage done."

"Are you a tapeworm in my guts?" demanded Ninth Master.

"The whole city knows you're so rich and powerful, sir, that silver means nothing to you."

With an oath Ninth Master forked out an ingot then. His servants pocketed half and gave half to the teashop. The money he had spent on tea for a hundred goats was as much as two hundred customers would have paid, amounting to two days' takings. The smashed teapots and bowls were not worth much, especially as some of them could be riveted and still used. Thus all in all the teahouse had made a profit. On top of which, when word of this got out, it became the talk of the town and everyone wanted to hear the manager's own account of this weird incursion. So for the next few days his business was brisker than usual. But this could only have happened to a tradesman who believed that politeness paid. No craftsman could have turned the occasion to such advantage. Craftsmen live by their skills, are scrupulous and stubborn, with a strong sense of self-respect. They would sooner break than bend. If one of them had been baited like this by Ninth Master, things would have turned out differently.

That was how Nie Xiaoxuan landed in trouble.

That morning, after scaring him, Ninth Master meant to let him go. But first he went to discuss with Prince Su the gifts for the Japanese. As it happened Xu Huan-zhang was there too, for he had recently gone up in the world and often called on the prince. He had suggested giving the Japanese unusual rather than valuable presents. Because when the allied troops occupied Beijing and looted the houses of Han officials, rather than fine calligraphy and painting they had taken the tiny shoes for women with bound feet; from Manchu houses, instead of jade miniature gardens, they had stolen opium lamps and opium pipes — they liked ingeniously made novelties. Hearing this Ninth Master remembered his snuff-bottles, and sent for them to show them to Prince Su and Xu.

Xu approved, "These bottles of yours will put all other presents in the shade."

"Are you trying to outshine me, Number Nine?" demanded Prince Su.

Ninth Master promptly answered, "If you'll condescend to accept them, sir, you can have them."

"What about you then?"

"I can always get another set made."

The prince saw that the seal on the base of the bottles was dated 1899. "No wonder they're so original," he chuckled. "I've never seen any like this before. Why should I grab something you treasure? Just tell the potter to make me another set."

Xu interposed, "Why not get him to paint some different scenes, so as not to duplicate these. You can choose contemporary subjects. Let me find some foreign pictures for him to copy."

The prince liked this idea. He asked Ninth Master to arrange with the potter to start work as soon as the designs were chosen.

Ninth Master went back to outside Qianmen and at once sent for Nie Xiaoxuan. Nie had been too worried to eat, even more on tenterhooks than when in prison. First he threw himself on his knees, then stood there in silence with lowered head.

Ninth Master asked with a smile, "Have you thought it over? Will you sell me one hand or your whole self?"

Nie went down on one knee, his head bowed, without a word.

"Well? Won't you agree to sell either?"

Still Nie said nothing.

Ninth Master bellowed with laughter. "All right, I'll give you a way out. If you won't sell either, make me another set of Guyuexuan."

"Eh?"

Unable to believe he was being let off so lightly, Nie stared at him blankly.

The steward prompted him, "Are you daft? Answer His Highness."

"Yes, certainly." Nie nodded several times. "I'll make whatever you say."

"How long will it take?"

"I can't say. Depends on whether I can buy the right kind of bottles. They come from Shandong. . . ."

"Never mind that. I want them in a hurry."

"I could scrape off some paintings I've done and do new ones."

"How long would that take?"

"Three months."

"No. Two months is the limit."

"I'll do my very best."

Ninth Master refrained from telling him that the subjects would be chosen by someone else. He said, "First fire one to show me. I'll only order a set if I like it, and then you can start work. You've been away from home quite a time, now go straight back."

With profuse thanks Nie left, drenched with cold sweat.

12

Because business was so brisk these days in Yi Shun Teahouse, Shou Ming filled one of the snuff-bottles Wu had painted with snuff, and wrapped up two others to try to sell them there.

The teahouse was not a large one, just three rooms with six square tables, and two trestle tables and some stools outside on each side of the door. It had a favourable location, however. For not far to the south was Joyous Pavilion where opera singers often went in the morning to exercise their voices. In those days actors, having a low social status, were not allowed to live in the inner city, so most of them lived in this area not far from several well-known theatres. Passing here on their way home they would drop in for a snack and some tea. So the teahouse was also patronized by opera fans, costume makers, make-up artists, theatre managers and all those who wanted to make contact with actors. Bird fanciers went there too. Like actors they got up early to go to a wood or the shore of a lake. No matter what birds they kept — larks, thrushes or orioles — they took them out first thing in the morning to sing. And on their way back from airing their birds they often stopped at this teahouse for a chat; so another category of customers were the men who made cages, caught grasshoppers or raised spiders and had something to sell the bird fanciers. As a result some of the teahouse's patrons could both sing and raise birds. If Beijing Opera was a man's profession and birdkeeping his hobby, what pleased him most was being told that he was a better bird fancier than actor. And vice versa. This was the unwritten rule. So men unconnected with either of these

professions generally stood outside to listen to the song
birds or look at famous actors, not venturing in to drink
tea with them for fear of infringing one of their taboos.

Shou Ming, having taken a seat and greeted his acquaintances, looked outside. When he saw two fat men
— one tall, one short — approaching, he smoothed his
gown and hurried out to greet the tall man with a bow
as Fourth Master, the short man as Master Wu.

Fourth Master Qian, who was carrying a big bird
cage, could not return his bow and simply made a show
of clasping his hands. Master Wu bowed back.

Some idlers had come over to look at Qian's bird
cage. Someone who recognized them pointed them out
as the well-known actors Qian Xiaoxian and Wu Qingchang. Both men were eccentric — when flush they
stopped performing. Wu Qingchang haunted curio
shops and was keener on acting as a middleman than
on singing opera. He and Shou Ming were both friends
and colleagues. Qian Xiaoxian was an animal lover,
unique in his way, who tried to reconcile natural
enemies. He had a large cage made with a partition
in it, in which he had kept a weasel and a hen in the
belief that gradually they would make friends. But
when he removed the partition the weasel ate the hen,
so that in fury he dashed out its brains. He then bought
an owl, put the partition back and kept a white mouse
on the other side. The white mouse had kept trembling,
hypnotized by the owl, until it died of fright. Now his
cage housed a tabby cat and a small song bird. The
partition was still in place and the bird was eating and
drinking; but its song was so plaintive that it drew tears
from your eyes. Since this cage had no cover, a crowd
always gathered round to stare at it. They enjoyed

watching this bird and beast, while Qian enjoyed watching the onlookers. He also collected unusual curios, so he and Shou Ming were half friends, half salesman and customer.

After greeting each other they sat down at Shou Ming's table. As Qian had a cat in his cage he couldn't hang it up with the other birds and put it on a table next to the wall. Having wiped his hands with a handkerchief and blown his nose, he reached for his snuff-bottle. This was a large one in keeping with his massive bulk and hung in a pouch from his waist. It took some pulling out. Shou Ming offered him the bottle painted by Wu. "Try mine, Fourth Master."

"Hundred Flower Dew, is it?"

"Hundred Flower Dew's no good. This is genuine Big Gold Flower from the West. Just its leather wrapper is worth a pair of fine boots. So this snuff costs the earth!"

"Come into money, have you, Master Shou?" Qian took the bottle with a smile and pulled out the stopper to sniff.

"Well? Not fooling you, am I?"

"It's Big Gold Flower all right. You can't have bought this! Tell me honestly how you got it."

Shou Ming put his head on one side, then nodded and whispered, "I'm buying it for someone. It's still half-full, so I'm keeping it for the time being. Put in another bottle it would lose its flavour."

Qian turned his attention to the bottle then. "What's special about this bottle?—"

Shou Ming smiled and said nothing. Qian picked it up again and held it up to the light. "It's painted inside, but that's nothing extraordinary."

"There are paintings and paintings. You wouldn't understand. Give it back before you break it."

Qian prided himself on his acumen and hated being suspected of having no money. He flushed.

"Afraid I couldn't pay up?"

"Of course not. Not to say this snuff-bottle, you could buy that big Ru vase from Prince Chun's mansion by giving just one performance. If you smashed it though, and I asked for its real price, you'd curse me for swindling you. If you paid the price of an ordinary bottle and I had to make up the rest, I'd lose my pants!"

"What's so special about it then?"

Shou Ming simply smiled. Qian picked it up again and shook his head, then asked sarcastically, "How much did you promise to get for it?"

"Fifty taels."

"I'll give you fifty-one."

"But I've promised it to someone else, I must keep my word."

"Find him another then."

"You're a good judge. If another painting like this were easy to come by, would you offer an extra tael? Give it back."

Qian pushed his hand aside. "Who told you to show it off to me, you sod? I'll add another four taels. You can come for the money backstage tonight."

"What a nose you have, Fourth Master, for a bargain!" Wu Qingchang had been looking on ironically. "Let me have a squint."

Qian handed him the snuff-bottle. Wu examined it carefully. "It's worth it. Buy it, Fourth Master! Since you're getting a big bargain, let me have a little one, give me the snuff in it!"

Wu produced his green jade snuff dish and emptied the snuff into it. As he was known as a connoisseur of antiques, Qian was pleased by his approval. He said, "I know you often sell curios for dealers. I don't, but if I did I'd grab half your business — do you believe me?"

"Of course. Good for you, Fourth Master."

In high spirits Qian invited Wu to go and eat fried dumplings. Wu said, "Thanks, but I've other business. See you tomorrow morning. Then we can go together to the Five Archways."

When Qian had left Shou Ming stood up as well to take his leave. Wu caught hold of his sleeve. "You're not getting off so lightly. Don't you owe some of that fifty-five taels to me?"

"Have a heart! I'm doing someone a favour — gratis."

"Asking fifty for that junk, and finding a fool to pay an extra five! How could you?"

"I'll tell you."

"If you can convince me, I'll pay for our breakfast. I'll drop out of business! Tell me, what made that bottle worth fifty-five taels?"

"It was painted by a friend of mine who taught himself when in prison for over a year. I believe in helping friends. If I make a cent out of it may I drop dead!"

Questioned further, he told the story of Wu Shibao without mentioning his name or the fact that he had been accused of being a "Boxer". Because Wu Qing-chang was now attending the Catholic cathedral by Xuanwu Gate, and people suspected that he would join the church.

Whether Wu was a Christian or not is irrelevant; he

was a warm-hearted fellow. He asked, "Now that your friend's down and out, will he go on painting snuff-bottles to make a living?"

"A bannerman like him, what else can he do?"

"Well, you can make a haul like this once or twice, but not as a regular thing. How many Qian Xiaoxians are there? Your friend needs a special style of his own if he's to make a name."

"What do you advise?"

"There are two ways. One is to take off some famous artist. Make it look like the real thing. That'll make money too. But why go to such pains to do something which will reflect badly on one's character?"

"Right."

"Another way is to strike out on his own. That bottle of his shows that he has it in him. That's why I butted in."

Shou Ming nodded. "I appreciated it. My friend's an impressionist."

Wu Qingchang shook his head. "Impressionists need scope to let themselves go. A snuff-bottle's too small, not as soft or absorbent as rice-paper either. It wouldn't come off. But realistic painting is too flat. It's like opera: two different actors have to play the same role differently. Do you agree?"

"Absolutely."

"Castiglione, now, has an original style. Why does nobody paint snuff-bottles like that? Don't listen to those critics who run him down. Anyone who could produce interior paintings like his would hit the jackpot. Times have changed you know. Who are our best customers? Foreigners! Not bannermen or high officials. When the newly-rich buy from us, nine times out of ten it's to give to foreigners. Right?"

"Right you are."

"The foreigners are fleecing us. The only way *we* can milk *them* is with our handicrafts, calligraphy and painting. So why not do it? Castiglione was an Italian. Italians, English and all Europeans are descendants of the Virgin Mary who have split up to live apart. So they all like his paintings. All have the same tastes. Tell your friend to cater to their fancy. Make the foreign devils cough up the silver they've stolen from us! If he takes my advice, I'll handle all his bottles and sell them for him for big money!"

Shou Ming respected Wu Qingchang's judgement. Since Wu had started mixing with Catholics he had had his suspicions of him. Evidently, Wu did it not in order to join the church, but to pick the pockets of those foreign monks.

As they were talking along came a man of medium height with a ruddy face. He was wearing a gauze gown, thin-soled shoes, and had his queue loosely plaited. He bowed and asked gruffly, "Am I addressing Master Shou Ming?"

Shou Ming returned his greeting. "Excuse me. Your face is familiar but I can't place you."

"Can I have a word with you?" the newcomer asked.

Wu said, "I have something to see to, I won't keep you company."

The other protested, "Don't go, it's only two short messages."

"Really I have business," Wu said. "You must excuse me."

When Wu was out of hearing the newcomer said,

"It's not that you can't place me, you've never met me. A friend asked me to find you." Offered a seat, he went on, "A friend of mine shared a prison cell with your friend Master Wu. He asked me to give you a message to pass on."

"What is his honourable name?" asked Shou Ming.

"It's Bao. He worked in the treasury. He wants you to tell Master Wu that Master Nie has been taken away by Ninth Master, and he doesn't know what has become of him. As he was leaving, Master Nie said he wanted Master Wu to pass on his craft. Then he could die content."

"What craft?" asked Shou Ming. "Who is Master Nie? Please explain."

"That's all he told me, word for word. All I know."

"All right. You said you had two messages. What's the other?"

The stranger produced a note for three hundred taels of silver. "Brother Bao has sent this for Master Wu to use as capital. He says he's never done anything of use to the world. If he can help Master Wu he won't have lived in vain."

"What does he mean?"

The other looked round and lowered his voice. "He's been sentenced to death and is now in the condemned cell, to be executed this autumn. For stealing silver from the treasury."

"Yet he has such a strong sense of justice!"

"What guard in the treasury doesn't steal silver? When he was caught they made a scapegoat of him. Well, I won't keep you. Thank you."

"Won't you tell me your honourable name?"

"It's Ma. I've an incense shop in Cherry Street. Do

drop in if you've time. Tell Master Wu not to let his
friend down. And please give me a receipt, so that
Brother Bao will be easy in his mind."

Shou Ming borrowed a brush from the counter and
wrote a receipt.

13

From the teahouse Shou Ming went to Liulichang to buy
pigments, palettes, glue and small jars for water, going
next to Pearl Market to choose some transparent glass
bottles. He took these purchases to Wu Shibao's small
inn in Pottery Market.

As Wu had been brought up in comfort, you might
suppose that he was in despair at being reduced to lodging in this little inn and working for a living. But no.
Although he had expensive tastes he was also adaptable
and contented with his lot, whatever his changes in fortune. In the ten days since Shou Ming had left him he
had smartened up his room by pasting the inscription
Bright Glaze Studio over the door, and hanging up a
dainty cage with a canary in it. Incense was burning
in an imitation 15th-century bronze censer on the low
table on the *kang*. On the window-ledge stood a genuine although chipped 18th-century vase holding two
sprays of tuber-roses; and by this was a fine stoneware
pot which had been broken but riveted together. On
the wall hung an unmounted couplet in his own calligraphy — two lines from an old poem.

Though the room was neat and cheerful, Wu's clothes
were shabbier than when newly washed in the bath-
house. His toes had come through his down-at-the-heel
cloth shoes. Shou Ming found him sitting cross-legged

on the *kang* intent on his painting. At once he put down his brush and jumped up. Unable to go down on one knee, as then he would have bumped into the *kang,* he simply clasped both hands in salute and said, "I didn't expect the honour of this visit, or I'd have gone to meet you."

Shou Ming replied jokingly, "Excuse me for coming so unexpectedly."

When they had sat down Wu took from under his pillow a folding fan with bamboo slats. "I wanted to ask you over to enjoy this," he said. "I bought this fan for three taels. Guess who painted it? Song Xiaomeng! If he knew his calligraphy had only fetched three taels, he'd turn over in his grave!"

"Where did you get the money to buy all these knick-knacks?"

Wu smiled complacently. "I earned it! As you didn't come for days and I hadn't a cent, yesterday evening I tried selling a bottle outside Hademen, and I got ten taels for it!"

Shou Ming looked grave. "Why not let me sell it for you?"

"I was just trying it out for fun. I didn't care how much he gave, I proved that I could earn money! You should congratulate me. Shou Ming, we bannermen have come down in the world. . . ."

Shou Ming sighed. "I don't hold it against you. When the allied army entered Beijing they carried off wives of princes and made high officials sweep the streets and groom horses — what could a bannerman like you expect? I'm a cavalry officer, but my official cap's worth less than these snuff-bottles you paint. You can see for yourself, there are bannermen now pulling rickshaws, carrying loads and minding camels — any job they get. You should thank Buddha that you picked up this skill."

Wu nodded.

Shou Ming went on, "It's not that I begrudge you my commission, but you mustn't sell too cheap. Not knowing market prices you'll be swindled. Guess how much I got for that snuff-bottle of yours? Fifty-five taels!"

"Really?"

"That's why I don't want you careering around yourself."

"All right, I won't."

"You stick to your painting and leave the sales to me. This isn't just my idea. Another of your friends is concerned for you."

"Who was that?"

Shou Ming passed on Ma's message from Bao, then piled the materials and silver he had brought on the table. "Master Wu, we're old friends. I want you to make a success of this snuff-bottle painting, not for the sake of a rake-off but because I can see that you have real talent. What does your cell-mate ask of you? That you'll make a go of your craft as you've no other means of livelihood. Today I met the actor Wu Qingchang, who wishes you well too. He's got some advice for you. . . ."

The news that Bao had been sentenced to death yet got Ma to send him silver had so upset Wu that he didn't really listen to Wu Qingchang's proposal. Finally Shou Ming urged him, "With so many friends wishing you well, just go ahead and give your whole mind to painting."

"You've got it wrong," said Wu. "Bao didn't send

that silver for snuff-bottle painting. Didn't he mention what Nie Xiaoxuan asked me to do?"

"Yes, but I didn't catch on. Ma wasn't clear either."

Wu explained what Nie had taught him in prison.

"This is great news!" exclaimed Shou Ming. "Why didn't you tell me earlier? Didn't you trust me?"

"Not a bit of it! Since Nie committed no crime I didn't think Ninth Master would have him killed. He feared the worst, so I had to agree to what he asked. But I was sure he'd get out and be able to find himself a better apprentice and son-in-law. The art of Guyue-xuan has been handed down in their family for genera-tions. Like a legacy. In desperation he entrusted it to me, but I can't take advantage of that. Besides, I can make my own living. I decided, so long as Master Nie lived, I wouldn't make those wares or tell anyone that I'd learned how to; but I'd look after his daughter. Master Nie saved my life. Now that I've got this silver let's both go and find her. They live west of Five Tiger Temple."

14

The liveliest places outside Chongwen Gate were north of Pottery Market and west of Garlic Market. Since the Ming dynasty, Fourth Lane in Flower Market was the centre for wig-makers, jewellers and traders in artificial flowers and wax fruit. East Little Market specialized in daily necessities and local products. Craftsmen, ped-lars, chairbearers and porters lived here, but few rich shopkeepers or celebrated actors and courtesans of the type found west of Qianmen. The dark, cramped houses, built of broken bricks with grey plaster roofs, were so squat that you had to stoop to enter. East and south of Rope Market were several temples which specialized in storing coffins until it was time for their burial. Five Tiger Temple and the King of Hell Temple were so dreaded for the coffins on their verandahs that even the most curious sightseers kept away. Inside Zuoan Gate was posted a garrison of intrepid bannermen. People were afraid of them because they pounced on anyone who did wrong and made him carry water — most Beijing wells were brackish, and sweet water had to be fetched from some distance away. So Beijingers thought this southwest corner a dangerous part of town. Whenever possible they steered clear of it.

When Shou Ming and Wu Shibao went out they found an unusual commotion in the streets. In Pottery Market and Garlic Market platforms of pine and matting were being put up. Both sides of East Little Market Street were lined with stalls selling incense, candles, paper effigies, imitation silver ingots, lotus lanterns and other offerings. At the gate of Fahua Temple was a Buddhist boat more than thirty feet long with a dragon prow and phoenix-tail stern, its cabins and upper deck thronged with dragon children, arhats and warrior attendants — a lovely piece of work. Wu realized that today was the thirteenth of the seventh month, when laity and monks alike prayed to Buddha to save the spirits of the dead from suffering. Each temple had its own distinctive rites, and everyone enjoyed this festival. So nobles, high officials and their ladies came out from town in their carriages to watch. Early as it was, the place was already packed. Shou Ming and Wu tried to push their way through the crowd, but were caught up and swept towards Sunset Temple. Shou Ming learned that when the imperialists had attacked Beijing there had been a battle here. For two days soldiers, civilians, old and young had joined in the fighting and killed a score of Germans. After the devils entered Beijing, they took reprisals by carrying out a three-day massacre. So at this festival each local household contributed a pint of rice to release the souls of the slain from purgatory. And even the monks performed their rites without collecting alms.

After an hour or so Shou Ming and Wu squeezed through to Five Tiger Temple and asked the way to Nie's house. Coming to a small gate painted black they knocked on it and called, "Is anyone at home?" A man's voice answered them. The door was opened, and out came Nie Xiaoxuan. He was wearing a grey cotton jacket, white trousers bound at the ankles, white socks and slippers. His newly shaved temples and plaited queue seemed to have taken ten years off his age.

Without giving Wu a chance to speak he said, "I've been making inquiries about you ever since I came home. Why didn't you come before?"

Wu apologized, "I couldn't help it. I had no money, I came just as soon as I got hold of some silver."

He introduced Shou Ming, who greeted Nie most respectfully. Then they went into the courtyard.

In this single-family compound only the south and west wings remained. The main rooms had been burned down and one of the two date trees had been scorched. The yard was neat and orderly with not a weed to be seen. Nie took his guests into the south room. Over the table opposite the door hung the portrait of an old lady in a red gown and pearl-studded cap. On the table were four plates of offerings.

"Is this your wife, master?" asked Wu.

Nie nodded.

At once Wu straightened his clothes and knelt to kowtow. Shou Ming would have done the same but Nie promptly stopped him.

"How long ago did the old lady die?" Shou Ming asked.

Nie told them that when the allied army came most people, including his daughter and himself, had gone to help the troops defend Zuoan Gate, leaving the old lady paralysed in bed. After entering the city the German soldiers killed everyone they could find. As the way home was cut and his daughter Willow was young, Nie had taken her to hide in the reeds north of Xingong Village. On the third day when they went home, half their lane was burning. By the time they and the neighbours put out the fire, their roof had fallen in and the old lady had been dead for hours. Since her face was charred out of all recognition, he had painted this portrait from memory.

"I couldn't lay her out decently," he said. "So I painted her dressed like a noble lady." He gave a bitter laugh.

Not wanting to upset him Shou Ming changed the subject. "Is your daughter at home?" he asked.

"She's gone to Sunset Temple to burn incense and pray for her mother."

Wu asked, "When did you come out, master?"

As Nie related his adventures his face cleared. He described rather sheepishly his horror at Ninth Master's threat, but laughed heartily over the order for another set of snuff-bottles. Just then there came two knocks and a crisp girl's voice called, "Dad, I've bought some wormwood."

Shou Ming and Wu stood up while Nie raised the bamboo door curtain crying, "Come in and meet our guests. Master Wu and Master Shou are here!"

Willow assented. Having put the wormwood and succulent lotus root she had bought in the west room, she tidied her clothes and came back to curtsey to the strangers.

"As soon as Dad came home he asked if Master Wu had been, and here you are. Sit down, Master Shou! Why, what is my old man thinking of? On a hot day like this you must be parched, and he hasn't brewed any tea! I'll go and do it." After rattling this off she went out with a big stoneware pot.

Wu had the impression that a radiant, scented figure had flashed through the room like a gust of wind, so that he was struck dumb and could hardly look at her. When she came back he sized her up. What he saw took his breath away, and he lowered his head. How could a humble family like this have such a beautiful daughter?

She was about twenty. In mourning for her mother she was simply yet tastefully dressed in a white tunic, white skirt and white brocade slippers embroidered with narcissus. She had bracelets and ear-rings of silver and tied her hair in plaits with blue silk yarn. She was so indescribably lovely that Wu felt bowled over. Her charm lay in her grace, her poise and radiant health, owing nothing either to coquetry or cosmetics. As both Manchus and Hans lived here the Hans had been influenced by certain Manchu ways, so that few girls bound their feet. And Willow had worked since her childhood. She was like a lotus springing up from a pool.

When Willow had poured them tea she sat on a porcelain stool at one side. "We've been thinking of you, Master Wu. Are all your family well?"

Nie exclaimed, "Of course. I forgot to ask, just talking about myself."

Wu told them, sighing, of his family's troubles, and Shou Ming helped fill in the gaps. Nie could hardly believe his ears. "So you never even saw your wife's body?" he asked. "And you still haven't seen your son? Your family broken up!"

Wu nodded. Nie asked, "In that case are you living with your uncle?"

Shou Ming told him, "His father and uncle never hit it off. Went their separate ways. Master Wu is staying now in the Du Inn in Pottery Market."

When Willow heard that the little boy had been taken away by his nanny, the rims of her eyes reddened. When she heard of the house being burned down she wiped away tears. And now she started sobbing.

Wu said, "Don't let it upset you. I'm doing all right, I enjoy painting snuff-bottles." But he also wiped his eyes.

Willow said, "A grown man can take it. It's your little boy I'm sorry for. When Dad was in prison I learned how hard it is to be an orphan, and he's such a little fellow!" She wept even more at the memory of her wretchedness, while Nie kept quiet.

Presently Shou Ming asked, "Are you busy now, Master Nie, working for Ninth Master?"

"I am indeed," replied Nie. "He wants me to fire bottles first as samples. I know where to get the materials, but I'm short of cash. In our trade the customer always pays in advance. This is the first time I've been asked to produce samples first."

Wu offered him two silver ingots. "Take this to be going on with. I brought it for Sister Willow."

Nie declined. "You're just out and must be short. If I were still behind bars that would have been different, but we can't impose on you."

Wu told him Bao's message and how he had sent silver.

Nie sighed, "Poor warm-hearted fellow, coming to such a bad end. You keep that silver. I asked him to give you that message. Now we can work together."

Wu was about to talk of Bao's execution, but Shou Ming stopped him by winking at him.

Then Nie asked, "Why not give up interior paintings and paint Guyuexuan with me instead?"

"You were afraid you'd have no chance to find an apprentice," answered Wu. "That's why you taught me your skill. Because of our friendship I agreed to set your mind at rest. Now you're home again you can make a careful choice of a successor. I've no right to horn in on your family craft. If you'd given me a sum of silver in prison so that if things came to the worst I could look after your daughter, now that you're back, of course I should return it. . . ."

Shou Ming cut him short by treading on his foot and throwing him a warning glance. Then he noticed that Nie had turned his head away while Willow was glaring at him.

Shou Ming asked, "Have you no sense? Other people kowtow, send gifts and plead to be taken on, but Master Nie won't have them. You, though, you drag your feet. Go on, while I'm here as witness, kneel down and kowtow three times formally to your master."

Shou Ming made him do this. And Nie bowed three times in return with a smile. When Wu rose to his feet Willow curtsied to him and greeted him spontaneously as "Elder Brother"!

Tactful Shou Ming hastily took out the two snuff-bottles he had not yet sold, and handed them to Wu. "Since this is so sudden, take these as your gift to your master."

Wu offered the bottles in both hands to Nie, who said, "Today is a festival, an auspicious day, and we've several things to celebrate. Prepare the meal, daughter, and we'll drink a few cups to drown the past years' bad luck."

While Willow fixed a meal, Wu trimmed the wormwood she had put in the yard, cut out some yellow joss sticks, and placed them among the leaves. Then he fetched two chairs and tied the wormwood stalks to their backs to make star lanterns. Shou Ming, entering into the spirit of the thing, went out to buy fresh lotus leaves, stuck little candles on them, then fixed them up on the trellis in the yard. As soon as darkness fell they heard Buddhist drums and the chanting of sutras. Children holding lotus leaves on long stems, with candles in hollowed-out lotus pods and water-melons, marched along singing and dancing. A bright moon cast its radiance all around, making the whole city a scene of rejoicing, so that everyone forgot that they were speeding the spirits of the dead on their way to the nether region.

With the candles on the lotus leaves and hundreds of incense sticks on the wormwood stalks, Nie's courtyard seemed sprinkled with stars. He made his daughter set the little table in the middle of the yard, and the four of them sat round to drink on low stools and hassocks. Nie invited Wu to move in with them to learn how to paint Guyuexuan.

Willow said, "Your inn can't be very clean, Elder Brother, you'd better move in with us. I'll clear out the east room for myself, and you can stay in the west."

Wu would have declined but once again Shou Ming stopped him, saying, "Master and apprentice are like father and son. This is an excellent plan."

Both Shou Ming and Wu drank heartily that evening. When they left, Shou Ming nudged Wu. "Now your troubles are over — all's turned out for the best. That's a lovely girl. If you're interested I'll act as middleman."

Wu answered tipsily, "Nonsense. We bannermen have a rule, Manchus and Hans can't marry."

"Rubbish. Didn't Emperor Qian Long take Iparhan as one of his wives? An honest-to-goodness Muslim from the Western Region!"

15

Wu Shibao never took the initiative, but given a lead he could follow. All his earlier enthusiasm for singing and interior painting was now transferred to painting Guyuexuan. It seemed to be magic the way Nie applied black or blue enamel, which after firing produced red blossoms and green leaves. Not only that, sometimes the glaze expanded or contracted. Small wonder that so many potters tried in vain to reproduce the technique. Wu gave himself whole-heartedly to learning, with Nie and his daughter to help him. Nie prepared the sketches and taught him to use enamel while Willow brought soup and water and did his washing and mending. One day she would make him a tunic, another a new pair of pants; every five days she urged him to have a bath, and twice a month to shave his temples. Shou Ming when he called found his friend a new man — plump, dapper and cheerful. Nie too was in good spirits now that he was out of prison, had found an apprentice and received a big order. He looked thoroughly content. As for Willow, no longer lonely, reunited with her father, she was happy cosseting her "elder brother". Shou Ming sensed the contentment of their little household. Wu's arrival had added a new zest to their life.

The first task Nie gave Wu was painting a saucer. When Wu had completed the outline Shou Ming asked Nie, "Won't it soon be ready?"

"You may be a curio-dealer, but you don't know the first thing about Guyuexuan. I'll get my daughter to show you her kiln."

With a smile Willow led him to the north room, the roof of which had been destroyed in the fire. In the middle of the well-swept floor stood a brick furnace the size of a large water vat.

"What's this?" asked Shou Ming.

"The kiln."

Shou Ming took a careful look. "You fire Guyuexuan in such a small kiln?" he asked incredulously.

"This is how our family has always done it. We keep it secret. I've only shown you because you're my brother's good friend. You mustn't give us away to anyone."

"Well I'll be blowed!" he muttered.

All porcelain had to be fired. Fastidious families had whole sets from lotus tubs to condiment saucers and wine cups painted with the same design and fired in the same kiln. Connoisseurs could distinguish easily between Ru, Ge, Jun and Ding wares, but it took discrimination to tell which of the same wares came from the same kiln. Guyuexuan, though relatively new, had puzzled many porcelain experts. No one had seen a whole set, or any piece more than half a foot high. Most were single bowls, cups or saucers. So Nie's set of eighteen snuff-bottles was unique.

"Do you mean to say," Shou Ming asked, "that Master Nie's eighteen bottles were fired eighteen different times?"

"Not eighteen, eighty-eight more likely," Willow told him.

"How could that be?"

"The enamels in Guyuexuan change colour during firing. Each needs a different heat, and a different heat for light or dark shades of the same enamel. A leaf needs one heat for the surface, another for the underside, yet another for the veins. Figure it out, how many times would you have to fire a bottle with twelve colours?"

"So that's how it is!"

"That's not all by any means. One moment's carelessness and your ware will be spoiled. You may only get two good pieces out of ten. So if you count in the rejects, think how many firings it takes for one bottle."

"No wonder a snuff-bottle often costs over a thousand. I'd always thought potters must be richer than princes."

"Other potters maybe, but we're always in debt."

"As bad as that?"

"Craftsmen have no steady income. An order takes

several months to carry out, and to buy material, charcoal, food and the rest we have to borrow. When we've sold our wares and paid our bills, how much is left? If we're paid in advance we haven't much in hand by the time we deliver the goods. Not to say we can't work every day in the year."

"Every trade has its drawbacks, that's true."

"There's no profit in Guyuexuan; my dad and I live on our interior paintings. From time to time we fire a few, partly so as not to allow this art to die out and let down our ancestors. Partly because we enjoy it, just as you and Brother can't do without singing. So sometimes we don't mind losing money on it. No matter how tiring or nerve-racking it is, producing a splendid, dazzling piece is a thrill that money won't buy!"

Shou Ming, struck by her reasoning and sure that she must be highly skilled, felt keener than ever to fix up a match between her and Wu Shibao. When Nie saw him out that evening, he broached the subject.

Nie said, "At first I had no choice but to teach Master Wu. I could see he had the makings of a fine craftsman. Though he's led a soft life he's keen to learn and a decent sort — not a wastrel who spends his time drinking, gambling and whoring. But our family has never married officials. Besides, he's a bannerman."

Shou Ming replied, "In prison he was struck off their register. And what if he were a bannerman? I'm one, that doesn't stop us from being friends, does it?"

"Don't get me wrong," said Nie. "We have Manchu and Han Chinese living here and we all get on fine. What I mean is, though now Master Wu is down on his luck, will he be content to go on like this instead of trying for a better job?"

"Aren't you getting mixed up? Bannermen have come down in the world. How many of your neighbours are really military officers? They've an allowance of rice twice a year and four taels of silver a month. Issued late and not paid in full. Wu Shibao likes to boast — that's a weakness we bannermen have. In fact he's talking about his grandfather's time. He's never had even the smallest post. When Prince Duan offered him one, he didn't take it; that's why he was in prison for over a year."

Nie liked the proposal and agreed to it. He told Shou Ming, "Let me sound my daughter out!"

That evening when Wu had gone for a stroll, Nie called Willow over and said, "What worried me most in prison was that I hadn't fixed up your marriage for you, or taught anyone to carry on my skill. Now Heaven has sent us Master Wu. Let's stick to our forbears' rules, accepting an apprentice and choosing a son-in-law at the same time. What do you say? Don't be shy. Are you willing or not?"

"Well!" declared Willow. "A spell in prison has made my old man see sense! But it's too late. You should have asked me before Master Wu moved in. Now we're eating at the same table and working side by side. If I refuse, how can you climb down? And think of the talk there'd be!"

But though Willow was frowning her lips had curled up. "If you're really against it I won't insist," said Nie. "I've already told people that he's my apprentice. I can say it's inconvenient living together and have him move to that inn."

"If I were to refuse to cooperate with him, he'd have no one to fire his paintings and then what use would he be to you as an apprentice? But why wait till now to ask me?"

"You're right, but it didn't occur to me. And who was it suggested he should move in here?"

They were talking and laughing when Wu Shibao came back. At once they dropped the subject. Willow went to the kitchen to heat water while Wu went into the south room to join Nie. The latter noticed that he seemed upset. There were tear stains on his cheeks. He urged him, "Tell me frankly, where have you been?"

Wu muttered, "To call on my uncle."

"Tell him you've become my apprentice?"

"No. I told him I mean to make a living by painting snuff-bottles."

"Did he disapprove?"

"Said I'd been struck off the register and cut myself off from the Wu family. He's through with me. I'm not to call myself a bannerman, and I must change my name." He hung his head, the picture of despair.

Just then the door curtain flapped and in darted Willow. Arms akimbo, half jokingly and half angrily she wagged a finger at Wu. "A man should have some self-respect!" she cried. "When your home broke up he didn't ask after you, yet now you go and seek him out! And after being snubbed you come back here to whine. He's on a higher level, I suppose!"

"Don't scold, Willow," said her father. "Blood is thicker than water. It's natural for him to love bannermen. Do you feel it's beneath you, Shibao, making a living this way? Don't you want to stay here with us?"

"If I ever change my mind about that, may Heaven strike me dead!"

"Fine," said Nie. "Then you must look on this as your home."

Wu knelt down. "You're like a father to me, master. I'll be your son."

Willow laughed. "Wait a bit. I make up half this house. Why don't you ask me if I agree or not?"

"You're not going to turn me away, are you, sister?"

"That depends. I shall have to see if you have guts."

16

Xu Huanzhang had many dealings with Japanese, but his only real friend among them was one of their sergeants. He invited this fellow to drink with him in a whorehouse and, over their cups, asked what pictures the Japanese preferred. The sergeant produced some photographs from his pocket. "These are what we like best."

There were two kinds of pictures. One taken with Japanese geishas; the other of the occupation of Beijing by the allied army. These showed the sergeant on horseback, his sword at his side, in front of various city gates. The first kind were too crude for Guyuexuan, but the second seemed just the thing. What better way for the Great Manchu Empire to abase itself to the invaders! Xu accordingly asked for two of these as souvenirs. Then he sought out an opium addict who could paint realistically, and ordered him to paint scenes of Japanese officers enjoying the sights of Beijing, with all their accoutrements faithfully executed. For this he paid him four taels and ten grams of opium. Xu delivered these paintings to Prince Su, boasting that since they had been chosen by the Japanese no other gifts would be so acceptable. Prince Su, very satisfied, asked how much they cost, but Xu insisted that they were a gift to show his respect. Thereupon the prince sent him to choose a fine horse from his stable, with saddle, saddle-cloth and all.

Prince Su had these paintings sent to Ninth Master, who found them highly original, sure to please the Japanese. Xu had recently also been trying to make up to Ninth Master. But he was too stingy to tip the steward and guardsmen, who despised him as a sycophant and bully.

Ninth Master was admiring the paintings when his steward commented, "You should be the last man to praise them, sir."

"What do you mean?"

"Those eighteen snuff-bottles of yours were the tops. But now that creep Xu Huanzhang has given Prince Su these to outshine you."

Ninth Master believed him and started cold-shouldering Xu.

Soon the Mid-autumn Festival came round. Under Nie's tutelage Wu had produced a snuff-dish and a snuff-bottle with excellent forms, colours and designs. Nie took them to Ninth Master's mansion for his inspection, and the steward led him to the inner gate. Ninth Master was watching his gardeners set out pots of fragrant osmanthus flanking the path while he fed a wolfhound, a new acquisition. It was a German dog brought by some Red-hairs from Macao. Tall and lean, with legs like iron rods, its paws thudded on the flagstones. Ninth Master had given in exchange for it two race horses and a couple of fighting crickets. A page boy, holding a red-lacquered dish filled with beef, was carving it up with a Mongolian knife. Ninth Master threw it up piece by piece, and the dog leapt to catch the pieces in mid-air. If one fell on the ground it left it, turning back to bark at its master.

Leaving Nie outside the inner gate, the steward brought in the snuff-bottle and dish. Nie, knowing the rule here, had slipped two taels of silver beneath the wrapper. Without even glancing at it, the steward whisked wrapper and silver into his pocket before going in to report.

Ninth Master, in a good humour, said, "I told him to come for the sketches, then set to work."

"If you don't pay earnest-money, how can he buy his materials?" asked the steward.

"Then give him two hundred taels. Don't trouble me with such trifles."

"He's presenting you with these two samples too."

Ninth Master looked at them, beaming. He called to Nie outside, "I'll give you an extra hundred, three hundred in all for part payment. And mind you don't give it back, I want the porcelain. If you botch it I'll cut off your hands!" He bellowed with laughter.

Nie answered with a bow, "Thank you, Your Highness. Just now the steward's orders were to copy the sketches you have. I don't know if I can till I've seen them."

"You must do it anyway," replied Ninth Master.

The steward said, "Don't worry, Master Nie. Ninth Master won't pick fault." He tipped Nie a wink to withdraw. Outside he whispered, "It's all right, I've seen the sketches. No problem for you at all."

From the counting-house the steward took three hundred taels of silver. Having given this to Nie and told him to make his finger-mark, he said, "Count it to make sure it's not short."

Nie counted it: 295 taels. He hesitated, then extracted five and put them in the steward's hand. "It's too much. Take this back." With that he left, taking the silver and a brocade case of sketches.

Ninth Master, still feeding his hound, decided to play a trick on it too. He tossed up the snuff-bottle Nie had given him, expecting the dog to bite it. Instead the hound leapt up but kept its mouth shut, so that the bottle fell on the steps and was smashed. Hearing the sound the steward came back to investigate.

"See how smart this brute is," chortled Ninth Master. "Throw anything but meat and it keeps its mouth shut."

"It knows the difference," said the steward. "A snuff-bottle's not the same colour."

At once Ninth Master tried out some beef-coloured objects — agate snuff-bottles, brown crystal wine-cups, dark amber mouthpieces of pipes and snuff-coloured pendants from his reception room. The boy had his work cut out sweeping up all the bits.

As it was still early when Nie left Ninth Master's mansion, he went to the Bridge of Heaven to buy offerrings and mooncakes for the festival. A month had passed since the festival for ghosts, and this festival for men would be very different, clear autumn weather with not a cloud in the sky. It was the season for fruits of every kind: russet, red, purple, yellow, orange and white — all the colours of the rainbow. From the north end of Happiness Street past the Bridge of Heaven stretched rows of bakeries and cake shops which had formerly catered for the rich. In these troubled times, however, business had fallen off and so they also set up stalls on the pavement. In the centre of a trestle five feet long was a huge mooncake over two feet high depicting the fragrant osmanthus tree in the moon and the Jade Rabbit preparing medicine there. Over this hung a square of red cloth with golden characters on it. Below were piled several pyramids of cakes. This spectacle drew crowds. And other stalls, not to be outdone, displayed all manner of festival delicacies. Then there were villagers selling cockscomb flowers, green soybeans, water-melons carved to look like lotus blooms. . . .

Nie was bargaining for a cockscomb when someone slapped his back. It was Shou Ming, a pouch over one shoulder, also doing his festival shopping.

"Let's have a rest in a teahouse," suggested Shou Ming.

The teahouses by the Bridge of Heaven were very different from those in town. Being small and cramped they set up big awnings outside, where most customers chose to sit. Under the eaves an oblong range boiled four or five kettles with long spouts. When the bellows were plied, flames and smoke spurted out. The tables were made of broken bricks; the benches were so broad and long that camel and mule drivers, wine and vegetable vendors and other working men could squat there to eat and drink. Today since it was so crowded the two friends went inside, for though it was dark in there it was quieter. When they tasted the tea served they frowned. It was inferior to that in town.

Nie told Shou Ming he had sounded out his daughter and she had not turned Wu down. Now it was up to him. Although both of them were living under one roof Nie could hardly propose the match to him directly. Shou Ming said he had also sounded out Wu, who had at first proposed to consult his uncle, then said that nobody need be consulted. So long as their horoscopes matched he would be most willing.

Nie nodded, thinking: So that explains why Wu called on his uncle. He said, "In that case, ask Wu Shibao to write out the date of his birth, and I'll write Willow's and take them to be compared. If they don't clash, the sooner they're married the better. If they go on living together tongues will start wagging."

Shou Ming asked him what he had in his brocade case. Nie told him it was some sketches he was to copy. Asked the subject, he said he hadn't looked at them yet. Now, at Shou Ming's prompting, he did, going outside where it was lighter. They saw realistic paintings of foreigners with nothing outstanding about the lines, colours and composition. It struck Nie that these foreigners with their guns and swords didn't fit in with the scenic sports of Beijing. Shou Ming sensed this too and shook his head but said nothing. By now several men were looking over their shoulders.

"Haven't we had enough foreign devils in Beijing?" demanded one. "Is the painter crazy or what?"

"What's that?" asked Nie.

A tall, lean man with a pale face and moustache laughed scornfully. "He must think the defiling of our temples an honour to paint muck like this. Disgraceful, I call it! If he goes and sells it to foreigners that'll be still more scandalous!"

Nie felt quite flabbergasted. Yes, the paintings were dated the year of the occupation. Just then the crowd around them melted away. Whispering, "We must scram," Shou Ming slipped back into the teahouse. Before Nie grasped what was happening a police officer came swaggering up to him. Those foreign police uniforms caught the eye, having only just been introduced into China. Nie shivered.

"Selling paintings?" the police officer asked.

"No," said Nie. "Just looking at some."

"Who was that man talking to you? Where has he gone?"

"I don't know him. Not even his name. He just came to look over my shoulder."

The officer took one painting and looked at it, then demanded suddenly, "Are you Nie Xiaoxuan?"

"What if I am?"

"You scoundrel! When the prince gives you pictures, how dare you bring them here to show them off! Clear out before I break your legs." He hurried away to order two of his police to catch the man with the moustache.

Nie stood there in a daze till Shou Ming called, "Come on in. Are you looking for trouble?"

Back inside Nie asked nervously, "Who was that? How did he know where I got these paintings? And why was he in such a rage?"

"That was Xu Huanzhang," Shou Ming told him.

Though it was broad daylight in the bustling street, Nie felt the sky had darkened. Shou Ming saw him turn pale and asked, "What's wrong?"

"Nothing. When I get worked up I come over dizzy. I'll be all right in a minute."

Shou Ming made him sit down, poured him some fresh tea and got him to drink a few cups while it was hot. Soon the colour came back to his cheeks.

"I'll see you home," Shou Ming offered.

"No, you have business of your own."

"Well then, let me hire you a cart."

"No, they shake you to pieces. I'll walk. It's early yet."

They parted, Nie heading east. He decided to make a detour to shake off his depression and clear his mind. He was not far from Goldfish Pond, and liked watching goldfish. This pond dated from the twelfth century, when there had been a palace here with painted balustrades and upturned eaves inside the Forbidden City. But it had long been neglected. The masonry had crumbled and the pool had been sold to the locals to raise goldfish. Like the flowers of Grass Bridge, the best fish were bought by nobles and the rich, the rest being sold to ordinary townsfolk, for Beijingers love fish and flowers. Nie found tubs and vats filled with goldfish of every kind: Four Tails, Lion Heads, Peacock Plumage, Three Whites, Seven Stars. . . . There were tco many varieties to count. Beside the pool the vendors of lantern-grass, insects to feed the fish, glass bowls and glazed basins added vivid touches of colour to the scene. Normally Nie enjoyed the sight so much that he could hardly tear himself away. Today, however, it made no appeal to him. He started home with dragging steps, in low spirits.

Willow had supper ready. She had set a chessboard on the middle of the table, draped streamers of tinfoil over the branches of a date tree and got Wu to set up two bamboo poles south of it, on which to hang lanterns. Arriving back Nie forced himself to smile as he produced the offerings he had bought. While his daughter set these out he washed his face. "I'm going to rest now," he said. "When you've sacrificed to the moon call me for supper."

It was growing dark by the time everything was ready. When the moon rose over the east wall Willow asked Wu to hang up the lanterns. She told him, "It's a woman's rite, sacrificing to the moon, so go indoors. And don't peek, or your eyes will drop out!" She laid plates of offerings on the chessboard, fetched a blue and white porcelain censer from inside, lit three sticks of incense and knelt down respectfully. Each time she put in an incense stick she offered up a prayer, as she had seen done in operas. All girls did this, though each prayed for something different. In operas the first prayer was usually for honest officials and peace. Willow had no such high hopes; she prayed for her mother's speedy reincarnation, for success in firing this set of snuff-bottles and a good price for it, and for harmony in her family, including Wu Shibao. When this was over she called him out to take down the lanterns and tinfoil, which she burnt. Then they carried the offerings inside, brought out wine and food and called Nie to this family feast.

Nie was feeling somewhat better after his rest. He managed to chat and smile during the meal. Then Willow asked what sketches he had been given.

"They aren't ready yet," he told her. "We'll first show a few samples of our own to Ninth Master. If he likes them he may not insist on his."

"In that case," said Wu, "let me have yours in good time."

"No, it's up to you now," retorted Nie. "Do you expect me to prop you up all the time? I'm leaving this to you, and shan't look at your work till it's finished."

"I'm afraid I'm not up to it," Wu demurred.

"You'll never get anywhere like that," scolded Willow. "Dad wants you to make the designs, he must have his reasons. If anything goes wrong it won't be the end of the world. Just do as he says."

Wu didn't insist. The next day he made four sketches in the impressionist style of "Four Worthies" — plum, orchid, bamboo and chrysanthemum. When he took these to Nie, the latter waved him away. "Don't pester me! I said I'd look when it's finished."

So Wu concentrated on his work, paying no attention to other household affairs.

Willow had eyes in her head. On the Moon Festival she had noticed her father's distraction. Since then he had often looked blank or shut himself up in his room to rummage about. His old habit had been "early to bed, early to rise". But now his light often stayed on till the third watch. One day, licking the window-paper, she made a hole to peep through. He was doing his accounts, with his ledger, silver and trinkets set out on the table while he flicked his abacus and wrote down figures. Another day she saw him poring over some sketches. She thought she recognized the brocade case he had brought back on the festival but not shown them. She told Wu what she had seen.

"For shame! How can you spy on your father?" he said. "Such sneaky behaviour! Just mind your own business."

Willow glared at him. "And I've saddled myself for life with a blockhead like you!"

She wanted to look at those sketches, but her father kept them hidden and whenever he went out he locked his door. She waited for him to slip up, and one day when he failed to lock the door properly she slipped in, found the brocade box and took out the sketches. She took two of them to show Wu.

"What are these?"

"Sketches," he said.

"I know that. But sketches for what?"

By the side of each were listed points to note in reproducing the sketch in porcelain.

"These are sketches for us to copy," said Wu. "Why did your father say he hadn't got them?" He examined the sketches again and frowned.

"Don't make that face!" cried Willow. "What do you think of them?"

"They show the occupation of Beijing by the allied army."

"Confound it!" She pounded the table. "I knew Dad had something on his mind, but you blamed me for prying. How the hell can we accept an order like this? How can Chinese paint such pictures?"

"Steady on. Your dad must know what to do. He may have arranged to use other designs instead. Hasn't he told us to go ahead on our own? When ours is ready maybe we can use it in place of these."

Not wholly convinced, Willow put the sketches back and locked the door. And Nie on his return appeared not to have noticed anything.

Ten days later Wu's "Four Worthies" came out of the kiln. Nie looked at them, nodding repeatedly. He fingered them for a while.

"Good," he said. "Good. I can set my mind at rest."

That evening after supper, though it was early, Nie said he was tired and would turn in. He closed his door without lighting his lamp. Wu, in high spirits after his success, did not light a lamp either but sat in the dark.

Willow, worried by her father's behaviour, also sat in the dark by her window watching his room.

At the second watch the lamp in that room lit up. Willow crept over and peeped through the hole in the paper. The next moment, with a scream, she kicked open the door and rushed in. Her father had a gleaming axe in his hands. He jumped when she burst in, and tried to hide it. But Willow seized hold of it.

"Dad, you mustn't." she cried. "Master Wu, come quick!"

Wu had jumped up on hearing her scream. Now he hurried to the south room. Taking in the situation at a glance he trembled and faltered, "What, what does this mean?"

"Dad must be out for someone's blood," cried Willow.

"Silly creature, I haven't the guts for that." Nie stamped his foot and let go of the axe.

"What were you going to do then?" Wu demanded.

"I hate these hands of mine!" With a sigh Nie sat down on his bed.

Holding the axe behind her, Willow seated herself on a chair. Wu stood there, both of them staring blankly at Nie, not knowing what to say.

Nie took a grip on himself. "You had a look on the sly at Ninth Master's sketches, didn't you?"

They nodded.

"And what's your opinion? Can we use this stuff?"

"What bastard made those sketches?" demanded Willow. "No self-respecting Chinese could do such a thing."

"What do you say?" Nie asked Wu.

"I'm flabby, spineless. When the foreign troops came

I hadn't the guts to take up arms against them. But I'd never sell out my country like this. At least I have that much sense of shame."

"If we don't do as Ninth Master ordered, will he let it go at that?"

"Why not pack up at once and clear out?" Willow proposed.

"I've always been open and above-board," said her father. "How can I sneak away? Especially as we've taken his deposit. I'd be sued for absconding, think of the disgrace."

"Can't you return his deposit tomorrow? We haven't touched it."

"Ninth Master won't hear of my returning it. I've got to deliver the goods or this hand of mine!"

Then Willow realized what the axe was for.

"I hate these hands of mine," Nie fumed. "I've worked them to the bone all these years, yet we've gone hungry, they keep getting me into trouble. If not for that fine set of snuff-bottles last year would I have landed in gaol? The day Ninth Master let me go he threatened me: I must sell him either my hand or my life. I was tempted to chop it off and fling it at him. But I couldn't bring myself to. If I let the art of Guyuexuan die out, I'd be letting my ancestors down. Now I've seen Shibao's work I'm easy in my mind. But we ought to chop off our hands sooner than paint such filth."

Willow sprang forward to clutch her father's hand to her heart. "Don't scare me like that, Dad. You must be out of your mind."

"That's not the way to look at it," Wu protested. "Ninth Master's known for his horse-play — no one takes it seriously. Tomorrow take his deposit back along with this set of 'Four Worthies' my sister and I have made, and beg him to settle for these instead. If he won't, we'll return his silver. At most he can cut off our heads."

They pleaded with Nie till the fourth watch, and finally he agreed to go and try. Willow locked the axe up in a chest in her room, then took her father some water to wash his face and urged him to turn in.

She and Wu spent a sleepless night talking things over. Since there was no knowing how Ninth Master would react, they could not decide on any definite plan.

17

After a nap Nie got up, washed his face, rinsed his mouth and had a hasty breakfast. He counted out the silver, wrapped up the sketches and new snuff-bottles, and hurried to Ninth Master's mansion.

These days everything had been going Ninth Master's way. Since the Empress Dowager had deposed the heir apparent and drawn closer to the pro-foreign clique, Ninth Master had found favour in her eyes. She had granted him a cap of the first rank, and the paint on his gate had been worn off by callers crowding to offer congratulations. For the first two days he had enjoyed this. On the third day he issued orders to admit no one except on urgent business.

Xu Huanzhang handed in his visiting-card, then sat waiting in the outer reception room till he ran out of patience. Then he saw the steward lead someone to outside the garden gate. They were whispering together. Xu leant out of the window as if admiring one of the miniature gardens, but actually to eavesdrop. Since his police appointment he considered it his duty to ferret out secrets.

The steward was reproaching Nie Xiaoxuan, but was willing to do him a favour as Nie was generous with tips and most respectful.

"Ninth Master is tired," said the steward. "You've picked the wrong time to come."

"Time is so short I dare not delay," pleaded Nie. "I'm afraid of offending him if I'm late."

"Make it brief then," said the steward, "and I'll report. . . ."

Just then Ninth Master shouted from the courtyard, "What are you muttering about, Li Gui?"

"Master Nie, the potter is here."

"He's been paid his deposit, what more does he want? Throw him out!"

"Very good." The steward glared at Nie. "I warned you. Clear off, quick!"

"I'm too tired to see anyone today," Ninth Master added. "Get rid of all visitors for me."

Nie's name had reminded him of Xu Huanzhang, and he was snubbing the latter deliberately to prevent further trouble.

In exasperation Xu left, not waiting for the steward to turn him away. When he saw Nie squatting at the end of the lane he vented his rage on him, thinking he had provoked Ninth Master. He called to him, "Hey, come here."

Nie was worried because Ninth Master would not see him and the steward refused to take back the deposit. What should he do? He didn't hear Xu calling. Xu came over and kicked him. "I'm talking to you!"

Recognizing the police officer, Nie jumped to his feet.

"Why did you call on Ninth Master?"

"About some snuff-bottles."

"Have you finished them?"

"No. The sketches won't do."

"Why not?"

Nie had answered without thinking. Now, sobering up, he summoned up his courage. "Because I'm a loyal subject of the Great Manchu Empire — that's why."

"You scoundrel!" Xu slapped his face. "I chose those sketches. Who are you to fault them?"

Nie let himself go. "Aren't you Chinese too?" he bawled.

"You rebel!" fumed Xu. "I spotted you that day plotting with another rebel. No wonder a piddling artisan has such a nerve. I'm not going to argue with you. Get those bottles made straight away. Any delay and I'll have your head. That fellow-plotter of yours is being beheaded today. We'll soon stop you rampaging."

Xu swaggered off. And Nie left in furious indignation. In Pearl Market Street he found his way blocked by a crowd. Above the hubbub of voices rose the sound of gonging and bugling. Hemmed in, unable to move, he stood on tiptoe and saw a troop of soldiers escorting some mule-carts with prisoners standing on them. The carts had stopped. The prisoners, all trussed up, had placards stuck on their backs. Some waiters from a nearby tavern carried out bowls of liquor and stood on a bench to raise these to their lips. One hefty prisoner downed a whole bowl in one gulp. "Another twenty years and we'll be stout fellows again!" he yelled defiantly. Some of the crowd applauded, but then the man collapsed like a heap of mud. Nie had recognized his voice, though unable to see his face. And now he saw the red character Bao on his placard.

On another cart a tall lean fellow with a moustache had also drained his bowl. It was the man who had commented on the sketches that day at the Bridge of Heaven. With a smile he cried, "Elders, brothers, descendants of the Yellow Emperor! I'm no robber, I simply opposed selling out our country! Piece after piece of our land they hack off to sell. The foreign devils kill us, rob us, shit on our ancestors' graves. They've even burnt our Yuanmingyuan, that grand old palace. Aren't we allowed to protest? I call on you, old and young, to save our country. . . ."

The crowd muttered sullenly. The prisoners shouted curses. At a signal from a junior officer, carters, troops, carts and spectators surged west — toward the execution ground.

Nie had sobered up. He wondered where to go. Back home? What could he do there? He felt utterly frustrated.

He turned north. As he was approaching Cloud Abode Temple, a carriage with a green felt awning and crimson mudguards appeared. In front rode a horseman, behind were some men on foot. The groom leading the horse was straining forward. Nie recognized Ninth Master's carriage and stepped aside. But as it drew near he flung himself on his knees in front of it. "Ninth Master!" he cried. "Have a heart!"

The groom reined in the horse. Ninth Master thought someone had stopped him to complain of an injustice. When he saw Nie he smiled. "What trick are you up to now, you wretch? Get up." Nie kowtowed, then stood to one side, raising the three hundred taels and the sketches over his head with both hands.

"I can't use sketches like these, can't accept your deposit!" he cried. "Have a heart and take them back!"

Ninth Master was in a good mood after drinking and being invited to an opera. He wasn't clear what Nie was up to, but laughed to see him red in the face, dripping with sweat and gasping.

"You ape, raving at me in your cups! Anyone else would box your ears for you. Get back to your work. I told you: If you don't deliver those snuff-bottles with pictures of the allied forces on them, I'll have your hands instead. I'm not taking back the deposit." He signed to the groom and let down the carriage curtain, laughing heartily to himself. The groom cracked his whip, and the carriage rumbled on. . . .

Nie stamped his foot and chased forward. "Wait!" he yelled. "You can have my hands!" Before the escort could stop him, he had thrown himself down between the horse and the carriage, his hand stretched in front of the wheels. . . .

Ninth Master didn't hear his shout, but the carriage lurched so that he banged his head. The groom let out a cry and reined in the horse. There was an uproar outside.

Without raising the curtain Ninth Master asked, "Now what is it?"

The curtain opened to show the steward's head, his face white. He faltered, "Nie Xiaoxuan's hand has been broken by the carriage."

"Eh?" Ninth Master laughed. "Trust him to be so pig-headed! Take him to the bone-setter. Prince Su is waiting for his snuff-bottles,"

The steward understood Nie's feelings and had a sneaking admiration for him. He said, "Ninth Master, Nie Xiaoxuan won't be able to make any more Guyue-xuan. Your set of eighteen snuff-bottles will be unique."

Ninth Master thought this over and nodded approvingly. "In that case," he said softly, "while he's passed out cut off his hand, and we'll report to the prince that he fell down drunk and was run over by a cart, so he can't make the snuff-bottles."

"Very good."

"He can keep the three hundred taels' deposit for medicine."

"Very good."

At a word from the steward the carriage moved on again.

Epilogue

The steward took Nie to a surgeon. The carpals of his right hand were smashed. But instead of cutting off his hand as Ninth Master had ordered, the steward asked the doctor to bandage Nie's wounds and prescribe some medicine, then hired a cart to see him home. He gave the silver to Willow, not only not subtracting a commission but paying for the medical expenses. Before leaving he advised them, "Move away as soon as you can, and find some other way to make a living. When Prince Su and Xu Huanzhang know of this they'll be out for your blood, and I shan't be able to shield you."

Wu Shibao had expected trouble with **Ninth Master**,

but had never dreamed of this outcome. He gazed in horror at Nie's bloody sleeves, closed eyes and face drained of blood. Then he paced frantically round, not knowing what to do or say. Willow had taken a grip on herself after her initial panic. She paid no attention to Wu apart from saying, "Keep an eye on things here." Then she went out. Not until lighting-up time did she return, bringing two red bundles with her. By now Nie had drunk some gruel that Wu had made him, and taken some medicine. He was in less pain, able to tell Wu disjointedly what had happened. When Willow came back they asked in surprise, "Where have you been? What's that you're carrying?"

She tossed one of her bundles to Wu. "You must go. Uncle Shou Ming's waiting for you in Yuelai Inn by Chongwen Gate. Tomorrow put on these new clothes and he'll bring you back here in a cart."

Wu, quite bewildered, wanted to ask her what she meant. He saw that she looked troubled. After a fractional pause she gave him a shove. "Get a move on! No time to act dumb. Once you've gone I've a lot to do."

Wu took the bundle in a daze and left. Willow told her father, "Dad, never mind how you feel, you must do as I say. Eat some more nourishing food, and take it easy. First thing tomorrow we'll be setting out."

"Where to?" asked Nie.

"Three Rivers County, to find Shibao's Nanny Liu. Isn't his son with her?"

With his good left hand Nie pointed at the bundle. "What's this?"

"What sort of loose woman would people take me

for, travelling with Wu Shibao? Tomorrow we'll get married before we leave."

"Get married? Leave? Is it up to you to decide such important matters?"

"You're ill and he's a dolt. If I don't decide, who will?"

"Is one night enough to get ready?"

"I've bought clothes, incense, candles and offerings. I'm getting Shou Ming to be master of ceremonies, and I've hired carts. We'll take everything we can, leaving the rest for Shou Ming to sell for us. He'll send us the money, he's a reliable fellow."

Nie could only fall in with her plans. That night Willow packed their things and set the offerings before her mother's portrait. First thing the next morning Shou Ming arrived with Wu Shibao in his new clothes in a horse-cart, bringing two mule-carts as well. Shou Ming presided over the wedding. The couple bowed to Heaven and Earth, then kowtowed to Nie and the portrait of his wife. This done, they thanked Shou Ming, and helped Nie into one cart. The newlyweds sat in the second. The third was loaded with luggage. So they left for Three Rivers County.

Thereafter Wu Shibao changed his name to Wu Changan, and made a living by painting snuff-bottles. Every year he and his wife also fired two or three kilns of Guyuexuan to carry on this art. But Wu never signed his name, never tried to make a profit. The base of each bottle was inscribed "Made in the Qian Long Reign", and he always stuck to traditional designs. Connoisseurs knew that very few Guyuexuan dated from the Guang Xu reign. It therefore caused quite a stir in Beijing when after forty-odd years some of these wares suddenly reappeared in the market. Indeed, this led to another story. Though the author would like to go into it, nothing might come of an investigation. Still there is no knowing whether or not a sequel will be written to this tale about snuff-bottles.

October 30, 1983

Han the Forger

HE hadn't walked down this road for more than thirty years. Now it was asphalted and lined with buildings and a school. In his youth Gan Ziqian used to come along here to Taoran Pavilion Park to sketch. Now, standing beside the historic lake, he felt lost. "Where on earth can Han be?" A man who would be useful for the country's modernization, Han had been ousted from the antiques trade decades ago. Like a sputtering candle, Gan knew his days were numbered. If he didn't find Han he wouldn't find peace even after death.

The misunderstanding between Gan and Han had started with a prank. Gan could paint well in the traditional style, and sometimes copied old works. Seeing a masterly copy of an early painting one day tempted him to do likewise. On an impulse he made a painting called *The Cold Food Festival* and attributed it to the celebrated 12th-century artist Zhang Zeduan, using a well-preserved sheet of Song paper and ink. Originally he did it just for fun, never expecting his copy would attract a newspaper correspondent, one Na Wu by name, who came from an impoverished Manchu noble family. Na Wu took it away and asked a famous craftsman to mount it, colour it with tea and then fake the seal of the Qing emperor Qianlong. When this was done he brought it back to Gan saying, "Look, it exceeds even Master Zhang's skill. And it's certainly as accomplished as Han's."

As a dealer, connoisseur of painting and well-known copyist, Han had been appointed assistant manager of the Gongmao Pawnshop.

"You flatter me. I don't think my skill is nearly as good as Han's," he protested.

"Flatter you? Never!" retorted Na Wu. "If you don't believe me, let's put it to the test."

"How?"

"I'll take it to Gongmao Pawnshop. If Han tells me it's a fake, then I'll say we were only joking. But if I can fool him, then it proves that you do have a remarkable skill. What's more we can share the money between us. Then you can treat me to a roast duck." With this, he carried the painting away wrapped in a blue cloth.

At first Na Wu had only wanted to pawn the painting in order to make the bet with Gan and it was only when he actually had it in his hands that he changed his mind. To fool people he needed to be dressed in his finest clothes, since the pawnshop looked first at the customer and then at the goods. So on the appointed day, he wore his silk gown, a fashionable waist coat, black satin slippers and white silk socks. Between his fingers he balanced an exquisite cigarette-holder with a fine cigarette, lit but unsmoked. Placing the painting on the counter, he asked a price of a thousand yaun and then turned away to look at the wall. From his appearance, Han assumed that he must be a ne'er-do-well from an impoverished Manchu family and that he had stolen the heirloom to pawn. Men of his ilk never sold things and usually never redeemed what they pawned.

Fooled perhaps by Na Wu's appearance, frightened by the high asking price or owing to sheer negligence, Han, after haggling for a long time, chanted in his Shanxi accent, "An antique painting. We can loan you six hundred yuan. . . ." In those days, a bag of flour was only two yuan forty *fen* and six hundred was an enormous sum. When Na Wu returned and told him the story, Gan laughed heartily. But on second thoughts, he was scared stiff. If the story got about, it would discredit him with his friends and offend Han as well. Although the relationship between them was not particularly close, they were still friends. And both were fond of Beijing opera, especially of performances by Sheng Shiyuan. Whenever an opera was staged starring Sheng, they would both go to see him. And as a result of their frequent attendance and vocal support, Sheng became convinced that if they were not at the theatre and cheering his performance would be below par.

Seeing Gan's misgivings, Na Wu coaxed, "Don't get so worried about it. Everybody already knows Han makes a living from fake paintings. It's time he got his comeuppance. If you're worried about your reputation, we won't do it again. Nobody will find out if neither of us let on. What we did this time wasn't to make money but to put your technique to the test. Now that he's offered us money though, we mustn't be so foolish as to turn it down. Are you really going to pay it back with interest and redeem the painting?"

"I can't afford to."

"You couldn't even if you had the money since the pawn ticket belongs to me now."

Gan had no choice but to give him three hundred yuan. Finishing his duck, Na Wu declared, "Now I'm going to take the ticket to the Japanese pawnshop. I should be able to bluff him out of two or three hundred yuan. So let me pay the bill."

"You're a little too clever at times," remarked Gan.

"Well, don't you agree that to cheat Japanese is patriotic?"

And soon Gan heard others gossiping, saying that Han was used to cheating people with his fakes, but that he had never expected to be swindled himself. Shortly thereafter Gan received an invitation from Han to celebrate his birthday on August 16.

When the day arrived, Han rented Listening to Lotus Hall overlooking a lake in a garden behind Beihai Park and set ten tables under a corrugated iron shade to treat his friends. Gan expected to find a dispirited Han but instead he looked more cheerful than ever. After three cups of wine, he stood up and bowed to the guests with his hands folded, saying, "It's not only because it's my birthday that I invited you here today. I also want to tell you that I've made a blunder.

"I'm sure you've already heard — I've been taken in by a fake. When I was poor, I lived on fake paintings. Now I've been caught myself. It is a sort of retribution, and I've no one to blame but myself. But I think all of us are basically honest men, so to save you from suffering a similar loss, I've brought it here for you to have a look at. Bear this lesson in mind and don't make mistakes yourselves." Then he ordered the painting to be brought out.

With this, his two apprentices approached, one holding the painting, the other carrying a pole with a double-pronged tip which he used to hang the painting on to a bronze hook. All the guests gathered round to examine the work. "Looks genuine all right. How amazing!"

"Don't you be taken in by it. Try to spot its weakness and then we will learn something from it." Turning to look at Gan, Han smiled, adding, "Ziqian has a good eye. You try first."

Gan's face had already turned crimson, but since he had been drinking, no one became suspicious. Moving forward, he first looked at the lower left-hand corner of the painting and spotted his thumb-print, positive proof that the work was his, but he was unable to detect any discrepancies. Had he known of any, of course, he would have corrected them in advance. Secretly he admitted that his brushwork was not up to that of the original painting. He commented, "The brush strokes are weak, and the style a little vulgar. Mr Han's really been deceived by the fact that the artist has used 12th-century paper and ink."

Han laughed saying, "I was duped this time not because the faker was so skilful but because I was too conceited and negligent. So today I'd like to advise you all, don't follow in my footsteps and always keep your eyes open. The painting looks genuine but if you're observant enough, its weakness can be easily detected. For instance, the subject is *The Cold Food Festival* and that takes place in spring.* The painter

---

* The Cold Food Festival used to be celebrated on April the fourth.

Zhang Zeduan lived in Kaifeng, where at that time of year people would have been wearing spring clothes. But look, the boy in the painting is still wearing a cotton-padded hat with flaps. Do you think Zhang would have made such a mistake? For another thing, the young woman by the grave is weeping over her dead husband. The word 'husband' has a closed syllable at the end, but her mouth is open saying 'ah'. Judging from this, I would venture to suggest that this painting is not by Zhang Zeduan."

It was an explanation that won everyone's admiration, even Gan's.

At this, Han threw a cup of wine over the fake, struck a match and set fire to it. Then he laughed again saying, "Getting rid of it saves anyone else from being swindled. Now let's have another drink before the opera begins."

With the destruction of the painting, Gan felt greatly relieved and calmly sat enjoying the entertainment. As a gesture of friendship, Sheng Shiyuan appeared and performed especially well. Han, on his part, cheered loudly and Gan couldn't refrain from following suit. When the performance was over, Han went backstage to express his appreciation. Sheng asked, "The man who often accompanies you to the theatre hasn't come to see me for a long time. Who is he? Won't you introduce us next time he comes?" Since he'd been cheated, Han had felt so miserable that he hadn't been to the theatre for several days and consequently wasn't aware that Gan had also been staying home. Sheng's words startled him. He knew that the faker must be someone from the same trade and had therefore invited a number of them in order to watch what would happen during dinner. However, he had never been even remotely suspicious of Gan. Immediately he looked around to search him out but was told by his apprentice that Mr Gan had just been called away unexpectedly.

Later, called to the side door of the garden by Na Wu, Gan was annoyed. "What the devil did you come here for?" he growled.

"I apologize but I must tell you. I went to pledge the pawn ticket with the Japanese but he asked me to let him inspect the painting first. Dare we run the risk? If it passes, then there's no problem. If the Japanese spots anything wrong with it though, he won't be as easy to deal with as Han — we'll be sent to prison."

"You're too greedy!" Gan scolded. "In any case, the painting has already been destroyed by Han."

At first Na Wu was stunned by the news. Then all of a sudden he slapped his thigh and exclaimed, "Wonderful! It's time Han got what was coming to him."

"What are you going to do? We've already made him lose six hundred yuan. Don't be so cruel! He and I are friends and see one another frequently."

"Friends? No. Business is business. It's foolish to let a good opportunity slip through your fingers. Come, stay awhile. I'll treat you to some crabs."

After Na Wu's departure, Gan was uneasy. Han was a better man than Na Wu and even if he himself had nothing further to do with this, he didn't have the heart to let Na Wu extort any more money from him. So he made up his mind to visit the pawnshop and inform him of Na Wu's intention in order to avoid any further trouble.

When he arrived at Gongmao Pawnshop, Han came out to meet him and graciously ushered him into a private room behind the accountant's office. Shortly an apprentice appeared bringing Gan a cup of tea. Han puffed at his hookah for a while before breaking the silence. "I haven't seen you lately. Where've you been?"

Before Gan could reply, the accountant, looking upset, scurried in and stuttered, "Something's wrong, sir!"

"What's wrong?" Han asked nonchalantly.

"There's a man here to redeem his pledge."

"Redeem his pledge? What's wrong with that? It's natural that people come here to redeem their pledges."

"But, he wants to redeem the. . . ." The accountant glanced at Gan, then approached Han and whispered.

"Speak up!" ordered Han. "Mr Gan is not a stranger."

The accountant couldn't help blurting out, ". . .that painting!"

"Which one?"

"*The Cold Food Festival* that you burnt yesterday."

Gan, shocked, felt a shiver run down his spine, for he had never expected that Na Wu would carry his trick so far.

But Han said calmly, "Tell him the painting he pawned is a fake and that he should be content with the sum he got from me. If not, I'll take him to court."

"I'm sorry, sir. But you can't speak to a customer that way. He came here to redeem his pledge and even if the pledge was a bit of toilet-paper, we are still supposed to return it to him. If we can't, then we should pay him twice the loan. Even if we do, I'm not sure he'll take it. How can I tell him we'll go to court?"

The accountant's argument reduced Han to silence. Just then they heard a commotion outside. Na Wu shouted, "What! You want to keep my heirloom, do you? If you're not going to return it to me, you'd better pay me a proper price for it!"

"Outrageous! I'd better go and see what's happening," said Han. "Excuse me, Ziqian."

Angry and embarrassed, Gan ignored form and followed Han out of the room.

The shop's counter was over a foot higher than the customer. Behind the counter stood Han, surrounded by his accountant and assistants, all looking down at Na Wu, who challenged, "If you have the painting here, then return it to me. If not, we'll have to settle the matter another way."

Gan peered out from behind Han and saw a swarthy, heavy-set fellow standing behind Na Wu. He was dressed in grey clothes, his sleeve cuffs covering his hands. Beneath his unbuttoned jacket Han could see a white calico vest edged with black trimming, and recognized him immediately as a police detective. It certainly looked as though Na Wu was determined to continue hounding Han. Winking at him, Gan began tentatively, "Oh, it's you, Mr Na. Well, we're all friends here. Why do you want. . . ."

"Mr Gan, what we're talking about is no laughing matter. Please don't get mixed up in this. I pawned a scroll painting inherited from my forefathers. Today I've come here to redeem it. First they tell me it's a fake. Then they promise I can get it back another day. Does it surprise you that my patience has run out?"

As Gan was about to try and coax him out of continuing, Han edged forward saying to Na Wu, "So you've run out of patience, have you? Well, I'm much more impatient than you are. I reckoned you'd be here as soon as the shop opened. Why did it take you so long? You want to redeem the painting, do you? Then first please show me the money!"

"So you're afraid I haven't brought it." With this, Na Wu threw a white packet on to the counter containing the principal and interest, amounting together to over eight hundred yuan. Having counted the sum and placed the interest to one side, Han handed six hundred yuan to the accountant, then removed a package from under the counter and handed it downwards.

"Here. Now take it away."

Hearing this, Gan and the assembled assistants were taken aback. Na Wu stood stunned before nervously reaching out for the package, his hands trembling so much that he could not even hold it. The detective reached out and steadied him, saying, "You'd better have a look. Is it the one you pawned?"

No sooner had he untied the bundle than the sweat stood out on his brow, and his lips trembled. Pretending to talk to himself, he said so that Gan could hear, "Wasn't this burnt yesterday?"

"If I hadn't burnt it yesterday, would you have come here today?" replied Han sarcastically.

"So there are two such paintings in existence!" uttered Na Wu.

"If you like, I'll produce another one for you to-night," added Han.

Incredulously Gan asked, "What on earth is it, Mr Na? Won't you let me have a look?"

Holding the painting, Gan blushed scarlet with shame. First of all, he examined the lower left-hand corner, and looked hard at the thumb-print, which though very pale could barely be distinguished from that in the destroyed painting and had they been placed together in front of him, he would have been unable even to identify his own work. It was said that some craftsmen were so skilful they could peel off the top layer of a painting to make two. "Can Han do that?" he wondered.

"It looks like there's nothing for me to do here." The detective was growing impatient. "Settle with me and I'll be off."

Paying him, Na Wu turned towards Han with a con-trite smile and folded his hands in a gesture of respect, "I've learned a lesson from you and paid two hundred yuan for the privilege."

"Take the interest back!" Han handed it over to him and laughed. "It was you who brought the paint-ing here and I imagine your slippers must be worn out, so you'd better use the money to buy a new pair. By the way, please tell the man who made the fake . . . ." With this he turned to the dumbfounded and embarrassed Gan before going on, "Does he think he's clever enough to fool me? Not until he can fool the painter himself with his fakes, will he be properly quali-fied. So I suggest he study for another couple of years."

Ashamed, Gan slunk out of Gongmao Pawnshop, head bowed, and from then on never appeared when

Han was around. Although Han was a man of good reputation, his master dared not run the risk of losing any more money and in the first month of the following year he was dismissed. Later he was reduced to working as a junk dealer for two years, but since business was bad, he finally supported himself by collecting and selling scrap. Gan, despite suffering a temporary loss of credibility, got a good job restoring damaged paintings.

As a result of his background, clear record, progressive ideology and loyalty to the Party, after Liberation Gan was elected to the leadership of the antiques trade and became vice-chairman of the trade association during the socialist transformation of capitalist enterprise.

To reinforce the leadership after the changeover, someone suggested that they should appoint Han to a job. But the authorities did not know much about his past and asked Gan for an opinion. Gan was evasive, saying he didn't know much about him and asked them to wait until he found out a little more. Returning home, he turned the affair over in his mind. Though he hadn't intended to cheat Han, he certainly wouldn't be able to explain it away. "If Han isn't hired, then no one will rake up the past," he thought. "If he is, however, he may raise it against me. What's more, I'm applying for Party membership. Why should I bother to recommend him?" But Gan also couldn't lie to the authorities. When asked for his opinion, he said, "Han lived on fakes and used to be an assistant manager in a pawnshop. He was quite well off before Liberation. On his birthday the famous Beijing opera actor Sheng Shiyuan even performed at his home. . . ,"

"It's said that he's an able man. What do you think about our employing him?"

"The decision rests with you," Gan replied evasively. "My political standard is low, and I'm not sure."

In the end Han was rejected.

According to the conventions of the antiques trade, people who had been vetted could do anything except assess or deal in antiques. From that day on Han sank into obscurity.

Many years passed. Gan didn't feel guilty and, as time went on, forgot about Han.

During the "cultural revolution", Gan was deeply wronged. After the fall of the Gang of Four, he was rehabilitated and had his savings, which had been confiscated, returned. What pleased him most was that he was able to go and work at an antiques studio, where he could put his knowledge to full use. But time takes its toll. When he was elected a people's representative, he was given a medical certificate stating that if he didn't rest, his chances of recovery were nil. At length he recalled Han.

In the antique world some old craftsmen had died, others had fallen ill. During recent years few talented successors had turned up, and a shortage of able people became a big problem. The international antique market was brisk. Han was good at both assessing and copying ancient paintings and should have had a position which would have given full play to his unique skills. If Gan had said yes before, then he would have been employed, but instead, the man had been barred for many years.

Gan was so filled with remorse that he confessed

everything to the Party committee. The secretary praised him and asked him to try and locate Han.

But Beijing was so big, where was Han? First Gan was told that he was a boilerman for a teahouse at Tianqiao, but when he got there he found the place had closed down. Then he was told that Han and another old bachelor had rented a house to breed goldfish near the Goldfish Pond. When he went to look for him, the house had been razed. Half a month passed but Han was nowhere to be found. All Gan knew was that he was still alive, and sometimes went to Taoran Pavilion Park to practise shadow-boxing at dawn.

He was determined to find him. Despite the doctor's warnings, he went with his cane first thing in the morning to the park. As the sun had not yet risen, only a few dim figures could be discerned running along the edge of the lake. Others were singing, walking or fishing. But whom should he approach?

Just then an old man with a beard and a cane, wearing traditional-style clothes, came towards him. He was so absorbed in humming a Beijing opera aria that he didn't notice the people around him. Out of habit, Gan spontaneously cheered, "Wonderful!"

The old man stopped to look up towards the shaded trees by the lake. "Why, that cheering sounds familiar to me, but I haven't heard it for more than thirty years."

"I haven't heard such a sweet voice for over thirty years either," Gan chimed in. "Aren't you Mr Sheng?"

"Oh my goodness!" The old man stepped forward, and grasped Gan by the hand. "It's you, the man who used to come with Han to see my performances."

"Yes. My name is Gan Ziqian,"

"I've heard of you. Once after a performance, I wanted to meet you, but you had already left. Thirty years have passed since that day. How are you getting along? Where do you work now?"

Told that Gan was an adviser at an antiques studio, Sheng said, "I'm with a Beijing opera company now. I lost my voice in 1945 when the Japanese surrendered and was jobless. But after Liberation, the government showed a lot of concern for us and gave us the opportunity to use our talents, so I became a teacher at a Beijing opera school, but that was interrupted by the 'cultural revolution'. . . ."

"Mr Sheng," Gan cut him short, "you mentioned Mr Han to me just now. Do you know where he is?"

"Why yes. He lives with me."

"Eh?" Surprised, Gan stared at him for a long time before he asked cautiously, "Really?"

"Of course. Anybody who comes here to practise shadow-boxing knows he's lodging with me. During the 'cultural revolution' the teahouse where he worked closed down. Since he couldn't earn a living, I told him not to worry and to stay with me for the time being. My wife died and my son was transferred to another province, so I was alone. I told him he could come and keep house and that as long as I had an income, he wouldn't go hungry. So he's been living in my place for the past ten years."

"If he's there now," Gan said impatiently, "may I go with you to see him?"

"No."

"Why?"

"Because he's gone into hospital with a stroke."
Gan heaved a sigh.

"Don't worry," Sheng added. "He's out of danger, but the doctor won't let him have any visitors yet."

Relieved, Gan asked again, "What caused it?"

"Overwork. Last year the doctor insisted that he take it easy, but he was busier than ever with his work. He said that his ancestors were connoisseurs of painting and had the knack of being able to tell genuine works from fakes. While he was able he wanted to write it down so that the knowledge would not be lost."

Gan sighed. "If only he could have done it earlier!"

"Years ago he used to complain to me that the higher-ups in the antique world were a bunch of laymen who'd insulted him and that he would rather die with his skills than teach others. But in the last couple of years, since I've been cleared of the false accusations made against me in the 'cultural revolution' and we've had a bit more money, he's changed his mind. Now he says he won't withhold his knowledge any longer and has decided to write it all down. I was delighted and provided him with paper, ink, fine tea and tobacco, but I forgot to remind him to take care of his health."

Hearing this Gan was moved. "You really have been a loyal friend!"

"Oh, I owe a great deal to the way things have improved since those chaotic years, otherwise I couldn't have afforded to help him."

With a heavy heart Gan walked silently beside Sheng for a while before asking, "Is he able to talk?"

"Yes. But his tongue gets a little stiff sometimes."

"So he can still be cured." Gan was cheered, thinking he should suggest sending someone to Sheng's house to have Han's speech recorded. When the next National People's Congress opened, someone should propose helping old scholars and craftsmen to pass on their knowledge.

Saying goodbye to Gan, Sheng promised, "As soon as I have the doctor's permission, I'll take you to see him."

On his way home, Gan felt much more at ease; at long last he had found an opportunity to make amends for his error. Now he could die with a clear conscience.

Translated by Song Shouquan

Na Wu

NA Wu's grandfather had been an official. So when his father Master Fu came to sell their mansion he raised enough to keep them for several years.

While Master Fu had property visitors flocked to his gate. From them he learned to raise pigeons, ride horses, the foreign game of billiards and the art of making kites. Best of all he liked singing Beijing opera or accompanying Kunqu opera. The well-known musician Big Head Hu often dropped in to train him to sing and applaud his performances. For an audience was needed to liven up these practice sessions. Often Big Head would play the opening bars, then as soon as Master Fu started singing would put down his bow to clap and shout "Bravo!" He would then continue playing. If Master Fu's throat was dry from lack of sleep, after this applause he might ask doubtfully:

"Why does it sound wrong to me?"

"You've not quite hit it off yet — stick at it." Big Head calmly went on playing.

Master Fu's wife died young. For his son's sake he didn't remarry. But one day he would buy costumes for actresses, another day would redeem a ballad-singer. The guest rooms in his back garden were constantly occupied. Naturally he was too busy to look after his son.

Na Wu for his part didn't want to be looked after,

He had a group of companions of his own age, all sons of nobles too. They complimented each other on their chefs or tailors; went to cock-fights, dog races, operas and flower displays. They outdid their fathers in some respects by picking up modern ways. They skated, danced, ogled women in Wangfujing, or frequented the most fashionable teahouse to fool around with waitresses. They had never known the value of money. When short of cash they smuggled out some bronze ware, porcelain painting or calligraphy from the back storeroom to sell on the sly, to keep themselves going for another couple of weeks. By the time Master Fu had sold off his property like so many pieces of bean-curd, young Na Wu had polished off all their antiques. When their creditors had them evicted from their last house, he realized that his sole skill — pawning goods — would no longer raise him even a copper cent or a coarse flour bun.

Master Fu breathed his last then and departed this earth, leaving Na Wu an orphan.

2

In his old age Na Wu's paternal grandfather had made a slave-girl, called Purple Cloud, his concubine, some eight or nine years younger than his son. On his death-bed he ordered his son to look after her. Master Fu, never stingy, made over to her a small courtyard once used as a stable, so that she could set up house there and live on her own.

Purple Cloud, the daughter of a tenant farmer, had been brought up to be frugal and hard-working. So she had taken in a lodger. A widow has to be careful of her reputation, must choose respectable neighbours. So she rented her rooms cheaply to an old physician named Guo. He and his wife had no children, and the old lady was consumptive. When the leaves fell she had to take to her bed. Purple Cloud saw that the doctor was so busy visiting patients and nursing his wife that their rooms were a shambles. She thereupon quietly took it on herself to brew the sick woman's medicine, to wash her and tidy up. At first Mrs Guo simply thanked her, meaning to make it up to her when she recovered. But her illness grew steadily worse.

One day she clasped Purple Cloud's hand and said, "It's not easy for you, a widow with no support. I feel bad the way you're nursing me every day. So let's settle this like sisters, and from next month on we'll pay you more rent. I'd not dream of offering you wages. Money wouldn't buy this kindness you're showing me."

The rims of Purple Cloud's eyes reddened. She helped the old lady to sit on the edge of the bed. "Elder Sister, I can get by easily, I'm not short of money," she said. "The old gentleman over there passed away not long after he'd married me. Apart from him, no one else has ever had any feeling for me. And I've had no one to care for. The fact is, nursing you I've been happier than when I'd only myself to think about. It's good of you to let me. Worth more to me than money."

Two years passed. The old lady knew that her time was running out. She made her husband go on an errand and called Purple Cloud to her bedside and tried to struggle up to kowtow to her. Purple Cloud made her lie down, exclaiming, "Do you want to be the death of me!"

"I've a favour to ask you," said Mrs Guo. "First let me bow to you."

"I'm the one who should be bowing to you, elder sister."

Mrs Guo sobbed that her husband and she had been married all these years, with never an angry word. Now she was done for, she couldn't bear to leave her old man on his own. He just wouldn't be able to cope. Apart from making his rounds, he couldn't even fasten his own buttons. In all her life she'd never seen anyone as kind as Purple Cloud; if she could only entrust her old man to her, she would pray to Buddha for her in the nether regions.

Purple Cloud replied, "Elder sister, if it's Dr Guo you're worried about you don't have to say any more. From now on, whether you're still here or not, I'll take good care of him. If you're still not easy in your mind, we can choose a day to invite the neighbours and the policeman to a feast, so that I can kowtow to the Guo ancestors before them all and recognize Dr Guo as my elder brother."

Mrs Guo hearing this felt most indebted to her. Her husband when consulted had nothing but admiration for Purple Cloud. On the Double Fifth Festival Purple Cloud seized the chance to take some sticky-rice dumplings to Master Fu, to tactfully sound him out about her proposal.

Master Fu said, "Since my father passed away you've had no connection with his family. They would raise no objection if you were to remarry, to say nothing of a nominal kinship like this."

She wiped away tears. "Though you're so open-minded, I can never forget the old master's goodness to me."

On the first of the sixth month the adoption feast was held. Purple Cloud could not remember her parents' names. For years she had been registered simply as the Woman Na. During the feast she gave the policeman a red package containing money, and begged him to add the character Guo to Na, to make her Dr Guo's younger sister.

Old Mrs Guo, as she had foretold, died soon after this business was settled. Then Purple Cloud took formal charge of the household. She was viewed with new respect then, addressed as Mistress Cloud.

3

Hearing that Na Wu was down and out, Mistress Cloud proposed to her Brother Guo that they should take him in. "Not for him," she said, "but for the kindness of his grandfather. We can't have the neighbours saying we've no sense of justice."

Dr Guo always fell in with her proposals. He tried to find out Na Wu's whereabouts and finally tracked him down in an inn, quite presentably turned out. Dr Guo had expected him to accept their offer with tears of gratitude. Instead Na Wu pulled a long face and tutted impatiently.

"I wouldn't mind moving in with you, but how could one of my family address a concubine as mistress?" he said.

Dr Guo's face darkened, he wanted to box Na Wu's ears. With a swish of his sleeves he marched out. Not liking to tell the truth when he got home, he simply said that Na Wu was doing all right and didn't want to come — no need to insist.

When Mistress Cloud persisted in asking questions, Dr Guo told her what Na Wu had actually said. She sighed, "Those pampered sons of the rich stick to those stinking conventions. Let him call me whatever he likes. We're not doing this for him but for his ancestors, aren't we? But if he's doing all right, let's leave it at that."

Yet a few days later Na Wu turned up at their gate. On entering he paid his respects and greeted her as did the neighbours as "Mistress Cloud" and Dr Guo as "Old Uncle". Though he should have addressed them as two generations senior, she was too happy to mind. She told him, "I'm afraid you've no one looking after you outside, so why not move in with us?"

Na Wu answered, "I'm ashamed to tell you this. I was doing business with someone and pawned my clothes to raise capital, thinking once the deal came off I'd have plenty in hand to buy you a little gift. But now I've lost the lot. . . ."

"Why talk of gifts, a young man on your own. I'm so glad you've come! If you're not comfortable outside, come and live here."

Was Na Wu capable of doing business?

His only attempt at it had proved a fiasco. A German in Tianjin had made quite a sum in China and wanted to take some porcelain home with him. He looked round several antique shops in Beijing without finding what he wanted. Na Wu spotted him in a shop where he had taken a curio to sell, and waited for him outside. He accosted the man, claiming to be the son of the Minister of Internal Affairs who was willing to part with some porcelain. Why not fix a time to inspect it? When the German suggested going to his mansion, he said his family mustn't know; they would have to meet outside. He would wait for him three days later in an inn in Xiheyan. Na Wu had no porcelain himself, but he knew that Suo Seven had filched a set of Guyuexuan from his home and cached it in Promotion Inn. Suo wanted to sell it but was afraid of the consequences if his family found out. Na Wu went and told him, "I've found a good customer who will ship the things out of China, keeping it secret, and should be able to pay a high price. If you appear your family may get to know of it, so I'll pose as the owner. When the deal's clinched I'll just take a small commission. But first you must lend me a few dozen dollars and book me a room in an inn, because if I don't cut a dash the foreigner won't fork out so much."

Suo Seven, being even a bigger fool than Na Wu, did exactly as he asked. When Dr Guo called, Na Wu had just moved into the inn and was dreaming of making a fortune. That was why he cold-shouldered him.

Suo Seven was a blabbermouth. This business came to the ears of the manager of the Old Curiosity Shop, Ma Qi. Ma knew that Suo had filched this set of porcelain and had been longing to get his hands on it, but hadn't offered enough to clinch the deal. He had seen the porcelain though, genuine Guyuexuan from the

same kiln as a few small bowls he had. As luck had
it, the German came to his shop for a look. Ma
secretly told his assistants to set out his Guyuexuan
bowls on the teapoys in their reception room. After
the foreigner had looked through his stock he invited
him in there to rest, and casually offered him tea in a
Guyuexuan bowl. The German was loud in his praise
and exclaimed, "The goods you have on display are
second-rate. How is it you use such an exquisite tea-
service?"

Ma Qi laughed. "If you like I'll sell it to you for
less than those wares you think inferior — it's not worth
half as much."

The German said, "You must be joking."

"It's a fact."

"How come?"

"These are fakes. Those pieces you don't think
much of are genuine; these are modern replicas. You
can't judge simply by appearances but must listen to
the sound a piece makes when struck, feel the base,
and examine the roughcast." With that he fetched
some porcelain from the shop by way of comparison,
and rattled away till the foreigner was quite bewildered. Finally he told an assistant to wrap up two bowls
which had not been filled with tea, and put these in
front of the German. "We may not have done a deal,
but to show my goodwill I'll give you these two fakes
as souvenirs."

The German took the bowls away and studied them
carefully. In less than two days he knew all the distinctive features of this "fake porcelain". When he went
to the inn and Na Wu opened up his casket, he laughed

— that ware was exactly the same as the "fakes" given him. Out of politeness he did not explain this, however. When he asked the price it was staggering. And seeing Na Wu living so shabbily, not at all like a nobleman's son, he firmly refused to buy and took his leave, most grateful to Ma Qi for having tipped him off. Going back to the Old Curiosity Shop he bought up all the fake porcelain, then returned happily to Germany.

Suo Seven blamed Na Wu for this fiasco, and insisted on the repayment of his loan, refusing even to pay for his room. Once again Na Wu pawned the clothes he had got out of hock, after which he asked Mistress Cloud to take him in.

Before long, through a middleman, Ma Qi bought Suo Seven's genuine Guyuexuan for half the price he had charged for his fakes. By the time the Suos discovered this and tried to get them back, they had been sold at a huge profit to a Tianjin exporter named Cai.

4

Mistress Cloud, being so modest and unassuming, thought it an honour to have Na Wu staying with her and regarded him as a treasure. Though he had been destitute outside he still lorded it over this former concubine, addressing her like a servant. For all his poverty he gave himself airs: refused to eat big muffin cakes, insisted on having his pickles finely sliced, and when served noodles with fried bean sauce kept back half the meat as stuffing for a sesame-seed cake. After

Mistress Cloud redeemed his clothes from the pawn-shop, he started changing three times a day again. Each time she had to wash and iron his clothes. If there was the least little crease he would complain, "How can I wear this? Looks as if an ox had chewed it." This young master kept Mistress Cloud busy from dawn till dusk.

Dr Guo still lived in the south room. After Na Wu moved in he tried to ignore him, but couldn't hide his disapproval. One day he told him, "Young master, we old folk have one foot in the grave and don't mind making do; but you're still young, you ought to find some way to make a living. You can't always expect meat pies to drop down from the sky. A doctor doesn't earn much, but it's enough to keep me supplied with cornmeal. Why not get off your high horse and learn medicine from me? And you should stop being so choosy."

Na Wu objected, "Those medical books of yours give me a headache. Isn't there anything easier? Folk prescriptions for instance, or charms. I could learn those."

"I don't know any charms," replied Dr Guo. "I know some folk prescriptions though. What sort of illnesses do you want to cure?"

"I want to be an abortionist. When young ladies in big families have lovers they'll pay a hundred dollars for an abortion so as to avoid scandals."

Dr Guo hearing that went off in disgust. And from that day on he ignored Na Wu. They had no family planning in those days, and doctors thought abortions illegal and criminal.

5

After Na Wu had stayed with Mistress Cloud for less than a month, though supplied with food and clothing he couldn't stand being hard up and felt intolerably lonely. As his clothes were out of hock he begged his friends to find some job for him. It was time for his luck to change, and while in a claque with Suo Seven he met Ma Sen, editor of *The Violet Pictorial*. Since Na Wu knew many actors and could take photographs, Ma asked him to be a reporter for the pictorial.

This pictorial published features on actresses, backstage gossip, romances, adventure stories and other sensational news. Its office, in a small shop in Coal Market Street, had a staff of only two: Ma Sen and his assistant editor Tao Zhi. The two men looked very different. Ma wore Western suits and leather shoes, Tao a blue cloth gown. Ma shaved twice a day, had a hair-cut every three days; Tao wore his hair down to his ears, and had a stubbly beard. The office contained only two desks and three chairs. Newspapers and magazines were piled on the floor. On the day Na Wu started work the editors invited him out to lunch and explained their rules to him. He would receive neither salary nor travelling expenses, and the pay for each contribution was nominal. But he was given a reporter's card and could start work in the name of the magazine, and make a living on his own. Na Wu felt he had been taken in. But having accepted he could hardly back out now. He decided to give it a try. After two months associating with other reporters he realized that he was on to a good thing. When he wrote cracking up an actress, he was paid not only by her but her backers too. In his wanderings through the town if he found empty rooms in some lodging-house or a restaurant selling some new delicacy, he would write an item entitled "An Empty Haunted House" or a letter denouncing the restaurant for maggoty dishes. He showed these to the landlord and restaurant owner, claiming that he had suppressed them for several days so that they could read them first and see if they could be hushed up. To keep out of trouble such men invariably paid to have these manuscripts suppressed, while Na Wu gloated over each new stroke of luck.

The Violet Pictorial was now serializing the romance A Pretty Young Lady by the popular writer "Master of the Drunkard's Studio". Sixteen instalments had been published, but he had failed to deliver the seventeenth. As Na Wu was in the office, Tao Zhi asked him to fetch the manuscript and pay the author.

6

The Master of the Drunkard's Studio lived in a narrow lane with few houses in it. His was an old-style two-storeyed building of brick. It overlooked a courtyard, in one corner of which was a rickety staircase just wide enough for one person. Several rooms opened off the passages upstairs and downstairs, each with a briquette stove, a water vat and a dustpan by its door. Na Wu was looking round when two people came downstairs. One was a woman with permed hair and pencilled eyebrows in a fancy, short-sleeved gown and embroidered satin slippers; the other was a middle-aged man in a grey cloth suit, cloth shoes and a felt cap. At sight of Na Wu they exchanged glances and halted.

"Who are you looking for, sir?" the man asked.

Na Wu said, "A novelist. . . ."

"Oh." Looking disappointed the man jerked his chin at the space below the stairway, then nodded to the woman and they left. Na Wu stooped to get under the stairs, and saw a door covered by a bamboo curtain, with a signboard engraved "The Drunkard's Studio".

Inside were two rooms, but it was too dark to see the back one distinctly. In the other room was a hardwood desk inlaid with mother-of-pearl, which looked out of place there. There were two chairs and a deck chair. The desk was crammed with books, papers, stationery, packets of cigarettes, ashtrays, inkstones and brush pots. Hearing footsteps, a man came out from the dark room. He was tall and thin with a pale face and a moustache.

"Who are you looking for?"

"Does the Master of the Drunkard's Studio live here?"

"That's my humble self. Please take a seat. Where are you from?"

"The pictorial. My editor's sent me for your manuscript."

"Well, sit down. The last couple of days I've been so busy, I forgot all about it!"

"Oh, we're waiting for your manuscript to go to press."

"Never mind, if you'll wait a bit I'll write it for you now. How far did I get last time?"

"Eh?" Na Wu flushed, not having read this novel.

His host laughed. "Never mind if you've forgotten. I have a record here."

He sat down at his desk and pulled out from a stack of papers a blue ledger. Leafing through it he asked, "Are you publishing my *Two Swallows*?"

"No," said Na Wu. "We're *The Violet Pictorial*. We're printing your *A Pretty Young Lady*."

"*A Pretty Young Lady*." The other riffled through his ledger, then shoved it aside and pulled out another. Leafing through this he exclaimed, "Where's my record of *A Pretty Young Lady*? Oh, I know!" He pushed aside the second ledger and pulled out from a drawer a thick stapled manuscript of rice-paper. Inserted in this was an empty cigarette packet, and opening it here he said with a smile, "You're in luck, I don't have to write a new instalment, just copy this out." With that he spread out a sheet of manuscript paper, picked up a brush and set to work copying. Na Wu was holding the dollar note he had brought. As soon as the novelist had finished copying and put the manuscript in an envelope, Na Wu laid the note on the table. The other glanced at it but didn't touch it. He turned to call towards the back room, "We've a visitor, brew some tea, quick!"

A round-faced woman in her fifties emerged and curtseyed to Na Wu. "Please sit down, sir! Don't laugh at our shabby place." Picking up a kettle she reached out for the dollar note on the table. "I'll go and fetch water."

Na Wu said, "All the tabloids outside are printing your novels, sir. How many do you write at once?"

"Eight or nine."

"Do you finish them all and keep them here?"

"No, I write an instalment at a time, and get paid for each instalment."

"But surely that manuscript of *A Pretty Young Lady* which I just saw is finished?"

"Well, that's second-hand."

"Second-hand? What do you mean?"

The novelist explained that writers who hadn't made a name were unable to get their work published. Others wrote for fun, not to make a reputation. Yet others were so desperate for money that they couldn't wait to be paid in instalments. So they sold their novels to him, and he made a profit by having them serialized.

Na Wu exclaimed, "So if you can afford to buy a manuscript, you can win fame without even lifting a finger!"

"That's how it has always been," was the reply. "A prince once published a number of operas, not a word written by himself."

Na Wu's face lit up. He said as if jokingly, "I must buy a couple of manuscripts myself so that I can enjoy being famous."

The other answered seriously, "In your profession, unless you have a name people will look down on you and you'll get nowhere. You need to make your mark. Besides, when you buy a manuscript you have to read it, then copy it out. You soon get the knack of it and can write yourself. There's nothing difficult about writing novels."

He had just bought an adventure story entitled *The Carp Dart,* and he offered this to Na Wu for a hundred dollars. As Na Wu happened to have with him a fake painting which he meant to pawn, this offer tempted him. As soon as he had raised three hundred dollars at the pawnshop he went straight back to the Drunkard's Studio and announced, "I've brought the money. Can I have a look first at the manuscript?"

"Don't be so naive!" said the other. "Buying a manuscript isn't like buying cucumbers that you can pick over and taste. Suppose you read it then refused to buy it, and went off to plagiarize it, what could I do? You'll just have to take it on trust."

As Na Wu fingered his money uncertainly, the other pounded his desk. "All right, we're friends!" He went into the inner room, rummaged in an old shoe box kept under the bed and took from it a manuscript on red-lined paper. He carried this outside to brush off the dust, then handed it to Na Wu. "Have a look at the contents first."

Na Wu read a few pages — it seemed really exciting. Then he weighed it in his hand and sized up its thickness. "This surely isn't enough for a hundred instalments," he said. "If I spend a hundred dollars on it, and it's only thirty instalments. . . ."

"How green you are! You can't expect to win fame and profit together. Don't you first want to make a name? This manuscript is well written. I guarantee it will create a sensation! Once you're famous you can make money."

Na Wu paid over the money and left with the manuscript under his arm. Without reading it through he asked the editors to serialize it. Ma Sen accepted it, then sat on it for a month. Each time he was asked about it he replied, "I haven't finished it yet, but it seems not bad." He said nothing, however, about publishing it. When Na Wu asked Tao Zhi about it, the latter laughed.

"Didn't the fellow who sold you this tell you the rule for getting a manuscript published?"

"We don't seem to have any rules for the Master of the Drunkard's Studio. We pay him a dollar for each instalment, don't we?"

The assistant editor laughed. "He's like a famous actor — as soon as he takes the stage people start applauding. But you're like an amateur — they don't make money acting, instead they have to pay for the privilege. Have to rent the theatre themselves, hire costumes and other actors; then throw a feast and hand out tickets — otherwise who'd come to applaud? Professionals perform in order to eat, amateurs to make a name or enjoy themselves. Of course the popular ones can turn professional, but only after they've paid to establish themselves."

Then Na Wu forked out another hundred dollars and asked Tao Zhi to draw him up a list of guests to invite to a restaurant. Only then did *The Carp Dart* begin to be serialized under the pen-name "Master of Windy Pavilion". After that some friends referred to him as a "writer" and congratulated him on "creating a sensation", predicting that he would go far. Na Wu answered modestly, though inwardly bursting with pride. His way of talking changed too and he walked with a lighter step, feeling that his two hundred dollars had been well spent. Though his painting had been exposed as a fake, and he had to sell a Western suit to square the pawnshop, still, confident that he would soon be famous, he did not lose heart.

When seven or eight instalments had come out, things

started to go wrong. Either Tao Zhi's list had been incomplete and he had offended someone, or people were out to make trouble. Some other tabloids printed reviews ridiculing and attacking *The Carp Dart*. Some accused him of plagiarism or writing nonsense. Someone wrote, "The Master of Windy Pavilion is the grandson of a former official in the Ministry of Internal Affairs. As his grandfather was indebted to a boxer of the Eight Hexagrams School, he has written this novel to crack up that school and run down the Xingyi School."

In his indignation Na Wu called on the Master of the Drunkard's Studio.

"What taboos did that manuscript of yours break?" he demanded. "Why has it given rise to all this talk?"

In fact the Master of the Drunkard's Studio had bought the manuscript from an opium addict for ten dollars without reading it. So raising clasped hands he replied, "Didn't I tell you it would cause a sensation? Congratulations! When people find fault that's good publicity. I used to commission articles running me down. Just think, if you simply publish a novel, your name only appears on the paper every three days. But when it gets reviewed, whether unfavourably or favourably, your name keeps appearing and readers remember it. Besides, success and failure go together. When some people curse you, others are bound to praise you. Leave them to fight it out while you cash in without lifting a finger yourself. You're in luck."

Na Wu thought this made sense and cheered up. But a few days later when he went to the office, Ma Sen handed him a letter and said sternly, "This is your letter, Master Wu.   We have all along co-operated well, so don't involve my partners and me in trouble. Leave us *The Violet Pictorial* to eke out a living."

At first Na Wu thought he was joking.   But the letter, when he read it, gave him a sinking feeling as if he had fallen into a deep well.

Written in thick black ink on a sheet of rice-paper with eight red lines it read:

"To the Master of Windy Pavilion.   On the sixth of this month, at three in the afternoon, I expect you in Happy Longevity Opium Den in Dazhalan.   If you don't show up, look out!   Don't say you haven't been warned!"   The signature was "Wu Cunzhong".

He asked Ma, "Who's Wu Cunzhong?   The name sounds familiar."

Without a word Ma tossed a tabloid at him.   An article in it was outlined in red ink.   The caption was, "Old age and ill health make Wu Cunzhong decline the post of bodyguard."   There followed an account of Wu.   He had been a boxer of the Xingyi School at the end of the Qing dynasty, had performed in Tianqiao in the early years of the Republic, but after the Japanese invasion had switched to making straw ropes.   Recently a county head had offered him big money to be his bodyguard, but he had refused.

When Na Wu had read this, Ma added, "Did you hear about that Russian strong man who used to challenge people in Sun Yat-sen Park?   He promised ten gold medals to anyone who could throw him."

"He was thrown by Li Cunyi, wasn't he?" said Na Wu.   "I heard he broke a leg."

"Right.   Wu Cunzhong and Li Cunyi were sworn brothers taught by the same teacher!"

Na Wu broke out in a cold sweat. He said wretchedly, "He'll break me in two when he sees me!"

"Why, in your novel, did you have to drag in that rivalry between the Eight Hexagrams and Xingyi schools?" Ma demanded.

"Heavens I didn't know a thing about it! I bought that manuscript."

Tao Zhi took pity on him then and said, "Don't get het up. With men like that you can usually appeal to their better nature. Just kowtow to him and don't defend yourself. Seeing you've knuckled under he'll probably let you off."

"You've got to go," declared Ma Sen. "Or I would not put it past him to wreck this office, and that would finish us off."

For the next three days Na Wu didn't eat a square meal, didn't have a night's sound sleep.

7

On the sixth a fiery sun shrivelled the leaves of the trees and melted tarmac roads as Na Wu dragged himself to Dazhalan. Turning into a lane he saw a big white porcelain lampshade bearing the name "Happy Longevity Opium Den". He went in. Opposite him was a stairway, dank and dark. He went up and found white curtains over the doors on both sides. Drawing one of these he poked his head in. A fat middle-aged man sitting in the doorway was fanning himself with a rush fan. "Want to buy opium?" he asked.

"I'm looking for Wu Cunzhong. . . ."

"In the second private room over there."

Na Wu drew back the curtain and entered that room. It was long with a wooden partition down the middle. On each side were four small doors, all with short cotton curtains on which a number was printed. He approached No. 2 and asked softly, "Is Mr Wu there?"

There was no sound inside. At this point a waitress came in carrying a brightly polished smoking-set. She indicated that he should go in. Nodding gratefully he raised the curtain and entered. This tiny room contained only a couch and a chair, but it was spotlessly clean. On the couch were a mat and a pillow, and paintings and calligraphy hung on the walls. An old man in a white cotton jacket, with a long beard, lay there on his back, his eyes closed. There was no knowing whether he was asleep or awake.

Na Wu said softly, "Mr Wu, I've come as you instructed!"

The old man's eyelids didn't even twitch. After a brief hesitation Na Wu withdrew to stand helplessly outside. The waitress happened to come back just then. Na Wu stuffed a one-dollar note into her apron pocket. "Mr Wu is asleep," he said. "Will you find me somewhere to rest and call me when he wakes?" With a smile she pointed at No. 2, then pushed him towards the door and left.

Na Wu went in again and stood silently waiting for Wu Cunzhong to open his eyes. After his long walk he was hot. But the rule of this house was not to open windows or turn on electric fans. The sweat poured down his face like creepy-crawly insects, but he had to hide his frantic anxiety. When five minutes had passed and still the old man did not stir, Na Wu in desperation fell on his knees.

"Mr Wu, Old Master Wu! I've come to apologize. I'm a scoundrel, an utter idiot. I talked through my hat. Please make allowances for me, I'm really beneath contempt. . . ."

The old man stretched then laughed. Hitching himself up he said, "Stop kneeling. Get up."

"I humbly beg your pardon!" Na Wu kowtowed, then stood up.

Smiling Old Wu said, "You had everything so well figured out, I thought you must be a boxer yourself."

"I'm nothing," answered Na Wu. "A fly licking a ladle."

"Well then you should have asked around before writing, instead of running people down right and left!"

"I'll come clean with you, sir. I didn't write that novel, I bought it from someone. I wanted to make a name, little thinking it was going to make you so angry."

The old man roared with laughter, mollified by the way Na Wu had knuckled under. "Sit down," he said more mildly. "Have a smoke?"

Na Wu sat down. Wu asked his family background and sighed on hearing that his grandfather had served in the Ministry of Internal Affairs.

"It seems we were fated to meet," he said. "Once I went to Mongolia on business, and brought back a gift from a Mongolian prince to your grandfather. When I delivered it he kept me to a feast. Of course I didn't see the inner apartments, but I was fairly dazzled by the outer courtyard! It struck me at the time as going too far — as if he thought his job would last for ever. The way he was pouring money out like water, he'd have finished off even a gold mine. And what would happen to his sons and grandsons, who'd no idea how hard it is to make a living? So you get by, do you, by writing rubbish?"

Na Wu flushed and nodded.

"You're still young," said Wu Cunzhong, "and you've enough education to learn a profession. A skill is worth more than ten thousand strings of cash. Why not get off your high horse and settle down to a job? If you earn your keep you can hold up your head no matter where you are."

"You're right! My father died early and I had no one to teach me. Thank you for putting me straight."

Though Na Wu was so glib, he struck the other as genuinely grateful. So Wu said, "I live by the Temple of Agriculture. I've bought a machine to plait straw ropes. If you can't make a go of it anywhere else, come and join me. I need someone who can read and write right away."

Na Wu thought: You rate me too low. Even if I'm down and out, how can the descendant of nobles work like a coolie! Not daring to show that he despised the job, he hastily said, "Just now I can manage all right, but I shall certainly ask for your help in future."

Seeing his reluctance, Wu did not insist. He said they could forget about that novel. Some of his sworn brothers had threatened in their rage to wreck the office of *The Violet Pictorial*, but he had persuaded them to wait till after he'd met "The Master of Windy Pavilion". Now that he'd settled the dispute, they'd have to let it drop. Na Wu bowed and thanked him profusely, then took his leave.

"Wait a bit," said Wu. "I can't have you coming all this way for nothing. China's martial arts are going to the dogs and the country's in a bad way. Still we do have a few good boxers in various schools. Go out and write us up to boost our morale. I'm no good any more, but I'll put on a little show for you. Number Three!"

"Here!" answered a booming voice behind the partition.

"Go and light the lamps."

Wu got up, put on his shoes and tightening his girdle, went out. Four or five men were waiting in the passage. The two youngest had brought a table, and the waitress made haste to light three opium lamps for them.

At sight of Na Wu these tough customers at once exchanged glances and grinned, making him rather nervous.

"Don't worry," said Wu. "These are all my apprentices. We thought you might know a trick or two, so they were ready to take you on. Now we've made things up, fine! We can all be friends."

By now more people had gathered round, crowding the passage.

The opium lamps, Taigu lamps from Shanxi, were about the size of a tea bowl, with brass oil-cups below their thick, tapering glass shades. You could only extinguish them by blowing straight into the aperture at the top. When the waitress had lit them and an apprentice had set them out in a row, Wu inspected them and adjusted their position. He then fell back five paces, took the "horse-stance" and breathed in so deeply that his belly underneath his girdle bulged. After slightly swinging his arms he stood stock-still and blew hard. The flames in the three lamps flickered, and one by one they went out, while the onlookers shouted "Bravo!"

Wu raised clasped hands. "I've made an exhibition of myself. Now I'm old, all I can do is raise a laugh."

Na Wu's legs were trembling, he was in a cold sweat. He staggered out to hire a pedicab to the editorial office. When he told the editors of his narrow escape they congratulated him and invited him out to Fengzeyuan Restaurant, where they ordered wine and dishes to help him get over his shock. Ma Sen returned him the manuscript of *The Carp Dart*, as they could no longer serialize it. They also said he was now too well-known to work for their pictorial and took away his treasured reporter's card.

8

Since becoming a reporter Na Wu had rented a small room in the south city and cut himself off from Purple Cloud. But now that he had no money for rent or food, he bought some cakes and went to call on her. The few months of his absence had seen big changes. The old doctor had died of a sudden illness, and the courtyard looked neglected. Mistress Cloud was taking in laundry. When Na Wu arrived she broke down.

"I didn't take proper care of you," she sobbed. "Fed you so badly that you left in a huff. But you shouldn't be narrow-minded. After all we still belong to one family, don't we? Who else is left of the Na family? When we were rich, carriages and sedan-chairs thronged our gate; but after we lost our money who would own us? We've only each other now."

Na Wu's nose tingled when he heard this. He exclaimed gruffly, "Granny!"

That reduced Purple Cloud to tears again. "You'll be the death of me," she protested. "If you've any pity for a poor lone widow, don't leave me again. With my washing and sewing I can make enough to keep the two of us. When you marry I'll look after you and your wife. And when you have a son I'll nurse him, if you don't think me too far beneath you. What you call me doesn't matter!"

When Na Wu agreed to this she gave thanks to Buddha. "Just stay here reading or amusing yourself. So long as you don't leave I'll feel secure. Sit down now while I clear out your rooms for you."

Purple Cloud made ready the doctors' rooms for him, then called him over to inspect them. The inner room was simply furnished with a bed, a table and a chair. In the outer room were two hardwood bookcases stacked with thread-bound books on medicine as well as a few works of literature.

"I sold everything else to pay for the old man's funeral," she told him. "His students wouldn't let me sell these books unless I sold them to them, for fear I'd be swindled. I thought maybe some were worth money, so I waited for you to decide which of them to keep. You can take your pick. Those you don't want we'll give to his students. When the old man was dying they helped me out, and I've no other way of thanking them."

"Tell them to take the lot," said Na Wu handsomely. "Just leave me the bookcases."

From that day on Purple Cloud wore a smile again. She got out all Na Wu's clothes to wash, starch and mend. When she had money to spare she gave him a few cents to hire a novel from the stall at their gate. The adventure stories he read reminded him of the manuscript he had bought from the Master of the Drunkard's Studio. He felt he shouldn't have let the man off so lightly. So one day he asked Mistress Cloud for some rickshaw money in order to call on a friend. She gave him two dollars she had just been paid, saying, "That's right, go out and have a good time before you fall ill of boredom. But don't go mixing with rowdies; remember we're a respectable family."

After the plain fare he'd been having, Na Wu's stomach was crying out for something richer. So first he went to Dongsi for a bowl of boiled offals. Then at Longfusi he had a plate of chitterling broth. When he reached the Drunkard's Studio and raised the curtain, its master hurried out in his slippers to greet him. Taking his hand he exclaimed, "So you made a pile! Where did you disappear to?"

"Made a pile, did I? On that book of yours *The Carp Dart*? I nearly had my back broken by Wu Cunzhong!"

"You'd only yourself to blame," was the retort. "Who publishes a manuscript he's bought without changing a single word? If you'd altered the names Eight Hexagrams and Xingyi, you wouldn't have had any trouble. But that's past and done with. Today I have a good proposal for you."

"Don't think you can fool me again."

"Whether you believe me or not, sit down while I see to some business. I'll be straight back." He poured Na Wu some tea then went out and could be heard going upstairs.

After the time it takes for a meal the Drunkard led in a stranger, telling him, "Didn't you want to meet this young gentleman? He happens to have dropped into my humble home. Let me introduce you: Manager Jia Fenglou."

Na Wu recognized the middle-aged man who had told him the way the first time he came. He stood up and nodded. "We've met."

"That's right. I saw at a glance that day that you were someone special. Someone exceptional! Don't take offence, but you impressed me so much that I'm overjoyed at this chance to talk to you. . . ."

"You're too polite, too polite, sir."

"It's the honest truth. When I heard later that you were the grandson of a high official, I was tempted to slap my own face. How could a nobody like myself presume to call on someone so distinguished?"

The Drunkard put in, "Young Master Na's most obliging, he never gives himself airs."

"Yes, he's told me several times that you never put on side, you're so tolerant. Now that you're here again, sir, you must do me the favour of coming to my home so that we can get acquainted."

"You do me too much honour," replied Na Wu. "I've simply cashed in a bit on my ancestors; apart from that I'm good for nothing. Please sit down."

Jia Fenglou suggested with a smile to the Drunkard, "Why don't you both come to my place?"

The Drunkard told Na Wu, "As soon as Manager Jia heard of your arrival he sent out to order a meal. It would be ungracious to decline. Let's go up."

"This is the first time we've met," protested Na Wu. "Why not let me invite you to a restaurant?"

"Won't you give me this pleasure?" retorted Jia. "My younger sister wants to meet you too. Shall I ask her to come and persuade you?"

The Drunkard took Na Wu's arm and he and Jia between them propelled him upstairs.

Jia had four rooms, one for himself, one for his sister, and two reception rooms. He ushered Na Wu into the northern room. On the wall hung enlarged photographs of his sister Fengkui in ordinary costume and on the stage. Stuck in the frames were cuttings from newspapers, all fulsome reviews of her performances. On a stand stood an octagonal drum with red tassels. By this hung a three-stringed fiddle. On the red-check varnished cloth on the red-lacquered desk lay some magazines and pictorials alongside musical scores and a list of performances. On one teapoy was a gramophone. Na Wu realized that Jia and his sister were artistes.

When they were seated the Drunkard said, "You're a Beijing opera and *pingju* fan, Master Na, you seldom go to ballads. When you've time you should go and hear Miss Fengkui — she's brilliant."

Na Wu bowed. "I will certainly give myself that pleasure as soon as I can."

"You must be too busy, sir, to do us that honour. And my sister's singing would grate on your ears."

"Now you're being polite!" the Drunkard said emphatically. "Fengkui is a first-rate artiste, very kind and warm-hearted too. Her fans are in luck, that's what I always say."

Na Wu thought: It's no use your trying to trap me. My father was the one to boost ballad-singers. Even if I wanted to I haven't the money.

Just then the door curtain swished and in came Fengkui.

Today her lips were lightly rouged but otherwise she wore no make-up, which made her look much younger than before, not more than seventeen or eighteen at most. She was wearing a short-sleeved gown and embroidered white satin slippers. Her hair, loosely swept back behind her ears, was fastened with a pearly clasp. Above one temple she wore a white orchid. With a cool smile she laid both hands on one hip and curtseyed to Na Wu.

"Excuse me, sir, for not being here to greet you. Please come into the next room for a snack."

Jia Fenglou led Na Wu into the next room where the table was laid with some dishes, a bottle of liquor and another bottle of high-grade Shaoxing wine.

As they drank Jia went on flattering Na Wu, who after a few cups of liquor relaxed and started joking with Fengkui. She neither responded nor cold-shouldered him but seemed completely detached, sometimes smiling at what they said, sometimes looking pensive.

After the meal Jia took his guests back to the other room. The Drunkard excused himself on the pretext of business, while Fengkui cleared the table. When Na Wu began to take his leave his host stopped him. "I've a favour to ask you," he said. "You mustn't go yet."

Na Wu had to sit down again.

Having poured him some tea Jia told him, "There's some easy money to be made if someone will lend us a hand. I was hoping to take advantage of your good fortune."

"What does it involve?"

"Recently a newly-rich upstart has been making a bid for my sister. We sell our art, not ourselves!"

"That's the spirit!" approved Na Wu.

"The fact remains, though, that artistes need patrons. We can't let him have her, but we want his money. Those people are stinking rich — all ill-gotten gains — so why not make him fork out?"

"Well, how can you get him to part with his money for nothing?"

"We need another money-bags who admires my sister too, who will outbid him. Since he's infatuated and can't bear to lose face, you may be sure he'll spend every cent he's brought. When he finds himself outmatched he'll slink away."

"I understand. You want me to bid against him."

"Exactly."

Na Wu laughed. "That's a fine idea, and I have the highest regard for your sister. The trouble is, I have no money."

"What are you thinking of? This is between friends. If we ask you to help we won't let you be out of pocket. And when we've pulled it off I shall express my thanks."

Na Wu perked up then. He asked, "Tell me your plan in detail. I don't want any thanks. I shall be only too glad to help a friend."

"The thing's as good as done then. Starting tomorrow I want you to go every evening to hear the ballad-singing in Qingyin Teahouse at Tianqiao. Someone will offer you a towel and some refreshment. Just take them. When my sister comes on and one of the audience calls for an encore, you follow suit. Do that each time he calls for an encore. But when he gives a ten-dollar tip, you must give at least fifteen or twenty dollars."

"Paid on the spot?" asked Na Wu.

"Of course. But don't worry. When the time comes I'll get a waiter to slip you the money. Give as much as he hands you, not keeping any back. At the end of the performance I'll be waiting upstairs to treat you to a midnight snack and settle accounts with you."

"Can do!" cried Na Wu eagerly. "Fine!"

"Only. . . ." Jia looked grave and lowered his voice. "This must be a secret between the two of us. And you'll need a different outfit."

"What outfit?"

"You're dressed like a young gentleman. Young gentlemen are open-handed, but they're in no position to outbid a rival, as their fathers hold the purse-strings. For you to spend too much would look suspicious. So get yourself up like a rich businessman."

"Can do!" Na Wu chuckled. "It's hard for me to pass myself off as a poor man. A rich merchant's more in my line."

"That's why I singled you out from the start."

As Na Wu left Jia thrust a red paper package into his hands. "You'll need some loose change in the teahouse. Take this to pay for tips."

When Na Wu declined politely, Jia retorted, "Friendship is one thing, business is business. I can't put you to any expense."

9

On his return home Na Wu told Mistress Cloud that a

friend of his wanted him to help out for a few days
with his wedding.

"At home you count on your parents, outside on
friends," she approved. "To put yourself out for friends
is all to the good."

"But my clothes are so shabby, I was thinking of
asking you for a little money to rent some second-hand
ones."

"You won't find any second-hand clothes to fit you.
And if you burn or tear them they'll make you pay
a big fine. I've some of your grandfather's clothes
here, all first-class material. When I've altered them
for you, I promise you'll cut a fine figure." With that
she measured him, then got out from her camphor-
wood chest some gowns and waistcoats of gambiered
Guangdong gauze, Hangzhou silk and other rich fabrics.
Na Wu chose those he fancied, and she sat up sewing
all night by a paraffin lamp while he enjoyed a sound
sleep. When he opened his eyes the next morning the
neatly ironed clothes were folded on his chair. He
leapt up to try them on. Not only did they fit, they
were in fashion, for Mistress Cloud knew the latest
styles, having recently been living on tailoring. Once
dressed he went over to thank her, but she had gone
out to do the marketing. He examined himself in the
mirror. He looked for all the world like a wealthy
young merchant, except that he couldn't afford a
suitable cap. To make up for this he went straight to
have a haircut and set, and put on pomade.

Qingyin Teahouse was off the beaten track in the
southwest of Triangle Market, a bowshot from the
centre of Tianqiao. To reach it he had to pass amusement stalls and refreshment booths with low stools and

canvas awnings. Then he skirted round a wrestling ground both sides of which were packed with more stalls run by chiropodists, professional letter-writers, fortune-tellers, dentists and oculists. There you could also find cures for acne, watch performing monkeys, or have your photograph taken in opera costume. In front of one shop was a cauldron in which an apprentice was pounding up a plaster, calling out, "A guaranteed cure-all!"

At the west end he finally spotted the wooden sign of Qingyin Teahouse which had walls of sorghum stalks plastered with lime. A short curtain hung over the door, and a man in a straw hat, his white cotton shirt unbuttoned, was rattling some coins in a basket-tray and yelling, "Who has a sweet tooth? Who has a sweet tooth?"

Na Wu wondered if they had switched to selling cakes.

But the fellow went on, "Jia Fengkui has the sweetest voice ever heard. Just come and try — it's sweeter than honey or crystal sugar. . . ."

A red notice on the wall listed such performers as Pearl and White Jasmine. Some names, including that of Jia Fengkui, had been cut out of gold paper and pasted up.

As Na Wu reached out to draw aside the curtain, the man with the tray barred his way. "Your honourable name?"

"My name's Na. What of it? Do we have to register to come to your teahouse?"

Ignoring his sarcasm, the man pulled back the curtain and yelled:

"Fifth Master Na is here!"

Shouts went up inside: "Fifth Master Na!" "A seat for Fifth Master Na!" Waiters hurried over to greet him and show him to a place slightly left of centre. The table was heaped with melon seeds and slices of water-melon. One waiter brought him a bowl of tea, another a hot scented wet towel. As Na Wu took the towel, a roll of bank-notes was stuffed into his hand. After wiping his face he looked down and saw twenty dollars folded round a slip of paper on which was written "Returning in Wind and Rain".

He settled down to size up his surroundings.

The teahouse was not too big, with seven or eight tables, most of which had plates of fruit on them. The few at the back were empty. Several customers were seated at the front tables. The man seated alone at the table next to his looked a few years younger than Na Wu. He was wearing a Western suit, leather shoes and a crimson tie embroidered with a gold dragon. On both sides of the room and at the back were benches which were packed; but just before each item ended the customers rushed out, tearing in again as soon as the collection had been taken.

There was no backstage. Some auspicious couplets hung on the wall behind the platform, with below them a dozen seats in a semi-circle for the women artistes in their colourful costumes. While one performed, others nodded, smiled or called out to friends of theirs in the audience.

A plump woman was performing a drum-ballad. When she finished she put down her castanets and bowed, her head on one side. As applause broke out below, waiters holding basket-trays darted down both sides of the room and to the back, calling, "All contributions gratefully received!" To the left of the stage were notices of the different performers' names, and during this confusion someone went over and picked out the one with the big characters Jia Fengkui. At once the young man in the Western suit cried, "Bravo!" He beckoned to a waiter who hurried over and stooped to hear his instructions and take his money, then shoved his way to the stage holding up a square tray. "Master Yan gives ten dollars to hear 'Golden Lotus'," he cried, At once the actresses on the stage and the waiters scurrying below it chorussed:

"Thanks!"

Jia Fengkui stood up and glided gracefully forward to bow with a smile to the young man.

Today she was wearing a loose-sleeved tunic and wide trousers of pale green with embroidered borders. Her wig, plaited in a thick glossy braid, was tied with a red ribbon and decorated with red tassels. She also wore long earrings of pearl and jade. Na Wu thought, "No wonder I didn't recognize her."

He was staring raptly when somebody nudged him. It was the waiter who had brought him a towel.

"Fifth Master!" The waiter handed him bank-notes for twenty dollars.

Na Wu nodded and promptly returned the notes to the waiter, who strode straight to the stage with his tray. "Manager Na has given twenty dollars to hear 'Returning in Wind and Rain'."

A roar of approval went up. Fengkui stepped forward to bow to Na Wu and said with a sweet smile, "We all thank you, Manager Na."

A buzz of speculation broke out as all eyes turned to Na Wu. The young man in the Western suit stood up to glare at him, not sitting down till the music started up. Na Wu felt transported back to the heyday of his family. In his pride and elation he no longer seemed to be acting a part — this behaviour came naturally to him.

The waiter came back several times with twenty dollars, on the pretext of offering Na Wu a towel, then delivered the money on his tray to the stage. After six repetitions of this merry-go-round, Master Yan was cleaned out. Huffing and puffing he pounded his table and left, escorted out by the waiters. At the door he looked back at Na Wu and declared loudly, "Reserve the three front tables for me tomorrow. I'm bringing a few friends to enjoy Miss Fengkui's performance."

Na Wu felt as invigorated as after a drink of iced sweet-sour plum juice in a heatwave. For months other people had cocked a snook at him; today he had cocked a snook at someone else — what a treat! But after his rival left, before he'd had enough of parading his wealth, the waiter stopped bringing him money. He listened listlessly to some more singing, then was told that Jia Fenglou was waiting for him at Two Friends' Tavern. Leaving a tip on the table he made off while the waiters announced his departure.

Jia was waiting in Two Friends' Tavern. As they went upstairs he said, "You're a born aristocrat — it comes natural to you. You've done us a very good turn."

Though there were only the two of them the meal was a lavish one. On parting Jia thrust a red package into his hands. When he opened it on the rickshaw he found it was the twenty dollars he had handed in so many times that evening. Since he reckoned that his rival had spent at least 150 dollars, this seemed to him niggardly payment. However, it was disgusting he reflected, for a gentleman to haggle with those low people. After all he had made a profit too, he gloated. When they reached a confectioners' he got off and bought two packets of plum-juice powder. He gave these to Mistress Cloud, who was waiting up for him, and urged, "You must try this." Mistress Cloud wrinkled up her eyes in a smile.

"Where did you get the money?"

"Won it at cards."

"Well don't play any more. We can't afford to lose. Gambling debts are no laughing matter. I've driven out the mosquitoes and put down your net. Have a good wash and turn in now. This hot weather is so tiring."

10

In a dozen consecutive visits to Qingyin Teahouse Na Wu made Yan spend over a thousand dollars. Today the young man arrived with a bulging briefcase and called for song after song until it was late. A curfew had been imposed and everyone had to be indoors by midnight. The manager and Jia Fenglou came down to explain this and invite both gentlemen back the next day. Na Wu nodded his agreement. But Mr Yan said, "I thought you were out for money. I've money to burn and haven't spent it yet."

In the confusion as the artistes were leaving, Fengkui stepped up behind Na Wu to warn him softly, "There's going to be trouble. Go back, quick!" He woke up then and hastily squeezed his way out.

Outside he realized how late it was. The stalls on either side had long since closed. The trams had stopped running. The place was so dark and deserted that he took fright. He cleared his throat and sang a few bars to give himself some courage.

"Anyone want a ride?" A pedicab for two had come alongside. Its fare, a man in a grey suit, was nodding and snoring. The driver asked Na Wu, "Want to go to the east city? I'll charge less, I'm packing it in."

Na Wu was tempted. "How much?"

"A dollar to Dongdan."

"Too much."

"Use your eyes. You can't hire a cab now for two dollars. This is no place to knock about on your own. If you don't run into robbers, the night patrol will nab you and fine you more than a dollar."

The pedicabman had kept going off-handedly and now had passed him. Na Wu called, "All right then, stop!"

The driver stopped and nudged his passenger. "Move over, will you? I've another fare."

"Another fare?" mumbled the man. "How many fares can you take?"

"Can't you see this is a two-seater?" The driver shoved him over to one side, then helped Na Wu on and pedaled quickly off. But when the time came to head north, he turned abruptly south.

"Hey!" called Na Wu. "Where are you going? This isn't the way to the east city."

"Don't move!" The man who had seemed asleep grabbed hold of Na Wu and in a flash levelled a knife at his middle. "One more squawk out of you and I'll knife you!"

"Ahh . . . you. . . ."

"Shut up!"

Na Wu kept his mouth shut but shook so convulsively that the pedicab creaked loudly. The man with the knife pounded his thigh and jeered, "Look at you! Not worth your salt, are you!"

The pedicab turned this way and that till it reached the foot of a high wall. There was a wood here with nobody in sight. As the driver drew up, the other man dragged Na Wu off. "Now, mate, do the handsome thing. Your money and your watch, quick!"

Na Wu faltered, "I've a watch, but it doesn't work. You can have it if you like. All the money I have is two dollars for my rickshaw fare."

The pedicab driver demanded, "Can a gentleman with no money play the patron? I've been watching you for days now."

"Cut the cackle and search him," snapped the man with the knife.

They searched him from top to toe but sure enough all he had was two dollars and an old watch which nobody would want, not even for spare parts. In a rage the man with the knife slapped Na Wu's face. "Take off your clothes!" he ordered.

Na Wu stripped down to his underpants, then stood there meekly, shivering. He was no longer afraid, but so cold that his teeth were chattering.

"Your shoes!" ordered the pedicabman.

"Won't you leave me my shoes to walk in?"

"Where are you walking to?" demanded the other. "To the police station to report us? Take 'em off!"

As Na Wu stooped to take off his shoes, a blow on the back of his head knocked him unconscious. When he came to he still had his shoes on. But it was pitch dark and where could he go stark naked? He stood up and did some exercises to warm up — he was frozen.

After a while he heard footsteps, heard opera singers exercising their voices. When some women walked towards him talking, he ducked behind a tree. In half an hour or so the sky was light. A stooped figure approached him slowly from behind. Na Wu called to him, "Sir. . . ."

The man stopped, looked his way and came over. Six or seven paces away Na Wu recognized him as Big Head Hu the fiddler.

"Master Hu!" He burst into tears.

"What's up, Master Na? Why haven't you been to see us for so long? Where have you been practising? Why are you carrying on like that? Is Mistress Cloud ill?"

"No, I've had all my clothes stolen."

"How on earth?" Master Hu took off his gown and passed it to Na Wu. Underneath he was wearing nothing but a patched vest. Looking from Na Wu to himself he said, "This won't do. You can't go about like that, neither can I. Why don't you wait here till I've borrowed some clothes from someone living near by. Don't stir from here. If the police see you and charge you with indecent exposure, you'll have to pay a fine."

"What is this place? Is it policed?"

"Your wits must be wandering, this is the Temple of Agriculture."

As Big Head Hu took back his gown, put it on again and left, Na Wu looked round to see where he was. Confound it, this was just one street away from the Qingyin Teahouse and at the east end, he recalled, was a police station with a red electric light. Now that the day was bright, more singers and strollers had gathered there. Na Wu skulked beneath a tree, not daring to move, less like someone who had been mugged than a thief himself.

11

In less time than it takes for a meal Big Head Hu returned with Wu Cunzhong, who while still some way off shouted, "Where is he? Where is he?" Na Wu stood up and at sight of him Wu burst out laughing. Tweaking his beard he joked, "So the Master of Windy Pavilion came here to swallow the wind? Hurry up and put some clothes on before you freeze."

Na Wu took a bundle from him and frowned when he saw that it was of blue homespun. Inside was a much washed and faded suit with sweat stains on the collar, which dismayed him. Wu told him, "These are my going-out clothes. Try to make do with them. They may not be too clean but they've no lice." When Na Wu had dressed Wu took them both to his place to have breakfast.

Na Wu asked, "How long have you two known each other?"

Big Head Hu told him, "I come here every day for a stroll and often see this old gentleman plaiting ropes. We were nodding acquaintances."

Wu Cunzhong lived west of the temple. Between the stacks of straw in front of his gate some youngsters were practising martial arts. Some boys were learning boxing from a young man, while two girls were practising sword-play on their own. As Wu passed them he gave them some tips. He took his visitors into a passage-way where he had two pedal-operated machines for plaiting ropes. On the ground were coils of new rope of different thicknesses. He led them past these to a small southern room, where a low table and stools had been put ready. On the table was a dish of hot sauce, a dish of pickles and a dozen flapjacks. As he sat them down his wife brought out a basin of millet gruel.

"We've nothing good to offer you, just village fare," said Wu. "It'll be a change for you, Master Na."

In all his years in Beijing Na Wu had never dreamed that there were places like this in the city, or people who lived like this. They were neither rich nor poor, didn't put on second-hand clothes to pose as wealthy or pretend to be hard-up for fear people would ask them for money, didn't give themselves airs or take advantage of others. They obviously enjoyed this way of life.

He asked, "Have you no addictions, Mr Wu?"

"You mean smoking opium?" replied Wu. "No such luck. Last time I went on business to that opium den so as not to attract attention. What I make each day on ropes isn't enough for even two pipes of opium. If I smoked, my family would have to live on air like the Master of Windy Pavilion."

Na Wu laughed. A few mouthfuls of gruel had warmed him and given him fresh energy. And the food tasted delicious. He said, "I like these flapjacks of yours. I must come and learn from you how to make ropes."

"You couldn't stand it, you're too soft. In one day you'd blister your palms. Take a look at my hands."

Wu stretched out a hand the size of a small rush fan. Na Wu felt it and exclaimed at its thickness and roughness. The calluses on it were harder than galvanized iron.

Big Head Hu asked Na Wu how he had come to be mugged. Not liking to explain what he and the Jias had been up to, he said he had stayed out late listening to drum-ballads. Asked where he had gone he answered, "Qingyin Teahouse."

The fiddler shook his head. "Why, you can listen to drum-ballads at the East Peace Market of the east city, or in that amusement centre at Xidan. Why go to the Qingyin Teahouse?"

"Just to pass the time. Aren't ballads the same everywhere?"

"No, there's a lot of difference," Big Head Hu assured him. "Who are the artistes in the Qingyin Teahouse? Riff-raff. You got off lightly just having a few clothes stolen."

Na Wu was secretly horrified to hear this. Now Wu put in laughingly, "If what you say is true, it should be possible to get your clothes back."

"Can you manage it for me, sir?" Na Wu brightened up.

"I can't promise." Wu chuckled. "But I may have a way. Those Tianqiao gangsters are all in cahoots with the police. Whatever they steal, whether cash or clothes, their rule is not to touch it for ten days in case the police send to look for it. After ten days they sell it or divide it up, giving one share to the cops."

"Then I'll go and report it at once," said Na Wu.

"If you do that they'll dispose of it straight away. They don't keep the loot for your sake. Only people with no connections would report them."

"What's to be done then?"

"I don't know, but I can have inquiries made. If something's stolen to settle a private grudge or from a rival gang, the police won't butt in. That's why I asked if you were telling the truth."

Na Wu flushed and shook his head. "It was true. No need to try to get those clothes back, I can afford to buy more. You mustn't go to such trouble."

With a laugh Wu dropped the subject.

After breakfast Big Head Hu offered to see Na Wu back. Na Wu, ashamed to be seen dressed like a coolie, said:

"If I wear these clothes home won't it be inconvenient for Mr Wu? I'll trouble you to go and fetch me some clothes from Mistress Cloud while I wait for you here."

Not understanding his scruples Wu promptly said, "Go on, wear them. Bring them back when you've time, or just keep them for the time being. I'm in no hurry to wear them."

Big Head Hu understood Na Wu and was disgusted by his insistence on keeping up appearances. "The fact is," he said, "I'm seeing you home so that I can drop in at my club on the way to arrange for a performance. This afternoon and evening we're putting on operas and I'd have no time. Time is money for us artistes. How can I have half a day off just for that?"

So Na Wu had to leave with Big Head Hu. As they walked out Wu's machines were already whirring. The dust and chaff in the air were choking and blinding. The young boxing teacher, stripped to the waist, was feeding straw into his machine as he pedalled it. The two girls who had practised sword-play, towels wrapped round their heads, had squatted on the ground to coil ropes. Na Wu could see that he wasn't up to such work. He hurried out of the passage-way and urged Mr Wu to go back.

Wu took his hand saying, "I met your grandfather. And I'm older than you, so let me presume on seniority to give you some advice."

"Please do, sir."

"As I see it, the bankruptcy of your family isn't altogether a bad thing. When we Manchus conquered China we had only eight banners of troops, ten thousand horsemen. It was our determination that won us the empire. After that, three hundred years of soft living finished off our enterprise; so it was only right for the Qing dynasty to fall. It should help us to overcome our decadence, our showy extravagance and our idle, ignorant ways. We must make a fresh start and become useful members of society. Changing our way of life is bound to be a bit hard, but however hard it is we mustn't sink to be swindlers. Above all, we mustn't suck up to the Japanese. Xuan Tong's become emperor now in the Northeast, and they say some nobles from Beijing have joined him. Mind you make the right choice. Millions of brave and loyal Chinese are still resisting the Japanese. How long can they last? We must leave ourselves a way out."

"Don't worry," said Na Wu. "I've never dared meddle with politics. I haven't the nerve."

Wu's advice had made him change colour. The more he thought it over the worse he felt. He'd imagined he was helping the Jias fool someone, whereas in fact he was the one who'd been fooled. He wasn't up to doing anything good, or even anything bad! He heaved a sigh.

12

Beijing opera clubs had their own hierarchy of rich and poor members. The first-class ones had time, money and pull. Time was needed for training, beginning on a mat; money to engage a teacher, buy costumes and be taken up by a maestro; pull to organize a claque, get your photograph into the papers and have yourself written up. The second class, those with money but no time, could also make a name, hire a theatre and fill it; and the ones who played female roles could pay to be taken up by a maestro and get famous actors to perform with them. The third class with no money or pull had to have good voices and practise hard until they were recognized by connoisseurs as well as the general public; then they could make a living. To which class did Na Wu belong? He simply went to the club as Big Head Hu's friend to pass the time. After a couple of years he learned to play a few parts which didn't need much acting. But when others hired costumes and theatre they gave him no look-in — he never appeared on stage.

Up to the Japanese surrender in 1945, Mistress Cloud

made enough by taking in washing and mending to buy flour mixed with beans and millet. But after the KMT's return, there was so much corruption and profiteering, such heavy taxation, that no one made new clothes or sent laundry out to be washed. Na Wu had to move into the north room with her so that they could let the south room. But this was easier said than done. As the People's Liberation Army scored victory after victory, all the rich and the officials fled south, leaving many houses empty. The common people made do with the rooms they had. For who wanted to move at a time when prices were rocketing? Mistress Cloud had pawned or sold everything she could, and they often found themselves on the verge of starvation.

Na Wu with no chance to go on stage still had to fill his stomach. Friends introduced him to sing in a teahouse, then to be an announcer in the radio station. The teahouse gave him a pittance for rickshaw money; the radio station didn't even give that, but he was paid for commercials.

One good thing about broadcasting was that the announcer had to give his name. So some of his audience remembered it. And the ground crew of Nanyuan Airport, when they wanted to start a spare-time opera troupe but didn't dare ask professionals to teach them, asked the radio station to send them an announcer. They offered board and lodging, plus two sacks of flour a month. This struck Na Wu as better than announcing and he accepted the job. He found that his lodging was only a straw pallet on the floor of the club with two army blankets on it. As for his board, at mealtimes he fetched from the kitchen two steamed buns and a bowl of cabbage soup. He wanted to chuck it but was afraid the angry service men would beat him up. So he stuck it out. It had its advantages. These veteran maintenance men would sing whatever he taught them, without picking fault. Na Wu hadn't finished teaching them one whole opera when, after a month, the PLA surrounded the city. Both sides kept up a barrage. If he didn't leave he was afraid the KMT would conscript him as cannon fodder or force him to dig tunnels. That was no joke. He demanded his two sacks of flour and left the airport, putting up in a carters' inn. But how was he to get his flour home? There were no more carts going into town, and a pedicab asked for one sack of flour, which he wasn't prepared to give. By the time he'd resigned himself to parting with one sack, the road was cut. Frantic, he pounded his thigh. Two days later he came down with flu. Then he had diarrhoea. The innkeeper, a decent sort, gave him incense ash as medicine and burned paper to exorcize spirits. But two weeks later, when he could get up, he was nothing but skin and bones. He had eaten up one sack of flour, and had to give the other in lieu of rent. The innkeeper made him two flapjacks and saw him off. Though it wasn't far to town, it took him three days to get there.

When he reached home the gate was bolted. He knocked and heard a woman's voice: "Who's there?"

The voice, though not Mistress Cloud's, sounded familiar. He looked at the number. Yes, this was the right house. He said, "It's me."

"Who are you looking for?"

"I live here."

The door opened with a creak. A young woman appeared. They stared at each other and both cried out. Before Na Wu had collected his thoughts she shut the gate again. He gave it a shove and stumbled into the passage. Having hastily bolted the gate she fell on her knees to him.

"Fifth Master, spare me, we've no old scores to settle. What happened was Jia Fenglou's doing. They bought me to make money out of me. I never had any say."

"Don't talk like that, Miss Fengkui. I did nothing to provoke you, why track me down here?"

Just then Mistress Cloud came out. She stared at them blankly, then pulled Fengkui to her feet and took Na Wu's arm, leading them both inside before asking what had happened.

Na Wu said, "I nearly died outside, barely escaped with my life. How should I know what's happened?"

Only then did Fengkui realize that Na Wu really lived here and hadn't come to seize her. Since in her panic she'd given herself away, she could no longer conceal her identity. She confessed that she hadn't told the truth when she rented Mistress Cloud's room. She had been sold as a child to the Jias, and had earned them enough to buy two houses. Now the city was blockaded, disabled soldiers were running wild, and as she could no longer perform, the Jias had decided to sell her. The Master of the Drunkard's Studio downstairs had tipped her off, and she had seized a chance to run away. First she had hidden with a friend, then come here to ask for a room. This said, she knelt to kowtow to Mistress Cloud. "That's the whole truth, madam. It's up to you whether you save my life or hand me over to the Jias for a reward.

I have a conscience, and if you shelter me, even if I can't repay you in this life I surely will in the next."

Mistress Cloud sighed as she pulled Fengkui to her feet. "I was sold too as a child. If I'd wanted to harm you I'd have driven you out long ago. Think I didn't see you were all on your own, with no relatives or friends coming to see you, terrified by each knock on the gate, too scared to go out, getting me to buy your vegetables for you? I soon saw you were hiding something, crying in secret all day; but not knowing you I didn't like to ask questions. I've no child of my own, you can be my daughter. Let me lay up treasure in heaven by doing what's right."

Fengkui cried happily, "Mother!" Then they embraced and wept.

Na Wu said, "This is all very well. But if we keep Miss Fengkui hidden here, word is bound to leak out."

Mistress Cloud said, "Can't you see there's a big change coming? When those troops march in these wretches will scurry into hiding. They won't dare go on looking for her or making trouble."

On his way back to town Na Wu had passed some units of the Liberation Army and sized up the situation. He nodded. "Right, they're a powerful force and they treat people decently. It looks as if there'll be a change of hands."

Mistress Cloud asked how he and Fengkui had met, and was annoyed by Fengkui's refusal to answer. "Do I count as your mother or not?" she demanded.

"The young gentleman heard me sing."

"I don't believe it! If that was all, why should you kneel in fright?"

Then, beating about the bush, Fengkui touched on Na Wu's masquerade. Mistress Cloud changed colour, her eyes fixed on Na Wu, who cracked his fingers and stamped his foot. Then he slapped his own face protesting:

"They fooled me too, didn't they?"

Fengkui spoke up for him. "It was Jia Fenglou's scheme. Fifth Master didn't know the ins and outs."

Mistress Cloud faced outside to bow and said, "Old Master Na, open your eyes. See what the descendants of your big house have sunk to!"

Fengkui was loyal to friends. She asked Na Wu to sell her trinkets so that the three of them could get by. Another month or so saw the peaceful liberation of Beijing. At last Mistress Cloud and Fengkui could breathe freely. But Na Wu still pulled a long face.

Fengkui told him, "Those rich, powerful local despots are afraid of the Eighth Route Army, afraid of being struggled against and having their property shared out. What have you to worry about?"

"You haven't been out or seen their proclamations," he answered. "Those say that the Eighth Route Army has a different policy for the cities than for villages. Rich people don't have to worry. But I've no way out. With the Eighth Route Army here everyone must work for a living. Seems I can't get out of that."

"You're still young enough to learn, aren't you?" she retorted. "Some people have to pull pedicabs or collect night-soil. With your education you shouldn't have to be a night-soil collector."

"So you say, but I'm afraid nobody will want me."

13

A few days later a policeman came to announce: All
KMT servicemen and civil servants in Beijing count
as having come over. Those sitting idle can register
with the authorities, who will assign work to those
fit for it and give the rest severance pay and two sacks
of flour. Na Wu saw in the street that the Eighth
Routers in army uniform and the cadres in grey
uniform treated people very decently. So he asked
Mistress Cloud to wash the ragged army tunic he had
worn at the airport, and having put this over his
padded jacket he went to the Nanyuan registration
office. There was a long queue there of old, young,
blind and crippled, all in shabby uniforms. He joined
the queue. After a long wait he got into the office.
Behind its four desks sat members of the military control commission. Na Wu went straight to the last desk
where there sat a teenage soldier.

"May I trouble you to register me?"

"What name?"

"Na Wu."

"What unit?"

"Nanyuan Airport. The KMT airforce."

"What post?"

"Instructor."

The young soldier stepped back and leafed through
a file, then put it down and picked up another.

"What did you teach?"

"Local opera."

"From what company?"

"None. A club."

At this point a man in his forties came over from

another desk. Eyeing Na Wu he asked, "Your monthly pay?"

"Board and lodging and two sacks of flour a month."

The older soldier told the youngster, "No need to look. The KMT army had no such posts." To Na Wu he said, "You need to have enlisted to count as an insurrectionary soldier. You're not registered."

"Then who will look after me?" asked Na Wu. "Won't some place give me two sacks of flour?"

"What operas did you teach?"

"Traditional ones. I played old men. Sang like this: His Imperial Majesty. . . ."

"I get it. Go to Qianmen Watchtower. There's a study group for artistes there, they'll probably see to you."

Though not issued with flour, Na Wu had sized up these PLA men. Even if they knew you were bluffing they didn't beat or curse you. His spirits rose. He went home to take off his army tunic and put on a padded gown, then took a tram to Qianmen.

Qianmen opposite the railway station was a sea of people. At the foot of the watchtower a skating rink had been fenced off with mats and tickets were being sold. He squeezed his way to the steps and climbed up to the tower, where he bumped into a spruce woman cadre in her twenties, her grey uniform clean and well pressed. She asked Na Wu, "Who are you looking for?"

"I heard there's a training class for artistes here. I've come to register."

"You're welcome. Come on in."

The watchtower had been partitioned into several rooms. He followed her into one. The woman cadre

sat down in front of the window and motioned Na Wu
to a seat opposite.

"What's your name?"

"Na Wu."

"What type of drama?"

"Traditional drama: it's called Beijing opera."

"What roles?"

"Old men."

"In what company?"

"Well, I haven't joined any company."

"Then how do you perform?"

"I've sung in the radio station and teahouses."

"Wait a bit."

She went out, returning shortly to tell him, "I just
rang up the old Theatre Trade Union, and they haven't
got you listed."

"But I honestly sang for a living!"

"Who can vouch for you?"

Na Wu rolled his eyes and said glibly, "My master,
Big Head Hu! I'm Big Head Hu's apprentice."

The woman cadre smiled. "You mean Hu Baolin?"

"That's right." Na Wu's heart missed a beat. He
had no idea of Big Head Hu's real name.

The woman cadre went out again. Presently she
came back with someone in a brand-new grey uniform
and cap. It was Big Head Hu. Na Wu at once
greeted him: "Master!"

"So it's you!" Big Head Hu stamped his foot.
"This is New China, and you must change your ways
too. Mustn't go on bragging and lying. What kind
of artiste can you call yourself?"

"Call me whatever you like, but I need somewhere
to study, so as to support myself."

Big Head Hu said, "Go and look up Wu Cunzhong. Two of his apprentices were underground workers. They've started a straw rope cooperative and may be able to fit you into it."

The woman cadre was intrigued. She asked, "What does this gentleman actually do?"

Big Head Hu replied, "He'd have no trouble filling up a form — he's never done anything."

Na Wu protested, "How can you say that? Wasn't I a reporter?"

Big Head Hu retorted, "Yes, you were a reporter. You published a novel too!"

The woman cadre stared in surprise. "Really? You published a novel?"

"Yes," said Na Wu. "Only it wasn't any good. . . ."

That cadre had a strong sense of responsibility. Although she was in charge of artistes, one of her colleagues was in charge of writers. She told Na Wu to fetch the manuscript of his novel with copies of the paper for which he had worked, and to write a brief account of his past history.

Seeing that there was hope, Na Wu thanked her profusely and left. That afternoon he returned with all she had asked for. After some dithering he concealed the fact that he had bought the manuscript of *The Carp Dart*. He could explain that later, he thought, if she found fault with it.

That same evening she read Na Wu's account of his past, and spent a few more evenings reading his novel and the pictorial. Her conclusion was: As this man's family went bankrupt in his grandfather's time, his class status is one of the urban poor. As he never joined the army, the government or any political party, his political record is clean. The pictorial he worked for was low-class and pornographic, but not politically suspect. Though his novel is absurdly far-fetched it is not reactionary. And he writes fluently and well. According to our policy we should unite with men of letters like this, to educate and remould them. By the time Na Wu came back three days later for news, she had got in touch with the appropriate department and written him a letter of introduction. She told him to go and register with the office in charge of popular literature.

Truly, his misguided hankering after fame landed him in big trouble! What ridiculous adventures Na Wu had in New China will have to be related in another story.

March 1, 1982
Beijing

Black Cat, White Cat

LIKE the Gang of Four, midnight raids were a thing of the past, yet the knock on Jin Zhuxuan's door startled him. Scarcely anyone comes in the daytime, so who can be looking for me at midnight? he wondered.

He switched on the light to open the door, amazed to discover the engineer Kang Xiaochun on his threshold, smiling and bowing. Why, only two recent wonders could be compared with this: the Tangshan earthquake and the rain of meteorites in Jilin.

"Excuse me for disturbing you so late." Kang sounded rather sheepish. "I've come to ask a small favour."

"Why, of course." Should he first invite Kang in or find some clothes to cover his nakedness?

"Don't put yourself out," Kang went on hastily, seeing Jin's embarrassment. "I'll tell you and then be off. I've come for your help."

"What help? Anything I can do. . . ."

"I've a bottle of brandy I want you to help me drink."

"Oh. What made you think of me?"

"If you agree, I'll go back first and you can follow, right?"

"Of course, if you say so."

"Many thanks, see you presently. Put on more clothes so as not to catch cold."

As Jin watched Kang go he pinched his thigh to make sure that this was not a fantastic dream.

While dressing he wondered what possessed the engineer. Was he unhinged, or had he some other favour to ask?

Since the setting up of Jinghua Construction Company thirty years ago, Kang had been the chief of the Technical Section with Jin as his secretary. For twenty-five years since the building of their housing they had been neighbours, but Kang had not once called on Jin, had only spoken to him in private twice.

Was that because of the engineer's arrogance? No! He was the most unassuming of their two dozen section heads. When he assigned Jin some task he never ordered him to do this or do that. Instead, holding a document in both hands he would walk up to Jin's desk and bow, then say softly with a smile, "Comrade Old Jin, do you think you can make two copies of this document? We'll be needing it at three this afternoon." Or he might say, "Old Jin, I think this might be reworded, why make it sound as if we're issuing orders? If it's worded as a suggestion, people will still carry it out. So I'll trouble you to change it."

Kang had become a section chief in his thirties, and before that, it was said, he had been a chief engineer under the puppet Manchurian regime. Earlier still, studying in Harbin Industrial University, he had distinguished himself. Who could accuse him of arrogance when he was so considerate to his subordinates?

Twenty-five years ago, when the two men happened to meet outside that had been their first private contact. After that, Jin's impression of Kang was not simply that he was modest and polite but that he liked to do people good turns.

Jin had a weakness passed on by his ancestors: he squandered money. Although a bachelor with no commitments, he quickly ran through his 52 yuan monthly pay. No wonder — too many people knew him! On pay day he never ate in the canteen. After work he would stroll to Happiness Delicatessen, meaning to buy a small portion of pig's head to take to the dumpling shop and wash down with some liquor. But the chief cook there knew him. As soon as he came in, the cook beaming all over his face would say in his ear, "I knew this was your pay day. I've some force-fed duck freshly braised in soy sauce. I've kept one for you."

So Jin had to fork out five yuan to go off with the duck. And then the manager of The Hot Pot, Liu Four, dashed out. Having known Old Jin ever since he became a waiter, after Liberation he still addressed him as a Manchu prince. "*Zhubeile!*" he called. "I was waiting for you. Fresh pork sausage and deep-fried 'deer-tails' just done to a turn. Come in quick, where else are you going?"

The mention of these dishes made Jin's mouth water. At Liu Four's insistence he went in and sat down.

Going back to his room that evening, when he counted his money he had 36 yuan left. After two weeks, apart from his meal tickets, he had barely enough for one bath and one haircut.

But don't imagine that Jin had a thin time of it in the second half of the month when he was broke. No, when forced to save he still knew how to enjoy life. After work he shut his door and imitating the calligraphy of the Song emperor Hui Zong he wrote some slogans for the Hygiene Committee to post up in the lavatories, embellishing these with delicately painted flowers and birds. On Sunday mornings he went to a stall to wash down a bowl of beancurd with two ounces of liquor, after which he spent most of the day looking round and chatting in Liulichang's antique shops. In those days you could look at rubbings for hours without being driven away by shop assistants.

One Sunday when Jin had no money he went to Liulichang. He was leafing through the rubbings in one shop when he noticed under the counter a pile of old yellow silk hand-scrolls. He picked one up, brushed off the dust and spread it out. It was half an imperial edict from Yong Zheng's reign. The half written in Chinese had been cut off, leaving instructions in Manchu on repairing the old buildings of the Eight Banners' yamen. Jin was no Manchu scholar, but his love for his ancestors and his national pride made him try to decipher such things. He mulled over it, unwilling to put it down.

The curio-dealer could read customers' expressions. He sidled over and said, "Trust you, Master Jin. I tossed that under the counter to see if anyone could tell its value. I wasn't expecting you, or I'd have hidden it!"

"Are you joking?"

"Don't try to fool me, you know what this is. If the other half weren't missing, would I have displayed it?"

"How much?"

"How could I make a profit out of you? Just pay me the cost — five yuan."

"Too much."

"You know very well it isn't."

"Not worth it."

"You understand what it's worth."

Jin said no more but put his hand in his pocket, knowing his pocket was empty but doing this for the curio-dealer to see. The latter knew he had no money but didn't let on, watching him quizzically.

Jin exclaimed in pretended surprise, "I forgot to bring any money. Suppose I take this with me and pay you for it tomorrow."

"Leave it here." The curio-dealer laid one hand on the mutilated edict. "You can take it when you've paid."

He was well aware that Jin always kept his word and had never taken anything without paying. He had stopped him to whet his appetite for this old edict. Jin kept hold of the scroll protesting, "For friendship's sake." The other stopped him from taking it, explaining, "Sorry, that's the rule of our shop."

They were disputing politely when a young man came in. With a smile he asked, "What's up, Comrade Old Jin?"

At sight of him the curio-dealer stepped back. Jin clutched the imperial edict to his chest and, looking up, saw it was his section chief Kang. He flushed.

"It's n-nothing," he stammered. "We were just talking business. I want to buy this but came out in such a hurry, when I changed my clothes I left my money at home. . . ."

For the last half year, Kang knew, Old Jin had worn this same suit. He doubted if he had other clothes to change into. He asked the curio-dealer, "How much is it?"

"Five yuan."

Kang got out his wallet, pulled out a five-yuan note and handed it over.

Jin, even redder in the face, reached out to stop him. "You can't do that!" he protested.

Meanwhile the curio-dealer had grabbed the note and stuffed it into his till.

Kang reproached Jin, "Why stand on ceremony with me, old comrade?"

Jin nodded repeatedly. "All right, I'll pay you back in the office tomorrow or before next pay day."

"Forget it, a small sum like this. Take it as a present from me."

They both left the rubbing shop then. As Kang was at a loose end, he took Jin to a nearby teahouse, where he ordered a pot of tea with melon-seeds and dates. Then the two of them started chatting.

"Before Liberation," said Jin, still red in the face, "I sold my family's property to get by. I've never worked in an office before. I must thank you for showing me such consideration."

Kang sat solemnly opposite him like a small school-child in class. Then he answered, "You're too polite. I'm young, and I'm a technician; I've never been in a leading position before. I hope you'll criticize the mistakes I've made."

"Fine, fine, you're sure to go a long way." As Jin said this he was thinking: He's been so good to me, I must speak frankly. Weighing his words he answered, "Well, between friends, there's something I'd like to raise."

"Splendid," said Kang, and meant it. "Go ahead."

"One day I was writing up minutes, the minutes of that meeting to discuss the Soviet expert's proposals for our new buildings. Everyone else, I discovered, had approved them and promised to carry them out. But you. . . ."

"I said they left loopholes, and a new plan was needed. I drew a diagram, too, showing where the structure wasn't strong enough and there might later be trouble." Kang spoke with unusual feeling. "I'm all for Sino-Soviet friendship, but that doesn't mean taking their experts' proposals as imperial edicts. He's an engineer, so am I. Shouldn't I give my honest opinion? If I spot faults and don't point them out, waiting for some fiasco, that wouldn't be the way to treat a friend."

"I'm not saying your opinion was wrong, just that no one else raised objections," said Jin. "Well, I muddled along for years in the old society, and I'm too old to catch up with the new, that's how it is. If I'm wrong just forget it. I'm talking through my hat." He laughed.

"No, you're right, I'll think it over. . . ."

"It doesn't matter. But you must make more criticisms of my work, give me more guidance."

Kang saw that Jin wanted to change the subject. Knowing his family background and his history, he did not expect him to be revolutionary. Half seriously and half jokingly he said, "I do have one suggestion to make to you."

"Go on, what is it?"

"You write our reports and minutes with a brush. When three copies are needed you'd rather make three copies than use carbon paper; of course that's up to you, but if I asked you to cut stencils what would you do?"

"You mean?"

"Why not make time to practise writing with a pen?"

"Don't worry, I am practising," replied Jin earnestly. "I don't use it yet at work, though, because I write much more slowly with a pen."

After that encounter they had no more to do with each other out of office hours. But each time Jin met Kang on the road he nodded and smiled to show that he had not forgotten his kindness.

Two years later, in the anti-Rightist movement, Kang got into trouble. Not big trouble, he wasn't labelled a Rightist, but one wall was covered with posters attacking him and at several meetings he was criticized for his anti-Soviet attitude, for deliberately finding fault with the Soviet expert's proposals, and undermining the Soviet expert's prestige. Kang made a conscientious self-criticism, admitted his faults with tears, and was finally let off lightly. Removed from his post as section chief he was sent to reform himself on a work site. During this movement Jin had said not a word, but when he saw others grinding their teeth and denouncing Kang he found it hard to take. Kang looked so abject, so intimidated, he wanted to comfort him but lacked the courage. This weighed on his mind for days. Later he found a chance to express his sympathy, which made him feel better. Since then he had had no further dealings with him.

Now that he was dressed he left his room. The draught on the stairs made him shiver and cut short his reflections. Going down to the floor below he knocked on Kang's door.

Kang was in the kitchen preparing a cold dish.

Since coming back from Jin's place he had chopped up the heart of a cabbage, marvelling as he did so at his own behaviour. How could he be so childish at his age? Inviting someone at midnight for a drink! Why had he gone off so impulsively to find Jin?

True, something had happened today to so elate him that he had to tell someone about it. His wife was on a visit to their daughter, and his son was away on business. But this didn't answer the question, "Why invite Jin and not someone else?" True, for over twenty years he had lost touch with all his old friends, so he had to find a neighbour to confide in. But as he had no dealings with his neighbours either, this still didn't answer the question. As Kang cross-examined himself and finished chopping up the cabbage he finally hit on the answer: I trust Jin Zhuxuan. Though I've scarcely spoken to him for twenty years, at heart I count him as a friend.

During the anti-Rightist movement Kang had been criticized, lost his post as section head and been sent down to the work site. Although he hadn't been labelled, most people regarded him as a dangerous character. This didn't count as a punishment, but it put heavy pressure on him. He had great self-restraint, however, and did nothing to make it seem that he was taking a negative attitude. He worked and studied harder than ever, behaved even more modestly. This was on the work site though. Going home on Sunday he let his family see his depression and frustration. They never questioned him but silently showed their sympathy and understanding. When he was angry, all three of them kept quiet, even going about on tiptoe. When Kang discovered this he was like a sick man who realizes the seriousness of his case from the consideration of those around him. This increased his exasperation. Not wanting his family to feel too depressed he would go out for a stroll.

One Sunday he went to Liulichang. When he came out of the rubbing shop it was still early, so he went into an antique shop. He looked casually at broken Qin bricks, Han tiles, bronze vessels, and painted pottery. Tucked away in one curio cabinet were some seals of Shoushan stone, one of them with a tortoise ingeniously carved on it. He asked a shop attendant to get this out, and examined it carefully as he fingered it. Someone beside him said with a laugh:

"Killing time here, Engineer Kang?"

Kang looked up. Jin had come in unnoticed and was standing next to him.

"I'd nothing to do so I came out for a stroll."

"Do you want to choose a stone to cut a seal?"

"I'm just looking. The carving on this intrigued me."

Jin took the stone and examined it with a faint smile, then asked the shopman, "How much?"

"Seven yuan."

Jin nodded, and without consulting Kang returned the stone to the assistant. Catching hold of Kang's sleeve he said, "Let's look somewhere else. We can come back if we find nothing better." Not asking if Kang agreed he steered him out to the street.

"That's not worth seven yuan, even if you have the money," Jin fumed. "If you need a stone I have some, I'll choose one tomorrow and bring it to your place."

"The price doesn't worry me," said Kang. "That tortoise knob. . . ."

"I know, I know." Jin gave him a meaningful smile.

Jin accompanied Kang to two stalls, then, seeing that he had lost interest, took his leave on the pretext of business. The next Sunday when Kang went home again to rest, his wife produced a paper package from a drawer and told him, "The other day that old fatty upstairs brought this. He said you'd understand."

Kang opened the package. Inside was a translucent brown stone, half an inch square and over one inch long. On the top was carved a tortoise, but unlike the one in Liulichang its head was tucked into its shell. On the base was carved the name Kang Xiaochun in the style of bronze inscriptions. And on two sides, in characters as small as the head of a fly, was the couplet: "Trouble comes from careless talk; vexation is caused by sticking your neck out." On another side in clerical script was the inscription: "Take the tortoise as an example."

Kang exclaimed in delight, "Jin Zhuxuan looks a fool but actually he's smart. He saw at a glance why I chose that seal with a tortoise knob."

Seeing his pleasure his wife asked, "Do you mean to use this seal?"

"Yes, I like it."

"If you leave it out and people see those inscriptions, won't they think you bear a grudge against the Party?"

Kang's heart sank. He turned pale.

His wife went on, "I advise you to put it away, and in future have less to do with other people. Though I've never spoken to that fat old fellow I hear he's from the same family as Pu Yi.* We're in trouble enough as it is, without looking for more. Better keep to ourselves. For his sake as well as our own."

---

* The last Qing emperor.

Kang felt as if doused with cold water, his pleasure completely spoilt.

Knowing that she had frightened him his wife hastily added, "I'm only playing safe. It may not be all that serious, don't take it to heart."

He stood there woodenly, not listening to her. He had decided to take her advice and lose no time in wrapping up the seal and putting it at the bottom of a case. Picking up the paper in which it had been wrapped, he discovered that it was the diagram he had drawn to point out the weaknesses in the Soviet expert's proposals. He had given it to Jin and asked him, when he had written an explanation to go with it, to hand it in to the Party committee to be filed. Later, other business had made him forget this. In the anti-Rightist movement his colleagues had searched for evidence against him and asked Jin for material, but Jin had insisted that this diagram had long since been thrown away.

It dawned on Kang that he had never understood Jin. That most people underestimated him.

Jin was generally considered like an old crock in the corner of a second-hand store, good for a joke but of little actual use.

Kang disagreed with this judgement. He had asked the Personnel Section about Jin's past. True, his uncle had been the son of a Manchu prince, but the Qing dynasty had collapsed when Jin was only four or five, and his family had no income. When he was twenty his uncle died, leaving him as his heir. But all he inherited was a mass of debts, the only right he could exercise was selling his property. So he sold his house using the proceeds to settle his debts. Unfit for manual labour, although a passable calligrapher and painter of flowers and birds, he was far from good enough to make his living that way. The only way out for him was sponging on friends. This was little better than begging in the streets, as it meant eating at the expense of his self-respect. After Liberation, since he came from a formerly wealthy Manchu family, the People's Political Consultative Conference and the committee in charge of national minority affairs decided to find him work.

A functionary asked him, "What kind of job would you like?"

Gulping back tears he said, "You don't have to ask. If the government's good enough to give me a job, who am I to pick and choose? I'll do whatever I'm told. I'd count it an honour to be a civil servant in the people's government."

"What special skills have you?"

"I was brought up to be a gourmet and playboy, but I can't afford this now."

Knowing that he was a calligrapher and painter, the functionary asked him for an inscription and two paintings, which he took to show the Ministry of Culture. They decided these were good enough to exhibit but not up to professional standards. So he was given a job in a construction company. Each time he spoke of this Jin expressed his gratitude to the government.

The post of secretary was the lowest in his section, but Jin took his job seriously. He worked hard and conscientiously, contented with his lot, with no extravagant hopes. He neither envied nor admired his young colleagues who always tried to get the better of others,

He enjoyed lending others a helping hand. Even when he knew they were scoring off him or using him, he turned a blind eye and cheerfully helped them out. At meetings in the section, those taking advantage of him criticized his mediocrity and lack of ambition — signs that he came from a decadent class. But instead of losing his temper or flaring up, he would promise to mend his ways. (In fact he never did. He didn't take such criticism to heart.)

As Kang saw it, Jin's way of life was decadent and he was slick and smooth, but one shouldn't expect too much of a man like him. As a secretary he did an honest job. Wasn't he more reliable than many people who mouthed political slogans? Kang thought it wrong to despise him, and therefore treated him as respectfully as he did everyone else. To his surprise this was enough to fill Jin with gratitude. And knowing how slick he usually was, it had amazed Kang that Jin had criticized him to his face in the teahouse. Now this seal and the diagram had once more revealed what finesse this apparently muddle-headed fellow could show in dealing with people.

Kang wanted to express his appreciation, but since that might lead to trouble he suppressed his feelings and steered clear of him.

In the "cultural revolution", Jin was paraded through the streets several times with a placard on his back inscribed "Dregs of feudalism" or "Filial descendant of the landlord class". Then he retired, while Kang went to a school for cadres. After the overthrow of the Gang of Four, Kang came home and saw Jin outside their apartment building — unchanged. To his surprise he looked no older and just as fit as before. They exchanged a few words on the staircase, then went their different ways. Kang returned to work in his office, and since Jin had retired they seldom met. Today Kang had needed somebody to talk to, and on the spur of the moment had knocked on Jin's door. Thus he had reason for this seemingly impulsive action.

A knock on his door. It was Jin.

"Come in, come in!" Kang called. He ushered Jin in, then brought in the cold dish and two wine cups. From the lowest shelf of his bookcase he took an unopened bottle of brandy, lit a match to burn off the seal, then opened the bottle and filled both their cups.

"I've three toasts to drink with you," he announced. "First to the two of us for coming unscathed through twenty years of turmoil."

"I'll certainly drink to that."

Jin tossed off his cup.

"Good stuff, this," he commented, then helped himself to a mouthful of the cold dish. He had meant to praise this too, but it tasted so bitter he nearly spat it out and, rather than lie, kept quiet.

Kang ate a mouthful himself, then pounded his forehead. "What the devil?" he swore. "I used saccharine instead of gourmet powder." He whisked the dish off to the kitchen and turned on the tap. Jin, following him there, found him washing his cold dish in a basin of water before adding more seasoning.

"Don't go to such trouble," said Jin. "Brandy doesn't need anything to go with it. Chatting as we drink will be better than you fixing another dish. Come on back to the table."

Having lost interest in the dish, Kang followed Jin back to the table and refilled their cups.

His hand on his cup Jin said, "With the second cup, please tell me why you invited me here to drink with you, or how can I enjoy this brandy?"

"I meant to tell you anyway. All my family are away, and I needed to unburden myself to someone. That's why I troubled you."

"What's on your mind?"

"All in good time. I'll tell you when we've drunk this."

Kang raised his cup to Jin, who had to raise his too. They clinked cups, then drained them. Kang smacked his lips, not being in the habit of drinking, and went back to the kitchen to cut up a turnip. Sharing this with Jin he relaxed and went on:

"Two months ago the Party committee sent for me to notify me that the verdict passed on me in '57 was wrong, I've been completely cleared."

"What was the verdict in '57?"

"I don't know, no one had told me. But the Party committee said I'd been classified as a fringe Rightist."

"Oh, so that's why you asked me here to drink."

"No, that wasn't reason enough. I didn't know at the time, and now that I've been cleared it means nothing to me."

"Ha, it's the Party committee who should be drinking, to stop them worrying."

"I told them, it doesn't matter whether or not you implement the policy in my case; what matters is implementing it for those buildings. I pointed out years ago that there were weak points in the Soviet expert's proposals, and you made me a fringe Rightist, so no one else brought up the question. I suspect that after that big earthquake in Tangshan those buildings may have cracked. Get the owners to investigate and have them reinforced before it's too late. Don't wait for them to collapse, or lives may be lost."

"So you still had that on your mind!"

"I spoke sharply, not that I thought it was any use. For twenty years and more I've been making proposals; each time they've said fine, fine, we'll look into that; but nothing ever came of it. Know what? This time was an exception!"

"Oh?"

"This morning the Party committee called me in again and handed me a letter, a letter with the big red chop of the Construction Bureau. It said the bureau had investigated, acting on my proposal, and had discovered three breaks plus a dozen flaws. I was commended for my responsible attitude, and put in charge of a group to study how to reinforce those buildings. . . ."

"Wait a bit," Jin put in. "I don't get it. When you were a section chief you thought nothing of it. Now you're to head a group, why get me up at midnight to celebrate? Do you think this group head's worth more than a section chief?"

"No, you've got it wrong, it's not because I'm a group head. . . ."

"I know! This shows that someone takes what we say seriously, eh?"

"Right!"

"Black cat or white cat, at least they count us as cats, right?"

"That's it!" Kang laughed. "Isn't that worth drinking to?"

"Bottoms up!"

The two men drained the golden brandy in their cups. Then Kang stood up and went to his bookcase to rummage in it for a while, returning to his seat to show Jin the seal with a tortoise knob.

"I took the two inscriptions on this as my maxim and steered clear of trouble," he said. "I wanted to thank you before but hadn't the guts. Now I'm not afraid to thank you, and that maxim is out-of-date. Do you mind changing those inscriptions?"

Jin took the seal and examined it carefully. "I don't think we need change them," he said. "Keep them as a memento. To celebrate your good news today I've another present for you. Wait a bit!" He dashed upstairs and was back in less than two minutes, a painting under one arm. He unrolled this by the lamp. At the top were two cats painted with fine brushwork, one crouching as if preparing to spring, the other leaping up with all four feet off the ground. They were painted to the life. Above was the inscription, "Black cat or white cat, a mouse-catcher is a good cat." At the side in smaller characters was written: "The Spring Equinox, 1979. This morning the Palace Museum invited me to check through its Manchu archives; this afternoon the Foreign Ministry asked me to go to an embassy to appraise the authenticity of its antiques. For years I had a sinecure, now that I am growing old I have found recognition and a useless crock has turned into two cats. With one foot in the grave I am finally prospering. I long to drink deep but, having no companion, have painted this to express my feelings."

Below this was a newly added inscription in large characters, "Having no better way to congratulate Engineer Kang on his good fortune, I offer him this painting as an encouragement to us both."

Kang burst out laughing as he refilled his cup.

March 1980